THE ANTONIDES LEGACY II

THE ANTONIDES LEGACY II

Charlotte Murphy

2020

Copyright © 2020 by Charlotte Murphy.
All rights reserved.
First Printing: 2018
ISBN 979-866-504-2602

DEDICATION

To the Wattpad readers who engaged and helped me to get to the end, chapter by ever long chapter...

Contents

Mortania & the Known World ix
Prologue 1
Defining Strength 15
Priya 28
Questionable Allegiance 44
Without Powers 57
Connecting 75
Unprovoked Attacks 98
Epiphany 112
Emerging Relations 126
Family Feuds 140
Desperate Measures 161
Trainees 175
Fragile Peace 186
On The Road 199
The Game Begins 215
What Lies Within 224
Crol 239
Ships In The Night 257
Tirnum Castle 267
Young Love 277
The Chosen 285
The Six 298
Words Left Unsaid 312

The Princess And The General 330
Age of Antonides 341
Pronunciation Guide 345

MORTANIA & THE KNOWN WORLD

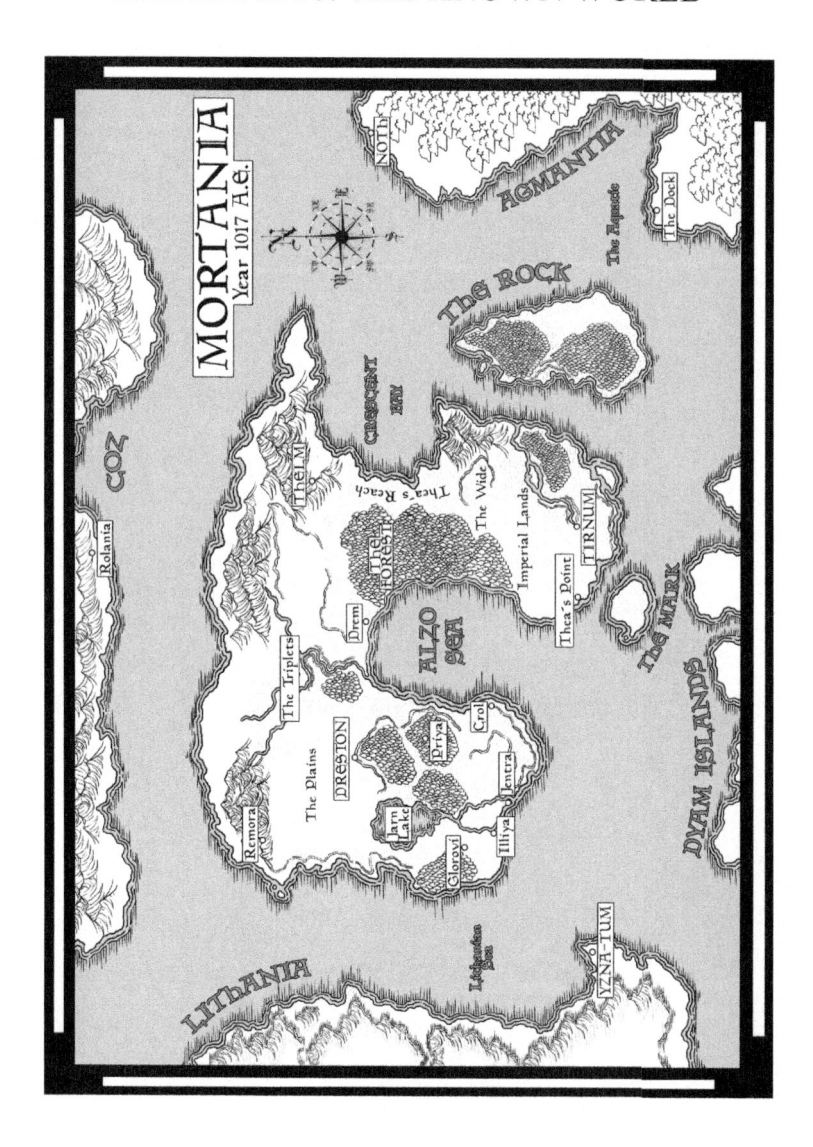

PROLOGUE

TIRNUM CASTLE, MORTANIA
1000 A.E.

She knew the exact moment that Alexander had been taken from her.

Although many knew and used the expression, few had ever felt their heart truly break.

The joining that Alexander and Rowan shared, was more than emotional but ordained by Thea herself.

The first Samaian Queen, Thea Antonides, had made intricate Everlasting-infused laws, that meant each ruler was destined for one particular person.

No one knew exactly how Thea had used the magic to create it, but all highborn Gifted were taught how to identify the people that would wed into the royal family. It was said, she made the magic laws to keep their lines pure; of people who only wanted the best for the Everlasting and the Keepers who would descend from her line.

Rowan remembered the day her parents had walked into her bedroom and told her that she was betrothed to the young prince. A royal messenger had left them only moments before and at only eight years old, had no idea what this new status would mean for her.

That was many years ago, and as she'd grown, she'd come to know how significant her new position was. Being named as Prince Alexander's Intended, meant that one day, she would be Queen.

Rowan had taken to her future position with vigour and vowed to be the best queen she could be. Subsequently, she met Alexander on her thirteenth birthday during a formal visit to the capital, and her heart had voluntarily belonged to him from that moment.

Being with Alexander had proved more than she could ever hope for. He had become a part of her in a way that was perpetual. She could no sooner stop loving him, then not take her next breath.

She'd lost a part of herself this night but focused on the very physical part of her that lay sleeping in her arms.

Blissfully unaware of the turmoil surrounding her, Crown Princess Trista Freilyn Mysten Antonides of Mortania, took a deep contented sigh and sucked her tongue.

Rowan, dressed in fitted dark trousers, long-sleeved shirt and leather overcoat trimmed in fur, took a ragged breath and finally called out,

"Minerva!"

A young woman rushed into the dimly lit, basement room they occupied and curtseyed low. When her eyes met those of her queen, they were weary and full of fear. They had been hidden there together and Rowan had begun to live through Minerva's tales of what happened above them. The young woman would escape into the castle to get news from the loyal guards posted there but it was deemed too dangerous for the queen to go herself.

"Yes your majesty?"

"The king is dead," she said simply making Minerva choke on the yelp that she stopped from escaping. "We must leave immediately. They are sure to advance on the castle now that he is gone."

Wrapped in a black velvet fur lined blanket, Princess Trista slept on while her mother strode out of the small stone room that had been their sanctuary for the last three nights.

Alexander had insisted she hide herself and their child in the depths of the castle so it would be easier to escape if he failed...

***

ROYAL APARTMENTS, TIRNUM CASTLE
THREE NIGHTS AGO

Rowan practically hissed at her husband's ridiculous words,

"You will not fail!"

She turned from him, desperate not to accept the words of defeat from the warrior she knew and loved.

Alexander walked to face her and took her delicate hands in his own to kiss her fists. No matter what, he always knew how to calm her down, with a kiss or a look. Alexander was her everything and that he was talking about leaving her alone, was more than she could cope with.

His deep green eyes bore into hers as he gently stroked his index finger along the side of her face.

"That fire inside of you is one of the many reasons I love you. I hope that our daughter takes that from you."

"Alex...please," his calm exterior suddenly evaporated and he snapped at her, moving his hand away from her face.

"Do not make me lie to you Rowan. Do not make me promise I will return when I don't know that to be true. Rowan please, do not ask that of me!" he turned away from her and in that moment, she knew she did not want their last moments together, to be filled with harsh words and fighting.

Rowan cast her eyes to their daughter lying on the narrow bed, content in her own little world, apparently not disturbed by the noise in the room; then turned to her husband. His back was to her and so she walked towards him to curl her arms around his waist and laid her cheek against his back. She could feel his heart beating and simply waited for him to receive her.

Alexander turned around eventually and pulled her into his strong arms. Rowan breathed him in then stepped back to look up into his face. She tried to burn his image into her memory: the slant of his eyes, the thickness of his eyebrows and the stark lines of this jaw that she'd kissed so many times and thought she would for countless more years.

"I loved you before I met you," he purred softly." My heart has always belonged to you." Rowan blushed and turned her face away him,

"I know the teachings…"

"No," he cut her off, turning her face back to his with his index finger on her chin." No teachings, no prophecies. I dreamed of you and Thea brought you to me. You are everything to me Rowan and I leave this world knowing that I have left a part of myself with you."

His eyes drifted towards his daughter before he stepped away from Rowan to lift her into his arms. She cooed and giggled at the faces he made before the little princess reached up and tugged a lock of his black hair that had escaped his warrior braid,

"My one regret is that I will not see her grow," he said quietly.

"Why Alex?" The question was torn from her, but she had to ask. "Why do you accept this?" Rowan watched her husband sigh and put their baby down after placing a kiss on her chubby cheek.

"You know our ways better than anyone, why you did not pledge to be Gifted I will never know," she smiled up at him before his face soured and he looked off into the distance; as though he could see through the stone walls.

"I have felt…different, these past nights Rowan. The Everlasting has called to me and I…I must answer."

"The Everlasting works *with* us, not against us my love."

"The Everlasting works in ways we will never fully understand but I have spent time with it, in the chamber and I understand and accept, that I will not survive this."

Rowan threw herself into his arms as the tears she'd held back for the last week, broke free. Alexander held her tightly,

"This is bigger than me, or us. This is what was foretold."

"It's not fair," Rowan cried out. "How will I live without you?"

"You will live as you have always done, as my Queen. You will make sure that our daughter sits upon her throne and takes back all that has been taken from us."

All Rowan could do was nod, she had no words left. Alexander lowered his head then and kissed her. It was a solid kiss, of possession and passion and his never-ending love for her. His lips were soft, the softest she would ever know and while they kissed so lovingly, more tears escaped Rowan's eyes knowing it was the last time she would ever feel his mouth on hers.

Regrettably, someone behind them cleared their throat and they broke their embrace.

"My sincerest apologies your majesties,"

Alexander sighed heavily and placed his forehead to his wife's, their eyes closed as they breathed each other in,

"Gorn?"

"We must leave now my King, Curian advances and we are at our last line of defence." Alexander spun to face him, eyes blazing with fury.

"You are Captain of the Guard, are you not? Deal with this that I may be with my family!" he roared at him making Trista let out a deafening scream.

Rowan rushed to her daughter's side as General Gorn Antos stepped back, crestfallen and silent.

"It's okay my darling, it's okay. Hush now,"

"Dada!" Trista reached for Alexander, trying to climb out of Rowan's arms. Alexander, all anger forgotten walked over to his daughter, his heart swollen with pride that she called for him.

He took the baby from her mother and held her tight against him, breathing in her scent.

"Papa has to go little one," Trista wailed her objection.

"Your majesty…please."

Gorn rushed him regrettably and so Alexander placed a kiss on Trista's head of dark curls, before handing her to Rowan even as the small child protested it. He kissed Rowan's forehead before stepping from the now screaming baby and marching out of the room.

Rowan, with Trista in her arms rushed to the open door of their apartment and watched her husband march down the long corridor, Gorn faithfully by his side attempting to get his armour back onto his tall lean frame.

I love you Rowan

She heard him as clearly as if he were still standing with her.

And I love you…always

Tears fell unforgivingly as she retreated into the room and out of nowhere, her Queen's Guard Captain, Lenya Sentine appeared to escort them to a prison of their own making.

***

Now, she hurried with Minerva and her child and the few belongings they could carry into the underbelly of Tirnum Castle.

She had changes of towelling for Trista, skins of milk that had been enchanted to keep warm, along with dried meats and a few pieces of salted fish. Anything else they would acquire when they were safely out of the city and the surrounding Imperial Lands.

The two women walked until Rowan stopped at a half moon shaped barred opening on the side of a cold and damp corridor. Through the opening, there was the castle sewer system and the smell that rose from it was more than unpleasant.

"Take her," Rowan commanded and handed Trista to Minerva. The baby stirred but did not wake as Rowan, closed her eyes and outstretched her arms.

She felt the power already ebbing away from her now that Alexander was no longer Keeper but she had to try. She had to believe that Thea would not abandon them so quickly.

Asserting her will, Rowan focused her senses on the iron bars and slowly, pried them apart. They bent slowly, until they were large enough for Rowan to fit through.

After throwing down her provisions, Rowan gathered her thick travelling robe into her hands and climbed down into the sewage system below.

Her fur lined, Phyn leather trousers protected her from any serious cuts on her way down but not from the smell. The odour threatened to suffocate her with its putrid essence, but she held her stomach strong before she released all inside it.

As she steadied her footing on the platform below, she peered up through the opening where Minerva was looking down anxiously,

"Give her to me,"

"What if she…" Minerva was cut short as they heard a loud bang overhead and she turned to look. Commotion could be heard from above as people entered the castle intricate hallways.

"Give her to me *now*!" Minerva nodded her head vigorously, fear apparent in her wide-eyed gaze as she attempted to lower Trista to her mother.

"It's too far!"

"Drop her!"

"She's just a baby!"

Another bang from overhead and the distinct sound of metal boots on cobbled stones,

"Drop her!"

Whether out of respect or fear, Minerva instantly let go and dropped Trista into Rowan's waiting arms.

As she caught her child, Rowan sent out a blast of power, knocking Minerva unconscious against the adjacent wall and slamming the metal bars back in place.

She staggered from the sudden force of it and let out a gloved hand to steady herself against the wall. Using her magic had not drained her like this in many years and the nausea was unexpected.

Trying to regulate her breathing while not trying to take in the rancid smell of human waste, Rowan turned to run towards some open tunnels but was stopped in her tracks as the sounds of boots overhead got louder.

Of course, not wanting to be seen, Rowan flattened herself against the wall beneath the barred opening as the people above her began to speak,

"What's this?" a gruff manly voice asked.

"Looks like she tried to run…she's out cold."

"What should we do with her?" a third man asked,

"I have a few ideas," the gruff voice suggested. There was no mistaking what he meant. Rowan closed her eyes, praying for them to leave Minerva alone.

"Hush man, is that all you think about? Only traitors to The Prophecy are given to you and we all know death would be better!"

"Looks like she's a servant here." the second man said

"Exactly, she served those Samaian dogs. Let me have her!" gruff voice interjected again but the third man was forceful.

"No!"

Rowan heard them shift around above her head and closed her eyes waiting for them to pass while she tried not to breathe too loudly.

"Pick her up and bring her to the cells, Sims," the third man continued. "Alun and I will continue on this way. That bitch queen has to be around here somewhere."

Rowan heard Sims grunt under the weight of something - most likely Minerva - and the other two men carried on down the stone corridor.

Rowan let out her breath slowly as she finally inched away from the wall toward the large opening a few steps in front of her. She had to walk through a shallow path of water to get to it and the feel of it beneath her booths was evidence enough of what the water was filled with.

She approached the large opening and tilted her head to look down into the abyss it disappeared to.

Rowan took a deep breath as she used her foot to feel for the muck coated rung of a ladder. Lenya, the Captain of her Queen's Guard had discovered the hidden tunnel when Alexander had commanded her to find an escape for the Queen should it ever be necessary. She had found this place that led out into a small cave in a cove along the coast.

Carefully, Rowan began to securely strap Trista to her chest with a purpose-built harness. It was easy enough to get the baby into and tie at the front before she turned to descend the ladder.

It was terribly dark, but she couldn't risk using her magic to make light in case anyone saw it. She didn't know who could be looking through the barred opening that led back into the castle.

With Trista secure, Rowan made her descent as quickly and carefully as she could. The bars were thick with algae and other things she didn't care to think about. She felt the grime even through her gloved fingers.

With her baby against her chest and provisions on her back, Rowan continued down the ladder when she missed her footing and slid down the chute.

She gripped hard against the next rung she felt but Trista was disturbed and cried out,

"Sssh sweetie, Mama's here," Rowan whispered to her, trying to slow her rapidly beating heart. "Mama's here,"

Trying desperately to keep Trista from screaming, Rowan moved faster until finally a slither of light came up from beneath her.

Rowan continued steadily until something grabbed her ankle. Rowan yelped with surprise and fear,

"Your majesty it is I!"

"Lenya!" Rowan picked up the pace with Lenya guiding her through the now curved tunnel that led out in a graveled cove.

Lenya stood, tall and proud in her Queen's Guard uniform but covered by a large hooded cloak. Rowan could see the gem of her sword hilt peeping through as she moved as well as the gem of the diadem hanging in the centre of her forehead.

The minimal yet still revolting sewage that came from the tunnel was spewed over the tiny rocks and the smell of salty sea air did little to cover it.

When she was finally free, she immediately unstrapped Trista and checked that the little girl was okay.

"Mama," she said with a little whimper,

"I know sweetie, just a little longer."

She handed Trista to Lenya,

"Get her clean!"

Rowan rushed to strip out of the dirty layers, caked with filth and changed into clothes that Lenya had waiting for her. She dressed quickly in the dim moonlight, the sound of waves so close by, crashing against the rocks that had held Tirnum Castle up for over nine hundred years.

When she was finally dressed in leathers and furs, Lenya had the little princess wiped down and re wrapped to keep her warm against the chilly night air.

When they were ready, Lenya led them steadily along the rocks and water until they came to a beach. Lenya raced up the dark sand to where two horses were strapped to a small abandoned boardwalk.

The horses were packed with their additional provisions and Rowan proceeded to climb into the saddle. Lenya handed Trista to her mother then mounted her own horse. When Trista was securely fastened against her again, Rowan and her aid set off quickly into the night.

***

"Mama!"

"Mama has to go, little one."

Rowan murmured a variation of the words she'd watched Alexander say only a year before.

She had known it broke his heart to leave them, but this was beyond anything she could have ever understood for herself.

"Mama stay!" Trista screamed again as Lenya peeled her from her mother's arms and mounted a horse. Trista kicked and screamed, reaching out for her mother with large tears dropping from her eyes. She was only eighteen months old, she didn't understand.

The three of them stood in a clearing, flanked by a multitude of trees that hung overhead creating an almost peaceful alcove where she knew their magic could not escape.

The void had been created long ago, by who no one knew; but it was here she knew she had to perform her last bit of magic for a very long time.

If only this place could shield them both forever, Rowan wouldn't have to abandon Trista, even if it were for her own good.

Rowan had been running for a year but the bond she shared with Trista was becoming too strong to hide. It helped keep their powers somewhat intact, but it made them vulnerable to roaming eyes and ears all through the power of the Everlasting.

Her long black hair was tied neatly away, but still hidden under the hooded bearskin cloak she almost constantly wore.

The winter had taken a drastic turn since Curian had taken the throne and seemed to be going on forever. Rowan was powerless to stop this change in magic, but Trista was not…if she lived.

Tears pooled in Rowan's eyes as she watched Lenya take her only child from her even though she knew it was for the best.

If she kept Trista, it would most likely get them both captured and killed.

Decisively, she reached out then and placed her finger in the centre of Trista's head. The little girl was immediately still and fell into a deep sleep.

Rowan muttered a quick spell and when she took her finger away, a tendril of smoky white magic came away with it before disappearing.

"She will not remember me," Rowan explained. "She has almost two years of memories, young…but memories all the same. She cannot know me lest someone extract those memories from her and deduce where I am."

Lenya nodded though it pained her to watch her queen suffer in this way. She climbed into the saddle with Trista in her arm and looked down at her queen with a reassuring smile,

"I will keep her safe until Remora; she will have a good life."

"Though not the life she was born to."

It was said with regret rather than bitterness.

"You hold the only thing that matters to me in this world Lenya. Keep her safe for my sake…and that of our kingdom."

Lenya nodded, rounded the horse and rode out of the clearing.

Rowan watched her only child disappear into the thicket and sighed heavily,

"Come back to me…I'll be waiting."

With that, Rowan simply disappeared.

DEFINING STRENGTH

TIRNUM CASTLE, MORTANIA
1017 A.E.

The sun appeared on the horizon as it steadily rose into the sky to shine over Tirnum Castle. The dawn brought with it, the crisp salty sea air from the coast as well as the calls of seagulls, soaring overhead in the early morning sun.

The common people who woke with the dawn were taking fresh loaves of bread from ovens and picking freshly laid eggs from chicken coops. Stables were checked and mucked out; the animals stored there made ready for their daily tasks.

The days had to continue as best they could even when there was a steady decline in available food and cultivable land on which to grow more.

While the land immediately surrounding the walls of Tirnum City had not seemed to suffer the effects of Curian's revolt, the rest of the capital was not so lucky. Miles beyond the city gates, spreading north into the Imperial Lands and south to Thea's Point; the land had all but died. Crops didn't grow as healthily if at all and the bitter winter that had descended on them didn't help matters.

The area known as the Imperial Lands which had once been the most sort after location after the city itself, was now nothing more than abandoned waste land between Tirnum and The Wide. Large mansions and family castles of nobleman had been raided during the rebellion, and in an act of defiance everything was burned and left to ruin.

The harsh winter had crept into the lush greenery of the Imperial Lands and had never left, leaving the lands barren.

Now, it was an eerie place, physically empty but filled with the memories of what once was, and the tortured souls left behind.

Bandits, general ruffians and the occasional Traveller could be found roaming the sparse lands either on their way to the capital or back north through Thea's Reach.

It was in this man-made wilderness, on a clear though bitter morning that Briseis had assembled her assortment of gifted human children.

There were twelve of them in total, the eldest no more than sixteen. They were a mixture of Mortanian, Agmantian and Coznian, girls and boys who had all manifested the Everlasting magic in one way or another. They all possessed heightened agility and speed along with the other powers that came with it.

Briseis Greybold sat atop Axus, her white stallion in front of the children with Captain Gardan Beardmore at her side and twenty other members of the Royal Sentry.

They had travelled behind Briseis and Gardan's horses on foot in the early hours of the morning. The princess was dressed in black thick fitted wool trousers and tunic with the matching fur lined leather boots that went over her knees with white fox fur around the top. The same fur lined the hem and neck of her sleeved and buttoned cloak with a thick hood that covered her against the icy winds around them. The children, in comparison were in black threadbare leggings and tunics with thin woolen boots that did little to protect against the frosted dirt beneath their feet.

"Face forward!"

At Gardan's command all the children were at attention, despite their shivering. At that moment, the princess gracefully dismounted and approached them,

"It might not feel like it, but I am proud of you. Of the hundreds of young people that were brought to me, you have passed every test."

Gardan motioned to the men closest to him and they each stepped forward to hand the children a sword and shield each.

"The twelve of you have made the most progress in using the Everlasting and so we elevate your training so you can better serve Mortania…and me."

She let the words settle with them a moment before beginning to pace all the way to the end of the line they had made and back again. The children were shivering from the cold but now from fear of why they had been given weapons. Their eyes looked warily at each other and the princess, their knuckles white from the intense grip they held on the swords.

"Soon, you will go up against men that have been fighting their entire lives. You will be expected to kill these men and return victorious to me. In so doing, you will be richly rewarded."

At the mention of reward, the children, perked up considerably. Many of them came from humble beginnings, some so humble they barely had enough food to eat. Whatever she asked of them, they would most likely do just for the promise of a meal.

"You will become my most special and trusted guard for you understand how to wield the power that was stolen from us and which has now been returned to its rightful Keepers."

Briseis turned away from them then to remount her horse. When she was perched high above them, holding the reins lightly in her hands she said,

"Remember that only the strongest survive but one cannot be strong only in strength. You must be strong in will, drive and mind."

She signaled to Gardan who in turn motioned to the Sentry who stepped forward and drew their own weapons. There was a collective gasp as the children looked on in fear,

"All who return to me by midday will have proved they are worthy to fight for me."

She turned her horse and with Gardan close behind her, set off at great speed back toward the city.

The children looked at the armoured men advancing on them and assessed the situation before them: kill or be killed.

There was only one option.

***

Lamya never realised how much she'd come to rely on her physical possessions until she had to give up most of them. She was finally on her way to meet the lost princess and as that involved extensive travel, she would have to do so lightly. She'd accumulated a wealth of possessions that must ultimately be left behind. She'd brought what she thought the bare essentials with her to Thea's Point but even that had to be halved.

In the end, she'd asked if she could leave some of her belongings with Alexia who had readily agreed. She'd spent the remainder of her time in Thea's Point with Alexia and her daughters who had promised to spread the news of the princess's arrival when the time came.

With Princess Briseis' declaration of war, it was becoming unsafe for Samai in Mortania once again. However, if Samai knew that their saviour was on the way, it might spark the survival instinct that had long since died out.

Although there were people old enough to remember the rebellions and the ruler before it – it had only been eighteen years - the absence of their link to the Everlasting had made Samaians weak.

No matter how they tried to regain a sense of bravery, there was only so much they could do to oppose the new regime. Lamya felt great sympathy for a people that had once been great, *chosen* to be great and had now been reduced to little more than peasants. For a people who had not treated their subjects the same when in they were in power, it was terrible to witness.

Decidedly, Lamya booked passage on a ship travelling west to Illiya. It was as far west of Mortania one could go by ship and once there, she would alight and travel on land back east; spreading the word of the Redeemer's arrival to all who would listen. She'd been instructed to go to Crol by the Council, but she knew she could be of better use if she got more people on side. So, despite it being a long-winded plan, Lamya knew it was the best thing she could do before meeting the princess. How she was meant to introduce herself to Trista and gain her confidence was another issue altogether, but it was what she must do.

Now, with her minimal belongings stowed on board, Lamya made her way up the gangplank onto the main deck of the ship. This vessel was a designated passenger ship and so had an eclectic mix of people on board. There were low and high born alike. She saw, from their dress and jewels, placed in clear view but not too large to be tacky, that the more affluent passengers were who she could get information from.

She wouldn't be so naïve as to trust them with her own political standing; but she would keep people close enough that they felt comfortable speaking with her. With her gifts, that would not present a great problem.

Decidedly, Lamya made her way towards a relatively young family of five; parents, two teenage boys and a little girl who currently sat in her father's arms.

"Hello," she said simply as she approached them.

She resisted using her gifts against them to get an uninhibited feel of their intent. She offered no more in her greeting in order to better determine how they would receive her without her forcing it in any way. The woman immediately smiled at her, as did the husband politely while the two boys nodded begrudgingly but did not say anything: teenage angst at its finest.

"Greetings, can we be of help?"

"No help, just friendship while aboard this ship," the woman smiled. "I'm travelling alone you see and just wanted to introduce myself to some nice people on board. My name is Lamya Rubio."

"Greetings Lamya," the woman replied happily, approaching Lamya to take her hand sweetly into her own. It was then that Lamya opened her awareness and felt nothing but good intent from the woman,

"I am Gracelynn, and this is my husband Edmere. Our boys Edmere and Julius and this is little Ellarie." Lamya shook Edmere senior's hand,

"It's a pleasure to meet you all. Forgive me, if I'm intruding."

"Nonsense, I would be grateful to have a female companion for the journey. We sail to Illiya, our home."

"Though our time would be better spent here."

Edmere the younger piped up with clear distain. Both parents made exasperated sounds, but Gracelynn buffered it with a smile,

"Edmere wants to join the King's Guard and so is reluctant to leave the capital."

Interesting

"Really, what interests you about the military?" Edmere looked at her as though she'd asked the most ignorant and mundane question in the wide world.

"What would not interest me about serving my king as I should and proving myself a man?"

"There are other ways for one to prove himself a man and not all of them involve fighting, destruction and death. Would you disregard your father simply because he is not a military man?"

All the family turned to Edmere who had turned a telling shade of pink. He narrowed his eyes at Lamya and pursed his lips together in defiance.

"I see you have met a worthy opponent in the way of words Edmere!" his father said good naturedly and readjusted the little girl in his arms. "Where is your cabin Lamya?" Edmere the senior asked.

"Second level," Lamya noted Edmere's distinct smirk that seemed to say her cabin status explained everything about her.

"Only one below us, would you be able to join us for dinner?" Julius inquired, clearly a much better natured boy. Lamya saw then, that in creating a minor enemy in Edmere, she had created an ally in Julius.

"I wouldn't want to intrude," Lamya repeated humbly.

"Of course not, we insist. Don't we Ed?" Ed nodded at his wife's invitation.

"Of course, conversation will be most interesting," he said laughing no doubt at Edmere's expense.

"Then I would be delighted to accept." Lamya said graciously and turned her eyes on Julius who blushed for an entirely different reason.

Infiltration complete.

***

There had been an escape from the prisons and a steady growth in rebellious brawls in the street, which meant that civil war was finally happening.

The streets of Dreston were alive with the passion of both Man and Samai as they struggled to deal with the impending change that threatened to upheave their lives.

Briseis' declaration of war had given some the fuel they needed to start fires of hatred and discrimination. Feelings that they had thought long buried had now risen to the surface and reared its ugly destructive head.

The people were getting brave; enough so to organise a mass rescue from the Dreston Castle dungeons. Although war was enough reason to fight back, the Samai had been isolated and restrained long before this, so what had changed? What was changing, that gave these people hope and strength?

The few Samaians they had captured had refused to speak and many had already been executed at Baron Dreston's word. If they could not be useful, then death was the price.

It was this situation he knew he had to leave soon and make his journey to Tirnum. He would always be safe in his city, but he did not have time to deal with an uprising when he needed to think about taking the throne. He would let his Dreston Council officials deal with the rioting while he was away, until he had claimed the Mortanian throne as his own.

"Lord, all is ready for your departure. Just send the word!"

Baron Lyon Dreston rolled his eyes as the temporary Captain of the First Quarter yelled his missive for the entire world to hear.

"Must you scream at me so? I am not deaf or dumb Elias." The large man stepped back in a slight bow to indicate his apology and so, wearied with the current travel plans, Lyon accepted it.

The previous week had been spent cultivating all they would need for the journey to Tirnum and its many obstacles. Though they would be travelling primarily by ship, Dreston was an inland city. His entire household and accompanying guard would have to travel the few hundred miles south to Illiya in order to board waiting ships. While Crol was closer, it was not large enough to accommodate him and his army.

They would march south to Illiya then travel the Lithanian Sea all the way to Thea's Point and march on to Tirnum. It cut their journey by days and although complex, much more desirable.

He was to travel with Lady Geneiva and her father behind his troops who would lead the journey to Thelm, arrive some time before him and anticipate his arrival.

His titthe for Princess Briseis had already begun their journey towards the capital and if all went well; he would arrive either in the midst of battle or at the end of it. Either way, he would be there to take praise for coming to the aid of the crown and consequently, take it for himself.

The thought pleased him so, that an intense laugh bubbled from inside him as he stood staring out of the window of his chambers. His city, his legacy lay stretched out before him so far that he could only just make out the edge of the city walls. In the immediate vicinity of the castle, there were wooded and grassed areas, along with farmlands that his personal work force developed, so not to venture out into the city.

For acres he saw vegetation and marvelled at how Dreston was surviving in the aftermath of the rebellion where other cities and towns had suffered. Dreston was inland and positioned near the desert. Its residents had yet to experience the bitter winters that he heard had spread from the southern capital and steadily north to Thelm. He was plagued with news of food shortages among the common folk but that was of little concern to him.

"We leave at first light," he said to Elias. "For now...leave me."

"Yes, Lord." Elias left him and Lyon sighed with deep contentment.

He was by no means close to achieving everything he was after, but he could feel himself getting closer to his goal.

With his pending marriage to Geneiva Thelm, he would have the might of her father and his forces to the north of Tirnum beyond The Forest. With Thelm holding the fort there and his own forces in the capital and some remaining in Dreston, he had more than enough power to hold the crown from all sides of the realm. There were no large cities to the south so all the other towns and villages would fall in line with the province they fell under.

Despite this, there was still the underlining question of how long he would be able to keep the crown once he had obtained it.

The thought entered his head unwillingly, but he knew it to be true.

How long before someone revolted against him to try and take the throne?

He needed to secure his ascension with an heir; preferably a boy but no one could predict these things. He had intended to marry Geneiva once he was crowned but if he already had a wife and a child on the way…

While he would have Alaina with him, it would be disrespectful to be seen visiting her litter too often; even he had respect for the old ways.

Geneiva may know he would have women grace his bed, but he was not meant to throw it in her face…or her father's. If Thelm were to feel disrespected and his daughter shamed, he may withdraw his support. He might not want to admit it, but he needed that old goat.

"Elias!"

The man returned in seconds with his armoured hand rested on his sheathed sword,

"Lord?"

"I will not be leaving tomorrow,"

"No…Lord?" the confusion was clear.

Lyon turned from the window. In his long black high collared tunic and black trouser covering black velvet slippers, Lyon looked like a shadow with the sun coming in from behind him. His long hair was tied back in a tight ponytail, accentuating his lean, cold features.

"Send the designated soldiers on to Tirnum. Baron Thelm, Lady Geneiva and I will remain behind with a select guard and members of our households in order to perform the wedding rites."

Elias did well to hide his surprise and the significant change in plans,

"Bring Aml to me," Elias nodded and departed once again.

A few moments later, the door knocked again, and he permitted Aml to enter.

His chief attendant was dressed in the customary grey woollen robe that promoted his station above the rest of the servants in the household. He had a thin chain of silver to signify his importance to the Baron. He bowed as he approached Lyon who was now sat at the small table that occupied a far corner of his chambers. Lyon motioned for Aml to take a seat and he did,

"I wish to be married within the week. Can this be done?"

"Of course, Lord, the priests have already blessed the union so this should not be a problem." Lyon nodded,

"Good, put the plans in motion. I wish to be married before we leave for Tirnum so the sooner the better."

"Yes Lord…" Lyon noticed the pause.

"What is it Aml?"

"May I speak freely?"

"As freely as your station permits," Lyon said simply. Aml looked at him with intense brown eyes, as brown as his smooth skin.

"Have you considered the consequences of this journey to the capital?"

"What consequences do you speak of?"

"The princess herself is a consequence and more so, her wrath. I have heard things Lord and none of them good."

"She is but a woman, what harm can she really do?" Lyon scoffed but Aml was adamant.

"I strongly believe that she is not to be underestimated Lord, but in all things, I will follow you." Lyon nodded so curtly, Aml took it as his cue to leave.

He had been short with Aml in that regard not because he was particularly mad at him but because there was a remnant of truth in his words.

He had heard over and over how much the princess was a force to be reckoned with, but he refused to let that deter him from his goal.

Aml would see, as they all would, that he would claim the throne and destroy this so-called warrior princess in the process.

PRIYA

It was difficult to do, painful in fact, but slowly Trista tried to open her eyes.

A flutter here and there allowed shreds of light to enter, but once she'd opened them fully, the harsh rays of sunlight cut through her vision.

Breathing steadily, she tried again until she was able to look at her surroundings with a hazy view.

She was lying on her back, that much was obvious as she stared at the long planks of narrow wood on the ceiling above her. She could hear birds and wind rustling through the leaves of trees. She heard distant voices outside the window that was somewhere above her alongside footsteps and the distinct banging of metal.

When she'd sat up slowly to look around, she realised she was in a perfectly square room. The walls were panels of polished wood and decorated with what looked like tapestries hung to give it some atmosphere. There was a three-draw dresser at the foot of her bed and the door was to the left of it. The sun that had almost blinded her earlier was coming through a small window just above her to her right so she couldn't look out of it without standing up.

When she finally turned her head all the way to the left, she saw Dana.

Her heart leapt with relief and happiness as she saw Dana asleep and safe in a narrow bed across the room from her. She had a bandage around her head with a distinct spot of red along the side. Panicked, tears welled in Trista's eyes as the guilt set in.

She'd put Dana in danger yet again and with that realisation came the fear that there was every possibility that they wouldn't be so lucky next time.

Would Dana make it out alive after another of her mess ups...would she?

Trista watched Dana sleeping and although she was worried about her, the fact that she was bandaged, and sleeping was a great sign. They were seemingly safe but now she had to find out what had happened to them.

She remembered the struggle to get out of Dreston but she also knew that it had cost Rayne dearly to do it.

Rayne!

Was she ok?

Her constant guilt flared up something fierce at having allowed Rayne to come to harm. Rayne had explained to them that while she still had her powers and knew how to do many wonderful things, doing so took its toll on her body as well as her powers.

Trista cursed herself and her injuries, for putting herself and Rayne in danger and not being able to do anything about it or check that she was okay. She could have tried scrying for her or feeling out for her magic. It might not have worked but at least she could have tried. She had to believe in the likelihood of Rayne being alive and well was high; as she was after all a Samaian sorceress.

Thoughts of Rayne aside for the moment, Trista tried to adjust herself more comfortably and a sharp pain shot up her back.

If she hadn't known before, it was clear from the pain that she wasn't up to using her powers. She had to find out at least if she was safe and if she wasn't, how she and Dana could get away. If she could just get physically better at least, that would have to be enough. Being locked away in the Dreston dungeons had shown her how much she still relied on others to help her and that was a terrifying thought.

As Trista lay there thinking, the handle on the door turned and slowly began to open. She hadn't even notice footsteps approaching, she was so lost in thought but as her heart beat fast with anticipation; a round face with big blue eyes and curly brown hair looked around the door. When the jolly faced woman saw she was awake, her eyes softened, and she stepped further into the room.

"Hey there, sleeping beauty, finally awake I see! How are you feeling?"

The woman now fully revealed was a bit on the large side. She had large breasts squeezed inside a corseted dark green dress with a long flowing skirt. The skirts weren't particularly big, but her hips were and jiggled as she walked towards them. Her eyes were a beautiful, sea-like blue and her eyes wrinkled at the corners as she smiled down at Trista. Her hair was piled on top of her head in a mass of brown curls that kept escaping whatever confinement was keeping it up there. She had an apron on and from the various marks over it; Trista could tell she was a worker; probably a cook or washerwoman of some kind.

"I'm…" Trista cleared her throat, surprised at the croak that escaped. "I'm fine, thank you…" the woman held her borderline chubby hand to her chest,

"Oh my, I'm so sorry sweetie. You must be scared out of your mind wondering who I am!"

Trista smiled uncertainly but the woman only smiled broadly, turned away from her, back to a small stool that she brought in between the two beds and took a seat on,

"My name is Iona and this is my home. I live here with Gorn and his son," Trista immediately piped up and tried to sit up,

"This is Gorn's house? Where is he, Rayne said we should find him-ahhh!" she suddenly had a sharp pain across her head and as she reached up, she realised for the first time that she had a bandaged over her head too.

"Okay, okay, calm down there Trista," Iona stood again and smoothed her hair as she got her comfortable under the sheets. Trista didn't bother to ask how Iona knew her name. "Calm down honey, I'll explain everything. Just take it easy."

Trista tried to nod as she lay back down, her heart beating wildly and panting. Iona left her for a moment and returned with a cup of water. A jug of it was on the table across from them that Trista hadn't even noticed. She helped Trista sip it then returned to her seat on the stool,

"That's better,"

"Wha…what happened to us?"

It was then that Trista saw Iona lose her smile completely and looked almost angry,

"You and your friend here were in a bad way. Gorn says some kind of power took a lot out of you, but I patched you both up real good. A couple of the Creekwood boys found you while they were out playing. When you screamed out Gorn's name, the boys called for me and, well…here you are." Trista nodded, she remembered that much at least so she knew Iona wasn't lying.

"Where is Gorn?"

"In his workshop, he's the blacksmith here in Priya. He works there with his son and I help run the house. You'll meet them both as soon as you're ready. He's dying to meet you, checking in on you and hoping to catch you awake but I said he had to wait until you felt better, you and your friend here…" she left the sentence unfinished and Trista slowly caught on,

"Oh, Dana. That's my friend Dana…is she okay?"

"She was much better than you that's for sure. Even woke up a few times and had some food…she was so worried for you; you were asleep so long."

Trista was suddenly terrified to ask,

"…how long?" Iona sighed,

"Three days, this the most we've heard out of you since the Creekwood boys heard you scream!"

Three days?

She'd been unconscious for *three days!*

Trista knew she couldn't continue to let her powers control her like this or she wouldn't be any use to anyone much less Mortania. Trista felt deflated and slumped further into the bed.

Iona must have realised because she reached out and placed her hand on her covered leg,

"Don't worry Princess, you'll be right as rain soon enough."

"Don't call me Princess!" Trista suddenly snapped, before turning her face away onto the pillow. "I'm no one's princess." Iona didn't seem fazed by her outburst.

"Don't think like that Trista, you're a very special young woman."

"No, I'm not. I don't do anything but get my friends hurt and pass out for three days while they lay there dying! What use am I?" She couldn't see her face, but Trista could feel Iona's pity.

"You'll see what use you are…one day."

Iona got up from the stool and after looking over at Dana and making sure she was okay; she made her way back to the door.

"Enough talk for now, I think. I'll be back to check on you both in a little while but for now, get some rest."

Iona left with a sweet smile and closed the door gently behind her.

Trista knew she shouldn't have snapped at her, but she was so frustrated, and it had just come flooding out. When Iona came back later, she would apologise to her; before then, she would focus on getting better.

Now she'd arrived successfully in Priya, there was no way she could give up. Rayne had sacrificed too much to get her here and now Iona and Gorn and his son were part of this too. There was so much on her shoulders at the moment; she honestly didn't know how she was going to deal with it all once she was well enough to do so.

Feeling completely overwhelmed, Trista took a last look at Dana then turned over onto her side, her body aching as she did so; and tried to go back to sleep.

She woke up a while later, she wasn't sure how long and this time; Dana was awake.

Her friend gave her a weak smile and Trista could see now that she looked very ill; she shuddered to think what she looked like when she finally looked in the mirror.

"Hi,"

"Hi back," Dana said before coughing slightly making Trista feel even more embarrassed. She'd done this to Dana and she needed so desperately to make things right.

"Are you alright?"

"I've been better," Dana smiled reassuringly as she turned only her head to look over at Trista,

"I'm so sorry Dana, I…I'm just so sorry," Trista felt the tears welling up,

"Trista don't cry, there is nothing to be sorry for."

"I did this to you,"

"No, *magic* did this to *us*. An excessive but necessary use of magic, nothing else."

"What did you do?" Dana looked sad, regretful as she replied,

"Rayne used a spell of some kind, a spell to travel someone from one place to another in an instant. I don't know what she did exactly, but I know it took a lot of power…power she didn't have."

The guilt just wouldn't end; more and more reasons that this was her fault just kept coming up.

"She wouldn't have had to use that magic if it wasn't for me. You and Rayne…you saved me at the cost of your own lives." Dana laughed before erupting into a fit of coughs,

"We weren't exactly going to leave you behind Trista, it was worth it. You are the Redeemer after all," Trista knew that Dana meant it as a joke but she couldn't deal with the title. It was just too much to deal with too soon and now that Rayne was gone, who was going to teach her what she needed to know?

"Don't say that…I'm no saviour."

"Maybe not now…but one day you will be."

Trista responded with a sigh but was saved having to fill the awkward silence when the door knocked and slowly opened to reveal Iona,

"There they are!" she exclaimed in her jolly way. "Feeling any better my little darlings?"

Iona was shouldering the door open and the girls realised she was carrying a tray with two steaming bowls on top of it.

The girls immediately tried to sit up as the delicious smell engulfed the room and Dana's stomach growled in response,
"Sounds like someone's hungry!"
"Starving," Trista agreed.
"Well, let me help you both up then you can eat."
The girls nodded as Iona rested her tray of goodies on the small table between them, then proceeded to help them both sit up in their beds. She placed a cloth over their laps then brought back a clay bowl that had a plate attached to the side; it had been crafted that way. Iona saw Trista looking at it,
"Made it myself, easier to put your bread on you see!" Trista did see as the steaming bowl of thick soup had a chunk of white buttery bread conveniently on the plate part of it. She could break a piece off and dip in as she pleased without having to find somewhere to put it.
"Take your time now, we don't want either of you getting sick from eating too much or too fast." The girls nodded as they tucked into their meal,
"Good?"
"Amazing Iona…thank you," Trista said.
"No need to thank me Trista, I just do what I can."
Iona sat on her stool again for a moment watching them eat, seemingly content with doing just that.
"When you both feel up to it, you can come out and meet Gorn. Like I said earlier, he's dying to meet you."
"I'm looking forward to meeting him too…I have a lot of questions."
"I'm sure he'll be happy to answer them sweet pea. Well," she stood up again. "I'll be back to get your dinner things and then you can rest some more. Tomorrow, we'll wash and dress you properly; then you can meet the family. Sound good?"

"Sounds great," Dana said making Iona giggle her way out of the door.

The following day, Trista lay in a large drum of warm water lathering herself. Bathing had never been a strenuous task but the entire process seemed like a never ending ordeal. Even after a few days of rest, she still ached in places she didn't know she had.

She would be eternally grateful to Iona and Gorn for taking them in as she didn't know how they would have survived their trip from Dreston to Priya. It was disconcerting that she was living in a man's house but had yet to meet him. She was anxious to meet him and express her gratitude.

As she bathed, the door to the washroom opened and Dana walked in. The washroom was next door to their own and Iona had shown them earlier that morning. They saw they were on the first floor of a large but simple house, the railing of the first floor overlooking a quaint living area. They would explore when they could once they were both washed and dressed for breakfast.

The tub Trista sat in was big enough for two and Dana joined her once she'd rushed out of her clothes. Iona had laid out clean dresses for them that she said would do until they could go into town and get them newer garments.

She'd explained that while they had landed with a few bags of belongings, there wasn't much.

The water splashed against the side of the large metal drum as Dana stepped in. She sank into it to soak her hair as Trista had done then came up again and rested against the side beside her friend.

"I feel a lot better today, how about you?"

"Much better, I can officially say I've had enough of that bedroom," Trista said with a smile. "I want to see Priya…and thank Gorn."

"Of course, we'll have a look around today. We'll ask Iona," Trista nodded and began to lather herself.

The girls were washed and dressed a while later, in simple woollen dresses and leather shoes that had arrived with them. Holding hands, they finally stepped out of the bedroom.

They were on top of a landing with narrow wooden stairs leading down. To the right of the stairs were two doors and to the left of it were two more. Peering over the bannister, they saw large cow skinned covered couches with bear skins on the floor. There were furnishings that depicted a life of wealth, but its surroundings were apparently of a working family. Before they could contemplate that in any real depth, the stomach grumbling smell of freshly baked bread reached them, and the girls looked at each other with a smile before making their way down the stairs.

When they reached the bottom, the rest of the house came into view.

It was large, as they could tell from the upstairs but with various sections cornered off with low fur covered walls. There was what appeared to be a reading nook with two large bookshelves filled with books. There was the enclosed centre area with couches and rugs that they had seen above, and in the furthest corner to their right, was the kitchen.

They entered the airy space to find Iona placing the loaf she'd just taken out of the oven onto the large kitchen table. She was fanning it when she looked up at them,

"There they are!" her smile was infectious as she motioned them to sit at the table. "Smelled the bread and came running didn't ya?" the girls laughed as they nodded.

"Well, breakfast will be ready in a minute."

Dana and Trista looked at each other, confused as to what more could be added to the table when there were already fresh fruits, steaming sausages, bacon and scrambled eggs alongside jugs of juice and milk. Iona cooked like she was feeding an army, not five people.

Trista noted the very large bowl and plate at the head of the table, the second largest bowl next to it. Three regular sized bowls were in the remaining spaces where she, Iona and Dana would sit.

"Gorn will be back in a minute." Iona continued as she turned back to a pot on the stove and added some sugar to it. "Had to get his lazy behind out of bed at dawn to sort some new shoes for Titan, that's our horse." Iona rambled on conversationally as she seasoned her pot. "Need to go into town today so couldn't leave him waiting any longer." The girls looked at each other again, an obvious question hanging in the air, but Trista was brave enough to ask,

"Iona…are you Gorn's wife?"

"Oh, Gods no!" Iona said with a nervous laugh, but the girls saw the heat rise up into her neck and face before she turned away from them. "I'm too old for that marrying stuff now!"

Trista didn't think she was that old,

"I work for Gorn, cook his meals; clean the house. I look after them, have done for going on twelve years now. It was easier to live in after…" Iona went silent and for the first time since they had met her, the girls saw her shoulders slump in sadness. She seemed to realise she'd let her mask slip and when she turned back to them, she was a picture of happiness.

"They're my family now…that's what matters." The girls nodded, not wishing to pry. Turning the conversation away from whatever had made Iona sad, Dana said,

"Your home is beautiful, who made all this?"

"Gorn," Iona replied from the stove as she outed the fire and turned back to wipe down the plates. "He started about a year or so after the rebellion and his wounds had healed properly."

"Wounds, he fought in the war?" Trista asked with clear enthusiasm. Not for war but for the fact that Gorn would have met her father. He could tell her about him…

Iona nodded as she carried the large pot to the table and set it in the middle on the cooling rack beside some honey. She set to cutting up the fresh bread as she spoke,

"Yes, he did, but I'll let him tell you that story."

The girls smelled the thick oats in the pot and couldn't stop grinning. Having a home cooked meal was a wonderful thing when they were so few and far between. They had travelled from Remora to Dreston through the desert with meagre provisions and even living with Rayne they had cooked themselves. Having Iona mother them felt like a dream.

"Forgive me but…you're not Samaian?" Iona laughed at Dana's question as she continued cutting the thick bread until it lay in perfectly even slices on the chopping board.

"No honey, I'm not but you don't need to be Samaian to see the destruction Curian has caused. If you can change that Trista, then I'm all for it." She gave Trista a wistful look, then as though she suddenly remembered where she was, went to wash her hands at the sink before taking her seat opposite Dana.

As Iona invited them to the bread, porridge and the assortment of fruits, the door behind them opened,

"Gorn, come get your breakfast before it gets cold!"

The girls turned to the doorway and it was immediately clear why Iona had made so much food.

Gorn was a large man.

A very large man but not that he was overweight, he was just…large.

He was over six feet easily, bald, seemingly by choice as there was shadow where hair should be and not the smoothness of old age. He had a thick black beard, slowly greying at the bottom that made it look like it had been dipped in flour. He wore leather trousers and a loose tunic that was partly covered by a blacksmiths apron.

When he finally laid eyes on Trista, his green eyes twinkled and the wrinkles at the corner of his eyes deepened before he said,

"There she is."

His deep voice was so soft; it was difficult to comprehend that a man his size was capable of such gentleness. He strode across the living area until he was in the kitchen with them and looked down at Trista, still smiling.

Trista noticed to her alarm that Gorn had tears in his eyes,

"I haven't seen you since…look at you," it was an odd feeling to know that someone you had never met loved you but that was the only way she could describe it.

Trista knew that this man had nothing but her best interests at heart and that he loved her more than she could ever explain or understand.

"Hello Gorn," it was all she could think to say but when she did, he practically beamed at her before pulling her out of her seat and into a bear hug,

"You sound just like her!"

Trista had no idea who he was talking about, but his excitement was so infectious, she couldn't help but smile,

"Put her down Gorn, you're frightening the poor girl!" Iona laughed as she ate her food,

"Okay woman keep your hair on your chest!" swiped her hand at him but she was by no means offended. Gorn put Trista down and turned his attention to Dana before grabbing her face and placing a delicate kiss on her head,

"Thank you for being with her, Dana?" Dana smiled with a nod.

Gorn looked back at Trista as though he couldn't believe she were really sitting there, before turning from them to wash his hands in the kitchen sink. When he was done, he finally took his seat at the head of the table and while he continued to grin at Trista, Iona shared out his food into the large bowl that now made sense.

"I'm sorry if I'm overwhelming you but I'm so glad you're finally here."

"We're all glad she made it to us Gorn but I think you should explain a bit more before you attack her again!"

"Yes, yes of course," he reached for some bread that he buttered before taking a bite. "How have you been, Iona been taking good care of you?"

"Of course, you're all really kind to us." Trista said,

"Kind?" Gorn chuckled as he shovelled some porridge into his mouth then added some honey, "I don't want to diminish my character but looking after you is my duty Trista!" Her confusion was clear when he said,

"You're our Princess, our heir and our leader and as former Captain of the Guard it is my duty to protect and serve you as I did your father and mother. Not to mention, I am your GodsFather…Rayne did tell you this?"

"She didn't go into much details and we didn't have time before we had to…leave," Dana said quietly. "She told us that Trista would have to meet you one day for training, but she didn't elaborate. We all thought…"

"We all thought that we'd have more time," Trista said regrettably and there was a moment of silence.

"We know you were the Captain of the Guard but not about what that means," Gorn smiled before he reached out to squeeze Trista's hand comfortingly,

"Then I'll start at the beginning. I lived in…" his sentence was cut short as the front door opened again and they all turned to look at the person who had entered.

"Your breakfast is here getting cold boy," Iona pretended to scold as the large person in the doorway stepped forward and into the kitchen with them. "Come say hello to Dana and Trista."

The girls watched as the boy - who was clearly not a boy and very much a man - walked into the kitchen and stopped to stand next to Gorn.

Trista swallowed as her eyes travelled up the mountain that was this young man. As she drank him in, she had the most peculiar sensation in the pit of her stomach that she had to fight to ignore. She shot a brief look at Dana whose eyes were transfixed on their new arrival,

"Trista, Dana, this is my son Oren. Son, this is Dana and the Princess." Trista shook her head,

"Trista is fine…really." She practically squeaked it out, and didn't know why, where was her voice?

"Hi," Oren said it with a polite though seemingly reluctant smile to each girl.

Oren was big, almost as big as his father but where Gorn had clearly softened with age, Oren was solid muscle. He wore the same leather pants with covering apron as Gorn but instead of a dirtied loose tunic, he was topless.

His biceps were the largest Trista had ever seen and he had a large tattoo going down his left arm all the way to his wrist. His pectorals were large and firm with a dusting of dark hair across his chest that sat above a taut and sculpted stomach from the groin lines that disappeared seductively into his waistband.

His skin was smooth and tanned, his bright green eyes shining out of a beautifully sculpted but coal smudged face. His long black hair was tied in top knot with escaped tendrils falling into his face. There was evidence of an early morning beard covering a lean jaw and a firm mouth with plump lips.

Trista swallowed again as she tried so hard not to stare at him,

"It's…nice to meet you," Dana was practically on fire the way her face was red. Oren nodded,

"I'm going to wash up Iona," Oren said quietly, his deep voice a smooth rumble as he left the room and headed upstairs.

"Odd," Iona said taking Oren's bowl to fill it with still steaming porridge. "He never usually washes before breakfast."

Gorn looked at her with a knowing smile before turning to the girls,

"Now, where was I?"

QUESTIONABLE ALLEGIANCE

"Again!"

The clash of steel against steel was deafening as Briseis ran through the training drills with the small number of children who had returned from the Imperial Lands. It seemed, however, that they were more than enough as none of her trained guard had come back at all.

The small group of six had proved their worth in that they had defeated trained soldiers as well as others of their kind. Four boys and two girls had returned who although barely sixteen; showed a lethal ability that Briseis couldn't help but admire.

They were currently in the training yard going over various blocking techniques both with weapons and magic. Briseis was there to provide the magic as the youths were volatile enough to hurt themselves irrevocably. Gardan and the castle guards were there for the combat training.

As they spared with their assigned partners; Briseis sent blasts of energy towards them at random intervals that they would have to deflect and so far, none of them had. They had been at it for hours and each time a force was sent to them; either seen or invisible; the youth were unable to block it.

The blasts couldn't kill them; but they left considerable marks, as all six had bruised faces and bodies.

"Enough!"

The six immediately halted their weapons and stood to attention, breathing heavily form their exhaustion. Briseis knew she was putting them through a lot, but she'd been doing more than this at their age. She didn't have room or time for weakness. She looked at hem now, enraged.

"What do you useless, pathetic ingrates call this?"

No one dared to respond.

"I recruited you to be a part of an army the likes this world or any other has ever seen and you can't block simple energy blasts!"

Still no one responded as Briseis paced along the lines of the coupled youths,

"Your next session will be at the end of this week. If I do not see significant progress by then, I will kill every single one of you. Do I make myself clear?"

"Yes, your Highness!" the chorus, although feeble echoed through the contained courtyard.

"You're dismissed."

The youngsters moved to replace their weapons while the guards went back to their regular posts. Gardan was by her side immediately as Briseis made her way back into the castle. He waited silently for her command and she found she liked that about him, he didn't ask questions.

"I want them ready Gardan"

"Yes Princess,"

"I want them ready to take on anything that, Gods forsaken Samai will throw at them. I can very well defeat her on my own, but I need reinforcements. I do not need to be worried about the battlefield while I rip the heart out of that bitch, do you understand me?"

"Yes Princess,"

"Leave me!" Gardan did not need to be told twice and so left her with her thoughts presumably back to Sentry's Keep. She watched him walk away for the moment and briefly wondered what he did do when away from her. She never had to worry about her tasks being carried out when it was given to Gardan but she'd never taken an interest in his life away from the castle. She shook the thought from her head and headed to the Great Hall.

The Great Hall was the melting pot of Tirnum Castle. While the Throne Room was reserved for her father's formal meetings and coronations and other such fancy affairs, the Great Hall was where everyone came to be seen and heard. Visiting nobles from around the country and other nations, congregated in the Great Hall, making their connections and small talk with who they deemed worthy. It was a hubbub of social climbers who wanted to remain at Court so they could imply they were in the King's favour.

In truth, her father had long retired from the cares of Court life, instead spending his days in his apartments and dealing with the administration of the kingdom from his study. He rarely spoke with the nobility unless it was impossible to avoid and so the Great Hall was a collection of people who just hadn't been told to leave yet.

Briseis tried to spend as little time there as possible, but there were times when being amid the kingdom's social nexus was beneficial.

As she sauntered into the large room past people waiting for audiences with her father; or her for all she knew about it, all eyes were on her. She didn't trouble herself with caring about that when she had more important things to do. Her father had told her a thousand times that these were the people who would support her if another uprising were to occur but Briseis argued that by focusing on their own forces, she wouldn't need them.

Surprisingly, when she reached the far end of the hall, Briseis found her father atop the raised platform where two elaborate chairs were placed for them. Their official thrones were of course in the Throne Room. He was talking with the commander of his armies and best friend, General Ignatius Rarno. Her father was in full regalia for some unknown reason, but she took her seat beside him in her fighting leathers. Servants were immediately at hand offering her food and drink, so she took a goblet of wine and drank deeply. She knew she'd need a lot more of that before the day was through.

"Princess, may I speak with you a moment?"

General Rarno approached her and while he looked respectful enough, she knew the older man despised her. She felt it radiating from him like heat but for once there was nothing, she could do about it. Rarno had never stepped out of line and never would as he was so loyal to her father, to kill him would be...unpleasant as well as unnecessary. He was her GodsFather she knew but it didn't stop her despising him and the way he followed her father blindly like a puppy.

"Speak," just because she couldn't kill him, it didn't mean she had to be nice to him. General Rarno cleared his throat as he approached her,

"There has been some unrest amongst the lords regarding your war."

The infliction on the word *your*, was not lost on her but she chose to ignore it.

"How so, General Rarno?" he sighed as though it were obvious,

"Fights have broken out in the cities amongst Men who have chosen to take this war into their own hands. Men from opposing sides are fighting in the streets; city watches have had to be on constant guard."

"And this is different to their usual duties...how?" Rarno straightened and adjusted his sword at his hip, gripping the hilt with a tight fist.

"They would not be fighting like this without the cause they see in this injudicious declaration."

Briseis was aware of her father listening in as was the rest of the present court.

So, they had sent Rarno to try and talk her down had they?

Briseis sat casually on her throne and took another sip of her wine before allowing her power to erupt in her hand and cloak around her fist. The grey fire settled there crackling faintly, a warning to all.

She sat there, reclined slightly in her seat, comfortable in her training leathers although it was far from ladylike and used her power to make a dagger materialise in her other hand. She'd used it earlier while she was training and liked the feel of it in her hand.

There was a hush that spread through the hall, like a wave.

"Would it be so *injudicious* General, if the power that I wield was to be used against us?" Rarno looked confused,

"What are you implying?"

"I am implying nothing. I am merely stating that if this power," the grey flame around her hand intensified and crackled, "were in the hands of those who would do us harm, would that not be a cause for concern?" Rarno scoffed as he shrugged his shoulders and looked around the room.

"We have always known the Samai possess abilities beyond our own, but those days are over." Briseis rolled her eyes at him,

"The fact that you believe that is both pathetic and irresponsible." As she finished speaking, Briseis stood and threw the dagger into the crowd. A collective scream from the ladies in attendance echoed into the air even as the dagger was brought to an instant stop in the centre of a nobleman's forehead. He froze with fear, tears instantly streaming down his face as his eyes focused on the dagger piercing his skin. He was shaking as the horrified crowd looked on. The dagger slowly began to turn, and a trickle of blood fell from the young man's head as it screwed into his skull,

"See how you cower from mere parlour tricks but you feel you are ready to face what is coming!" she yelled at them in disgust as in an instant, the crowd let out a collective gasp and began clawing at their throat.

Men and women fell to their knees as they clawed at their throats, trying to take breaths that just wouldn't come.

"This, is what the Samaian threat is to us; to *all* of us!" Briseis yelled at them; her voice echoing through the Great Hall. "Lack of air, ready to choke you to death, ready to destroy everything you hold dear!"

People were turning blue, passing out on the floor as they struggled to try and breathe. The fire in her other hand flared with its power.

"Is this what you want?" Briseis continued with rage as she stared down at Rarno who had collapsed at her feet, his mouth gaping like a dying fish as he tried to get some air

"You wish to be held captive by their power and your pathetic fear?"

"Enough!"

Briseis turned just a fraction towards her father's voice before she was knocked back by an unseen force against the wall behind her. As she hit the wall, a collective intake of air echoed around the Great Hall as her hold on the court was lifted. Splutters and coughs resonated all around as the people tried to recover.

Briseis looked toward her father, furious at his interruption and immediately Enflamed and her father did the same.

People began to scramble to their feet to get to the open door, unsure of what would happen next. Guards helped desperate people evacuate as Briseis advanced on her father.

Curian sent a blast of power at her, pushing her back. It infuriated her further as she charged towards him and threw a ball of fire at him. He dodged with incredible speed and it hit the opposite wall cracking the wall instantly. She did it again but Curian threw his arms up and the fire disintegrated against the shield he had quickly created. Undeterred, Briseis sent another and another while her father successfully deflected or dodged them, destroying the Great Hall in the process. She knew he wouldn't be able to fight her one on one, so he was trying to keep her as far away from him as possible.

Curian sent another energy blast at her, knocking her back but this one was stronger. She hadn't expected it and it winded her. Furious she shot fire at him again before using her Everlasting aided speed to get behind him. Briseis materialised a dagger in her hand again and went to plunge it into her father's back. He dodged just in time before unsheathing his sword, but she shook her head, they wouldn't be fighting that way. Briseis reached out her hand and tried to choke her father but she felt his magic resist her - he had learned from before – but she battered her power anyway trying to get her grip around his windpipe but he fought her all the way.

They both pressed their power onto one another, Curian focused on stopping her and Briseis intent on getting through. Her father buckled suddenly, falling to his knee where the floor cracked. Sweat was on his brow as was on her bottom lip as they both concentrated on killing and not being killed. The crack splintered the harder she bore down on him until with a force, she couldn't explain; her father closed his eyes and when he re-opened them; sent out a current of power that sent her flying across the Great Hall and against the stone wall behind them.

The wall cracked and splintered all the way up the ceiling; splitting a hanging rafter in two. It came crashing down into the middle of the hall, shattering into pieces. Briseis lay there, unable to get up as her head spun from the force of the impact. She glared at her father even as she felt blood seeping from the back of her head.

Haggardly, Curian rose from his position on the floor, breathing heavily as he clutched his side.

"Do what you will with this war Briseis, it is clear I cannot stop it!" he yelled after her; his flame subsiding and seemingly out of nowhere, Rarno rushed to his side. "But I will not let you hurt Mortania's people."

Curian exited the Great Hall on the arms of Rarno who helped keep him upright. When they began their ascent to the Kings Rooms; Curian turned to his General and said,

"We must destroy her...by any means. Briseis must be killed."

***

"Through the mighty power of the Gods, I pronounce you Baron and Baroness Lyon and Geneiva of Dreston. May the Gods bless this union, and the prosperity it shall bring onto your people!"

The High Priest concluded the marriage rights that finally united Baron Lyon Dreston with the Northern power that was the province of Thelm.

He turned and kissed his bride who was dressed in pure white silk with blue trimming as was custom for a virgin bride of her status. She was as formal and rigid as Lyon had come to expect from her, but he still held the hope that she would loosen up once they were alone.

If that were not to be the case, he always had Alaina to satisfy his sexual appetite. Geneiva Thelm was a means to an end and many men of his stature took multiple mistresses and he was unlikely to be any different.

They departed the Grand Temple and entered their ornately decorated gold litter, to be paraded through the streets of Dreston and up the adjoining hill back to the castle.

The ride was a tedious one as the men carrying the roofed litter had to get through the tight crowds. As was tradition, the procession was full of guards, priests and the anticipated low-ranking priests who threw coin into the streets to showcase the wealth that would bequeath to the city and its people because of the union.

They reached Dreston castle almost an hour after the ceremony where the Baron exited the litter with his new bride and led her up the castle steps and straight through into the banquet hall. He and Geneiva took their seats on the large decorated chairs atop the dais. They could not readily be described as thrones, as they were not royalty...yet.

Lyon took his new wife's hand as he addressed the room of nobles and servants alike, ready to begin the feast.

"Greetings to you all!" he said and instantly there was quiet. The Baron fixed his eyes on a few people in turn, before continuing,

"I am both pleased and thankful for this most joyous union of the houses Dreston and Thelm. Will the sons of this union be prosperous and reign supreme!"

"May the Gods keep you!" the crowd thundered with the common blessing before Lyon took his seat and the procession of gifts and well-wishers begun.

Nobles approached the dais with declarations of fealty to Dreston and its cause for the crown. Some had travelled far in order to be at the wedding in person; as the date, had been moved so suddenly. The ones that had made it were ready to express their excitement at the trip to the capital and what they would have to encounter there. He assured them that they would be justlyrewarded.

When the appropriate time had passed for him not to be considered rude at an official wedding banquet, Lyon declared that he and his new bride would be retiring as they would be departing for Tirnum first thing in the morning.

As was custom, the high and lower sect priests, Baron Thelm and the resident Keeper of Law, Judge Mormund followed them into his rooms.

He and Geneiva parted ways so her ladies could get her ready while the priests did the rites over the bed. When Geneiva returned, Lyon was waiting for her. She got into the canopied bed dressed in a sheer nightdress that while covering everything showed enough to whet his appetite for her. She was young and supple and would bare many sons of which he was certain. Lyon immediately took her into his arms to kiss her.

Not surprisingly, she was rigid beneath him as there were people including her father looking on; but soon enough he had discarded her underclothes and claimed her as his bride. She bit her lips to contain her scream and tensed her entire body before looking up at the ceiling and beginning to pray. Lyon had to fight not to roll his eyes, why did virgins have to be so dramatic?

He drove himself into her fully, forcing her legs further apart to accommodate him causing her to cry out. There were mumbles from the priests and the judge while her father cleared his throat.

Lyon continued without further notice of them until he released himself within her and finally pulled out.

Without wasting a minute, the priests pulled the coverings aside to inspect the sheets. When they were satisfied with the very blatant display of Geneiva's virginity; they said the appropriate blessings and rites and left them alone.

Geneiva sat up slowly and pulled her nightgown back down. She went to move off the bed, but Lyon stayed her with a hand on her shoulder,

"Where are you going?" she held her arms across her chest and looked away from him as she answered.

"The rites are complete. I wish to return to my own rooms."

"Oh no my dear, you are now my wife. You will sleep here and perform your marital duty until I say otherwise."

The horrified look on her face was almost comical as he drew her back into the bed and lifted her nightgown again,

"Lord husband...I am sore and I..."

"And," he cut her off. "I do not care."

Lyon lifted her nightclothes again and without any preamble, penetrated her again; this time with no one to observe him.

They departed Dreston early the following morning with his entire household in tow to begin to the journey to Tirnum. Immediately behind the armed guard came the litter with the two Barons and behind that were Geneiva and her ladies and then the rest of the household. The early morning sun beat down upon them as they rode the initial streets out of the city gates and into the vast wasteland of The Plains.

The two Barons were in deep discussion, lounged against a mountain of cushions drinking wine in their finery when Erik said,

"You are confident in a victory for our people?"

"Of course. I have deployed forces ahead of our arrival; I am bringing another four thousand men with me and have towns across Mortania under my jurisdiction and control. The Greybolds will not know what hit them." Lyon was confident as he continued to sip from his heavy goblet.

"You seem so confident of a woman who I have heard can kill a man with a simple look." Lyon shrugged and asked

"Does she bleed?"

"Excuse me?"

"The question is simple enough Erik," Lyon took another sip of his wine before twirling it around in the golden goblet he held. "Does this woman bleed?"

"Well of course she can bleed, she is human after all!" it was clear how ludicrous Erik thought the question as he looked at his new ally with confusion.

"If she can bleed, then she can be killed Erik. It's as simple as that."

"The Princess is powerful, she can…"

"She can be killed Baron Thelm," Lyon turned his attention to the outside world whipping past them through the small fabric window of the litter that carried them. "It's as simple as that."

***

Rayne watched with a heavy heart as the Baron and his household departed Dreston and the remaining guard closed the city gates behind them.

She shook her head with a sense of deep impending dread about what would happen next. She wondered at how quickly things had changed and would continue to change now that Trista had left her.

She'd been waiting eighteen years for Trista to come into her own, to meet her and teach her all she needed to know to defeat their common enemy. With Trista's capture and the pressing need to escape to Gorn in Priya, in many ways; Rayne felt she'd failed her princess...and her family.

She closed her eyes at the pain that pierced through her heart. As she stood wallowing in her sorrow, Rayne dug deep; deeper than she'd had to do in many years and tried to summon her power but felt virtually nothing.

Getting Trista safely out of the city had cost her more then she realised. She couldn't even begin to contact her mentally, the effort and magic it would take could cost her even further.

A tear escaped Rayne's eye and she took a shuddering breath,

"Forgive me Rowan...I'm sorry I couldn't be with her all the way."

Rayne turned from the narrow alley she stood in and leaning heavily on a pair of wooden crutches, she made her way back home.

WITHOUT POWERS

The morning after meeting Gorn and Oren, Trista was in the kitchen with Iona helping to make breakfast. It was clear that all meals were a big affair as Iona seemed to be constantly cooking.

Gorn and Oren spent their day in the forge where they worked as blacksmiths and Iona looked after everything else in their home. She cleaned and dusted and looked after the animals that roamed the surrounding grounds. She made them breakfast, lunch and dinner and always with a smile on her face. Trista and Dana found her good nature infectious and found themselves smiling more than they had in a long time.

They'd spent the previous day getting to know each other and Trista had explained about her life growing up in Remora. She explained how she had to leave Remora once she Ascended and that Avriel had helped her escape. Gorn had been familiar with the name but not so much so that he could comment on her. Trista explained what she'd learned from Rayne but that she was unsure of what she would do now she'd found Gorn.

Gorn said he would explain everything once they were settled in and spent the rest of the day resting as they were still so very tired. Oren didn't say much during their conversations, nothing at all if truth be told but Trista found herself stealing looks at him, trying to gather what he was thinking about her and her life.

Both he and Gorn were back in the forge, as they had been before the women had woken up. Dana was out in the yard collecting eggs from the coop and Trista had been tasked to make the porridge while Iona got to work on the bread.

"Gorn will get you started with your schedule today," Iona offered with a smile.

"Schedule?" Trista asked looking up from the porridge pot.

"Yep, he has it all planned out for you. There's so much he wants to share with you and teach you." Trista stopped stirring for a moment before she voiced the question that had been burning in her throat since yesterday,

"Will he be able to tell me about my parents?" Iona's face softened at that as she reached out and pulled Trista into a hug; or as well as she could do with dough on her hands.

"Gorn will tell you anything you wish to hear my girl," Trista smiled back at her and went back to stirring. "He just wants you comfortable before we get into all this…stuff." Iona made a movement with her hand, gesturing to all around them. Trista determined that referred to her finding and killing the Princess of Mortania.

At that moment, Dana walked through the front door with a basket full of eggs and set them on the side of the table,

"Thank you Dana!" Iona said turning to look at her but as she did so, her eyebrows knotted.

"That's all you got…from both coops?"

"Both?" Dana said innocently but Iona only laughed,

"I told you there was another outback; closer to the wall. What you got between your ears; wool?"

"Sorry Iona…erm, Trista. Could you get the rest of the eggs for me?"

Trista looked over at her friend,

"I'm in the middle of…"she cut her sentence short as she realised the look on Dana's face as she shifted her eyes to the door. "Oh, erm…sure. I can get them, here."

She handed Dana the wooden spoon who took it with a satisfied smile. Trista took the egg basket from Dana and headed back out the door toward the chicken coop.

Priya was warm and as Trista stepped outside, she delighted in the warm rays of sunshine that washed over her. It wasn't dusty and stifling like the heat of Dreston, but here, the air was moist and the trees a lush green; still thriving with life in the heart of summer. Gorn's house was surrounded by a few acres of land that while a short ride into the main, was still quite connected. The surrounding acres were used to graze their livestock and grow fruit and vegetables. A path led through the trees and into the main town, a lot like Trista's home in Remora.

She turned to the right of the front door towards the back of the house where the chickens were kept and quickly filled her basket with the remaining eggs.

She was almost done, wondering why Dana had wasted her time coming out here when she finally saw the reason why.

Oren.

The back of the house, where the coops were kept, shared space with the back of the forge where Gorn and Oren worked. There was a low brick wall separating the two areas so the animals wouldn't go over. It was over this wall, that Trista could see Oren in the forge.

He was topless again, not unusual considering the forge got ridiculously hot, and he was currently banging away at something on the anvil. She could only see his profile, but that was enough to send her heart racing. The bulge of muscles as he hammered the metal into shape, the sweat dripping off his arms making them shiny as he worked, was all a little too much.

When he turned slightly to dip what she could now see was an axe head into the water bucket; she caught a glimpse of his coal smudged face.

Gods, he was gorgeous, Trista thought as she ogled his solid abs and thick muscles. She'd never thought of a man in such a blatantly sexual way before and it was admittedly rather exciting. Oren was unlike any other man she'd seen before. In Remora every man was a gentleman and more of the academic persuasion like her father. Oren was young, powerful and sexy in a rugged, no nonsense way that she'd never encountered.

Trista stood watching him for a long while when he sharply looked up from the anvil and looked directly at her, startling her. For some reason, she stared back, unable to look away from his penetrating gaze. As she watched him, the most peculiar sensation erupted in her stomach and unthinkingly to grab her stomach, she dropped the egg basket, smashing some instantly. Crouched on the floor behind the wall, holding her stomach, Trista took a few deep breaths to calm herself, but it was such an odd sensation. She stayed crouched there for the moment until eventually, the feeling stopped and when it did; she stood up slowly to look back over the wall, but Oren had gone.

She picked up what she could salvage of the eggs and with a bemused shake of her head, made her way back into the house.

When she got into the kitchen, Dana was there with a huge grin on her face that Trista couldn't help but respond to,

"Behave," she hissed at her friend.

"What's that honey?" Iona asked as she bent to put the bread in the oven.

"Oh nothing, here are the eggs...I'm sorry but I dropped a few." Trista ignored the splutter of laughter that escaped Dana.

"Not to worry darling, we have more than enough. Could you go and ask the boys to come in. I want them washed up, before breakfast today. Then we can all have a nice chat."

With a polite nod, Trista headed back outside.

The workshop was off to the right at the far end of the front yard, leading toward the path that led into Priya. Trista walked up to the front steps and Gorn was there, sweeping them. When he saw her, he smiled,

"Trista!"

"Morning," she replied with the same big smile as she walked up to meet him. "Iona said to come inside to wash up before breakfast."

"That woman," he said rolling his eyes mockingly as he turned into the workshop to put the broom away. "Boy, come out here, breakfast is almost ready."

Gorn bellowed into the forge as he busied himself with organising his tools. Trista looked around at the metal work and tools that lay around,

"You made all of these?"

"Some, not so much anymore. Oren does most of it now."

Trista ran her hand over a sword hilt shaped like a dragon with his mouth open and the sword came out the other end. Its eyes on either side were bright red jewels.

"They are beautiful,"

"Know much about metal work, do you?"

Trista looked up at the sound of Oren's sarcastic comment. He stepped out of the forge wiping his hands onto a dirty rag, throwing it down on the table closest to her as he came to stand in front of her.

"No," Trista steeled herself against his ridicule, not sure why she was so nervous that he was speaking to her. It was the most he'd said to her since they'd arrived.

"I have eyes. I can see if something is beautiful or not. It doesn't mean it has any substance to it." Oren looked at her from the tips of her toes to the top of her head without moving his head.

"Funny…I was thinking the same thing."

He walked away from her and out the door towards the house. Trista stood with her mouth wide, in total confusion before looking at Gorn,

"He's a little cranky in the morning," he said apologetically as they walked towards the door. "Don't pay him any mind."

Trista nodded although she was a little confused and almost sure, that Oren had been talking about her.

They ate breakfast once everyone was washed up and dressed around the kitchen table. Chatter and jokes were thrown around the table mainly by Gorn and Iona, while Trista and Dana laughed and asked questions, and Oren sat in silence. Trista found herself watching him every not and then but when Gorn mentioned his old home, her attention was switched.

"You haven't always lived in Priya?"

"Goodness no, I was born and raised in HighTower, it's an estate under the Illiyan jurisdiction. The lords of Illiya were our liege lords and us their bannerman. I left there when I went to live in Tirnum, to join the army. That's where I met Alexander for the first time. He was only a little younger than me but even then, I knew he had spirit and a good heart as any young prince should do"

Trista hung onto his every word, eager to learn anything she could about the father she would never know. She realised that while there was always the possibility that her mother, Rowan may not have survived the last eighteen years, there was the same possibility that she had. There was a hope that she would see Rowan one day, but her father was dead. Lost to her forever and so she wanted every piece of information about him that she could get.

"When his royal duties didn't call him away," Gorn was now saying, "Alex was up at the crack of dawn for his training, doing drills and he was always the last to leave; always wanting to do better. I befriended him in a way that a lot of the other recruits were afraid to befriend him; because he was the crown prince. I think he came to see in me; someone who would always tell him the truth...never baby him or just agree with him because of his station. He admired that about me, and I admired that he actually wanted that from me."

Gorn had a sincere and wistful look on his face as he spoke,

"Alex and I spent our early training days together and many more years after that. We went through almost everything together. He was my…my very best friend."

There was a moment of silence as Gorn sniffed and blinked a few times to compose himself before continuing.

"When he'd completed his formal military training, a year later, he married your mother Trista, as was Intended. Soon after I married Lorma and soon enough, we had this one."

He turned his eyes to Oren who merely huffed but everyone could see how much Gorn adored his only son.

"We lived a good life in those years before the rebellion; things were peaceful. Your father took his throne very early on in life and for a long time, it was the most wonderful kingdom to belong to."

"What was it like in the castle?" Dana asked, clearly taken in by the notion of grandeur and royalty. It was so far removed from anything they had experienced; it was exciting and overwhelming to say the least.

"Life was...hectic!" Gorn said with a laugh and Trista saw Iona smile at the way Gorn laughed at the fond memory. "When Alexander became King, he appointed me as Captain of the Guard and so I always had something to do. Managing security; training new recruits; sparring with your father and organising scouting missions throughout the kingdom."

He took a sip of some type of warm ale that Iona had made for him before continuing,

"When we eventually had time off though, they were the best times. Feasts and parties and festivals like you would never imagine. The Great Hall would be lit to the rafters with candlelight and had musicians playing. Your mother was a wonderful hostess Trista, no one wanted to miss any of her parties. People from all over the kingdom wanted to be there see what Queen Rowan would do next and…"

Trista suddenly pushed her chair back from the kitchen table and stormed off outside. The others looked at each other, confused before Gorn sighed, seemingly realising what was wrong and got up from the table. Gorn used a cane sometimes when his injured leg was playing up. He used it now to head out the front door and looked around the front yard for Trista.

He found her, sitting under the shade of a large tree picking at something on the ground. He approached her slowly and with a little difficulty, he took a seat down beside her. He placed his large hand on the top of her raised knee, giving it a squeeze,

"I might not be able to wield the power like I used to but even I can tell when kin are feeling down. What's wrong Princess?"

"Please don't call me that," she replied faintly as a tear escaped and rolled slowly down her cheek.

"Why not, it's what you are."

"No," she turned her face up to him, where tears pooled in the rims of her eyes. "No, it's not what I am! A princess would have enjoyed those parties and heard those musicians. A princess would have been a part of that wonderful kingdom and celebrated in its happiness! That's *not* me; that wasn't my life!"

Gorn was silent for a moment as he looked at Trista's sympathetically.

"And you wish it was."

It wasn't a question.

Trista looked away from him then, letting the tears fall that she'd tried to hide for so long.

"I spent my whole life feeling left out; feeling like a nobody and to hear about the life I should have had; it makes me...it makes me..."

"Angry?"

"Furious!" Trista shouted but not at him. "I grew up without any real friends or my birth parents for so long and hearing you speak about how great my life could have been with them, just makes me feel...resentful."

Sympathetically, Gorn placed his arm around her shoulders and pulled Trista in for a hug. She readily accepted it as she finally let her tears out.

"The day you were born...it was the happiest I had ever seen Rowan and Alex. Once they cleaned you up, they both lay either side of you in their bed, just watching you, happy that you were finally with them. I don't think any child was loved more than you."

Trista wiped her tears and looked up at him,

"When they named me your Godsfather, I felt privileged that they would entrust me with the care of such a precious little thing as you. Oren was only five or so at the time, I wasn't even sure I was doing the right thing as a father, but they trusted me to care for you, to look after you; their most precious possession."

Gorn held Trista's face by her chin,

"The past doesn't matter now Trista. You were born a princess and so you *are* a princess, and no one can ever change that…but only you can embrace it."

"That's just it Gorn," Trista protested, feeling defeated. "It's not just about the parties or titles. It's about an entire way of life that I will never understand; that will never come naturally to me. How am I meant to lead an army and rule a kingdom when I don't know *how* to be a princess?"

"No one knows how to be anything Trista, one must learn and practice with all things. You're learning right now, as you did with Rayne and how you will with us."

Trista nodded, knowing that he was right but still feeling angry at everything that could have been.

"You're angry at having your life taken away from you; no one can blame you for that. I even ask that you build on it." Trista leaned out of his embrace to look up into Gorn's face,

"What do you mean?"

"You know why Rayne sent you to me?"

"Yes, to learn to fight."

"Yes, Oren and I are going to teach you how to fight with and without your powers."

Trista tried to take that in but for the life of her all she could focus on was that Oren would be teaching her.

"Without my powers?"

"Briseis has become very powerful in the years that you haven't even begun to learn your fighting ability. We have to find a way for you to defeat her should your powers ever fail you."

Trista was all to aware of how her powers could fail her, even more so how she could fail them by overexerting herself. She needed to get stronger so she could be of more use to everyone.

"Okay, but why does Oren have to teach me?"

"Because Oren doesn't care who you are and won't go soft on you," the sultry voice that belonged to Oren travelled as Trista looked up to see him coming towards them.

Trista's face reddened as she watched him prowl towards her, now dressed in dark brown leather trousers and boots and a tight sleeveless vest. His hair was left loose, hanging haphazardly more to one side than the other as though he'd just run his fingers through it.

"Excuse me?"

Gorn held out his hand for Oren to help him off the ground and even as he pulled his father up, Oren didn't take his eyes off her.

"Oren," came Gorn's steady warning.

"Don't worry Dad, I won't hurt the precious little princess but I won't go easy on her either."

Trista looked directly at him defiantly and got up from the floor to glare at him,

"I didn't ask to be treated specially in any way. I didn't ask for any of this!"

"That makes two of us," Oren retorted, green eyes full of mockery and distain.

"Oren!"

Gorn was firmer this time which clearly stopped the next words to come out of Oren's mouth, but it didn't stop the venomous look that he directed at her.

"I'll be back by nightfall, make sure she's ready."

Oren looked at her dismissively before turning and walking towards their small stable where their horse, Titan was kept. Moment later, Trista watched as Oren rode away down the path leading into Priya. Her heart pumped rapidly with the rage that built inside of her.

"What did he mean? Ready for what?" Gorn sighed as he looked back at her apologetically.

"I'm getting old Trista and since my injury;" he motioned to his leg and the cane he used. "I don't move like I used to." Trista put the dots together,

"So, I'm stuck with him!"

It didn't matter how good looking he was, Oren was a surly, moody person and she didn't want to spend any time with him; especially not alone.

"Trista, I've trained Oren since he was three years old and for the last twenty years he has grown into the most powerful and incredible fighter."

"How would you know; it's not like he has anyone to compare himself to!" she was being spiteful now and realised how futile it was because Oren wasn't even there to hear her.

It was then, that feeling in her belly came back again but felt as though it had clenched into a fist, making her wince.

Gorn sighed,

"I realise Oren can be difficult but right now, he is the best thing for you. Your training must be fast tracked, and he can do that with you better than I ever could."

Trista looked up at the large man as she held her hands across her stomach and saw something in him that upset her more than anything Oren had said, fear.

Gorn, this larger than life male who had been nothing but excited and happy to meet her and teach her about her heritage was afraid. He was afraid that she wouldn't be up to the task of saving them all from Briseis. Hadn't she thought the same thing a thousand times since she'd left Remora?

She couldn't let everyone down, especially not Gorn and so she knew that she would handle anything Oren or anyone else threw at her.

"What do I need to do?" she asked Gorn and with a relieved smile, he explained what was required of her.

Once they'd helped Iona with some of the chores in the house, Dana and Trista followed her into town. Iona wanted to get them some new things and once Trista started her training with Oren, she didn't think they would have time.

Priya was in the south of Mortania and so was nearly always hot. Right now, in the middle of summer, the sun was blazing overhead and so they were all dressed in the lightest of dresses with their hair pulled casually away from their faces. Trista's black curly hair refused to be tamed at times but alongside Iona's mass of brown curls, it didn't look quite so hectic. Dana's once bob length brown hair had grown out in the weeks since they'd left Remora and she held it back with a simple yellow band that matched the dress she wore.

The women walked the short path into Priya, and the girls delighted in the quaint little town that seemed to accommodate a large Samaian population.

Where Dreston had been a mixture of races and cultures, here there were more Samai than most.

"It became a haven after the rebellion," Iona explained when Trista asked why so many were there. "Its why we haven't been effected as much by the changing weather and dying crops; Samai together generates good magic and so we survive." Dana looked confused,

"If everyone knows that, then why not just all congregate in one place and create magic to fight the king?" Trista waited for the answer, as she'd wondered the same thing.

"When I asked the same thing, Gorn said that too much puts a target on your back in some way. Like it sends a signal that the king could track, its why Samai magic is banned in so many places. The longer it's not used, the easier it fades."

"But magic is everywhere," Trista insisted. "Rayne told me that I can draw power from almost anything as long as it's connected to the Everlasting."

"So what happens when new generations aren't connected?"

The answer was staring her in the face: the power might be everywhere but no Samai could harness it if they weren't born under its rule.

"Don't think about it too much Trista. Let's just get you girls some new things then we can get something to eat."

As they walked down main street, Trista had a peculiar sensation in her stomach again and instinctively, she turned to look into the busy crowd.

She saw him instantly, walking towards a tavern with a very pretty girl on his arm. Trista watched as Oren nuzzled his face into the girl's neck and disappeared with her into the establishment. Trista blinked away her embarrassment and caught up with Dana and Iona.

The women spent the day in town and returned with a variety of trousers and tunics that they had either lost or left behind in Dreston. When they returned home, Gorn gave Trista a large box and said she should change into what was inside for when Oren got home.

True to his word; Oren returned by nightfall.

Trista was in the washroom when she heard Iona scold him for smelling of perfume,

"You waste your life away in that sin pit with Nyron and the others!" she snapped even as Trista heard her washing up their dinner things. She strained to listen but only heard Oren's mumbled reply. She stayed in the washroom until she heard him climb the stairs and disappear into his bedroom and told herself that it was none of her business who Oren spent his time with. She was still in there repeating her mantra when she heard him leave his room again and go down the stairs.

She stood now in the outfit that Gorn had given her: a pair of fitted dark green leather pants with the matching long sleeved shirt. It was called a shirt but had no buttons and was kept strapped to her by little laces at the sides that she had to loosen to get into it. Along the forearms, shoulders, stomach, thighs, shins and back were what looked like metal guards. They moulded to the shape of her arm so were flexible, but she couldn't dent it with her finger.

Once she'd tied her hair back into a tight ponytail, nervously she left the washroom and went to meet Gorn in the workshop.

Dana and Iona were in the living room talking and when she arrived downstairs, they both went silent.

"That bad?"

"Not at all," Dana said, almost in awe. "You look amazing Trista."

"Thank you…I'd better be going; I'll see you soon." Iona smiled warmly at her as she walked out the front door.

Trista walked the short distance to the workshop but as she went to open the door she heard Gorn and Oren talking,

"You can't blame Trista for something she has no control over Oren!" Trista's hand stopped at the workshop door as she heard her name. She leaned forward to listen better,

"I'm not blaming her for anything!"

"Then what was that about this morning? You had no right to speak to her that way!"

"Oh because she's the princess?"

"No Oren, because she's lost. She's lost and has no one but us to turn to and teach her our ways. You of all people should understand that!"

"I do!"

"Then do right by her and put aside whatever it is you're feeling. I realise it's a lot to deal with now that she's here but you knew this day would come."

She knew she should stop listening but what on earth were they talking about?

Her belly went funny again and suddenly, she heard footsteps and jumped back from the door just as Gorn opened it.

"Trista."

"H-Hi...I'm ready."

She looked away from his eyes guiltily before looking into the workroom where Oren stood, now in much the same attire as her but all black. His hair was slicked back into a ponytail away from his face. He lifted a large pack onto his shoulder before reaching out and picking up two swords; one significantly smaller than the other so it had to be hers.

He stepped toward them and Trista had to jump out of the way before he barged into her,

"Let's go!" he called over his shoulder and with a last look at Gorn who smiled at her reassuringly; Trista followed him into the night.

When they had walked for what felt like forever into the dense overgrowth of the surrounding bushes, Trista finally built the courage to ask where they were going.

"It's not far," was Oren's reply.

"But where *is* it?" she asked again. Even though his back was to her, she knew he had rolled his eyes by the sigh he made.

"Excuse me!" she snapped making him come to an abrupt halt and turn to look at her.

"What?"

"I'm talking to you, that's what!"

"And I'm ignoring you!"

"Well that isn't going to work for me!"

"Oh no, what ever will I do!" his mocking was her undoing.

"What is your problem with me, what have I ever done to you!"

This time she saw him roll his eyes but completely out of the blue, he outstretched his hand and a blueish green flame erupted there; making Trista step back in shock.

"How did you do that?"

"That doesn't matter," he moved his hand away and the flame stayed where it was, hovering between them and generating the light he seemed to have created it for.

"We don't have a lot of time, but we have a lot to get through, so please don't start with all the questions unless they relate directly to your training."

"Asking where we're going to do this training isn't directly related?"

"No, you don't need to know where or why. You just need to do it!"

"Stop being short with me!"

"Why, not used to hard work?" Trista stood back and looked at him disdainfully.

What did he have against her?

"You don't know anything about me or what I've been through." He scoffed as though she was talking absolute bullshit.

"I know enough,"

"And that's enough to condemn me?"

"Until I say otherwise, yes!"

"That's not fair!"

"Life's not fair Trista!"

It was the first time he had ever said her name and Trista was deeply ashamed at how that made her feel despite how he was talking to her.

"It's not fair that I have to be out here teaching some clueless princess how to fight but here we are. So just do what I tell you and be quiet."

Trista didn't bother to respond. If he wanted to believe she'd been sheltered growing up or was choosing to stay ignorant to her past, then so be it. She would just have to fight tooth and nail to prove him otherwise.

"Lead the way."

Without another word, the flame went out and Oren took off again. She had no choice but to follow him.

CONNECTING

That same night, Lamya lay on the bunk in her cabin and connected with the Council to explain to them her plan. She relaxed herself and slipped into her meditative state and in moments she was in communication with the Council.

"Greetings Chief Justice Yeng."

"Greetings Lamya, to what do we owe this pleasure?"

"I wanted to let the Council know that I am on my way to Illiya."

"We told you to go to Crol," her grandmother said just as she felt the presence of the other Justices; Lorien who she'd spoken with the last time they were connected along with Justices Lobos and Antyen.

"I am aware of my orders, Chief Justice but I feel my time and gifts would be better spent recruiting followers from across the kingdom, influencing others to join our side."

"Your orders are to meet the princess and guide her to Thelm, that was all. We have the rest under control." Justice Lorien replied curtly.

"Is that why you don't know where she is?"

"Lamya, you overstep your mark."

Lamya felt her grandmother's disappointment and so apologised immediately,

"My apologies Chief Justice...and Justice Lorien."

She knew Justice Lorien disliked her, feeling that her advancement in the Council was due to nepotism when that was entirely untrue. What was true, was that Lamya had bettered his son at almost every exam and test during their schooling years and he hated her for what he saw as embarrassing his kin.

"Justice Lorien is correct," Justice Antyen chimed in, her childlike voice distinctive from all others. "However, there is always more that can be done to enhance our fighting force across the kingdom for when the time comes."

"I see no harm in Lamya spreading the word of the princess' return." Justice Lobos added.

"And what happens when the Greybold princess discovers that her enemy is now in the open rallying forces, will she not rally more against us?"

"She is already doing so, Justice Lorien, it is us who are lagging behind." Justice Antyen chimed in again, her melodious voice making Lamya smile despite the seriousness of the situation.

"I agree," her grandmother said and Lamya held her breath. "I agree that there is no harm in letting the common people and Samaian population in the far reaches of Mortania know that their salvation is near. Lamya, you may continue with your plans."

"Thank you, Chief Justice."

She was told to reconnect with them once she was on land then bid them good night.

***

By the time they came to a stop, Trista was exhausted. She and Oren had hiked through the bushel and hilly terrain behind Gorn's home without seeing or hearing another person. Once she thought she saw a light that could have come from a cottage or inn, but it soon disappeared and all she had was the sound of Oren's footsteps in front of her to guide her.

She'd almost crashed into him when he stopped abruptly but caught herself at the last minute and took in her surroundings.

They had emerged into a clearing surrounded by trees that loomed overhead creating an almost peaceful dome above them that she could no longer see the sky. As Oren dropped his large pack on the ground, Trista had the most peculiar sensation of having been there before. She placed her fingertips to her forehead as it began to pulsate with a dull pain.

Mama has to go little one
Mama stay!

The voices slammed into her head causing her to sway so she steadied herself, hiding behind the motion of lowering her own pack to the floor and taking deep breaths. She didn't want Oren to know anything was wrong; before he think she was already complaining.

When he turned back towards her, he created the blueish green light again but this time, made a gesture of throwing it away from him and it landed in the centre of the alcove and blazed there like a campfire. She tried not to look impressed as she slowly stood up, trying to fend off the feeling of nausea.

"We're camping here?"

"Yes. We'll stay here for the next week or so, depending on how you do; so, I can train you without any interference."

"You mean from Briseis."

"Exactly, I haven't been able to feel your power since you got here but it doesn't mean that she doesn't have something up her sleeve that will allow her to locate you. This place, will help with that."

"What is it?"

Oren looked up and around them at the dimly lit alcove and shrugged,

"It's like a void I guess, a place of no magic; no power."

"Then how can we use our powers in here?"

"Okay, wrong explanation. It's not that the space doesn't have any power; it's that it can't let power out. There's a barrier; all around us that absorbs the power that's sent into it. Watch," Oren clenched his hand into a fist before opening it and a blueish green fireball erupted in his clawed hand. He threw it into the trees and a way off, it disintegrated into thin air.

"You try," Trista's eyes widened,

"Throw a fireball?" Oren shrugged. "I can't do that,"

"There's a first time for everything," he said as he flicked something out of his fingernails before folding his large arms across his massive chest.

"Okay," Trista mumbled as she turned away from him and closed her eyes, willing the fireball into her hand.

"Stop thinking about it, will it."

"How can I will it, if I'm not thinking about it?"

"Just humour me, okay Princess," Trista gritted her teeth against the title that she was beginning to hate, especially coming from him.

She took another deep breath and when she opened her eyes, her fist was aflame, but it wasn't a standalone ball as Oren's had been.

"Too much power, don't Enflame; rein it in and shape it," she nodded as she drew in her powers, making sure not to Enflame and tried to shape her power the way Oren had done. A few moments later, she opened her eyes again and a small blue fireball was in her hand.

As she turned to Oren with a smile on her face; it disappeared.

"W-what happened?"

"You lost concentration. You must learn to be able to maintain your power in each form you wish it; without losing focus. There will come a time when you'll be required to use both your physical strength and your magical strength, and you won't have time to take a breath or close your eyes. In those brief moments, Briseis will kill you."

"These forms have to be consistent," a fireball suddenly erupted in his right hand. "Damaging and swift," he threw the fireball into the air as he immediately conjured another one in his left hand. With his right hand that had released the first fireball, he drew his blade from his across his back, then threw the ball in his left hand before creating a shield of pulsating air as soon as the ball had left it.

Oren stood there, battle ready quicker than it had taken her to blink. As she was about to be thoroughly impressed; she felt a kick in her back that propelled her towards him and into his shield. She bounced off it, falling onto her backside in time to see the ball of energy that he had sent to hit her with; disappear just like the shield.

Oren put his sword back and powered down before stepping forward and looking down at her.

"Just because my hands were occupied; it doesn't mean my mind was."

"Okay I get it" Oren smirked down at her and strode away.

"Get some sleep, we start at first light."

Trista blocked a overhead strike from Oren; what felt like the fiftieth in a row and ground her teeth together.

"Again!" Oren commanded,

Her arm felt weak, like her bones had decided to vacate completely; but she couldn't let him know that she was in pain.

They had been training for the better part of two days and she didn't feel as though she were getting any better; if Oren's feedback was anything to go by.

"Stop!" Trista stopped and eagerly caught her breath as Oren sized her up. She went to walk away to get her water skin, not wanting to deal with his penetrating stare any longer.

"You think there's water available on the battlefield?"

"Excuse me, I can't take a break now?"

"There are no breaks in war, when are you going to understand that?" Trista looked at him as though he were crazy,

"Oren, we're training,"

"So that means you're not taking it seriously?"

"That's not what I meant, and you know it. Why are you being so hard on me?"

Oren raised his longsword again and lunged at her. She barely registered what he was doing before she dropped her water skin and lifted her own sword to block the attack.

The force of the connect rattled her teeth as she combined the strength of physically holding her weapon and sending power into it to help match his own.

She pushed him away from her, blasting him with a small energy ball that barely made him stumble.

He advanced on her again and swiped at her, once; twice, three times and each time she blocked.

You can't always play defence

Oren had said this to her the very first day when he realised that she relied on his moves to decide what to do next. Decidedly she charged at him, but when he shielded high as she knew he would, she went low and sent a blast to knock his feet apart, this time making him stumble.

Oren growled at her before advancing on her again and raining succinct and calculated blows until he was too fast to keep up. Oren crashed his blade down on to hers and she buckled into the ground before he leant over her with what would have been a death strike.

"That was being hard on you. Get it together Princess, or you would have doomed us all"

Oren stormed away from her and as she got up off the floor and dusted herself off; she felt his frustration.

"I'm sorry,"

"I don't want your apology, Princess." He spat at her,

"I know…but I'm giving it any way." He didn't say anything as he took a seat by his bed roll on one side of the now outed campfire.

There was an unnatural quiet in the alcove that she'd begun to get used to. Sometimes she forgot that there were people other than she and Oren in the entire world.

She took a seat opposite him and watched as he began to sharpen his sword,

"I don't have the…attachment to this as you do and for that, I'm sorry but I want you to know that, I am trying and I will do my best to save you all from this." Oren growled at her and threw his sword down before turning to look at her with anger in his eyes,

"That's where you're going wrong! This isn't just about us! This isn't just about me, or my father or even the entire Samaian population; this is about *you*. This is about you claiming your birth right and taking what is rightfully yours and not complaining about how hard it is!"

"I'm not complaining!"

"That's all it sounds like," Oren dismissed her with a disdainful look that had her face heat up.

In that moment, she felt a rage of the likes she couldn't begin to explain. How could he dismiss her like she was nothing; like she wasn't even trying?

Trista stood up and picked her sword up as she straightened up,

"Get up," she said simply but Oren didn't even look at her.

"I'm done playing with you."

Trista let out a ball of energy directly at the side of his head, knocking him sideways. As he skirted across the ground, she advanced on him and went to strike him but was blocked by an invisible shield,

"Argh!" she growled her frustration as she watched him get to his feet and stretch his arm out, for his blade to materialise in his hand. She didn't have the time to question how he'd done it, but it infuriated her further; that he was so in tune with his powers and she wasn't.

Again, she went after him and attacked him with her sword in the ways he had taught her only days before.

On and on, she attacked him while Oren expertly blocked, parried and dodged each blow as he saw fit. She couldn't possibly beat him, and it enraged her. In a fit of fury, she stepped away from him and without another thought in her head, threw her sword at him.

In the instant it left her hand; Trista felt a vibration in the air and suddenly, her sword was aimed at her. Instinctively, she threw her arms up to block her face and as she did so; the blade stopped mid-air. Looking fully at the long blade that was inches from her face, she realised that she hadn't stopped the sword but instead shielded herself against it.

While Oren was still sending the blade towards her; she was beating against his own power and trying to stop it penetrating her shield.

She could feel its power in the vibration between shield and sword, pressing against her entire body like intense gravity. Her head began to pound at the pressure of keeping her shield up against his incredible strength when he didn't even seem to be breaking a sweat.

A piercing pain shot through her head and Trista collapsed, dropping her shield and the sword flew over her head, embedding itself in a tree behind her.

"You could have *killed* me!" she gasped.

"Stop exaggerating, I'd never kill our precious princess."

He said walking over to and then past her to retrieve her sword from the tree. He handed it to her when she was upright again, trying to catch her breath.

"How did you make your sword materialise in your hand?"

"That doesn't matter, what matters is that I saw true strength from you just now. Keep that up, and you won't be such a failure after all." He walked past her,

"I'm not a failure," she said through her teeth, although she wasn't sure she believed it as she hung her head in defeat.

"Hey," Trista looked up and turned to look at him even though tears were threatening to fall. Expecting distain or further ridicule, Trista was surprised when she saw actual remorse on Oren's face.

For a second, she forgot her piercing headache or his humiliation of her and everything else for that matter. All she could see now were the intense teal green of his eyes and the thick lashes that framed them as she looked directly into his face.

Gods he was beautiful.

"I shouldn't have said that," his voice was so low she barely heard him. "I…you're doing better…keep it up."

She nodded but he turned away from her almost instantly and Trista almost called out to him. What she would say, she wasn't entirely sure, but she felt…something.

She watched as he walked over to his bedroll, took a few things out of his pack and said,

"I'm going down to the river, I'll be back."

Again, she nodded and let him walk away without another word.

Oren didn't return that night before she fell asleep, but when she awoke the next morning, he was asleep in his bedroll opposite her. Not sure why he had stayed away so long or whether she should address it; she decided instead to get ready for the day's lesson.

She gathered her things and made her way down to the small river where they washed and gathered water. Oren had shown it to her their very first day and she was glad of the privacy it offered even for a little while.

She could sit on the rocks after a day's training and just think about all that had happened to her in the weeks since she'd left home.

She thought about Thorn, and whether he was thinking about her and she thought a lot about her parents and how they were coping without her. Her father, she knew would survive anything but her mother…Trista was all her mother had and now that her only daughter was gone, Trista wasn't sure how Gwendolyn Freitz would cope.

In the farthest reaches of her mind, she accepted that she missed the certainty of Remora. The same rigidity that she thought stifled her, she missed with a yearning that she'd never known. Everything was different now; everything was new, and it terrified her.

Trista didn't spend too long in the water as it was so cold, rushing down from who knew where but when she finally emerged from soaking her whole head; she saw Oren looking down at her from the top of the ledge they had to climb to get back to camp. It was a few metres up so was unlikely he could see anything, but she instinctively covered her breasts although only her shoulders were above the water.

They looked at one another for a few minutes until he called down,

"Hurry…we need to get started." she nodded,

"I'll be right up!" she called back as he turned and walked away.

She saw him drop his own things near his feet before disappearing back into the growth all around them. For a split second, Trista was disappointed she hadn't walked in on him bathing.

It was obvious that she found him attractive, more so then she had any boy she'd ever met. With Thorn it was a friendship that had grown into something because of how he treated her. Thorn had treated her with respect when no one else did and for that she'd grown to love him. Of course, Thorn was good looking with his large blue eyes and dark hair, but there was something magnetic about her attraction to Oren that she'd never experienced before. Still, however obvious her attraction to him, it was clear that he didn't feel the same about her.

He had been unfriendly to her from the very beginning and unless it was regarding her training, he didn't really speak to her. She did not necessarily want to have deep rooted conversations with him, but it would be nice to have a friend; specifically, a Samaian friend who could tell her about her heritage and her legacy.

She would be forever grateful to Dana for being her friend when no one else cared about her; but there were things she could learn from Oren about herself and her powers.

Trista decided then, that despite his treatment of her; she would put more effort into befriending Oren and not be so in awe of him.

She finished getting ready for the day's lesson and was back in her fitted uniform, her hair still wet but drying steadily in the warm air around them.

When she walked back through the trees up to camp; she found Oren in the middle of his warmups.

He was topless again, something she'd had to get used to in the few days she'd known him. He was going through a series of slow, fluid movements that he had briefly explained stretched his muscles.

He was stood in his fighting stance, with his eyes closed and with his palms up; he made the motion of pushing away from himself then turning his hands as though he were pulling the air back towards and simultaneously moving back with the movement.

When he brought his hands back, still in their cupping shape to his chest, he reached his large arms outward, so he eventually shaped a circle. He brought his palms together above his head and brought it down again, so his hands were in the centre of his chest.

He begun again with the pushing motion but this time to his left when he had previous started pushing to his right.

All the while he completed these movements, a ball of blueish green light – his power - hovered between his palms. When he separated his hands, the ball split and when he connected his palms again, the ball came together again.

When he had completed his choreography in all four directions and completed his last circle; he brought his hands to his centre and opened his eyes.

The energy ball disappeared,

"Who taught you that?"

Although his eyes had opened, he hadn't really looked at her or focused on anything until she spoke. When his eyes focused on her, she could see that his pupils had flames that slowly died away; Trista gasped.

Had he been Enflamed without being on fire?

If he had, then Gorn had been right; Oren was indeed very powerful.

"My father, it was part of my early training...before the war."

Oren walked toward her but not to continue the conversation; she knew he was going down to the river.

"Tell me about him and the castle, about everything before the war...about growing up there."

Oren stopped as he walked past her and although he didn't turn around, she could see him contemplating it.

"Rayne only talked about my powers and how to use them," she added in a rush. "She didn't tell me anything about what should have been my home." She took a step toward him, wanting to turn him to face her but she thought better of it.

"Maybe...maybe if I understood it better, I could...*be* better."

He was quiet a long time, still not turning to look back at her until he let out a pent-up breath and said,

"Complete your training to a satisfactory level today and I'll talk to you about Tirnum."

He went to walk away,

"Thank you," he stopped again then continued down into the trees away from her.

Training under Oren's watchful eye was tough at the best of times, but when she knew getting information out of him was dependent on her progress, she was determined to do her best.

They continued steadily through her physical drills, using her sword as well as a variety of weapons that Oren had brought to see what she liked and used best. When she'd asked to use the bow and arrow that he had yet to present to her, Oren had declined.

"You need to be able to handle a close contact weapon before you can proceed to a bow." He had said. "We'll get to target practice when you can best me with a short sword."

Disappointed, Trista focused on the tasks at end and focused on the main things that Oren had taught her.

Don't think too hard.

Calculate every move.

Be light on your feet.

Remain firm and balanced.

Be aware of your surroundings.

Stay focused on the task at hand.

All of that, as well as simultaneously using her physical and magical strength without depleting herself as she had in Dreston. Trista had to remain focused on her weapons, her magic, her body and of course protecting herself from Oren's attacks. It didn't help that he was more powerful than her and as such, was getting bored with her inability to challenge him.

They had only been training for four days, but it felt like an eternity and she wanted to get better quicker.

If she was honest, she wanted him to like her quicker.

"Stop!" Oren called out unexpectedly.

Trista was in the middle of sending a blast of energy toward him and stopped it mid-air. It disintegrated before their eyes and she lowered the sword she was using to strike him. She was breathing heavily, and her hair was plastered to her head with sweat but somewhere, in the back of her mind; she felt proud of herself.

This was the first time in four days that she hadn't been metaphorically watching the clock. She'd been so engrossed in her training, she hadn't noticed the time or the pain in her wrists, arms and legs.

Almost as if thinking about them, made them physical; Trista shook the pain out of her right wrist and flexed the fingers in her left hand.

"Well," she said loosening her stance and placing her weapon on the floor. "Does that qualify me for a history lesson?"

Oren looked up at the hanging branches overhead and where a sliver of light from the sun usually got through, there was nothing.

"Sure," he replied before walking over to the campsite and placing his own weapon on the floor beside his bed roll.

He took a seat on the floor beside his things and when he held out his hand, his sharpening stone appeared in his hand. He set to sharpening his blade as he did most evenings once their training was finished.

It would forever amaze her at the things Oren could do; at the things, she would be able to do one day.

Rayne had explained to her early on that while Samaian magic was primarily mental and molecular it could be manifested in any way that the wielder wished.

For example, a Samai would not need to say the word 'fire' to create fire but some found it easier to do so. Rayne had said that most were able to create whatever they willed just by thought.

There were of course exceptions to this. A Samai could not materialise or summon something they had never encountered or seen. Oren could easily summon fire at the campsite because he both knew what fire was and had experienced it; the same as he could with his sword. Heat, air, metal, wood were all things that were around them to make the magical blueprints of what he wished to create. He could not however, summon a member of the Phyn in the middle of the sea if he'd never met one. He'd have no blueprint of what it should be for his magic or his will to summon it.

Again, there were limitations on summoning in terms of distance and size. If one could see their discarded sword on the battlefield, they could summon it into their hand, and it would fly toward them. If one couldn't see their weapon, it would have to materialise from how and where they had seen it last.

It was all very complicated and intricate, but Trista put those thoughts to the side for a moment, as she took a seat on her own bed roll and looked expectantly over at Oren.

"What do you want to know?"

"Everything," Oren looked at her as though she were stupid, so she laughed nervously and looked away. When she looked back at him she said,

"Tell me about yourself then, and I'll ask questions."

It was clear he didn't like the idea, but he didn't say no. He continued sharpening his sword,

"I was born in the Imperial Lands, an area just outside Tirnum City. My parents lived there before I was born but once the rebellion and the war got underway, my father moved me into the castle into his personal apartments where he could keep me safe."

"Just you?"

Oren looked up at her so quickly, she almost didn't see it and even though she knew he didn't want to say it, he spoke anyway.

"I've never met my mother...she died while having me." Trista wasn't able to hide her shock.

"I'm sorry," he didn't respond but then she hadn't expected him to.

"I started my training with my father very early on and continued with my weapons tutor in the few years before I moved to Tirnum. Every day my father told me, that one day, my people would need me and that I would need to be ready. So, once we left the city with the rest of our family after the war; we trained, and we fought and I did everything my father said in the hope that one day I would be worthy to fight for the Redeemer."

Trista blushed but he just continued,

"King Alexander, your father was killed when I was four years old and in order to save my life, my father escaped with me and my cousins to Priya. We've spent these last years preparing for your arrival."

"You have cousins? Where are they?"

Oren seemed to realise he had said something wrong and Trista felt a sudden tingling over her skin, like something was about to happen.

"What is it?"

"It doesn't matter," he looked away from her and continued sharpening his sword, clad in his all black leathers.

"No Oren, tell me…please."

Reluctantly he looked back at her and sighed,

"My cousins, Nyron and Naima Antos; they are my uncle Theon's children with his wife… Renya Illiya."

Trista looked at him confused,

"So, what's wrong with that?"

Oren stopped sharpening and looked at her quizzically,

"You really don't know anything, do you?" Trista blushed, unsure whether he was being mean to her but unable to deny it.

"Know what, Oren?"

Oren looked directly into her eyes,

"My uncle, Theon Antos was married to your aunt, Renya Illiya and her sisters, are Rowan and…Rayne."

Trista's heart stopped right in her chest as she contemplated what that meant.

She had…*family*.

It also meant that…wait…

"Rayne?" Oren just stared at her. "Rayne is my aunt…my mother's *sister*?" Oren said as he put his sword away and stood up,

"I think that's enough revelations for today." Trista scrambled to her feet, reaching out to grab his arm and thinking better of it once her fingers touched his skin. She snapped her hand away as though it had shocked her,

"No please, tell me more."

"Another time," he said, though not unkindly and walked away before she could say anything else.

Trista was reeling with this new information. *Rayne was her aunt…her* aunt!

It was so laughable; she knew it was true but still incredible.

Trista now prayed more than ever that Rayne was okay because she was family and the best link to finding out about her mother.

She told herself to ask Oren about her two cousins another time but couldn't help the feeling of finally feeling like she belonged to something, to someone.

When Oren returned, from the river it seemed because his hair was wet, he was in his normal clothes again. She turned to him before heading there herself.

"What's my family name?"

"What?"

"I assume Theon Antos is your paternal uncle?" Oren nodded. "So, if your uncle's name is Antos then that's your name, but what's mine…who do I belong to?"

If she didn't know any better she would have said that Oren smiled but it was gone too quickly for her to be sure,

"You are from the Royal House of Antonides…that is to whom you belong."

With a nod of thanks, she left him to go down to the river with a small smile on her face as she decided that Trista, daughter of Matthias and Gwendolyn Freitz was no more. She was Princess Trista of House Antonides and by the time she reached Tirnum Castle to face Briseis; everyone else would know it too.

Mama!

Mama has to go little one.

Mama stay!

Trista tossed and turned in her sleep later that night, as she murmured the words she saw in her mind. A sense of loss and dread seeped through her body, as images came to her in the mist of her dreams. Long black hair in a braid, resting on a feminine shoulder; a scent of jasmine and something else she couldn't identify.

Mama!

Mama has to go little one.

Mama stay!

More images of a woman whose face she couldn't see, a small house; a simple house that was warm and inviting...a house that was *home*.

Come back to me...I'll be waiting.

Mama!

Mama has to go little one.

MAMA STAY!

Trista bolted out of her sleep into an upright position and screamed into the night

MAMA!

Blue flame consumed her before shooting out of her in all directions, hitting the protective barrier around them. It beat against it, as it continued to absorb what she was putting out.

Trista sat screaming into the night as her power blazed around her; her chest heaving in and out heavily as she breathed. Images and noises flashed before her eyes and she realized that she knew who they were; she understood what was happening.

Trista

Her name sounded like an echo underwater, but she could still manage to make it out, but not who was saying it.

Trista

She heard it again but couldn't find her way to it out of the din that was her memories. They came flooding into her head like a dam had been broken. Almost two years of memories of a mother and a woman who was always there to protect her and running...always running.

Trista come to me

The voice was closer now and as Trista opened her eyes, conscious that what she'd been seeing was in her head, she saw a large figure walking toward her flame. No, she realised. Not towards it but *into* it.

She stared out through the flames that continued to blaze around her and watched as Oren stepped through her fire and towards her; his hand outstretched,

"Trista, come to me. Take my hand," he said.

I can't

She hadn't said it out loud, but Oren responded,

You can, take my hand Princess

Unsure, Trista reached out to Oren who seemed so far away but as soon as she reached out, she felt his hand take hers; he pulled her into him and as all her flame receded; she collapsed onto him.

Oren fell backwards, his arms wrapped protectively around her as Trista landed on top of his chest, both struggling to catch their breaths. Her hair that she'd taken out of her braid to wash, fell all around them, cloaking them in a blanket of dark curls so that all they could see was each other.

They looked down into each other's eyes and Trista struggled to breathe as more than her ordeal made her breathless. She watched as tiny flames erupted in his pupils and the most peculiar sensation erupted within her. In an instant it was gone, as were the flames in his eyes,

"W-where did you go?" Oren said, still holding her against him

"I was…I was...I don't know...how did you get to me?" Oren's eyes shifted slightly,

"I don't know," he was lying, and she knew it. She didn't know how she knew; she just did. "Trista what happened?"

She was still so disorientated; she didn't bother to question him about it. She answered him though, because she couldn't keep it in.

"I saw...my mother. She's alive Oren...my mother's alive."

***

Briseis was marching through Tirnum on her way to Sentry's Keep. She had a few more training drills she wished Gardan to implement with the new trainees and needed it incorporated into their training schedule as soon as possible.

After the altercation with her father, she realised that she would have to fight more than the Samaian threat as there was unrest on her own doorstep. She would deal with her father in due time, but she needed to focus on the bigger picture which was of course the former Samaian princess.

As her plans took root, Briseis suddenly felt as though she'd been punched in the gut and doubled over onto her hands and knees. She was winded and crouched there on all fours as she tried to catch her breath,

"Your highness!" an approaching guard called out to her and as she looked up into his concerned face; she laughed.

He was weary to reach out to her but did so anyway, and surprisingly she took his hand to stand up right. Slowly she dusted off the sleeves of her dress and the front of her full satin skirt before looking up at the guard,

"She's stronger,"

"Y-your highness?"

"The redeemer...she's stronger." Briseis was speaking to herself more than anything as her mind began to work quickly.

"Go to Sentry's Keep and tell Captain Beardmore I wish to have a formal military meeting in the morning."

"Yes, your Highness,"

"And send a messenger to Baron Dreston and tell him that I want all Samaians apprehended from Priya. The redeemer is among them and I want her dead."

"Yes, your Highness."

The guard rushed off to do as he was bid, leaving Briseis to make her way back to her room, in indescribable pain.

UNPROVOKED ATTACKS

Lamya sat with Gracelynn, Ed and their children aboard the Mayflower having their evening meal. They sat in the dining cabin with a few other passengers when the most incredible and positive wave of energy passed through her.

"Trista," she smiled with relief as she cradled her cup of warm sweetened ale.

"Excuse me?" Gracelynn turned to her while attempting to feed her daughter Ellarie, but Lamya shook her head, dismissing it.

"I just had a thought about my...cousin. I will be seeing her very soon,"

"Does she live in Illiya?"

"Oh no, she will be in the capital when I return there in a few weeks."

"I see, well I ho—" Gracelynn's reply was interrupted when a loud bang shook the dining cabin, causing people to yell in surprise.

Almost instantly, there was continuous banging and shouting followed.

"What in the world was that?" Ed questioned as his wife picked up their daughter and ushered the boys toward her.

"Come here boys, stay by me."

There was another loud bang, this time against the cabin door making everyone jump and call out in shock and confusion. The noises outside the cabin grew louder and Ed and the other men in the room stood and drew their swords,

"Wait here; I will see what is going on."

"I will come with you," Ed turned to Lamya quizzically.

"I beg your pardon; we don't know what is out there. I will not have a lady walk into it."

"I appreciate your concern Ed, but I can take care of myself." Lamya reached inside the sleeve of her black robe and produced the small dagger she always kept with her.

"If she is going then I will come too!" Edmere stepped away from his mother and siblings to be near his father.

"You most certainly will not!"

"Father, I wish to fight!"

"We do not even know if there is a fight!" Ed snapped at him and the boy was clearly not impressed by being spoken to that way. "We do not have time to discuss this!"

Another bang against the door and everyone yelled, getting more afraid as the noises outside grew louder, accompanied by the clashing of swords.

"IN THE NAME OF THE KING!"

The voice echoed through the door and all eyes looked around at one another. Edmere and Julius looked fearful at their parents, as did the other young children around the room.

"Oh my!" Gracelynn cowered into her seat, her baby in her arms and Lamya abandoned all thought in going outside; the elder woman would need her help.

The men looked back at them with confused and worried eyes before Ed took the lead.

"Stay here, do not come out until I call for you!" he said to his wife. He kissed her, then left with the four men who had joined him, slamming the door behind them. Lamya had the sense to lock it behind them, although she had doubts it would be helpful. They'd seen nothing when the men exited but two wooden barrels at the bottom of the steps leading into the dining cabin. That had to be what had caused the banging.

"What are we going to do?"

"Wait here like father said," provided Julius and Lamya smiled in his direction before closing her eyes where she stood.

"What are you doing Lamya?" he asked

"Concentrating. Could you please give me a moment?"

"O-of course..." Gracelynn said worriedly as she held her daughter tightly in one arm and held Julius' hand with the other. Young Edmere stared after the closed door with terror in his eyes. The remaining women and children had gathered together, all unsure of what to do.

Lamya ignored them for the moment to clear her mind and reached out into the commotion outside the door. She almost choked on the anger that she felt there: rage, dismay and death. Too much feeling was out there that she didn't stay connected long and broke the bond to turn to the women and children around her.

"We have to get out of here."

"Father said to remain here!" Edmere replied forcefully although Lamya could feel his fear and apprehension.

"Yes, Ed said we should not leave until he returned."

"I know Gracelynn but there are terrible people out there that would do us harm. We have to get everyone off the ship!"

"How do you know this?" a woman asked curiously from the back of the room, as she clutched her baby to her chest.

Lamya was saved having to give an answer as there was a tremendous bang on the cabin door that shattered the wood down the middle of it.

The women screamed and little Ellarie began to cry. Another bang and the wood splintered again as whoever was on the other side, rammed it open and finally barged through.

Three large men stood in the doorway with blood splattered across their faces and bloody swords in their hands. They wore no colours or banners to identify where they were from or who they were fighting for, but from the look in their eyes, she doubted it would matter.

The one in front, had a thick black beard and the two either side of him weirdly enough were blonde bearded twins; twins with scars over their faces to match the missing right eye on each man. Lamya wondered unhelpfully whether this was intentional.

"Bring the young women, kill the old and children!" Black Beard said.

The women screamed as one of the twins stepped forward and when he did, Lamya stepped toward him. The other twin sneered at her,

"Aren't you a pretty one," Lamya didn't reply and kept her face neutral. "You won't be so pretty once I'm done with you." He growled at her before reaching out to cup her face. Lamya simply placed her right hand on the back of his own and the man went rigid.

"Take my hand Gracelynn, now!"

"Burrich?" Black Beard looked on in confusion.

Lamya reached her left hand behind her to take hold of Gracelynn's hand.

"Everyone hold onto someone's hand and run when I say!"

"What are you doing? Bulloch, get them!"

The other twin – Bulloch – stepped forward but as he did so, Burrich turned away from Lamya and swung his sword at his brother, immediately catching him off guard; slicing cleanly into his brother's arm.

"What the hell is going on?" Black Beard yelled as he marched into the room but Burrich marched forward and struck at him too.

"Stay close to me and follow, quickly!" Gracelynn gripped her hand determinedly with Ellarie in her other hand as Lamya followed in the wake of Burrich as he chopped his comrades down. His twin and his leader lay injured and bleeding on the floor behind him as he worked as a human shield and protector of the women and children behind him.

When they climbed the small steps onto the deck of the ship, the scene they walked into was carnage.

There was destruction everywhere as these men - whoever they were - ransacked the ship and proceeded to set it on fire. The mast was already alight and everywhere, men were fighting and shouting as they battled with swords and axes. It was horrific as she recognised men she had spoken and dined with during the voyage be cut to ribbons. Lamya also saw at the corner of her eye, that not all men were fighting, but also looting.

Barrels and bags were being carted across planks onto the much larger ship that had moored beside it.

Pirates!

"My Gods, what's happening?" Gracelynn screamed but Lamya didn't bother to reply, she could *feel* what was happening.

"Stay close!" Lamya shouted above the din as the small group of people tried their best to stay close to her. Lamya touched Burrich again and said,

"Get us to a life boat; everyone must be accounted for!"

Burrich didn't reply but again he went rigid and marched down the deck of the ship, slicing at anyone who got in his way. Finally they reached a large lifeboat at the far end of the ship and everyone climbed in.

Burrich stepped aside as though waiting for something but was incredibly still despite all that went on around him,

"Get in, *quickly*!" Lamya urged them into the boat. "Hurry!" she yelled again as she kept her eye on Burrich who gently began to sway. A trio of men finally saw them and their attempt at escape. They charged towards them so Lamya touched Burrich again and said,

"Protect us."

Burrich stepped forward to attack the men and although he was a large man, three people were two much to handle on his own. While he fought two, the other man came toward Lamya and in an instant, she had her dagger out and threw it directly into his chest. The man was stunned as he went still and collapsed to the ground with the dagger right through his heart. Lamya abandoned her escapees for the moment and rushed to retrieve her dagger. It amazed her how easily it slid from his chest and his blood oozed onto his filthy tunic. She wiped her dagger clean against his chest, looking around her quickly as she did so. To her utter horror, she spied a red painted symbol on the side of the ship's panelling.

There was a circle with lines emanating from it and a large 'X' across it. Lamya knew instantly what it meant and felt sick at the idea.

Hurriedly, she turned to get back to the lifeboat when she heard her name. She turned in the direction and her heart broke to see Ed clutching at his side as he tried to crawl to her.

"Edmere," she breathed out as she rushed towards him.

"Take any loot you can find. Any Samai can be...!" a voice suddenly bellowed across the chaos, but his last words were cut off by an explosion that rocked the ship.

Lamya stumbled, trying to get to Edmere over the fallen men and splintered wood that lay on the deck. She looked around, trying to identify who was leading the attack but to no avail. These men were pirating of their own accord, there didn't seem to be a leader behind it.

Lamya, trying to get over to Edmere without being seen by the men infesting the ship, turned as the most tremendous crack echoed overhead. The mast was burning steadily, and it wouldn't hold for much longer.

Quickly, Lamya got to Edmere, ignoring the burning mast for the moment and took his hand,

"Where are my family?" he was struggling to speak. Lamya checked where he was clutching his side and saw the gigantic bleeding wound. He wouldn't make it, that much was abundantly clear.

"Oh Edmere,"

"My family?"

"S-safe, they're in a life boat. Come with me," she attempted to pull him with her, but he was too heavy and cried out as she did so.

"I cannot...I cannot," at that moment, Lamya hated her skill and the fact that it was so incredibly limited. She couldn't heal Edmere or even compel him as she'd done Burrich to make it to the lifeboat if his body wasn't physically able to do so. It just didn't work that way…

"Protect them, please."

An incredible crack came from above them and Lamya watched in horror as the mast snapped and plummeted toward them, making a noise that she knew would haunt her for the rest of her days. It was a groaning, like a beast in pain as the large beam descended upon them.

Edmere, with the last of his strength pushed at her and sent her rolling away from him onto the deck, just as the mast came crashing down.

It was catastrophic as the mast split the ship in two, sending people and fractured wood flying into the air in every direction. Lamya was flung clear across the deck, into the air and crashed headfirst into the darkened water below.

The Antonides Legacy II

It was odd how quiet it was beneath the water, even as chaos raged above it. The light from the fire blazed overhead as Lamya kicked with all her might towards the surface. She took a draw of much needed breath when she broke the water.

Treading water, Lamya tried to get her bearings among the floating wood and bodies around her before she finally laid eyes on a large piece of fractured wood and swam towards it. Swimming was difficult with her thick sodden robes and climbing onto the wood without it toppling over was something she never thought she'd have to experience.

She collapsed onto the makeshift raft, her long red hair plastered over the wood and her face, but she didn't have the energy to move it. She took several deep breaths to calm herself down even as screams and shouting echoed all around her. Despite the fear that ripped through her, screams meant survivors and hopefully they consisted of Gracelynn and her family.

Once she was calm enough to do so, Lamya extended her senses and in an instant felt Gracelynn's presence not too far away. She felt the direction she was in and while laying on her stomach, began to paddle. Within a few strokes she was close enough to another panel of wood she could use as an oar and so set on her course to Gracelynn.

She found the survivors a while later, the boat at least and called out to them, waving her arms as she did so. They yelled back when they spotted her and within minutes they had made their way to her and lifted her into the boat.

"Thank the Gods!" a woman cried out in relief as Lamya caught her breath and slumped against the side of the boat. When she was finally able to open her eyes, and concentrate she realised that the boat wasn't nearly as full as it should have been, but thankfully Gracelynn and all her children were accounted for and they were all dripping wet.

"Where are the rest of you?"

"W-when the ship cracked, we were thrown from the boat...we were the only ones able to get back in."

Lamya felt Gracelynn's guilt at having survived when so many others had not but it wasn't her fault; she told her as much.

"What will we do now, Lamya?" Julius asked fearfully. His older brother said nothing as he stared out into the black waters of the sea.

"We get to land; it won't be far. When the sun comes up, we'll find the coast and head for it. We'll survive this...we all will."

"Father didn't," came Edmere's sombre and angry reply and Lamya saw tears pool in Gracelynn's eyes.

"No...he didn't, and that's why you should all be strong for one another. Your father would have wanted you to take care of your family Edmere."

Edmere looked at her and while there was anger and sorrow in his eyes, it dissipated into the fear of a young boy who had just lost his father. Lamya felt also, that Edmere felt guilty for his behaviour towards his father, and nothing she or anyone else said would save him from that guilt.

Lamya closed her eyes to drown out the fear and worry around her. She had to concentrate on building her strength for when they made it back to the mainland.

She didn't want to admit to herself that she was afraid that once they got to land; they may not be safe from the people they would encounter there.

It was a long night for everyone but especially for Lamya.

She had the now unfortunate gift of being able to detect the emotions of everyone in their small boat. The fear, uncertainty, anger and despair were in full force from the women and children and a few injured men who had managed to escape the ship.

Once the sun rose and they were able to determine the thin strip of land that was the Mortanian coastline, they aimed for it. It was exhausting work for Lamya but for the other woman, many of whom had never worked a day in their lives, it was backbreaking.

After hours trudging through the savage waters, they finally came up on land and clambered out onto the gravelly sand.

They lay there for long while, catching their breath until Lamya turned to the young boy beside her,

"Julius?"

"Are you alright?" she smiled at his concern as she knew by now that he had a little crush on her.

"I'm fine Julius, but I need your help."

"W-what can I do?" he asked fearfully.

"You and your brother must head in that direction," she pointed to her right into a long line of trees. "When you find the town, you must find a physician or healer and tell them that there are injured people that need their help." Julius' eyes looked into the trees frightfully and said,

"What if they don't believe us?"

"They will," she assured him as she placed a hand on his cheek.

"I will do as you ask."

"Thank you," she got onto unsteady feet and made her way to Gracelynn, who was trying to calm Ellarie down.

When Lamya explained of her request to her sons she was apprehensive but understood that there was no one else who could. The three men with them were seriously injured and the women were not fast enough to get the message to any who could help in time.

"How do you know they will go in the right direction?"

"I have gifts," was her reply and lay back down beside the other woman to watch as the two young boys set off in the direction she had said.

It was closing in on dusk before the boys returned and when they did Gracelynn ran to them; thankful that they had arrived safely. She had already lost her husband and wouldn't have survived if anything had happened to her boys.

The wagon they arrived in, was driven by an old man with two other younger men in the back; one with the grey robes and black sash of a physician.

"Who is the most injured?" he asked as he jumped down from the wagon and approached them determinedly. Lamya stood up shakily to meet him,

"The three men with us, they were hurt during the fight."

"The women and children?"

She knew it was inappropriate but Lamya felt her face flush as she came face to face with the physician and realised how attractive he was. He was very tall with thick dark blond hair and mesmerising hazel eyes a lot like her own. She reached her power out to him and appreciatively, she felt his attraction to her.

"Hungry and tired mostly, but we'll live."

He nodded and left her to attend the men who were lying on the sandy ground. Once he had seen to them and dressed their wounds as best he could with the supplies he had; the men were loaded onto the cart along with the rest of the group. Lamya was the last to approach but before she climbed up, the physician took her arm.

"Excuse me, Miss…?"

"Lamya,"

"Lamya, I am Ardus." He shook her hand before continuing. "Before we head back to Jentra; I need to ask…what happened here?" Before answering, Lamya did the calculations of their location and it was a lot better than she thought; Jentra was just a town or two away from Illiya.

"I don't know exactly. We were having dinner and pirates attacked us. They were looting the ship and killing any who opposed them." Ardus was clearly shocked as he asked,

"Who were they pirating for?" Lamya shrugged,

"We didn't even see another ship once ours was wrecked but from the little I heard they seemed to be royalists." Ardus was thoughtful,

"What would the king want with a ship carrying passengers and small trade goods?"

"I don't know Ardus, but then I'm not entirely sure the King even knows about this…there were no banners."

"I see," he rubbed at his smooth face contemplatively before turning his attention back to her. "We best get everyone into town and fed and into a warm bed. I'm sure I can call in some favours."

Lamya went to climb into the cart again when Ardus stopped her,

"I see you are attached to no one."

"Excuse me?" Ardus looked apologetic as he blushed,

"I mean, there are small families and of course the injured men but you, you are alone." Lamya blushed and hated herself for it,

"Yes, I was travelling alone…to Illiya." Ardus cleared his throat,

"I have a room spare…at my home if you were willing to stay…before you continue your travels. Only if you wish it," he added quickly and Lamya smiled shyly,

"Thank you Ardus, that would be most welcome."

She smiled at him then as she felt that his intentions were true and when he smiled back at her just as shyly, her heart beamed.

***

Their journey to Illiya was becoming a bore.

The relentless travel and meetings with Baron Thelm were becoming intolerable so it was a welcome change when news was brought to Baron Dreston from the capital.

"What does the Princess have to say for herself?"

Lyon wondered at the fact that the princess hadn't communicated with him with her power as she had before, but he was not one to question the ways of magic. He'd never delved in magic or the Everlasting power that he had been taught about as a child. It was disconcerting enough thinking that someone had the ability to invade your mind whenever they saw fit, before thinking about what else they could possibly do.

"The letter remains sealed Lord,"

"Give it here then," he reached out and took the letter as they continued their journey toward Illiya.

Aml had informed him that they would arrive within the next few days, so he was prepared to not kill anyone with his impatience for now.

He opened it and read quickly, a smile appearing on his face as he reached the end. He handed it back to the guard who had given it to him and said,

"Give this to Baron Thelm and have him meet me in my tent once we camp for the night. Before you return to me, command a group of one hundred men to set out for Priya."

"Their instruction Lord?"

"They are to find and kill any female Samai in the area, aged between seventeen and eighteen; on her highness Princess Briseis' order."

"...as you wish Lord."

The confusion and dismay at the request were evident on the guard's face but he had the sense not to voice it, before turning his horse and heading back to his men.

Lyon marvelled at the interesting turn that this trip had taken. Priya was perhaps a few days away from their current location. They had left the Jarn Lake behind them many miles ago and dependent on how fast a hundred men could travel, his men would be able to attack Priya and kill the Samai girl before they reached Illiya.

When they were successful, it would be another reason for the princess to trust him, which brought him another step closer to the crown.

EPIPHANY

She knew everything.

Everything was as clear as a summer's day, as though she'd never *not* known.

She was a princess, for a short time at least, born to a loving King and Queen, the latter, forced into exile and lived the early years of her life in a small town in the middle of nowhere.

Memories came back to her, of she and her mother in a small cottage where they lived and played with another woman constantly on the lookout, for what; she hadn't understood at the time.

The cottage had been temporary, the first in many attempts at trying to make a home away from roaming eyes. They had been running, always on the move after leaving the cottage until they had arrived…here.

In this ancient place, a place that contained magic so Rowan could perform one final spell to save her child. Why they couldn't have stayed there she wasn't sure, but the lack of provisions may have played a huge part.

Trista reeled with the new information that flooded her mind and suddenly felt ashamed that she'd been hiding in a remote mountain village for most of her life.

She knew deep down that she hadn't been hiding, but even deeper than that was the knowledge that those years in ignorance had been wasted. There was also the sense of betrayal, that if Rowan hadn't taken her memories from her, however small they were; she would have been prepared for this.

Her mother.

Rowan was another issue altogether. She now had memories of someone she'd technically never met and while they were all good memories, there was something that bugged her about the way Rowan had let her go.

Even with the minimal recollection of her, Trista knew Rowan Illiya was alive and she was determined to find her, to finally get answers to her burning questions.

Rowan, her heritage and everything else that had come back to Trista was not nearly as significant as the memory she now had of her father; of a man with loving eyes who told her regrettably that Papa had to go…

Three days went by since her mind had been opened, and Trista had brought a new determination and vigour to her lessons with Oren.

"Shit!" Trista cursed as another of Oren's blows crashed into her sword and rattled the bones in her arm so hard, she thought they would break.

They had been sparring for almost an hour and she wasn't bettering him. He was in loose trousers, boots and topless while Trista fought in the same style of trousers and a cropped short sleeved top.

Her taut stomach muscles were on display as sweat dripped down it. The hair that had escaped her braid were plastered to her face as she shook out the tension in her arms.

"You're still blocking too hard!" Oren snapped at her.

"How can I block *too* hard? Either I'm firm or I lose my footing!"

"No," he fired back. "You have to be fluid enough that you don't rely on your footing. If I pound at you with a weapon; the physical power it takes to maintain that strength, isn't worth it if you can get out of it instead."

Trista nodded her understanding as she regained her breath,

"Again!"

Oren was on her immediately as she raised her sword to block his strike then immediately danced out of it.

"Good!" he praised as he charged at her again and she met him blow for blow.

Oren was an excellent fighter as far as she could tell; and while she spent her time concentrating on not being bested by him; she couldn't help but admire his skill.

He swiped low making her dance back to avoid the blade of his longsword and as she skipped back, she threw up an energy shield; skirted around it; fired at him with an energy ball that sent him flying clear across the clearing.

Quick reflexes had Oren on his feet in seconds, but Trista was already on him. With a burst of energy, she knocked his sword out of his hand when his grip was loose. His eyes widened in momentary shock and in that moment of hesitation, she summoned her dagger and threw it at him.

Oren was back in the game and stopped the dagger mid-air, dropping it to the floor just as Trista suddenly appeared behind him, grabbed his head back by his hair and aimed her sword at his throat.

"Very good," he complimented panting ever so slightly. His words seemed to bring her out of her zone and she quickly let go of his hair, recognising how disrespectful and almost intimate it was. In all their days of training; she'd never been able to best Oren.

"I'm so sorry, I…I don't know what happened."

Oren turned and for the first time, she saw him smile at her. Not a big smile but she could see he was amused,

"You Shifted," he sheathed his sword. "It's a way to travel from one place to another almost instantly but as with all our powers, there are restrictions."

"What kind of restrictions?" she asked putting her own sword away and hurrying to walk beside him as they headed back to their camp.

"We can only Shift to places we can see, as you just did or for example from here," Trista hadn't blinked before he was a few yards ahead of her, looking back at her. "to here. You try."

Trista nodded and as Rowan had explained to her a million times, she willed to be beside him. She felt a tug in her stomach before she crashed into Oren's solid body.

"I did it!" she laughed to herself and when she looked up at him he nodded,

"Yes, you did."

They stood looking at each other for a few short moments before he cleared his throat and stepped back from her.

"We still need to work on some things though,"

"Like what?"

"As great as it can be in battle; you're still not conscious of the things you're doing, you just…do them. You beat me which is great, but you're not entirely sure how because you didn't plan to. That's what we need to work on next; your strategic battle mind." Trista was thoughtful,

"Won't you be there for that?"

They arrived back at their bedrolls and campfire and Oren put his sword by his things before turning to her,

"Excuse me?"

"If I become Queen, wont I need my own General, like your father was to mine."

If she didn't know any better, Trista would've thought that Oren was embarrassed. He seemed to straighten as he cleared his throat,

"*When* you become Queen and yes…I guess you would."

Oren stepped away from her and began to go through his weapons. He took to sharpening a dagger he found, and Trista went back to her things.

They had been together just over a week and during that time they had made a nice camp for themselves. They had their designated sleeping area that was cut off from where they trained and they took turns down by the stream to not get in each other's way.

In the time she'd spent with him; Trista had learnt a great deal from Oren and not just in the ways of combat. She now knew how to create and control energy balls and raise shields and of course summon weapons. She was comfortable using a short and longsword but was yet to touch an axe or bow and arrow. Outside of using weapons; Oren had also taught her physical fighting and those were the lessons she hated the most.

It was during these lessons that she had to touch him - that he touched her - Trista found she liked it very much.

She'd never been physical with any man other than her kiss with Thorn, and to have Oren touch her body even while fighting was strange but also exciting in ways she couldn't explain.

Despite her growing attraction to Oren, she was technically engaged to Thorn and whenever she thought about him, she felt guilty. She thought about him a lot and wondered if he was still thinking of her or he still cared about her. Would he still want to marry her once this was all over with…would she still want to marry him?

Trista looked toward Oren and her heart jolted. He was so good looking it dishevelled her a lot of the time, but she had to look past it.

He was her trainer, her teacher in all things Samai in many ways and nothing more,

"So, would you be my General?" she asked sitting crossed legged on her bedding.

"Are you asking me to be?" he didn't look over at her.

"Well yes…yes I am." She said firmly.

She realised that with Oren it was always best to be honest and straight to the point; he didn't have time for games. He chuckled to himself,

"If I am considered worthy, I would consider accepting; there is protocol for things of this nature."

"Protocol?" she began to sort through her clothes in preparation for a wash; she was in desperate need of bathing.

"Advisors, Gifted and ministers etc.; members of various councils would have to choose candidates and elect who they wished to be the new General."

"Wouldn't that be my choice?"

"Ultimately yes, but a leader always listens to their counsel."

"Listen sure, but it doesn't mean I have to do what they say all the time does it?"

"I suppose not," he finished sharpening the dagger and blew the residue off the top before looking up at her. Trista swallowed as he did so, his eyes always disarming for her.

"Well I intend to change things," she said decidedly

"Oh really," she heard his disbelieving chuckle, but chose to ignore it.

"Well…one can't do everything the same all the time and if there are changes to be made, I won't be afraid to make them."

She didn't hear anything for a long time and when she looked up to see if he had heard her; Oren was looking directly at her.

"Now you sound like a Queen."

Heat rushed to her face making her look away and stand up with her wash things finally together,

"I'm going to go wash up," she heard him huff his response and so she rushed off towards the river.

Trista was bathing a while later and was suddenly very aware of her body. She looked down at herself in the water, at her breasts and stomach and legs and wondered absentmindedly if Oren found her attractive.

Her fighting leathers had grown restrictive in their time in the jungle and so she'd begun to train in the loose trousers and top she had on earlier but had never stopped to wonder how she looked in it.

Did Oren like the lines that had suddenly begun to appear down the sides of her stomach. Did he even notice the beauty mark just to the right of her belly button?

Stop it!

She tried to think of something else but soon enough, she betrayed herself and her mind and hands wandered into places that had previously been unexplored. She wondered what it would feel like for Oren's hands to explore her body the way she was, to have him caress her skin, her breasts…between her legs…

"I'm insane," Trista snapped her hands away from her body to cover her face from the shame and guilt that took over her. She'd never thought of Thorn like this, so why was Oren any different?

Trista plunged herself under the water, trying to purge her sinful thoughts about Oren and his incredible muscular body.

Dramatically she kicked and punched at nothing to vent her frustration, screaming into the water, creating a mass of bubbles as she thrashed about.

She continued her tantrum, loving the pressure it released from her head, when suddenly she felt something long and thick under each of her arms dragging her to the surface.

She came up spluttering and coughing from the water she'd unexpectedly inhaled and when she'd finally cleared her hair out of her face and realised that the thick objects were Oren's arms still around her; she screamed again.

"What are you doing here?" she pushed at his chest, but he held her tight,

"Are you alright, I saw you struggling under the water!"

He was still holding her tightly and her breasts were flattened against his large naked chest. Her legs were right up against his, along with everything else…

Trista pushed at him in alarm and unsteadily found her footing in the not so shallow water before quickly covering her breasts and lowering herself into the water. Oren stepped back, looking away, clearly embarrassed,

"I'm sorry, I thought you were in trouble, hurt…or something…I'm sorry."

"It's fine, I was just…"

Letting out my frustrations under water because I find you ridiculously attractive and don't want you to know about it.

Trista lowered herself further into the water and tried to forget the feel of her breasts against his bare chest as he'd lifted her from the water,

"I'm fine."

She didn't bother to elaborate. In the week, she'd spent with him, Trista had got used to the weird feeling she got in her stomach when Oren was around but, in that moment, it exploded into something she'd never felt before.

She gripped her stomach in surprise as the most peculiar sensation turned her stomach over and when she did so; she heard Oren take in a sharp breath.

She looked up at him, but he was still looking away from her,

"I didn't mean to…I'm sorry."

He waded out of the water until he climbed out completely and headed seemingly back to camp and because she was still very naked, she couldn't even go after him.

The feeling soon dissipated as it always did, and she finally caught her breath. Once she did, the first thing that came to mind was whether Oren had seen anything just now and whether he liked it?

Oren was up and dressed when she opened her eyes the following morning. She rubbed the sleep out of her eyes to look over to where he was packing the last of his things into his large leather pack.

His hair was loose for once and Trista admired how he could still look so masculine and strong with long hair. Now it was wavy so he must have already washed down at the river.

He was wearing a dark brown wool tunic, but it had no sleeves and so his large arms were bare except for the thick leather cuffs he sometimes wore around his wrists, usually when working or fighting.

Idly she admired his intricate tattoo and felt odd at how looking at it made her feel. The design was like nothing she'd ever seen before and she'd planned to ask him about it, but there never seemed to be suitable time.

Trista sat up on her bedroll; pushing her hair out of her face and called out to him,

"What's going on?"

"We're heading back." He replied without looking at her and she immediately knew something was wrong.

"Why, I thought we had a few more days here?"

"We can continue your training back at the house. I want to discuss your progress with my father."

While he continued to pack, it wasn't lost on Trista that he was consciously trying not to look in her direction.

"Oren?"

He stopped packing for the moment, his back still to her before he straightened up to turn and look down at her and what she saw in his eyes was unsettling.

His bright green eyes that, though serious a lot of the time, were always alert and now they seemed…vacant somehow.

She couldn't explain it, but something had changed in Oren and she knew somehow that she was the cause of it.

"What's going on…really."

"I've helped you as much as I can. I need to consult with my father about how to further your training."

She knew he was lying, but the abrupt way in which he said it; she knew he couldn't be made to say anything else. She didn't have the energy or understanding to fight him about it so she gave in.

"Fine. I'll be ready in a moment."

He nodded and turned back to packing his things.

They packed in complete silence and while the ever-present sensation she had when Oren was around was still there, it felt faint. She'd given up trying to figure out exactly what it was, and while it made her feel connected to him, she pushed it into the depths of her powers and tried to ignore it as best she could

Once they had all their things together, Trista and Oren made their way back through the jungle terrain towards home. As they had been in the alcove for over a week, Trista hadn't had much time to do any exploring. She'd done as much as she could without taking time away from her training, but she knew, as they walked through the lush thicket of trees and large plants that she was missing out on a lot. The exotic landscape was so different to both Remora and Dreston, and she would have liked to have spent more time there.

Not wanting to spend the rest of the long walk in silence, she struck up a conversation,

"Have you done much travelling?"

"Yes," his reply was sharp, but she wouldn't be deterred. She knew he was upset about something but if he wasn't going to tell her what it was, and it had nothing to do with her; then his anger had nothing to do with her either.

"Where have you travelled?"

"Mortania mainly but I've been to Agmantia. Here, I spent some time in Dreston with my father to visit Rayne and went to Thelm once with friends when I was eighteen."

"You have friends?" Trista laughed at her own joke, but Oren didn't even react.

"I returned to Illiya, to visit my uncle's home…or what was left of it."

"That's my aunt Renya's husband?" Oren nodded. "Where did they live…what happened to it?"

"They lived in the Lord's Mansion of course, but by the time I got there, it had been left to ruin while the new so-called lord moved into a manor of his own making."

"That's Lord…" her memory failed her as she thought back to her school lessons. "Balkin!" the name finally came to her as he asked,

"Hasn't he always been the High Lord of Illiya?"

It was then that Oren stopped walking and turned to look at her coming up behind him. The look on his face was a cross between confusion and outright anger,

"You're serious, aren't you?" Trista shrugged

"About what?"

Oren didn't say anything but took a deep breath and turned to carry on walking. Trista was just about to ask him what he meant when he said,

"The province of Illiya and the surrounding lands have been governed by the Illiya family for hundreds of years. Josef Illiya, your grandfather had three children; three daughters and when he passed, the lands and titles went to his middle daughter Renya, making her High Lady. She married my uncle Theon Antos and they had twins, our cousin's Naima and Nyron. As Naima is the eldest, she is the rightful successor to that seat."

Trista mind was buzzing with this information. Not only did she have family, but that family had history…a lot of history.

"Lord Balkin," Oren continued. "Is a traitor and a thief, just like that king he follows. The only difference is that he didn't take the name of the lands he pillaged or was given as a prize after the war."

"Who else took a family name that wasn't theirs?"

"Lord Tyus Priya formerly Ragland, Lord Rinly Crol formerly Bester and Baron Erik Thelm formerly Van Raylen all did this. Baron Dreston is the only human to have true ancestral control of a barony."

Oren cut his way through some overhanging branches and Trista followed quickly so not to be hit by the backlash.

"Tirnum was of course held by the reigning royal family and Thelm by the Thelm family who with the murder of their

Baron Justin and his son and heir Thantos during the war, now have no true successor."

As he spoke, Oren charged his way through the trees mercilessly without stopping for a break.

She took a moment now to reflect on all the destruction and deaths that had occurred since her birth and how unaware she was. Growing up in Remora, they were never taught about the Samai. They were mentioned in a way that explained they were another race but their history; the achievements had all subsequently been attributed to Curian. In as little time as eighteen years they had wiped out her entire history.

"Why didn't Rayne become High Lady of Illiya; she's the eldest, isn't she?"

"Rayne pledged herself to be Gifted when she was a little girl. People who pledge to follow on the Gifted path can hold no titles or lands and can never marry or produce heirs. Your mother was of course betrothed to the crown prince and so the responsibility fell to Aunt Renya."

"I would like to meet my cousins when we get back."

"You will," Oren said in a way that halted the conversation.

It was clear he didn't want to speak but she felt closer to him and their shared history than ever before and she just wanted him to keep talking.

"My father will explain anything else to you when we get back, we should hurry." She didn't bother to argue with him but asked instead,

"Did you ever meet my parents?"

"You mean did I ever meet your father?" he effortlessly bent a low hanging branch out of the way with his powers and stepped passed it. It snapped back into place once Trista had gone through as well. Oren stopped again and turned to her.

His green eyes seemed to glow that much brighter as he looked down at her.

"Yes…there's so much I'll never know about him."

"And there's equally as much that I can't tell you. I met him when I was three years old, I can't help you paint a picture of him Trista."

Trista hung her head and looked away but was surprised when she felt Oren's hand on her shoulder. She looked up at him, suddenly overwhelmed by how beautiful he was. As each day went by, she stopped thinking about Thorn more and more and thoughts of Oren replaced him. It wasn't just how he looked either; she was attracted to his strength, his power and his knowledge of a world that she was just discovering.

She swallowed; her mouth instantly dry at having him so close to her.

"I can't tell you what your father was like, but your mother can. Do your best to find her and she can tell you everything."

Trista nodded her understanding and he smiled sympathetically before tapping her comfortingly on the shoulder. She was about to thank him when a tremendous sound echoed through the trees.

Birds flew out of the branches overhead, screeching as they did so and Oren snapped his hand away, immediately alert,

"What was that?" the ground rumbled beneath their feet.

"I don't know…but we need to get back. Let's go!"

Oren took off into the trees and Trista followed close behind wondering what on earth they would find.

EMERGING RELATIONS

Briseis sat atop Axus looking down on a small piece of the army she was banding together to defeat the Samaian Redeemer.

In the days since she'd felt the power surge from the warrior that had almost crippled her, she'd arranged for her army to be ready for the war to come. Briseis had no idea the true strength of the opposing army but she was determined to not be outdone.

It was the midst of summer and yet, there in the Imperial Lands and indeed the rest of the southern lands surrounding the capital; it was cold and the winds bitter.

Her growing army, recruits coming from these same regions, was steadily being camped in the Imperial Lands, and so she was dressed in leathers and furs to keep out the chill.

Briseis turned from her troops for the moment and looked toward the north. If they rode farther, they would reach The Wide, the infamous battleground when countless wars had been fought, the most notable of which was the one between her father and the Samaian king.

Where her father had killed the Samaian king Alexander, Briseis would in turn take the life of that king's only child.

It was poetic really.

The thought brought a rare smile to her face as she listened to Gardan give out her instruction. She watched him now and wondered, again briefly what he did when away from her? The thought suddenly took root and she wondered how he had come to be in her service? Did he have a wife, children; where was he from? What did her captain do with his time other than carry out her orders?

She watched him, doing just that and marvelled at his dirty blonde locks. He was good looking she supposed, in a low born type of way but nothing to really consider.

"The princess has received word of aid from Baron Dreston who will arrive in the capital very soon. With him, he will bring a further four thousand men to add to the two thousand that will arrive in Tirnum before his formal arrival."

Dreston, although a nuisance in having to contact him when she had become so magically weak had proved his worth in the last few days Briseis thought. She would need his help immensely to add the significant numbers to her army that currently only stood at ten thousand, and not all were even trained soldiers. While she planned to have the advantage of the Six, they may not be as ready as she wished them to be.

As Gardan continued giving the information and instruction as to why they were here, Briseis turned her eyes to the Six who stood in a cluster at the front of the forces, closest to her. They were doing much better in the short time they had been training and were now effectively blocking energy attacks as well as creating ones of their own.

Currently, Briseis was not concerned with perfecting any skill in their magic wielding but that they could fight. There was no point in being magically skilled if someone could just run them through with a long sword if they got close enough. If they could defend themselves physically, their powers would develop as a consequence of that skill; she had learnt this in her own training.

"The war to end all wars will begin soon and you must all be ready. You will train day and night, but you will also be on guard for a threat that could come at any time. I have divided you into sections best suited to your skill; report to my guards in an orderly fashion to receive your station."

As he brought his speech to a close, Briseis called out to Gardan,

"General, a word if you please."

Gardan's eyes widened in shock but he came to her without question; a tendency that she admired in him; he knew his place.

Briseis dismounted in her black leathers and fur trimmed cloak; her white blonde hair in a thick braid down her back; to come face to face with him. He was a lot taller than her of course but she was still able to stare him down if the occasion called for it.

"Make sure to appoint a new Captain of the Sentry from your own men, one of your best and most trusted. You are now my General and as such will accompany me in all aspects of this war. Is that understood?"

"Yes, your highness...thank you Princess." Gardan said humbly as he bowed his head.

While the word General was used, the actual title was Captain of the Guard and therefore held immense power and privilege as the head of the Royal Army. There was in fact only one General position and that was currently held of course by Rarno.

Despite the fear she evoked in others with her Sentry, Briseis knew that they had no real standing against her father's official guardsmen; and were still considered a lesser group.

During battles, the reigning monarch would have their general by their side; in her father's case it was Rarno and she wanted Gardan.

The fact that Briseis had appointed a Captain of the Guard without going through the proper channels and while one was already in service, was impudence that wouldn't go unnoticed.

She officially didn't have the right to do so because she wasn't Queen...

"General Beardmore, have the Six brought to my tent immediately."

"Yes, Princess."

Briseis turned from him and made her way across the dead frost covered ground to the elaborate tent that would serve as her base camp when she was in the field. It had compartments that served as rooms that housed her bedding and of course, a wash area.

In the main meeting area was a large table with a map of Mortania, spread across the top. The four corners were held down by elaborately decorated weights and the pieces signifying her army, Dreston's forces and what may be the Redeemer's were in the centre ready to be placed where she wished.

As she leant over the top, running her fingers lightly over the word Priya, she heard commotion outside. She had two guards posted outside the tent and within moments, one had entered.

"What is it?"

"Forgive me Princess but your father has arrived with General Rarno and an armed guard."

"I see...you may leave." The guard exited as quickly as he had come and within seconds of the canopy falling; it rose again to permit her father.

He was again in full regalia, his large crown atop his thick dark hair. His cloak was navy with their symbol of a crow clutching an orb stitched elegantly onto the back. He was armoured but not in full battle gear and had his longsword by his side.

"What in the Gods' names do you think you are doing?" he hissed at her.

Briseis didn't bother to look up as she did some calculations in her head.

"ANSWER ME!"

Briseis raised her eyes to him without raising her head, "What, do you want?"

Curian stared her down as he pointed back towards the canopy opening,

"There are thousands of men outside preparing for battle, some who aren't even old enough to have seen battle. What on earth are you doing?"

"Acquiring an army, is that not what one does in a war?"

"A war of your own making! There was never any declaration of war Briseis. I rebelled so that there never would be again!"

Briseis rolled her eyes and straightened up to look down her nose at him,

"While we all appreciate what you did all those years ago father, times have changed, and a new threat is upon us."

"The Redeemer?" he scoffed, "You truly believe that nonsense!"

"It's not nonsense and the sooner you accept that the better. You know the stories; you know the prophecy!"

Curian began to pace the room just as Rarno entered. He bowed respectfully to Briseis but kept his distance.

"It's been eighteen years, *no one* is coming!"

"How long do you think it takes for a child to grow? Just because you've been sitting around for all these years doing nothing, doesn't mean that they have been!"

"I have been running this kingdom!"

"YOU'VE BEEN RUNNING IT INTO THE GROUND!"

As Briseis shouted at her father, Gardan and the Six entered the tent. Rarno turned angry eyes toward them while Curian stopped pacing to look in their direction.

"Who are you to enter unannounced?" Rarno challenged knowing full well who Gardan was,

"This is General Gardan Beardmore and a special unit of my forces."

"General?" was Rarno's response,

"Special unit?" was her father's as they both looked at the six youths in confusion. Rarno let out a laugh,

"Are you serious, your majesty...this has to be a joke!"

Briseis stepped from around the table and her hand immediately enflamed,

"Come a little closer and I'll show you how funny it is."

"Briseis enough!"

Briseis didn't move but kept her eyes on Rarno who audibly swallowed and diverted his eyes away. Slowly he raised his hand to his throat and rubbed at it, remembering.

Curian couldn't take his eyes away from the youths as he said,

"What do you intend to do with these...*children?*"

His scepticism was justified as to the eye; they did not look like much. They were dressed in navy blue hooded robes with white sashes around the middle and all varied in height.

"These Six were born with the Everlasting power...I have been training them to use it to fight the Redeemer." Curian's eyes widened,

"Why did I not know of this?" Briseis raised her eyebrow at him and Curian, for once didn't respond.

"They're children Princess, little boys and girls. How can they be expected to fight?" Rarno jumped in.

"Their type of fighting will not only require physical strength but strength of the mind, Father."

Briseis turned away from her father and Rarno and back to the map in front of her. Gardan moved to her side, a move that didn't go unnoticed by Rarno.

"I have felt the Redeemer, getting closer to Tirnum every day and I will be ready for them with this team and my army…even if you aren't."

Curian was clearly intrigued. He looked down briefly at the map then back up at his daughter who couldn't seem to take her eyes off it She was completely still, staring down as though transfixed by something on the paper that only she could see.

"*Felt* her…how?" Curian interestedly crossed the room to stand on the other side of his daughter and looked down at the map.

"I can't control it and I don't know why it happens but when it does…I know where she is. I can feel everything about it, the taste, the smells and I just know." Briseis ran her finger over the words Priya again.

"The last time I felt her she was here, then before that, she was here," she ran her finger across the map to Dreston.

"Then the very first time, she was here."

Briseis' finger ran along the map again all the way to Remora in the high mountains.

"Extraordinary," Curian said in awe as he looked at the map then finally up at Briseis.

"We could get rid of them for good. With this knowledge we could finally rid ourselves of the Samai."

"Your majesty, I don't think you should rush into anything just because her highness has had a *feeling*."

Gardan shifted his footing and placed his hand on his sword hilt while Briseis looked up at Rarno with her eyes again,

"If you have nothing to contribute here Rarno, then I suggest you leave." Rarno squared himself up and looked directly at them,

"As the Captain of the King's Guard I have every right to be here."

"And if her highness, who is in fact leading this war should wish it, I have every right to throw you out." Gardan replied forcefully.

Rarno's eyes moved from Gardan to Briseis then to Curian who was still looking down at the map. Rarno looked to Gardan,

"You have no standing here *boy*" he sneered at him. "I serve the *reigning* King!"

"Rarno enough!" Curian finally looked up and walked over to Rarno to take his shoulders in his hands.

"Briseis commands this army and I command my own. You will head our forces as General Gardan will head hers."

Rarno was outraged, his face turning an angry shade of red as he looked at his king in disbelief

"Curian, these are children playing a man's game!"

"A man's game that can finally be won, Rarno!" Curian hissed at him as he stood closer to him.

"Think of it, finally ending the Samaian threat, getting what we wanted...ruling in peace."

Rarno was silent for a moment before looking over at the six youths, then Briseis and Gardan who were still consulting the map.

"This is what you truly want, friend?" Curian's voice rang true,

"Yes,"

"Then I will follow you...as always."

Curian clapped Rarno's shoulders together in happiness before pulling him into a hug. Rarno was taken by surprise when into his ear, he heard the faintest,

"She is still the enemy."

When Curian pulled away from him, he had a large smile on his face,

"Come Rarno," he exclaimed loudly. "Show us how a seasoned man will win a war!"

***

Lamya spent the night in Ardus' home as he had offered, once he had seen to the other injured people from the lifeboat.

She regrettably left Gracelynn and her family in the care of the local hospice where Ardus worked and there, other healers took care of her and her children. Gracelynn had quickly written a letter to their relatives in Illiya and once she heard back from them, she and her children would make the journey there.

Lamya left them with an emotional farewell and told them to ask for her if they were ever in Tirnum City again.

She hoped she would even be there to receive them if they did.

Ardus had shown her to his home and while he left her to wash and rest, he returned to the hospice to help the injured. It wasn't until later that evening upon his return that she was able to speak with him.

She had changed into a light shirt that Ardus had lent her before he left. He was much taller than her of course so it looked like a very loose dress more than anything, but would serve until her robes dried. She used a shawl she'd found on the bed in her room to cover herself up.

She heard a light knock on her door and once she felt the shawl was wrapped as much as could be to protect her modesty; she opened the door to greet him.

Ardus smiled down at her, hazel eyes twinkling in the dim candlelight of the cabin.

"You are still here?"

"Where else would I have gone?" she asked quizzically but when he blushed she realised what he had meant.

"I brought some food…would you like to eat?"

"Yes, thank you."

Ardus' home was simple but nice; a wooden cabin with two bedrooms, an open kitchen and sitting area, and a separate room for bathing.

In one corner of the kitchen/sitting space, he had created a work area dedicated to his craft. She saw bottles of ointments and tonics and leaves for salves among countless papers and books of his medical findings. There were two large chairs and a table to the far side of the room closest to the fire and it was here that he invited her to sit. Lamya took a seat as he left her to busy himself in the kitchen.

"It is just stew and bread, I hope that's okay?"

"That's fine, thank you." She said with a smile as he put a pot on the stove and lit the hearth beneath it.

"I rely a lot on the charity of my patrons. The healers, they give me a lot of what I eat."

"That's wonderful although, doesn't healing pay well? You have a nice home."

Ardus busied himself with cups and plates as he spoke to her, his back to her; but Lamya watched him anyway. The movement of his blonde hair seemed to have mesmerised her along with the movements of his arms and the strength of the muscles in his back through his shirt.

"This house belonged to my father who was paid very handsomely as a healer. Too handsomely some would say. So when he died, I paid who I needed to keep my home, but I stopped taking the extortionate payments he charged. I did not think it right to charge people for their right to live."

He turned to her suddenly making her blush as he handed her a mug,

"Careful, it's hot."

She took it between her hands and sipped, it was sweet but with a hint of something spicy.

"What is it?" she asked appreciatively before taking another careful sip.

"I don't know exactly," he said with a laugh as he sat in the chair next to her with his own mug. "The women call it *nougy*. It's an evening beverage we have in Jentra, calms the nerves and things like that."

"I see," Lamya took another welcome sip then set the mug on her lap. "How are the people I arrived with?"

Ardus sighed with a small smile that didn't reach his eyes,

"They will all live, and that's what's important but what on earth happened out there?" he wasn't looking for a response as he continued, staring into the fire.

"So much has changed in the last few years…so much destruction and discord amongst the people."

"I've travelled across Mortania and the Known World and I've seen a lot of the destruction you speak of. It seems to stem mainly from Man and the Samai." Ardus nodded,

"There are many who take sides when it comes to our most recent political history."

"What side do you take?"

Ardus turned his hazel eyes away from the fire and onto her face,

"I take the side of what's right."

He placed his mug of *nougy* on the low table between them and got up from his seat to walk back to the kitchen.

He stirred the pot he had left there before turning off the fire and serving the stew into two bowls. He cut two thick slices of bread and placed them on a small wooden plate. He brought the bowls and plates to set them on the low table before taking his seat.

"Help yourself," he said with a smile as Lamya reached out and took a bowl and slice of bread. They did it at the same time and their hands touched briefly. Lamya snapped her hand back as did he,

"I'm sorry go ahead,"

"Apologies, please take it"

They spoke at the same time, making each other laugh and Ardus gestured to the bread,

"Please, I insist." Lamya reached out again with a faint blush in her cheeks.

"Thank you so much for your kindness."

"It was the least I could do for someone so…alone."

She knew that hadn't been what he meant to say but she didn't question it as he tried to cover his tracks.

"I didn't mean that as it sounded!"

"It's fine, I know what you meant. I am usually required to travel alone in my line of work."

"What do you do?"

"Well, I'm a teacher I guess. I work at a school in Thelm when I am there, but I travel the world learning all I can to give that knowledge back to my students. I was on my way to Illiya with new information as it happens." Ardus nodded his understanding,

"Yes, you mentioned you were heading in that direction. My brother lives there; I'd be happy to accompany you."

"There's no need, I wouldn't want to put you out," she rushed to refuse his help but Ardus cut her off.

"You wouldn't be. Any excuse to spend more time with you."

Lamya blushed furiously and looked down at her bowl before taking a large mouthful just to have something to do with her face. Ardus continued to eat his own food and when both bowls were clear he took their dishes back to the kitchen before returning to his seat.

"If we leave early tomorrow morning, we can get to Illiya by nightfall."

"That would be amazing, the sooner the better."

"I hope you don't mind me asking but, what's so important there?" Lamya sighed as she thought of her answer.

"It's more so that I need to be there by a certain time, not that the place is significant. I'm on a tight schedule…it's difficult to explain."

"Will there be someone to meet you in Illiya at least?" Lamya nodded. She had spoken to her grandmother while Ardus was at the hospice and there would indeed be another Lithanian who would equip her with new provisions since she'd lost all her belongings on the ship.

"Good, then you should get some rest. We have a long day ahead of us."

Lamya nodded again and stood up from her chair. She walked the short distance to her room and when she opened the door and stepped inside, she waited in the threshold a moment.

"So close to the sea, there can be a lot of noises at night so try not to be too alarmed. I'll be right next door if you need me."

Lamya turned to face the wonderfully kind man and blushed for the thousandth time that day. She was unused to being so attracted to a man, but she couldn't deny that she found Ardus very appealing. Her life was devoted to the Council and the knowledge she both found and brought there, there was no room in her life for romance, but it didn't stop it feeling wonderful.

"Thank you very much Ardus…for everything." Lamya turned away before her face could betray her feelings any longer and closed the door gently behind her.

She rested her head on the door once she'd closed it trying desperately to steady her breathing.

Stop it Lamya, it's no use thinking about him this way!

She would be rid of him tomorrow anyway so, thinking about a romance or a simple life by the coast of the sea, that could never be, really didn't matter.

With that thought, Lamya got into the bed and fell into a dreamless sleep.

FAMILY FEUDS

They'd run for what felt like forever, but even then, they didn't reach the town centre until the evening was onset.

On the journey into the training area, they had travelled at night and so time hadn't had much meaning. Trista finally noticed how far they'd travelled when they emerged from the overgrowth of trees and plants into the hottest afternoon sun; knowing it had been morning when they left. She and Oren had been so cut off from civilization, it was almost a shock to see other people.

Travelling across The Plains, she and Dana had been fortunate enough not to run into too many people who would ask too many questions or wish them harm; other than those men just before they'd reached Dreston.

Dreston therefore, had been her first real sight of the kingdom and all the people that lived in it. Priya was less of a surprise after the excitement of Dreston and had been relatively quiet in comparison to what she and Oren walked into.

They stepped out into the town square, with travel weathered walkways lined by buildings of various uses; taverns, inns, a God's House and a mail house to name a few. People were running around in a panic although it wasn't entirely clear what had happened. The two of them scanned frantically before Trista noticed a column of smoke rising into the air a few buildings down towards the town. Oren saw it too and quickly looked around before turning his attention to Trista,

"Go in there," he nodded his head towards the tavern. "Wait for me there while I go and see what happened."

"No, I'm coming with you!" she protested and while she'd expected him to argue with her, he merely nodded and took off down the road toward the smoke.

They passed men and women who rushed past them covered in dirt and in some cases blood.

She's found me again!

Trista hated that her first thought was of her own wellbeing and that the princess had discovered her location.

They hadn't run too far before they arrived at a strip of buildings on fire and it looked like they had been for awhile.

People were evacuating horses and other animals from what they could now see were stables, but various other buildings were on fire and steadily spreading. People were trying to douse the flames, but the smoke and heat was unbearable.

"I don't think swords can help with this Oren!" a voice called out.

Both Trista and Oren turned towards it and a man ran up through the crowd towards them.

Trista's eyes bulged out of her head at the sheer size of him.

He was more muscular than Oren and a little taller with the same black hair and green eyes identifying him as Samaian.

His long hair was tied away from his face and from the smudges of soot over it; it was obvious he had recently been near that fire. He had a thick and healthy beard and thin crows' feet near his eyes showing that he was older than them, but Trista wasn't sure by how much.

"Nyron!" Oren reached out to clasps forearms with the other man, who after clasping it back firmly, pulled him into a tight hug.

Nyron…this was her cousin.

"What happened?"

"We don't really know. A few hours ago, an explosion went off and set the granary on fire that led onto the weapons chamber and has been spreading ever since. People are struggling to stop it."

"Where's Naima?"

"Helping the injured back at the inn. I've been evacuating animals and trying to get things out of people's homes, but the water isn't working fast enough, and we don't see any other way to stop it."

"Why don't you suffocate it?"

It was only when she spoke that Nyron seemed to realise she was there and when he did, his eyes widened in immediate recognition.

"Gods above!" he cried in astonishment as he stared at her. "It's you." Oren confirmed

"Nyron…this is Trista. Trista, this is our cousin Nyron."

Trista reached out to shake his hand as Oren had done but Nyron pulled her into a bear hug, picking her up and squeezing her to his chest,

"Gods be praised, you're safe!"

"Nyron put her down!" Oren chastised and even though she couldn't see him, Trista thought she heard amusement in Oren's voice. Nyron put her down in front of him, dusting of her arms apologetically,

"I'm so sorry but I…it's great to finally meet you Trista."

Trista beamed at him, she couldn't help it; she liked him immediately.

"As wonderful as it is to meet you too Nyron, we need to do something about this fire."

"Of course, what did you mean?" he asked although he was still grinning at her with excitement; it was infectious. Even in the middle of a crisis, she couldn't help but smile back at him and she couldn't wait to be able to talk with him properly.

"We need to cut off the air," the two men looked at each other then turned to her, confused.

"Fire breathes, if we cut off the air it can't spread."

Nyron smiled, clearly the idea had never occurred to him. Without waiting for their approval, Trista took off towards the buildings until the heat was dusting against her skin.

She surveyed the damage in front of her and her ring began to glow,

"I need these people out of the way…please."

Oren didn't respond, instead nudging Nyron and the two of them began to clear the way of people trying to save their belongings.

"Get out of the way, stand clear all of you!"

There was a hubbub of resistance as people struggled, not wanting to leave their possessions behind but soon enough, the volunteers and residence were out of the way of the flames while the buildings continued to burn.

Rayne had told her repeatedly that her power was through her will, that she could do anything she put her mind to, if it was in the realm of the Everlastings reach.

Fine, she wanted to starve the fire of air and that meant cutting off its supply, so Trista closed her eyes, raised her arms out by her sides until the air around her went still.

She willed the air to be cut off around her and as she opened her eyes to focus on the closest flame to her, she moved the vacuum of air so she could slowly engulf the building with it.

She felt power wrap steadily around the building, making the flames hiss away as she did so,

"Trista, you don't have the strength yet, you shouldn't be doing this." Oren protested.

"Put out the fire of the building next to it," she replied, ignoring him completely. "I won't be able to hold this for long, so we have to make it count for something."

Annoyed, Oren jogged away from her with Nyron at his tail as they roped in helpers to put out the fire closest to the first one that Trista was suffocating. They proceeded to wet the thatched roofs and wooden buildings in an attempt to stop it spreading.

On she pushed the block of air to engulf the fire that was rapidly spreading through, in and around the building like a monster, threatening to destroy everything around it.

She knew she was using too much of her power too quickly, but Trista was determined not to allow the fire to best her. Beads of sweat appeared on her upper lip until finally, the entire building had been smothered and she watched as the flames, slowly died.

Trista held it there for the moment, watching as the flames slowly extinguished until she was confident that no naked flame was left.

Her heart continued beating rapidly in her chest as the energy it took to stop air, took its toll. It was air, light and frivolous in its nature but it was exactly that, nature and Trista was stopping its course.

She took her eyes from the building briefly to see where Oren, Nyron and others were quickly putting out the remaining fire.

With an exhausted breath, she let go of her hold on the air and collapsed to the floor.

She could barely lift her head or her arms as all the energy she'd been filled with, left her completely. She struggled to breathe but for the first time after using her powers for such a big task, she was still conscious.

Believe in who you are.

The thought came back to her, always in the back of her mind.

"Trista?" she felt Oren's hands on her shoulder, lifting her onto her feet.

"I-I'm okay," she replied faintly before swaying a little and folding into his arms. She was so concerned with not falling over she barely registered how it felt to be there… barely.

"I'm taking you home!" Oren snapped,

"I'm f-fine Oren," she said, even as she grasped her head to stop it pounding.

"No you're not, yo—"

"Oren!" Oren turned at the sound of his father's voice and what looked like fear flashed across Oren's face. "Bring her to The Phyn."

Gorn snapped and simply turned in the direction of the local tavern. Trista looked up at Oren who was looking down the road after his father and saw the look of sadness on his face.

"Come on," he muttered and helped her back down the road toward The Phyn with Nyron following close behind.

They arrived at the local tavern on Main Street and entered a circus. Dozens of people were running in and out looking for and after loved ones who had been caught in the blaze. Trista was vaguely aware of people with bandages on their heads being escorted presumably back to their homes, but the place was packed.

While Priya was large, it was a far cry from the magnitude of Dreston and the people lived more widespread in the surrounding countryside than in the centre. The Phyn was where they would congregate until they made their way back to their countryside residences.

The Phyn was run by a man named Markus and his wife Joy, who was also the Madame of the brothel that was attached next door.

While the tavern maintained a level of respectability the working girls and the men who used their services were not allowed in the main bar until after hours, but before then; all were welcome.

Gorn, who was walking angrily ahead of the group held the door open for Oren and Trista to walk inside; Nyron entered after them but Trista saw a young woman walk in beside him and she seemed vaguely familiar.

When Gorn led them over to a large wooden table in the corner of the room; Trista saw that Dana was there waiting for them.

"Dana!" a smile spread across her face even though she felt so weak. Dana rushed from her seat and barrelled into her with a hug.

"Are you okay?"

"I will be…I would like something to drink though. I feel…dried out."

"Water?" Trista nodded. "I'll be right back."

Dana left to go to the bar, leaving them to talk. Oren helped Trista onto one of the benches and sat beside her, holding her up against his shoulder. Trista tried to ignore that leaning against his powerful arm made her feel…funny. Gorn sat on the opposite side of the table,

"Are you okay, Trista?"

"I'm fine Gorn, just a little…tired. That took a lot out of me."

"Of course, it did! That was an incredibly *stupid* thing you did back there."

Oren looked over at his father but didn't say anything.

"S-stupid?"

Her eyes shot to Oren then back at Gorn in disbelief just as Dana came back over with a jug of water, a mug and took the seat next to her.

"Yes, stupid."

"Father, Tri—"

"And you!" Gorn snapped again turning his angry eyes back to his son. "How could you let her do something like that; knowing what she means to us!" Gorn shouted making the other patrons look up then quickly look away, even Dana looked uncomfortable.

"I know exactly what she means to us, me more than anybody!" Oren shouted back as he gently leaned Trista away from him towards Dana, to stand up from his seat. He stormed over to the bar, Trista's eyes never leaving him, to where Nyron stood, waiting patiently with the girl that had walked in with him.

Trista didn't want him to leave; having him beside her made her feel stronger somehow. She watched as Nyron and the girl took the stools either side of him, and the three of them were hushed in conversation.

Trista turned back to Gorn, a new breath of fire in her belly as she raged at Oren being in trouble because of something she did.

"It was my choice to use my power Gorn, don't blame Oren!"

"I do blame Oren; he should have known better!"

"He told me I shouldn't use them but I did it anyway! If anyone should be yelled at it's me, or am I too precious to be told off?"

"Princess..."

"No Gorn, I'm *not* a princess so stop trying to treat me like one! I wasn't raised a princess; I don't know what it is to *be* a princess!"

She looked him square in the eye, knowing she needed him to understand how she felt about this.

"I did what I felt was right and you couldn't have stopped me anymore then Oren did, so don't blame him for my judgement!"

Gorn cleared his throat and she could see that he was shocked she was speaking to him like this but it had to be said.

"You can't go around protecting me and acting as if I can't do anything wrong because I can and I will make mistakes. If I'm grown enough to make them; I'm grown enough to suffer the consequences for them."

Gorn looked at her in astonishment and then undisputed pride,

"I'm sorry…I should have known better. I was just so frightened for you Trista. Our powers, they're volatile and are not to be used lightly unless you're really prepared for them. Why do you think no one in town thought to do it themselves?"

She realised then, that she *hadn't* thought about it. She had barrelled in to use her powers when there was an entire town of Samai who had chosen not to, why?

"I realise there are reasons why you can't use power collectively, but I need to use mine to get better at them. If I'm going to fight Briseis, I need to be able to *beat* her or what's the point in all of this?"

Gorn nodded his understanding and reached out to take her hand across the table. He rubbed the top of her hand with the base of his thick calloused thumb and sighed heavily,

"I wasn't able to protect your father and that is something that I will regret until my very last breath," Trista saw it pained him to even think about it. "I want to protect you Trista, at any cost." Trista smiled at him,

"Protecting me doesn't mean smothering me Gorn," Trista smiled sweetly before turning serious. "I need to grow up. I have my memories back; however small they are and I know now that I have to embrace them. I have to embrace who and what I am, to be able to do what I need to do…what my mother needs me to do."

"You saw her?" Trista smiled,

"You don't sound surprised that I could have?" Gorn smiled back and shrugged his large shoulders.

"The last time I saw your mother, she had you in her arms and said she needed to hide you one last time. She disappeared into that jungle and never came out. What she did in there, I can only imagine…she was very powerful Trista and maybe some of her was left behind." Trista nodded,

"Well I didn't see her as much as I felt her…she'd been in that place before."

Trista kept it to herself that she thought she'd had memories of her father. She didn't want Gorn to tell her that that was impossible or even that who she'd seen wasn't Alexander. She wanted to keep the image she had of him, just for herself.

"Don't be so hard on Oren okay…he's helped me so much."

"I'm sure he has," there was a look on Gorn's face that neither of the girls could comprehend but before they had a chance to dwell on it, Gorn rose from the bench.

"Well, I'll get you something to eat before we head back to the house. I assume my niece and nephew are hovering around for a reason?"

Trista grinned as she turned to look in their direction and even thought they were still stood with Oren who was facing the bar, the young woman was looking over at them.

Naima Antos was Nyron's twin sister and that's why she'd looked familiar. Trista smiled at her and the woman took that as her cue to walk over. Nyron followed a few moments after seeing his sister leave but Oren stayed where he was.

"Don't overload her with too much information you two," Gorn mockingly told them but the siblings just laughed.

"We won't Uncle Gorn."

He slapped a large hand on Nyron's shoulder before giving Naima a kiss on the cheek and going over to join his son.

The brother and sister sat on the bench opposite the girls as Trista finally took a sip of the water Dana had brought her. She did so with a shy smile as she looked at two members of her family.

Family.

"That was an incredible thing you did back there." Nyron said first. His voice was deeper than Oren's and despite his size, he looked incredibly lean and athletic in his angular face and jawline. Naima in comparison was all femininity and grace and for the first time in a long time, Trista thought of Avriel. That same innate elegance exuded from her, from her emerald green eyes that were large in in her angelic face. She had long curly black hair as Trista did but it was pulled back, slicked at the front into a ponytail that exploded into curls at the back. She was as tall as her brother even when she sat down beside him.

"Thank you, although Gorn didn't seem to think so."

"Gorn is a worrier; has been our whole lives. Family means everything to him." Naima said, her voice light and pleasing to the ear; like a song.

"I see that…I'm just happy to even have any family."

Nyron and Naima beamed at her, their faces looking so much more alike when they were smiling.

"You've always had family Trista, even if you didn't know us." Naima said gently and Trista felt their sincerity as they looked over at her. "We've waited a long time to meet you too Trista. We've thought about you every day; not knowing where you were or if you were even alive."

"Why wouldn't she have been alive?" Dana asked quietly, and Trista remembered her manners.

"I'm so sorry, Nyron, Naima; this is my best friend Dana Black. Dana this is Nyron and Naima Antos…they're my cousins." Dana smiled, not letting the revelation shock her too much and shook Nyron and Naima's hand over the table.

"We will consider you our friend too, but to answer your question Dana; we hadn't heard of Aunt Rowan or Trista since they left Priya over sixteen years ago. We had no way of knowing if she were alive or dead."

"We used our powers as best we could to try and get a location on her, but nothing worked and for a long time, it was dangerous to even try."

Trista's heart broke at Nyron's words; there was so much she needed to understand about her past.

"There's so much I need to know…please tell me."

Nyron and Naima looked at each other with smiles on their faces before turning back to Trista and Naima began speaking,

"Well, you know Nyron and I are your first cousins as our mothers are sisters. As members of your closest family, we were one of the few who saw you when you were born; considering the rebellion that was going on at the time."

151

"Exactly, the entire kingdom was in upheaval that Aunt Rowan had to have you in relative secrecy. Aunt Rayne had to put wards around the birthing room, so that you would be protected." Nyron added

"Protected from what?" Trista asked just as a young man came over with a plate of food in his hand and placed one in front of her. She stole a glance back to the bar where Oren still sat with Gorn in a seemingly heated discussion but turned back to the twins.

"Thank you," she said to the boy before he disappeared again. "Go on,"

"From anyone, Tris," Trista liked the nickname Nyron had seemingly just created for her. "Curian was rebelling; people were rallying behind his cause all over Mortania so father, Uncle Alex and Uncle Gorn fought to keep things in order, but it just wasn't enough."

"They underestimated the dormant hate that some humans had for the Samai." Naima added. "They didn't count on the fact that people would turn and fight against us. In the end…it got too much for them to control."

"What happened to your father?"

"He died alongside his men during the Battle at the Wide. After your father and General Antos or Uncle Gorn to you and I, Father was the next most powerful man in the kingdom. He fought, as they all did until his very last breath."

"He was very brave," Dana said gently.

"That he was, but he was also a man of honour. There were only two ways he was leaving that battlefield: victory or death."

"What about Gorn…he was injured and left."

Naima shook her head instantly at Dana's question,

"No Dana, Uncle Gorn was injured terribly and had to be pried off the battlefield. His leg had already been run through when he got news that the king had fallen…"

"It took ten men to follow through on the king's order that if he were killed, Gorn was to take us away."

"He never would have agreed to it if it wasn't an order. He, like his brother our father is a man of duty. If those men never dragged him off the field; he never would have left."

Trista looked at the twins in dismay,

"I don't blame him Naima but even I can see that Gorn blames himself."

"As any Antos would, you should have seen this one when our father said he couldn't join the Royal Army at ten!" Naima laughed at the fond memory but Nyron just rolled his eyes,

"Antos men will not apologies for being honourable warriors. I saw my father and my uncle as the greatest soldiers who ever lived…I wanted to be like them."

Trista nodded her understanding with a proud smile

"Please tell me more about our family."

Nyron and Naima proceeded to tell Trista and Dana all about growing up as Samaian nobility; as niece and nephew to the Queen and the children of a military Captain.

The twins were born in High Tower, their father's hometown in the province of Illiya. While those lands were officially governed by the High Lord of Illiya, the Antos family oversaw the area on behalf of the reigning lord. As the eldest Antos brother, HighTower was Gorn's inheritance and all its lands and titles would one day pass to Oren. The twins mother, Renya was High Lady of the Lands of Illiya as Oren had previously explained.

The twins had been educated at the Illiyan Academy along with other high-born children of the southern regions but moved to Tirnum after their mother died when they were eight years old. Their father had wanted them closer to him while he worked, and so left HighTower and Illiya in the hands of the advisors who were trained to do just that until the Antos children were finally of age.

"Our father spent most of his time in the capital and we would visit him during the summer or when he had official leave. In those early years, we spent time with our aunt and uncle and once Oren was born, we took him under our wing."

"You took him under your wing you mean," Naima countered to her brother. "I wanted nothing to do with your antics and the corruption of a four-year-old."

"What you call corruption dear sister, I call man training."

The quartet laughed and spent the rest of the afternoon laughing and talking about Trista's family.

The twins opened up a world of family, frolicking and fun that seemed like a dream. While they were related to royalty, they weren't in fact royal and so Naima and Nyron had a relatively normal upbringing. They'd learned to ride and hunt and fight very early on and their parents had instilled in them a love for their king and country. They were loyalists through and through and even if they weren't related to her, Trista knew she would have adored them.

Where Naima was, stern and followed rules and protocol, Nyron was the prankster, the joker who always wanted to make everyone laugh, but he was fiercely protective of his family and of course his sister, the only immediate family he had left.

They talked about the rules and privilege of being high born and all the traditions that they were expected to follow. Oren didn't join them at the table for any of this, instead choosing to eat a meal alone and then leaving the tavern altogether.

Gorn, who had also left the tavern returned later in the evening to ride Trista and Dana home with the promise that Nyron and Naima would visit soon.

Trista had never felt more alive and happy then she did at that moment and her feeling of giddiness only heightened when she lay in her bed across from Dana that night.

"Something happened…with Oren."

Dana shot upright in the bed, closing a book she was reading on a hundred uses for wolves bane.

"Tell me everything!"

"Hold on, don't get carried away!"

"What do you mean, this is huge! Did you kiss him?" Trista almost choked on her words

"No, of course I didn't kiss him!"

"Did you want to?"

"No!" Dana raised her eyebrow at Trista with a smirk. "M-maybe."

"I knew it!"

"Dana, it's not that…okay it's not *just* that. It's something different with Oren, like a-a feeling. When he was near me once, I think he felt it too, but I don't know what *it* is!"

Trista went on to tell her the few incidents with Oren in the river and when she'd had her nightmare and how it had made her feel around him.

"So, what exactly are you telling me?" Dana said with a giggle.

"I don't know really," Trista sighed heavily. "Do you think I should talk to him about it?"

"If you have something specific to say or ask then sure. He doesn't like stuttering," Dana laughed but having spent the last few weeks with him, Trista knew this to be true.

"True," Trista worried her lip. "Okay, I'll ask him about the feeling. Either it's his power or it isn't right?"

"Right."

"...right...here we go."

Trista got out of bed and put on a robe that Iona had given her and went to the bedroom door,

"Good luck,"

"Thanks," Trista replied nervously into the dimly lit room as she opened the door and stepped out.

Terrified, she walked the few steps to Oren's bedroom but when she got there, the door was open, and he wasn't in there. She didn't bother to peak into his sanctuary which was virtually impossible without candlelight and so went downstairs to look for him. Iona had already gone to bed and while Trista didn't find anyone in the living rooms or the kitchen, she saw a light outside the kitchen window coming from the forge. Deciding it was now or never, Trista left the house and made her way over.

It was cool outside and all the nocturnal creatures of Priya were making their calls as they bustled through the trees and bushes. Trista approached the forge but the door was ajar through which she heard voices; Gorn and Oren's voices.

"...matter. I expect you to be more professional." Gorn was saying,

"I'm always professional,"

"Usually yes, but we both know Trista is different, special"

"You don't have to tell me that Dad, I know she is."

"Then make sure that this doesn't interfere with her training."

"It hasn't, and it won't!"

"Then why do you wish to stop training her?"

There was silence from Oren for a moment and Trista struggled to listen closer as she didn't want to miss his answer.

"I've taught her all I can,"

"That's a lie."

"I told you what happened! Dad...she's more powerful than I ever could have understood, she needs *you*, not me!"

"You know I can't move like I used to, you're the only one who can do this."

"Nyron can teach her, it doesn't have to be me."

"But it *should* be you and I'm done talking about this; do your duty!"

Gorn was clearly irritated but it wasn't clear why; if Nyron could easily train Trista, then why was he so adamant that Oren do it?

"I have always done my duty, but it's not about duty anymore Dad, can't you see that!"

"What are you saying? Do you want..."

"No, of course not!" Oren seemed to be angry that his father would suggest whatever he was suggesting. "Sure, it's a little different now that she's here but now..."

"Now what Oren? You always knew you would have to do this."

"But *she* doesn't know. I thought she'd know as much me but it's very clear that she doesn't, and I don't want to be a part of that!"

"You don't have a choice son."

"I know that!" Oren bellowed at his father but the silence that followed was more telling than the outburst.

"I know that Dad, I just...listen," he seemed to have made up his mind about something. "I won't spend this time with her, training her until she understands what this all means."

"You *know* we can't tell her yet!"

"Until you do, I won't be alone with her…I *can't* be alone with her." Trista's heart stopped at his emphasis.

What had she done so terrible that Oren didn't want to be around her? Trista moved closer to the door, trying to get a look at Oren's face; to try and understand whether he was angry with her.

"We can talk about this another time…I think you should rest." Oren was now saying,

"Oh uh…yes…I will."

They walked toward the door and Trista quickly backed away from it, terrified of them finding her eavesdropping when she suddenly remembered her ability to Shift.

Please work!

The first place that came to mind in her panic was the reading nook in the living room and so with every fibre inside her, she tried to Shift there.

The reading nook was just behind the front door and Trista arrived just as Gorn opened the door and headed slowly up to his room, leaning heavily on the crutch he sometimes used. He always walked with a slight limp due to his injury anyway but the crutch helped on particularly bad days.

Crouching, Trista waited for him to get upstairs before she stood up, took a deep breath and stepped out to head upstairs as well. It wasn't until she heard the front door shut behind her that Trista let out a yelp and spun around to see Oren standing there.

"What did you hear?" was all he said as she stood there, quivering in her slippers and robe. She wrapped her arms instinctively around herself, suddenly very conscious of her body no that he was near.

"Gods Oren, you scared me!"

"What did you hear?"

"N-nothing," she stuttered but she knew he didn't believe her so she gave up the charade. "Nothing I understood anyway."

"Good, let's keep it that way. I don't appreciate being spied on."

He barged past her towards the stairs. She should have let him go but instead she called out,

"I didn't mean to!"

"It doesn't matter what you meant, *don't* do it again!" he turned to hiss at her in the dark of the living room.

The only light came from the moon outside, casting an eerie shadow on everything and what made Oren look even more imposing. She knew she shouldn't have spied on them but Oren was angrier with her then was necessary and she didn't understand why.

He went to walk away from her but she called out to him anyway, frustrated and upset.

"What did I ever do to you; why do you dislike me?"

Oren stopped in his tracks but didn't turn around to face her. He stood there for a long time, while her heart was caught in her chest. She had known this man for only a few weeks but she couldn't explain why she needed him to like her and be on her side. It was more than finding him attractive or just wanting to be liked; she wanted Oren to respect her as she respected him.

When he turned to her, his eyes were cold and distant again and Trista knew she wasn't going to like what he was going to say,

"I dislike you Trista, because you're not ready to take on the responsibility that is expected of you and because you aren't, we're most likely going to lose this war."

He looked her up and down before adding his final blow,

"I don't want to train you because you're not worth it."

If he had shouted it might have hurt less but he was completely calm. Trista took a deep breath and squared her shoulders, she wouldn't let him see how much his words had cut her. She wouldn't let him know how weak he made her;

"You said I was powerful…you told Gorn I was more powerful then you realised." Oren sneered at her,

"You might be powerful Trista but you're useless and I don't have time for useless."

Despite her efforts, Trista's eyes clouded over, the moonlight making her eyes shiny with the tears resting there.

"I'll train you because my father wishes it but that's it."

Oren turned away from her and marched up the stairs, without another word slamming his bedroom door behind him.

DESPERATE MEASURES

Lamya woke the following morning to the sounds of muffled movement outside her temporary bedroom.

She got up, quickly wrapping the shawl around her shoulders to poke her head out of the bedroom door to see what the commotion was about. She didn't see Ardus so she returned to her room to pick up her clothes that had now dried and left again to go into the washroom.

When she finally exited the washroom, washed and dressed, she found Ardus in the kitchen area serving up some bowls of steaming porridge.

"That smells wonderful," she complimented to alert him to her presence and he turned to her with a smile. Despite herself, Lamya felt her face heat up again as his eyes focused on her. She put her hair behind her ears nervously and went to stand next to him.

"Thank you, oats are my one speciality." He chided himself playfully as he handed her a bowl and they walked together back to the chairs near the fire place.

Lamya took a spoonful and hummed appreciatively, "Good?"

"Just what I needed thank you," he smiled at her again as he took another mouthful.

"I hope I didn't wake you earlier, I was trying to be as quiet as possible." He seemed to realise that he had failed in that regard and Lamya didn't correct him. They laughed at that before she asked,

"When will we head out to Illiya?"

"After breakfast if you want. I've got the wagon all packed up with my supplies, so we can go as soon as you're ready."

"You should have woken me properly; I would have helped."

"I wouldn't dream of it. I would never let a beautiful woman do any heavy lifting." Lamya blushed but Ardus was polite enough to look away.

Lamya usually turned her Empathy off when interacting with others; she didn't need to feel everyone's emotions all the time and so she'd never looked into Ardus' appreciation of her since yesterday.

Curiously, she did so now and the intensity of his attraction to her was overwhelming. She immediately tuned out again, it was invasive after all.

"Well, I appreciate the lay in." He nodded his acknowledgement but didn't look up at her.

They finished their breakfast in companionable silence until Lamya insisted on taking the dirty dishes and washing them before they left. A few minutes later, they were both fully dressed; Ardus had lent her an overcoat and they climbed into his wagon. It had a high leather roof covering the back where Ardus had perfectly packed his supplies. He invited her to ride in the back, but she politely refused and said she would ride up front with him. They set off moments later onto the long, well-travelled road from Jentra to Illiya.

They passed through the main street where crowds were crammed together; busy going about their morning duties. They were setting up market stalls, sweeping front steps of more permanent establishments and washing windows alongside the regular hustle of the town.

It both warmed and broke Lamya's heart that towns like this that still existed in ignorant bliss to what was going on in the kingdom around them; and that that peace could be shattered at any moment. Their journey took a few hours but with chatter and flirty teasing, the time flew by.

Lamya revelled in having intelligent conversation with a man she found so incredibly attractive. It was a shame that nothing would come of their meeting each other.

They arrived in Illiya closing on nightfall just as Ardus had said, and the sea front town was fit to burst with people, even at this late hour.

"You won't be findin' no lodgin' that way I tell ya!" an old man moaned up at them. He tottered along the cobbled path beside them on his walking stick, covered in filthy and tattered clothing.

"What's going on, friend?"

"Ah bit ah gold and I'll tell ya!" he smiled a row of crooked and missing teeth. Ardus reached into his coin pouch and threw the man two coppers. The old man huffed as he caught them; a little too nimbly for Lamya's liking and motioned his head in the direction of the town behind him,

"Dreston's household, on their way to the capital tomorrow with his army. Taken up every inn and tavern we have."

Lamya was intrigued,

"Baron Dreston, is here?"

"That's what I said, aint it!" the old man huffed, annoyed and hobbled off.

Ardus turned to her once he'd set the wagon in motion again,

"What concerns you about the baron?"

"I'm not sure just yet. Can you please bring me to the River Maiden?"

"Of course."

Lamya had spoken with the Council the night before and been told to meet a fellow Lithanian at the named inn. She'd been told they would give her lodging for the night and all she would need to continue her journey to eventually meet Trista in Thelm.

They arrived at the River Maiden within minutes and Ardus got down from the wagon to help her down into the street,

"You can't stay here for long!" a random man shouted over at them who was trying to get by with a wagon full of hay.

The streets were heaving with people buying, selling and bargaining various items. Samaian, Coznian and Man alike, mingled together in relative comfort Lamya observed. She was aware of course that Illiya had been a primarily Samaian town, the rightful rulers being High Lord and Lady Josef and Mysten Illiya; Queen Rowan's parents and their descendants.

"I will assist the lady then I will move." Ardus replied calmly.

"Make it quick," the man grumbled going about his business. Ardus turned back to Lamya with a roll of his eyes and pressed a small piece of paper into her hand.

"This is my address if you ever need me…for anything."

Without any warning, Ardus leant down and kissed Lamya on the side of her cheek, so close to her mouth it might as well have been there. She raised her hand to place her fingertips gently against the skin he had kissed as he straightened up to look down at her,

"It was a pleasure and I hope to see you again."

Lamya looked up at him and saw regret in his eyes. He turned from her then, got back onto the driver's bench and set the horse in motion; disappearing into the dense crowd.

Lamya watched after him for a long time, thinking of all the reasons she wished him to turn around and come back to her. She knew if she had the choice; she would have wanted to see what a life with Ardus could be like.

"Lamya Rubio?"

Lamya turned at the sound of her name and came face to face with a woman who looked almost exactly like her. She had the same red hair and amber eyes identifying her as a Lithanian but her hair was short and her face much rounder. Where Lamya's hair was red with hues of orange like fire, this girl had more auburn tones.

"Yes?"

"I'm Cynthia, I'm here to show you to your room. The Council sent me."

"Oh yes, thank you," Cynthia smiled back at her and led her straight into the tavern.

Cynthia brought Lamya directly to a comfortable space above the tavern. It had a bed with actual feathered pillows and a wash basin to perform the essentials.

A larger communal bathroom was at the end of the upstairs hall where Lamya had seen at least four other rooms but was not sure of the occupants.

A young serving girl came to the door a few moments later and took their orders for supper. By the time she'd disappeared and reappeared with the requested meal, Cynthia handed her new clothing, coin and provisions that would last her until she reached the princess.

Cynthia explained that once Lamya made it to Crol, she was meant to book passage across the Alzo Sea to Drem and carry on her journey from there.

Cynthia left Lamya not long afterwards, bidding her as safe journey. Lamya made sure to get some much-needed rest but despite her weary body, her mind kept conjuring images of a young and handsome physician with hazel eyes. She flipped around in her bed, restless until she fell into a much-needed sleep.

The following morning, Lamya washed and dressed herself against the brisk seaside air and left the tavern to make her way towards the docks. There she found ships, a multitude of ships baring the sigil of House Dreston and with a heavy heart, she eyed the men who were loading provisions onto it.

She saw crates labelled as swords and axes as well as ones with dried fish and meat. These were the provisions for an army and the amount of boats told her that it was no small size.

Did the Council have enough supporters to rally against the Baron who commanded a force this size? She had no clue and she had no way of finding out.

What Lamya did know, as she made her way back to the River Maiden was that over a hundred ships were leaving Illiya this morning and would arrive at Thea's Point in a matter of days.

Lamya could only hope that Trista was out there; prepared for when that happened and what it would mean for everyone who relied on her coming out victorious.

***

Baron Lyon Dreston awoke in his suite bright and early the day after he arrived in Illiya.

He and his household had arrived in the large coastal town in the late evening and everyone had been so travel weary; they immediately retired.

He made sure to satisfy his appetites once his rooms had been set up and lain with Geneiva. Once he'd released himself within her; he'd dismissed her and brought Alaina to his bed. He had enjoyed the young woman until he could barely see straight and fell into a dreamless sleep. He awoke now to her supple naked body beside him, covered barely by the thin cotton sheets.

She was on her back, one arm by her side and the other over her taut midriff. Lyon reached out to palm her stomach before reaching under the covers and manoeuvring his hand between her legs, prying her soft lips apart to penetrate her with his fingers.

Alaina was instantly awake, eyes wide as she registered where she was,

"My Lord," she said instantly as she spread her legs further to accommodate his intrusion. Lyon worked her until her formality was broken and she was nothing but all feeling woman.

Despite loving that she was under his control, there were times when her complete abandon to her feelings was more of a turn on than her submission. Alaina exploded around his hand that was punching into her and before she had a chance to come down from her climax, he mounted her and drove up into her.

She cried out and instantly wrapped her legs around him while grabbing at his forearms that were either side of her slim frame. Lyon was relentless in his rhythm; pounding into her with an aggression that lacked any passion or romance but pure lust.

This session, thankfully for Alaina was to be a short one; merely a release before he got ready for the long voyage to Tirnum.

Once, twice; three more pumps into her had him burying himself to the hilt emptying himself until his legs were weak.

Lyon slumped onto her and once he was ready; pulled out of her. Alaina winced but said nothing and lay there until he was sat upright in the bed.

"You may get ready," he said simply, catching his breath as Alaina moved slowly off the bed, buckling as her legs hit the ground. She said nothing and headed out of his space to wash and dress wherever it was that she did those things.

She would be ready and waiting for him again tonight whenever he wished it, but Lyon had a thought that he wouldn't be calling on Alaina tonight. He would have a lot more pressing matters to attend to before they arrived.

They were days away from the capital; days away from the first real implications of war since the Rebellion and Lyon needed to make sure that everything was in place. Two thousand of his men had gone on ahead but nothing would be solidified until he personally arrived. He had his own men; he had command of Thelm's forces if needed and once he got rid of that pesky princess; he would have control of the royal forces as well.

He realised this would be a lot more difficult to obtain but he was willing to do whatever it took to establish himself as the rightful successor.

Lyon rang the bell for his attendants and when they all hurried into the room; Aml entered behind them.

"Greetings Lord,"

"Greetings Aml, fire away."

Aml went into his normal routine of reporting any significant changes that had gone on in the household or anything that needed his attention. While they were travelling of course, he would receive words from the ministers back in the city as well as any men he had deployed anywhere else.

"The men you despatched to Priya are days away, we received a raven this morning. Are the orders still the same Lord?"

Aml's eyes shifted a moment and it was the only indication that he had any thought about what was being asked.

"Yes Aml, all young women aged seventeen and eighteen are to be killed."

"As you wish Lord," Aml said simply as he continued his report.

"The ships are ready when you are; we had men working through the night to have everything loaded up."

"Fantastic, are the cabins of Alaina and Geneiva as I wished?"

"Yes Lord, either side of your own."

"Fantastic," Lyon said again. "I couldn't be asked to have to travel too far if I wish to visit either one. Any news from her highness?"

Aml noted the distain in Lyon's voice as he said it,

"None as such, other than that his majesty the King has now joined forces with the princess?"

"His forces were against her?" Lyon asked in surprise as he sat in his chair to be shaved. One of his man servants proceeded to lather his face while another laid out his fitted trousers and shirt with matching jacket.

"Not against Lord just…separated. They are now occupying the same camp in the Imperial Lands."

"I see," he said simply as the shaving blade was now at his face.

"Any orders before we depart, Lord?" Aml waited patiently as his master's face was finished and wiped clean. Lyon sat up once they were finished and fixed his amber eyes onto Aml's smooth brown face.

"None Aml, just let me know the instant the previously departed men have arrive in the capital."

"Yes Lord," Aml bowed before taking his leave.

Lyon sighed as he rose from the chair so that his servants could dress him. Life would be so much easier once he was king, he thought.

***

The King sat with his most trusted advisor and friend, General Rarno, discussing the growing strength of Briseis' army over their own, over breakfast that morning. They were eating in the king's private quarters so not to be disturbed or overheard by prying ears.

"They get stronger every day," Rarno admitted as he poured himself some thick black coffee; the strongest kind in all the world; all the way from Coz. "The power among them is unbelievable, even in these early days."

Curian was inclined to agree even as he swirled his own coffee with disgust. They had been sat in his private seating room since dawn; discussing all that they intended to do now that they knew Briseis was serious about her war.

"How have I let it come to this?" Rarno smartly said nothing. "How was she able to amass this level of power, right under my nose?"

"She is smart," Rarno replied simply if not reluctantly.

"To think that my little girl…could be…this." Curian's voice was barely a whisper.

"We have to focus; we have a plan and we must stick to it."

"How long will she be fooled? How long can we keep this up?" Curian snapped at his friend, but a fire rose in Rarno's eyes as he looked at his friend square in his.

"We'll keep this up for as long as we have to, because we know now what she is capable of; what power she holds over this land. If ridding the world of Briseis Greybold is what needs to be done to give this country peace, then that is what must be done!"

"She's my *daughter* Rarno!" Curian thundered as he rose from the table; pounding his mighty fists on the table top as he did so. "My own flesh and blood; do you not understand that?"

Rarno remained in his seat, looking up at his friend of over twenty years; his king and commander for only a little less than that. They had become brothers in arms once Curian joined the military and Rarno had recognised in him a passion to do what was right. When Curian had come to him, speaking of banding the Prophecy, he knew he would follow this man into any battle.

"I understand that the blood of your blood and flesh of your flesh would rip yours away in a heartbeat if it would get her what she wanted. I understand that as evil as that girl is; Briseis tolerates you on that throne she so clearly covets."

Curian slumped back into his chair as he knew his friend's words to be true. Briseis would sooner cut his throat to get to the dais than help him retain it.

"I will follow where you lead Curian, friend…but you only have two options left: kill your daughter or be killed by her."

Curian held his head in his hands and without any preamble, wept. He wept as though his heart had shattered into a thousand pieces that he could never in his life hope to find. Rarno said nothing as he allowed his friend to process his words and come to his decision on his own. He wouldn't push for what he wanted or even what Mortania needed without Curian's say so.

Soon, the tears came to a stop and the young man turned old king that he had grown with and admired was back; if not feebly, but back none the less.

"If she is to use her new recruits against us, then we need to take them out before she discovers our true intentions." Rarno nodded, holding his breath.

"Find out their weaknesses, other than their inexperience and find out how we can use that to kill them."

"Yes Sire,"

"If worse comes to worst, we need a backup plan…we need reinforcements."

"Reinforcement, from who?"

"Agmantia."

Rarno caught the breath he was already holding as he shook his head,

"They do not fight any wars but their own. They are ruthless warriors and vicious assassins yes but they are a secluded people; their Queen does not involve herself with our affairs."

"She will…if the offer is right." Rarno was intrigued,

"What do you propose?" Curian shrugged,

"My crown."

Rarno's eyes bulged out of his head as she stared into the face of his best friend.

"Are you *crazy*?" he hissed at him, looking around as though speaking about it would somehow make it happen that very instance. Curian said nothing and looked off into the distance, contemplative. The lines on his forehead were deep, heavy with the worry of all that plagued him; all that he regretted.

"I have nothing left to give Rarno. I offer Agmantia my crown, the run of Mortania after my death; if they can rid us of Briseis."

"You would give up everything you have fought for, what *I* have fought for, to foreigners; our enemies if recent history is to be read!" Rarno was furious but Curian didn't seem deterred.

"Agmantia have always been a friend to Mortania,"

"The Mortania ruled by Samai!" Rarno spat at him. "I will not be a part of this Curian, I won't!"

"What is the alternative Ignatius, tell me?"

"The alternative is to fight, to fight for what is ours!"

"And when we lose?" Rarno gaped like a fish. "We will lose, because Briseis is stronger than us, even without her band of merry man. She has the kingdom on her side and with the right offer we can have Agmantia on ours!" Curian stared his friend down,

"You're either with me or against me,"

"Cur..."

"You are either with me or against me General Rarno...which is it to be?"

Rarno looked at his friend and king in utter defeat. It went against his very nature to bend over and die, but he was nothing if not loyal. He would never leave his friend, not now.

"We lose nothing by asking," Curian said suddenly, seemingly saving Rarno the actual words of surrender.

"Except our anonymity," he murmured, thankful that the Gods wouldn't hear him utter the words of a coward. "If she knows we are against Briseis, she could very well tell her we mean to kill her."

Curian was silent for a moment, thinking it over before he looked up at Rarno with sad eyes, just as his hands ignited with black flame,

"It's a chance we'll have to take." Rarno nodded, although every fibre of his being was against this plan.

"Send word to Queen Nucea of Agmantia," Curian was saying. "We request the aid of the Agmantian Assassins to aid us in ending the life, of my daughter…Crown Princess Briseis Greybold."

"As you wish…your majesty."

TRAINEES

Briseis looked on with pride as her special fighting team held a shield of solid air in place against an onslaught of her personal guard. The Six as she'd begun to call them, concentrated and centred their power to add strength to the shield and prevent anything from coming through it or breaking it completely.

So far, they had done remarkably well but this was only to shield themselves against attacks they *knew* were coming. Briseis wanted them to be able to shield strongly at will, over her entire army if necessary. A skill such as that would be invaluable in any fight.

Despite her disregard of her father; he was right in his assessment of the teenagers that made up the Six. While she could train them to use their powers and in general combat; it took years to be ready for the battlefield; time she simply did not have to spend with them. While they may not have the appropriate expertise to fight on the battlefield; she was determined they would be useful in other ways; namely their control and use of the Everlasting.

As her guards continued to batter at the shield with their weapons; swords, bows and arrows, Briseis finally threw off her black velvet cape and stepped from her viewing spot at the side of the training ground. She was in her Phyn leather armour, dyed with the faintest hint of green that cost a small fortune in gold.

Around her wrists were steel cuffs that she could use to block or deflect oncoming projectiles. The same steel cuffs were strapped around the ankles and made up the high neck of her suit. Her hair was tied back in a long ponytail that began to billow in an unseen wind as she approached the Six and their shield.

Her men were tiring; she could see the sweat dripping from their brows but now came the next step of the test.

Briseis braced her feet a few steps apart and outstretched her hands before instantly igniting into flame. Her entire body on fire, Briseis pushed out and sent a stream of grey fire at the shield. She watched as the Six buckled, if only a little as they channelled more energy into the shield. Even though it hadn't blasted through; Briseis' power was bending the shield; pushing it inward, back towards the Six.

Briseis watched them; watched how they decided without even speaking how best to deflect her attack. Just as she registered a decision being made and they drew power to centre it to their purpose, Briseis parted her hands and while a stream of energy poured heavily against the shield in the centre, two more blasts from seemingly nowhere attempted to penetrate the shield.

Briseis continued to batter it with three outbursts of energy, the floor around her cracking from the intensity of her blaze. Harder she pumped her own magic into the blasts as she watched one of the Six; Orla collapse to her knees. Once Orla was down, the rest of the team began to crumple; weakening the shield as they did so. The shield was strained under Briseis' attack and lack of people to strengthen it.

Soon enough, only one of them; Jaysen remained, maintaining the shield as best he could until with just an extra bit of pressure, Briseis crippled it and Jaysen fell to his knees; the shield instantly dissipating from in front of them.

All six of them were clutching at their chests; gasping for breath.

"See to them," Briseis said to no one in particular as she recoiled her flame and stood as she was before. Seconds later, two nursemaids were crouched on the cobbled floor beside the teenagers.

"You did well," Briseis complimented as she approached them still gasping. "You kept that shield up for almost two hours before I attacked and that is commendable."

Six pairs of eyes looked up at her in disbelief at her praise,

"While you've shown new strength in defending against physical attacks, you still need to work on your defence against magical ones."

"Excuse me, your highness?" Briseis turned her head at the sound of Gardan's voice but did not fully turn around.

"I have news of the King." Briseis turned her attention back to the Six,

"Get yourself cleaned up for breakfast. I want you back here working on your magical defence for the rest of the morning."

"Yes, your highness," they chorused although a little feebly and made their way, seemingly to the Infirmary with the nurses.

Briseis turned to Gardan, his dark blonde tresses lightened in the morning sun overhead. She had arranged this morning's training on her own so hadn't seen him yet and marvelled at how fresh he looked. Briseis shook the thought from her head as inappropriate as it was…

"What is it General?" Gardan approached as close to her as was necessary and began speaking.

"I've had news that your father deployed a messenger this morning."

Briseis raised her eyebrow as if to question why this was of any importance.

"He sent a messenger to Agmantia your highness; to her majesty Queen Nucea."

That piqued her interest,

"Any idea what was written?"

"No your highness, the messenger left before we could get a look. We were informed too close to his departure." Briseis nodded.

What could her father possible want with Agmantia?

Queen Nucea Voltaire was notorious for her want to stay out of conflict that did not immediately involve Agmantia. While her resolve was infamous, so was the elite company of assassins that resided in a remote city in the Agmantian mountains…

"Keep an eye on my father's movements," Briseis decided. "I want to know what he's up to."

"Yes your highness." Gardan bowed and took his leave and Briseis briefly noticed, that she'd have liked him to stay.

***

Trista was *exhausted*!

Nyron and Naima had arrived to help Trista train. She'd been surprised at their early arrival but had willingly began working with Nyron on her sword technique. She was focused on her form but couldn't help Oren's words from the previous night creeping into her mind.

I don't want to train you because you're not worth it
Not worth it

How long had she felt like that while growing up on Remora?

How long had she felt like there was no real purpose to her life and now that she'd found one, she seemed to be failing at that too.

She knew she was missing something in order to be truly invested in this fight but she didn't know what it was. Even with her new-found memories of her early childhood; she still didn't feel connected to her powers or her people.

She had trained with Oren and now Nyron and had learnt all she could from Rayne before she was violently taken away from her, but it still wasn't enough.

A lot had been taken away from her Trista realised, and she was the only one who was able to exact revenge for that fact. She was the only one who could help a nation of people redeem themselves after years of enslavement and ridicule from others.

Thorn, both sets of parents, Rayne and Kemar; she'd lost so many people in so short a time and it was only going to get worse if she didn't get her act together.

The fact she felt so unprepared to do anything made her so angry, it was difficult to control. She hated that she wasn't in control, that she wasn't good enough; that she couldn't make Oren think she was worth it.

Trista

Faintly, she heard her name being called and turned towards the sound, though the feeling felt too slow; as though she were swimming in molasses.

"What?"

Trista let go!

Let go of what?

In that moment of thought, Trista seemed to come back into her own body that she hadn't realised she was out of and found herself bearing down on Nyron with her sword…but it wasn't her sword, not exactly.

The sword in her hand was made entirely of power, of a pulsating energy that was shaped exactly like her sword. Her weapon had somehow been discarded and in its place, was a humming blade of power.

Nyron was underneath it under his large energy shield trying to stop her slicing into him but was clearly failing. His teeth were clenched as he focused all of his power into stopping the energy sword slicing through him.

"Trista, stop!" it was Dana screaming her name and as the realisation hit her, Trista took a deep breath and just, let go.

Instantly, her flame subsided and it seemed as though all the sound in the world came rushing back to her all at once; the birds in the air, the wind rushing through the trees was all deafening. She swayed slightly and felt a pair of hands on her elbows, holding her upright and turned to see Naima behind her,

"W-what happened?"

Naima looked down at where her brother was getting up, his shield now dissolved and dusting himself off. They exchanged a glance that was both shock and fear.

They were in the middle of the yard in front of Gorn's house, just a few metres from the forge.

They'd been training since sunrise, Nyron teaching Trista and Naima showing Dana the basics in using a staff. Oren was working as usual but stepped out of the forge and walked towards them; just as Nyron straightened up.

"Did you know about this?" Naima asked quietly, directing the question at Oren who was now standing next to Nyron. Dana was now by Trista's side,

"I suspected," Oren said simply, his face showing no emotion at all.

"Suspected!" Naima snapped. "Did you tell Uncle Gorn?"

"Yes," simple again as if he couldn't care less.

"Oren, why didn't you tell *us*? This is...this is...I don't know what this is!" Nyron exclaimed as he ran a hand through his hair.

"What's going on?" Trista said, regaining her balance and looking between her cousins and Oren. Naima gave her brother that look again and she exploded,

"Will someone tell me what the hell is going on?"

The twins went silent but Naima moved slowly to stand in front of Trista, ready to share whatever detrimental piece of information Trista was now sure was coming.

"Trista...we think you could be a Master."

Trista looked to Dana then back at the twins, confusion clear on her face.

"Master...master of what?"

"Everything," Nyron said prophetically

"I don't understand...what does that mean?"

Naima sighed, looking from her brother to her cousin then back at Trista.

She was dressed much like Trista in trousers and tunic but hers were a light brown with a dark brown wide leather belt around her waist. She had dark brown leather straps tying her boots to her feet. Her black hair was braided down her back and the loose strands at the front held away from her face by a last piece of leather.

"Trista, the Antonides family were more than the Keepers of the Everlasting. They were...they *are* an old line of gifted mages who were able to use magic in ways that others couldn't."

"Yes, so what?"

"What you did just now…creating your weapon from magic…only Masters can do that."

"I-I didn't do anything. Nyron I'm sorry," Nyron jumped in, shaking his head as he did so.

"Tris don't apologise, I'm fine. That's not what my sister is trying to tell you."

"Then what are you trying to tell me?" Oren made a sound and Trista looked up while everyone else rolled their eyes.

"Ignore him," Naima said. "Trista, you created something with your powers. You didn't summon it, or make it appear from someplace else. You used magic in its rawest form to create something you wanted and only Masters can do those things. Gods, Trista…there hasn't been a Master in the Antonides bloodline in almost sixty years."

"Woah," that came from Dana who was still by Trista's side

Trista was stumped,

"What am I supposed to do now?" Naima shrugged but was apologetic as she spoke,

"I don't think there's anything you can do, none of us would know where to begin with teaching you…it's beyond us."

"It wouldn't be beyond Rayne, she would know." The silence meant they were all inclined to agree. "Why didn't she tell me?"

"Have you done this before?" Nyron asked

"No,"

"Then it's unlikely she could have known. As I said, we haven't had a Master in years; she probably thought it wasn't worth bringing up."

"What about him, he knew!" Trista fired at Oren who was still standing there with a look of nonchalance on his face.

"She's right Oren...how did you suspect as you said." Nyron said, folding his own arms towards Oren.

Everyone looked towards him, the twins irritably; Dana expectantly and Trista angrily.

"When we were training she had a nightmare, a vision of some kind, I had to get her out of it."

"What does that even mean?" Naima's question although they all thought it.

"While she was in her nightmare, she manifested what she could see. I saw it as clearly as I'm looking at you now. She made this...shield around herself; solid...unyielding."

"So how did you get her out of it?" Dana asked quietly and almost swallowed the question as Oren turned his eyes onto her. He turned to Naima and Nyron and something exchanged between the three of them that had the twins looking away; Nyron clearing his throat as he bent to pick up his sword.

"I was the only one that could." Oren said and walked back to the forge.

Angrily, Trista growled in frustration and marched away from the remaining trio into the house.

"Things just got very interesting," Nyron mumbled.

"What?" Dana asked looking between the twins for an explanation but Naima shook her head.

"It's...complicated. Do you want to finish training?"

"Shouldn't I go after her?" Dana looked towards the house but Naima shook her head.

"Not right now Dana...I think Trista needs some time by herself. Come on, let's get you fight ready,"

Later that night, Trista lay awake long after everyone else had gone to bed still angry about the way Oren was treating her. While she'd cooled off later in the day and continued her training with Nyron, Oren's rudeness was really starting to grate on her. That he could be so dismissive of her when she was trying her best was frustrating to say the least. The fact he hadn't told her something so important about herself was another issue altogether. Why would he keep something like that from her? She was honestly beginning to wonder whether Oren was even on her side.

As she lay there, looking into the darkness feeling betrayed, angry and frustrated, she felt the most peculiar sensation in her head; almost like a headache pulsating at her temples except it wasn't painful. No sooner had the feeling appeared; she heard a voice, no…voices.

Trista bolted upright and shut her eyes, holding her hands to her ears as the conversation between two people got louder until it was a clear as if they were standing in the room with her.

"*It's been days Gardan, why have they not arrived yet?*"

"*I am not sure; I have been informed it is only a matter of time.*"

"*You have our own ravens dispatched?*"

"*We have a post just outside the town that will send word as soon as they arrive.*"

"*Good, I need to know this is done Gardan. It will be one less thing to worry about!*"

"*Yes your highness.*"

"*Leave me; I want the Six back in defence training before dawn. Do you understand General?*"

"*Yes Princess!*"

The words finally faded and the feeling subsided. Trista shook her head, trying to clear her thoughts and as she opened her eyes; she saw her family ring glowing gently on the dresser beside her before it stopped completely.

She wasn't sure what they had been talking about but Trista was sure of one obvious thing; she'd heard the princess.

Somehow, she'd heard a conversation between Briseis and a general of some kind hundreds of miles away but what were they talking about and who were the Six?

It was too much for the middle of the night, she thought but even as she turned over and tried to sleep; she knew that everything had changed.

Whether for the better or for worse, she didn't yet know.

FRAGILE PEACE

Trista and Dana fell into a routine of sorts; a schedule more than anything and it gave them both a sense of being and purpose that they had considerably lacked before.

The girls would help prepare and have breakfast with Iona, Gorn and Oren at dawn; once Gorn and Oren had come in from working in the forge in the earlier hours.

After breakfast they helped Iona with the chores before she went into town; even when she insisted that she didn't need their help but let them do it anyway. Once that was done; Dana and Trista would do their weapons training with the twins and Oren when he wasn't working the afternoons in the forge with his father.

While they did hand to hand combat with Nyron as well as using swords and even an axe; Dana stuck with trying to master the staff Naima had given her.

"It makes more sense to me," she'd said when Trista asked her why she favoured it over other weapons. "A sword seems to invite danger; with a staff, no one would necessarily think I could do anything with it."

Trista had smiled at that because it was so Dana; straight forward and to the point. She needed that right now; clarity in a time of a lot of confusion; namely about her new connection to Briseis.

She mentioned her hearing voices to Gorn the day after it happened and three days later; she hadn't heard it again. He'd said not to worry about it; especially if it didn't cause her any pain and that there were a million different ways that the Everlasting could be working in order to prepare her for her battle with Briseis. Maybe being able to hear her plans was one of them.

She had been comforted with that thought but it still weighed on her that if she could hear Briseis, Briseis could hear her. She'd known of course that Briseis had been able to track her somehow, but since she'd learnt to shield her power that was no longer a problem. Whether or not she could hear her conversations was an entirely different matter. Still, until she knew for sure, there was no point worrying about it if she was safe.

She was training now with a bow, having taken a break from hand to hand combat with Nyron to try her hand at it. Naima had given her one she said belonged to her mother, Renya; saying that a bow was in some ways the most difficult weapon to master. The tiniest things mattered when it came to firing a single shot: wind direction, the sweat in your palms; the reach of your hands and balance in your hips. One used their whole body to release an arrow, so it had to count. So far, she hadn't had the best luck and so not to waste the precious time she had, stuck to perfecting her swordsmanship.

Alongside their weapons training, Dana also practiced her healing with the notes and books Rayne had given her before leaving Dreston. Dana had explained that when they'd packed before rescuing Trista from Dreston's dungeon's; Rayne had given her some books and scrolls that she knew would be helpful. Dana was becoming a novice healer and Trista was extremely proud of her best friend who seemed to have finally found her place in the world.

When the sun finally began to set and Naima and Dana had gone to help Iona prepare dinner, Nyron and Trista were still outside in the yard. Oren and Gorn were still in the forge making who knew what.

Their horse, Titan, was grazing lazily around in the open field opposite the road that led into the town.

Trista blocked a blow from Nyron when she saw Oren step out of the forge. He bent down to wash off his arms and around his neck in the bucket of water that was placed outside for that very purpose. With her eyes, still on him, she continued her varied blocking moves as Nyron had shown her until suddenly, she felt something like a ripple in the air and Nyron was suddenly behind her. She anticipated his blow however and blocked that too, Nyron laughed.

"What?"

"Just checking you were paying attention,"

"I was, I…" her eyes darted to Oren who was walking towards them. Trista looked away. "Shut up." She mumbled but Nyron just chuckled to himself;

"You can use that you know,"

"Use what?" Trista snapped at him as she struggled to look up at him and dropped her sword to the floor, training was over.

"Your feelings…" he didn't say the words *for him* but they both knew what he meant. Trista's face blushed furiously and she turned away as Oren approached,

"Drink at The Phyn, Oren?" Nyron asked turning to his cousin with a cheeky grin on his face. "I've got an appointment with Marcella."

The way he said Marcella it was obvious what that appointment would consist of,

"Again, that's every night this week. Haven't you run out of coin yet?" Oren did not sound amused,

"I have the same amount you have, to grace Tysha's bed three nights in a row, brother!" Nyron teased as he slapped Oren on the back and wrapped his arm around his shoulders.

Trista's face was on fire as she continued taking off her outer training armour. So, that's where he'd gone every evening, to Jo's…with Tysha. At the corner of her eye, Trista saw Oren shrug off Nyron's arm,

"Grow up, Nyron," he stalked into the house while Nyron threw his arms up and laughed in the merry way he did; deep voice rumbling,

"Why, where's the fun in that?"

Despite her embarrassment at Oren's movements, Trista couldn't help but giggle to herself as she followed Nyron inside to get ready for dinner.

Trista sat down to eat that evening with Gorn, Oren, Iona, Nyron, Naima and Dana and for the first time in her entire life; felt like she belonged; that she was part of a family.

She had never had meals like this with her parents back in Remora and for the first time in a long while; she allowed herself to miss them. She missed her mother's cooking and the way her father pretended not to indulge in her peach pie when she made it on weekends and special occasions like his birthday. She missed the smell of their kitchen and the warmth of their living room on winter nights when her mother knitted by the fire and her father quietly read a book. She would sit on the floor at his feet, reading her own book as her father would intermittently stroke the top of her head lovingly.

She might have felt alone in Remora but she'd never felt unloved.

Trista had been through so much in the weeks since she'd left home but she didn't allow herself to dwell on it when she had so much to do and learn.

Sitting there, with the others made her feel warm and a part of something and it was wonderful.

Since she'd had that small glimpse of her mother and the memories that came with it; Trista was more determined than ever to do what needed to be done to find Rowan. If only to ask her all the questions that were bubbling up inside of her.

"...we thank Thea that she arrived to us safely...to Trista."

"To Trista!" everyone at the table chorused although Trista was vaguely aware that Oren hadn't. She hadn't even heard the initial toast but smiled anyway,

"Thank you but...it's not necessary."

"It's not necessary to toast to your good health and all the progress you've made? Nonsense girl!" Gorn chuckled and even Iona nodded,

"He's been waiting for you a long time girly, be proud of what you've done."

"I am, I just...thank you. I just want to be able to do what's needed before I celebrate anything." Gorn nodded his understanding,

"And you will Trista, it will take time but you will. You'll have us and an entire army ready to fight in your name."

"Army?" Dana and Trista said it together.

Gorn chuckled and Trista saw the way Oren sighed to himself as though he knew she would asked something stupid like that. It made her blood boil that he was right but also because it was so unfair. He wasn't even bothering to educate her and instead was ridiculing her for her lack of knowledge. Instinctively she picked up a bread roll from the middle of the table and threw it at him; hitting him on the side of his head. Everyone went silent as Oren looked back at her in outrage, so much so that a ring of fire ignited in his eyes as he breathed heavily.

Suddenly, the twins burst into laughter but Dana, Gorn and Iona tried to hide their mirth with no luck. Oren looked around before he cleared his throat but said nothing and turned back to his plate,

"Okay calm down you two," Iona giggled to herself

"You didn't think you were fighting Briseis one on one, did you?" Gorn asked as he forked some steak into his mouth. Iona had made a huge spread for them of steak and mashed potatoes and every kind of vegetable. They had roast chicken and roasted potatoes and fluffy white Coznianrice to go with it.

"Where will this army come from?" Trista asked but Nyron answered,

"All over the world. Once you and Aunt Rowan disappeared, the rest of us knew we had to secure forces that would fight in your name. Thousands fled when and where they could so they could return one day to fight for you."

"There are Samaian warriors located here in inland and coastal cities and towns," Naima added. "We've maintained contact with those that live off the grid as Nyron said, these last years, we had to make sure that able bodied Samaians were still training and keeping themselves ready to advance on the capital."

Trista was thoroughly impressed. So much was being put into place before she'd even realised the part she would have to play.

"We have assigned messengers to dispatch the command to move when the time is right." Nyron concluded.

"Move to where?" Trista asked.

"Initially to Thelm," Oren provided the answer this time as he finished chewing some vegetables. "Soldiers will be ordered to get to Thelm where we'll come together to march our full force through The Pass and into The Wide."

"Isn't that dangerous? People have died from the sharp drop into the ocean." They all looked toward Dana as if she'd grown a second head,

"My father's a tailor, he travelled to get fabric from the city when he was young and said it was a dangerous trip." They all nodded and Nyron replied,

"It can be dangerous Dana but it's the only option we have. We don't have the luxury of ships to bring people in from Thea's Point and even if we did, we'd be sandwiched between Tirnum and the sea." Dana nodded her understanding,

"We do have a few advantages though," Naima smiled at the two young women. "We'll have The Forest at our back for endless supplies of wood; The Pass of course for any emergency supplies from Thelm and of course, higher ground."

"Higher ground?" Dana asked again. Nyron smiled and positioned his hands as though he were shooting a bow and arrow.

"It's a lot easier to shoot and overpower from uphill Dana."

Trista let that thought settle for the moment before she said,

"How many men do we have?"

"And women," Naima cut in and Trista looked at her, "Women fight in Samaian armies too," she said proudly, and even Trista grinned.

She knew she'd been training to fight Briseis and Dana to protect herself should anything happen to her but she never questioned how Naima knew how to handle a weapon. She'd assumed she knew how to fight because her father was a military captain.

"Apologies, how many Samai do we have waiting in the wings?"

"Twelve thousand at last count," Nyron replied although it wasn't as proudly, and it wasn't hard to figure out why

"Briseis will have more I take it?"

"Most definitely. During the last war, Curian had a hoard of thirty thousand rebels and now he has command of the Royal Army."

Nyron seemed to see the worry in Trista's eyes as he added,

"We'll have our powers Tris, or we will do once we're all together again. We hope to generate more as time goes on." Trista nodded.

She was aware that Samaians gained power and energy when they spent enough time around each other; a lot like conductors of the energy around them. Despite being all about will and feeling; their powers were still limited by their own physical health and strength. An army of well trained, Ascended Samai would generate a lot more power than a group of Samai untrained in their magic for eighteen years and among many who may not have Ascended. It was more of a gamble now than it had been during the last war.

"That's enough war talk for tonight, I think. Makes me sad thinking about my babies going off to fight," Iona scolded as she stood up and went to get a jug of ale.

"Hush woman; nothing's going to happen to the children!" Gorn laughed.

"You say that but you don't have to patch up their cuts and bruises when they've done all their fussing," Iona grumbled back at him as she re took her seat.

They went on like that; arguing like an old married couple as everyone continued with their meal. Later, Iona served up desert and when they finished eating; Nyron and Oren did the washing up before they went to get ready to go the The Phyn.

Trista went to drop a cup into the wash basin just as Iona was handing Oren a large bowl to wash,

"Make sure its spotless you hear me?" Trista watched Oren smirk and lean back to kiss Iona's fluffy cheek,

"Yes Iona," Iona swatted him away although Trista saw the smile she tried to hide. Iona of course wasn't Oren's mother, but Trista saw then that she was in all ways if not biologically.

Soon, the washing was done, Nyron and Oren had disappeared to get washed and dressed while Gorn sat in his chair smoking his pipe and Naima, Dana and Trista were in the reading nook talking. Iona had gone to bed,

"Naima?" the young woman looked up at Trista. "What's the deal with Iona?"

"What do you mean?"

"She's not Gorn's wife but she lives here." Naima nodded as she settled herself more comfortably in her chair and leaned towards the girls who instinctively leant closer to get the gossip.

"Iona got caught up in some scandal and has lived here ever since." The other girls' eyes widened,

"What kind of scandal?" Dana asked worriedly,

"Years ago, Iona worked as a washerwoman to support herself as she had no family but had managed to secure an engagement and was due to be married. The story is that she came to wash for Gorn one day but when she got here, he had collapsed, and Oren wasn't home. She helped fix Gorn up, tended to him but by this point had been away for a long time."

Naima paused her story and the girls were hanging on her every word, their hearts in their throats.

"As I heard it, her fiancé came to find out where she was and found she and Gorn in a, shall we say compromising position."

The girl's eyebrows raised as they looked at each other and back at Naima,

"We can never get either of them to admit what actually happened, but what we do know is that Iona's fiancé called off their engagement and no one would use her services anymore."

"That's awful," Naima nodded her agreement as she snuggled into her chair.

"She had nowhere else to go and of course, feeling responsible, Gorn allowed her stay and she's never left."

Trista felt sad for Iona, being shunned like that knowing exactly what they felt like growing up in Remora.

"They say nothing happened but on nights I've stayed over, I've seen Iona leave Gorn's bedroom so who knows." Dana giggled but Naima just laughed along with her.

As the girls sat laughing, Nyron and Oren approached them, freshly washed and dressed and heading towards the front door. Trista hated that Oren looked so handsome. He'd put on dark pants and a shirt and his hair was loose. It hung in that un-kept way that she loved.

"Don't wait up sis!" Nyron said wiggling his eyebrows, Naima just rolled her eyes.

"We get it Ny, you're going to have sex! Big deal, when will you grow up?"

"Why does everyone keep saying that?" he chuckled as he ruffled his sister's head and dodged the slap she threw his way.

"See you tomorrow ladies," Nyron said before heading out of the door. Trista looked up just before Oren followed behind him. He didn't look in their direction but he hesitated before closing the door then swiftly disappeared into the night.

Dana laughed as the door closed;

"Your brother is a character," she was looking at the door where he'd just been.

"Do you want to take him off my hands?" Naima laughed but when she saw Dana's blush, she stopped. Naima looked to Trista who shrugged before turning back to Dana

"Dana, do you like my brother?"

"No!" came her too swift reply making Trista snort out a laugh she'd tried to hold back. Naima winked at her,

"Don't worry, I won't say anything."

"Good, because theres nothing to say!" Dana protested even with the smile still on her lips.

"W-who is Tysha?" Trista stammered the question out as she played with the hem of her dress; willing herself not to blush.

"Tysha? Why do…oh, Tysha's a barmaid at The Phyn."

"So, not a…working girl then?" Trista asked what she hoped was casually.

"Not officially but she's been known to take payment for private drinks if you know what I mean." Naima wiggled her own eyebrows making Dana laugh again.

"Have either of you…?" Naima left the question hanging in the air and Dana shook her head,

"I was engaged," Trista said. "All we did was kiss…once. Have you…?" Naima laughed as though the question were absurd,

"Of course, I've lain with a man, but…no one special for a long time." Naima clearly went to another place that had Dana and Trista look at one another questioningly.

Naima was clearly a smart and beautiful woman, but they knew virtually nothing about her; or her brother.

"I'm waiting until this war is over before I think about taking on anyone serious."

"Why?" Trista asked.

"I don't want to start a family in a world where my heritage is a sin or that my child will not have the powers, I was blessed to be able to Ascend to."

"Isn't that a long time to have waited, you're what twenty…"

"We're thirty-one," Naima replied with a smile. "While I would like a family, I want a safe world for it even more…I can wait a little longer."

The other two girls nodded their understanding, feeling suddenly sad for Naima and the life she'd put on hold.

"We'd be shunned if we weren't married by your age." Dana admitted, filling the silence but Naima only laughed; her beautiful face lighting up as she did so.

"It's a good thing your best friend will be making the rules now isn't it? Don't worry Dana, the right man will find you; there's no rush at all."

Iona had made up a bed for Naima, Nyron was sleeping in Oren's room and by the time everyone had gone to bed; the boys still weren't home.

It was during the night, as she lay in a dreamless and peaceful sleep that Trista awoke to banging and shouting from downstairs;

"WAKE UP, EVERYBODY! WAKE UP!"

"Oren," she breathed as she recognised his voice and rushed out of bed. Dana was right behind her as they peered over the balcony just in time to see Oren running up the stairs towards them.

"DAD, TRISTA!" he bellowed,

"Oren I'm here, what's going on?" Gorn hobbled out of his room and interestingly enough, Iona was behind him in the doorway, her shawl wrapped around her nightdress.

"What's going on boy?"

Everyone, including Naima was now in the upstairs hallway outside their bedroom doors so Oren addressed them all;

"Soldiers. Ransacking the town." He said through sharp breaths. "Killing Samaian girls." Oren's eyes turned to her,

Trista's eyes widened in horror; they were looking for *her*. "We have to leave now!"

ON THE ROAD

"Get your things together quickly," Oren continued. "We'll head to Crol."

Dana and Trista stared at him wide eyed. "Anything that won't fit in a saddle bag has to stay behind; bring furs if you can. Dana," Dana's eyes shot up to Oren's and he reached out to place his hand gently on her shoulder. Trista felt incredibly guilty that she was annoyed by this,

"Get any supplies you need for your healing too; ointments, salves; anything but don't make it too heavy."

"I will," she said obediently turning to go back to their room.

Oren turned away from them then to approach his father, Naima and Iona who was wringing her hands together in worry.

Trista realised he wasn't going to say anything else to her and so followed in Dana's footsteps. They both dressed in their fighting leathers, Dana's a little less severe than Trista's but practical. She tied a utility belt around her waist that had space for various viles and small jars.

Dana was dressed before her and rushed out of the room to get her healing things but within minutes, the girls were packed and heading out into the yard.

They saw three horses waiting, Titan, Oren's horse was saddled and one of the other two horses was strapped to a small wagon.

They questioned nothing as they tied their belongings to Titan and the free horse and threw their clothes into the wagon.

Trista rushed to the forge where Oren kept her weapons and strapped her sword around her waist and another across her back along with a bow and a quiver of arrows. As she was stepping out of the door, she saw a strap of different sized daggers that she picked up and headed out with.

She was adding the daggers securely and safely in Titan's saddle bag when the front door opened, and Oren stepped out with Iona close behind him.

He had changed from his usual dark tunic and trousers and was now in a set of armour that Trista had never seen before.

He was essentially still in black leather but there seemed to be an iridescent look to it that had Trista thinking of fish scales. Around his ankles and covering up to his knees were metal guards obviously meant to protect. These same guards covered the tops of his thighs and biceps and made up a large portion that covered his chest and stomach.

The coverings were also across his back; covering his shoulders and while the casings were metal, they didn't seem to restrict the movement of his clothes; flowing freely with his movements as he walked. Around his wrists were two metal cuffs; one of which Trista could see had a teal stone welded into the top of it.

He had two swords strapped across his back in the designed spaces, so they didn't restrict his movements and another strapped around his waist. Oren had tied back his hair into what Trista had learned was a warrior braid that fell down his back between the two swords.

Oren helped Iona to the wagon and told her to get on,

"Get to the safe house like we told you and stay there for a week at least before coming back to the house."

"No, Oren I won't leave you!" Iona wailed; her eyes puffy from fearful crying.

"You have to!" Oren snapped at her making the girls jump. They had never heard Oren speak to her this way and the fact that he had done, seemed to bring the seriousness of the situation to the forefront.

In the silence that followed Oren's outburst; they all distinctly heard violent screams of whatever atrocities were taking places only paces away.

"Iona please," Oren placed his hands either side of Iona's face and looked down into her eyes pleadingly, "If anything happened to you..." he didn't finish but they all knew what he meant. Iona smiled sadly and pulled him into a fierce hug before kissing him on the cheek.

"I love you like my own. You better come back to me." Trista heard her whisper to him, and it broke her heart to see Oren shut his eyes and breathe her in.

"Go," he said finally and helped her onto the horse.

"Where's your father?"

As if on cue Naima and Gorn stepped out of the house, Naima helping him walk quickly toward the wagon with his stiff leg.

Oren rushed over to help his father as Trista and Dana strapped their belongings to one horse and Naima left Gorn to strap a bag she was holding to Titan. As they did so; everyone suddenly turned at the distinct sound of hooves approaching them on the road coming from the centre of town.

Trista drew her sword and instinctively stepped in front of Dana while her eyes shot to Oren who had finished helping his father onto the wagon and walked toward the road.

"Dana, get on the horse and keep hold of Titan. Naima, Trista either side of me now!" Oren snapped as the girls took their positions beside him.

No sooner had they got to his side, the approaching hooves got louder and were soon accompanied by four men on horseback.

"Where's my brother?" Naima asked quietly as the men slowed their approach.

"I left him by The Phyn, he's going to make the preparations." Oren murmured back as the soldier spoke.

"What do we have here then?"

They were dressed in colours that Trista immediately recognised but it didn't begin to make sense what Dreston soldiers were doing in Priya. The lead soldier scanned them all, judgement in his eyes and clearly annoyed by their preparedness.

Finally, his eyes focused on Trista and then Naima, eyes that were appreciative for more reason than one.

"Take those two and get rid of the others."

Two of the soldiers behind him dismounted and approached the trio but Trista felt her hand hum where her family ring was securely on her finger.

One of the soldiers made to approach her and so Trista took a deep breath and attacked.

She swung her sword outwards causing the guard to jump back to avoid the swipe. He was in a full suit of metal armour and the strike would not have got to him, but he at least realised she wasn't going to go without a fight; if at all.

Naima to the right of her, took on the other guard who had approached her and Oren advanced on the two remaining guards still on horseback.

Trista saw in a split-second, Oren reach out and drag both men off their horses with his power. Swift and easy no fuss, just as she'd done in Dreston and had both men come crashing to the ground. One wasn't able to recover before Oren had stabbed his sword through his thigh, leaving him writhing in pain. The other guard had managed to get to his feet as Oren stabbed his comrade and was in his fighting stance as Oren approached him. They both attacked at the same time but the soldier seemed to underestimate Oren's strength because when their swords clashed and he dug his heels into the ground; they moved backwards a few inches.

Oren kicked out at him causing the man to stumble backwards before swiping at him again, once, twice before hitting him with an overhead strike that connected in the thin space between his neck and shoulder. The man cried out as blood splattered everywhere.

Trista on the other hand was having a harder time of it as she finally understood where Nyron and Oren may have been going easy on her.

She had no time to gather her thoughts or her next move; it was all instinct and in the moment. The man swung back at her and quickly Trista dodged, keeping her movements light as Oren had taught her. Their swords clashed against each other a few times before Trista spun out of the embrace, ducked low and sliced at the space behind his knees. The soldier screamed out in agony as his leg buckled and he bled out; dropping his sword in pain.

Stepping away from her victim, Trista turned her attention to Naima who while Oren had had two opponents; the biggest of the men had approached her.

Trista caught the end of the dance of swords as the big man went to stab right into her stomach but Naima spun out of his range; as agile as a dancer and stabbed the man, straight up into his armpit. Blood squirted across her face but she didn't seem to care.

"We need to get to town!" Oren shouted. He mounted one of the soldier's horses. "Dad, Iona, this way!"

Gorn who was in the driver's seat of the wagon with Iona, his face a picture of anger and frustration whipped their horse into gear and directed it after Oren and down the road into town. Trista immediately mounted Titan while Dana, who was still atop the other horse Oren had brought, followed her friend down the path. Naima took another of the soldier's horses and headed in the same direction leaving two dead soldiers and two critically injured left on the ground.

The scene that awaited them when they reached the town centre was of complete and utter despair. The first thing that came to mind to Trista was the outbreak from Dreston prison.

Everywhere, people were running and screaming from the multitude of soldiers who were ransacking the houses and buildings in the town centre. The Phyn was on fire and Trista could see that there were still some people inside. Soldiers were dragging young women from the brothel into the street; some fully clothed and others not. She saw one young girl already dead in the middle of the road; with a small child wailing at the top of her lungs as she hugged the body.

Gorn and Iona were already off down the road and Naima had seemingly gone with them because Trista couldn't see her. Only Dana was with her; eyes frantic at the destruction in front of them.

Trista's fist clenched tightly and began to heat up as she observed the mayhem and as anger built inside her of the injustice of it all; Oren was suddenly by her side. He had discarded his horse somewhere and was now on foot, both his swords out.

"No, no powers!"

"Oren we have to …" she was cut off as a terrific flash of lighting cracked across the sky, followed by a roll of thunder. The rain came down immediately, creating a sense of doom that was otherwise only implied. Oren ignored it even as rain splattered against his face.

"I know but we can't afford to do that right now. You see the' Lord's Mansion?" Trista turned her eyes towards it and nodded,

"Yes,"

"Head there and if I'm not there in twenty minutes you and Dana you leave without me. Get to Crol, get a ship to Drem then make your way to Thelm." Trista shook her head immediately,

"No, come with us. We'll get Nyron and Naima and we can all go!"

"No Trista, get to the Mansion *now*. That's an order Princess!"

She knew there was something significant in him using her title but she didn't have the time to dwell on it as she nodded curtly at him and Oren took off into the night.

"Trista come on, we can't stand around like this," Dana cried out urgently and Trista quickly kicked her horse into movement and headed towards the Mansion.

Despite being able to see the Lord's Mansion from each point in Priya it wasn't particular close to any one place as it was on a hill. The distance was deceptive and the path there was not a straight one. Now that the town centre was littered with Dreston soldiers in torrential rain, it wasn't going to be an easy one either.

Trista and Dana raced through the town centre, avoiding soldiers as best they could. Most were occupied with pillaging homes and businesses and weren't paying too much attention to what was running past them outside. Still, when one soldier finally caught sight of her black curly hair blowing in the wind; all eyes were suddenly on her.

"That one's getting away!" she heard a soldier shout.

"Come on Titan!" Trista urged him until she felt a sharp pain graze her arm and fell from the horse.

"TRISTA!" Dana screamed out even as her horse carried her off into the depths of town.

Instantly, Trista reached for her power and shielded herself with a cocoon of solid air, causing her to bounce off the puddling ground from an impact that would have surely broken bones if not killed her.

Trista rolled out of the fall; clutching at her arm as she did so. Groaning in pain, Trista looked at her hand as she pulled it away from her arm and saw her own blood. She held her hand there but her blood came oozing through her fingers as her whole arm began to ache from the arrow wound.

Shakily she got to her feet as two horses caught up to her, one with a seated archer.

"Fire at will," the other soldier commanded indifferently and his comrade obeyed.

Even as pain shot up her arm, Trista raised her right palm and like her very first time using her powers; halted the arrow coming her way. When it stopped inches from her face, she swatted it out of her way.

"What in the Gods…" the non-archer said as Trista, now enraged and in pain walked towards them.

As Oren had done earlier, Trista dragged the archer from his horse with her powers and smashed him violently into the floor. She reached out with her left hand to the discarded arrow on the floor and with a flick of her wrist, moved the arrow from the ground into the soldier's throat. He gargled and choked on his own blood as he lay there dying.

The other soldier tried to flee and without a second thought, Trista created a large fireball in her left hand and threw it at him, setting him on fire. The soldier screamed, writhed and burned until there were no more screams left in him.

Breathing heavily, Trista looked around for Dana even as soldiers littered around, dragged women into the street and fought men who tried desperately to protect them. Forgetting about Dana and the Lord's Mansion for the moment, Trista approached the first soldier she saw and drew her sword.

Trista hacked through them like a blur; dodging, swinging and blocking where and when her body told her to, even with her right arm screaming with pain.

As she ducked from a blow from her opponent, she heard someone call out her name and after she stabbed her sword into the soldier's foot and knocked his sword out of his hand; she turned to find who it was.

Nyron came running up to her, sword in hand and his face splattered with blood. From a quick scan of his body, she could see that none of it was his.

"Trista what are you *doing* here?" he was angry with her she saw and felt instantly guilty. "You should be at the Lord's Mansion."

"I got shot from my horse," she showed him her bleeding arm. "I lost Dana and I couldn't just leave!" Nyron shook his head in disbelief but also understanding.

"Where's Oren?"

"I just left him getting women out of The Phyn, everywhere is burning Trista; they're looking for you!"

"I know that Nyron!" her eyes darted behind her cousin; looking for Oren.

"Get to the Mansion; Oren will be with you soon."

Trista didn't bother to ask how Nyron knew but hugged him anyway,

"You're not coming, are you?"

"Not today Princess; there's a lot to do before we can leave. Naima and I will meet you in Thelm when the time comes."

Trista nodded; unsure of how to thank him for helping her in the short time she'd known him. She pulled him back into a hug, praying that she would see him again as she had failed to do with so many others.

"Get to the Mansion," he repeated.

Trista backed away from him and Nyron smiled as he backed away from her and waved his fingers,

"See you later Tris!" he blew her a kiss before turning away and heading back into a group of soldiers who were approaching them from behind and Trista took off once again into the night.

Trista had never run so fast in her entire life. Even as she sprinted over the cobbled stones of the road over discarded bodies of people and animals alike, she felt the rapid pumping of her heart in her chest. She used it to keep her going, to push through the pain screaming through her legs as she tried to get to the Mansion.

When she finally approached the road that led directly up the hill to the Lord's Mansion, she came to a sharp stop as she saw an unwelcome sight.

Gorn, Iona and Dana had been stopped by a group of soldiers and were seemingly being interrogated. Funnily enough; Titan had found his way there too.

As she approached; face bloodied, black hair wild and eyes wide with worry for her friends; it was clear she was with them as one of the soldiers turned at the sound of her approach.

"Stop right there!" he yelled out as he walked towards her.

Her friends turned to face her and what started out as relief slowly turned to fear and disappointment. As Nyron had said, she wasn't meant to be here. The relief turned disappointment was clear on Gorn's face.

"Let them go!" she ignored the soldiers order completely as she approached her friends

"Who are you to give us orders? You're coming with me."

The soldier drew his sword and in answer, Trista drew her own. The surprise was clear on his face, but he was over it quick enough to block her first blow.

Pain rattled up her arm even as it lay relatively limp by her side. She had lost a lot of blood, and she was beginning to feel the effects of that as her vision got cloudy.

He fought reactively, defending against whatever attacks she dished out, but it was clear from the onset that she was at a disadvantage. She knew she couldn't beat him with her physical strength, but she didn't feel strong enough to use her powers without passing out.

The soldier ducked from another of her sword strikes until unexpectedly, he banked left but hit right and pummelled her head with his sword hilt.

Trista stumbled back; her head howling with pain as the man advanced on her. She tried to reach for her power; but she couldn't concentrate on anything but the pulsating pain in her head and arm.

The soldier raised his sword to drive it down into her chest but as his arms raised, an energy ball flew from overhead; knocking him backwards; violently onto the ground behind him. He crashed into some nearby crates, splintering word everywhere as Gorn, Iona, Dana and the remaining guards looked on in fear.

Trista turned her head as best she could to see Oren approaching; his black armour glistening in the moonlight overhead as he jumped down from the horse he had ridden in on.

He was by her side in an instant, holding out his hand to her even as he kept his eyes on the remaining soldiers that were still around his family and Dana.

"Get up," he helped her to her feet, and she swayed where she stood. He didn't stay to help her, but instead blasted at a soldier who had recovered from his initial shock and charged towards him. The others stayed by the cart, pulling Gorn and Iona out of the carriage, pushing them into the dirt along with Dana.

Oren growled with anger as he saw the disrespect and Shifted over to them instead, running one of the soldiers through. Oren looked into the man's eyes as he twisted his sword in his gut and violently pushed him off the blade as the man gargled and choked his way to death.

Oren turned his attention to the rest of the men as Trista, her head still pounding stood in the way of the first soldier that Oren had Shifted away from. The soldier, confused where Oren had even gone, focused his attention on the easy target in front of him and continued charging at Trista.

She braced herself for the impact as the man barrelled into her and knocked her to the ground. Even with her head screaming, she scrapped with him on the ground, punching him over his head, trying to disorientate him as she was. She screamed out as he punched her in the gut when they'd rolled into a position with him on top, winding her and making her curl into the foetal position on the ground.

Trista coughed up a mouthful of blood as she cried out in pain and with nothing else left to do, mustered as small amount of power and repelled him away from her. It was enough to get him off her, stumbling onto his back.

Trista lay on the ground in pain before rolling onto her front to try and gain some equilibrium. She could hear screaming but was so focused on trying to get to her feet, she didn't hear someone calling her name. Shakily she got to her feet just as Gorn appeared, *Shifted* she realise in front of her.

"Gorn?"

His hold on her went stiff, then lax as his eyes widened and look toward the sky.

"Gorn!" Before, it even registered what had happened, she heard Oren cry out,

"FATHER!" Oren screamed just as Gorn coughed, and blood spluttered out.

"G-Gorn?" She didn't realise he was falling until his entire weight started to collapse onto her, but before it did, she felt something lift him and watched as he was laid gently on the ground, on his side in front of her.

It was only then, she saw the arrow sticking out of his back.

Her eyes darted up to where the soldier she'd repelled, stood with a muddy bow and arrow in his hand.

Oren brushed angrily past her and skidded to his knees beside his father, before raising his right hand sending a fireball towards the soldier.

The man was engulfed in intense teal coloured flames, screaming as his flesh instantly began to roast inside his armour. The rain did nothing to diffuse the flames and he fell to the floor screaming, until the screams died away.

Oren took the arrow out of his father's back and set it alight in his hands before discarding it onto the ground and turning Gorn onto his back

"N-no," tears flooded Trista's eyes as she realised what had happened, what Gorn had done for her.

She dropped to the ground, scrambling to Gorn's other side as Oren took his father's hand in his own. The ground was wet and cold with the continued rain, but no one cared, no one knew what to say

"Gorn?"

"Dad?"

"G-get Trista to Thelm," Gorn gasped at his son as rain continued to come down on him, making it even more difficult to speak. "That's all that matters."

"Papa...no," Oren murmured so quietly Trista wasn't even sure she'd heard it. She knew Oren would never be the same after this moment.

Gorn turned to look at her, reaching out to cup her face which she leaned into,

"Please don't go," Trista cried, her heart breaking. "Please don't leave us."

"I c-couldn't save your father but…" Gorn spluttered again as his breathing got laboured. "A-at least I could s-save you."

"Dad," Gorn turned his eyes back to his only son who knelt looking down at him, tears flowing freely from his eyes. His hair was plastered to his face, water dripping off his armour, and Trista had never seen such despair as she did in Oren's eyes.

"Trust your heart son…you are an A-antos…y-you know what is right…e-even if it's hard to do." Trista watched Oren take hold of his father's hand and squeeze it tightly,

"You were my greatest gift Oren…I love you."

"I love you too Dad," Gorn looked at Trista once more and smiled before taking a last laboured breath.

Trista watched as his mighty chest rose and fell one last time. Oren closed his father's eyes before collapsing onto his chest and behind them, Trista heard Iona wail out in misery.

She turned to see Dana looking on, crying as the rain around them got heavier and continued pummelling them.

Trista looked up and saw more soldiers, this time on horseback approaching them, before turning back to the man who had been a father to her for the last few weeks and the son that had lost him.

"O-Oren..."

Oren looked up and in the second he looked in the direction of the coming soldiers, she saw the flames ignite in his eyes.

Oren growled, got to his feet and extended his right arm just as the horses advanced on them and attacked them with a force no one could see.

Soldiers fell from horses, the legs of the animals crumbling beneath them as Oren blasted them with his power.

Trista watched in amazement as their armour caved into their chests and arms crushing them inside it. Men cried out in torture as Oren clenched his fist and the ten or so men, were crushed to death by their own protection.

When every last one was dead, Oren lowered his hand and stumbled back, clutching his hand to his chest.

"Oren," Trista said quietly, not sure what to say or how to approach him. The power had weakened him, she was sure. He was taking deep breaths to try and regulate his breathing again.

She was saved having to do anything as Oren completely ignored her and knelt back down beside his father. Oren laid Gorn out straight, closed his eyes and rested his hands on his father's chest and began to speak. Trista didn't understand the words, but she recognised them as an ancient language that

Rayne had briefly explained that Samai used for their more intricate spells.

Oren spoke slowly until Gorn's body began to glow until it transformed into tiny specks of light that eventually disappeared.

Oren got to his feet and walked away from where his father had been and approached Iona in the wagon who was so clearly distraught,

"You need to get out of here Iona." He said quietly, uncaring, void of all emotion.

"Where's your father; what happened to him?" she cried hysterically,

"That doesn't concern you now, leave here as I told you before…please."

He marched her back to the wagon until she was safely back in the driver's seat and even while she protested, he slapped the horse's behind setting it into motion and sending Iona on her way. Trista's heart broke that she might never see Iona again and she hadn't even said goodbye.

Oren turned determinedly to swing himself onto Titan before turning to look down at the girls,

"Get on a horse and follow me!" Oren commanded and took off into the adjacent trees in the opposite direction.

Still broken from her fight with the soldier but knowing it didn't matter now, Trista approached the closest horse, Dana got back on the one she'd been made to discard and both girls took off after Oren into the rainy night, leaving a pile of melted soldiers and a dead father in their wake.

THE GAME BEGINS

They rode steadily until morning, pushing their steeds as far and as fast as they could.

It wasn't until the sun began to rise that even Oren, with his unrelenting strength finally slowed down. He brought Titan to a slow trot along the country road, walking into the rising sun. From behind, he was just a figure of solid black against the bleeding orange and red of the horizon. His silhouette was as dark as the feelings that thread through him, like a vine; choking any ounce of happiness he had left in him. The girls said nothing, not knowing the words even if they tried; and so, as the sun rose; their spirits lowered.

They'd left Priya through the vast countryside rather than follow the main road out of the town. Once through the initial overgrowth, to avoid any lingering eyes on the town exits, they emerged onto the main road and left the town for dust.

No one said anything for a while after they slowed their horses until Dana braved the tense atmosphere and approached Oren, still in her saddle,

"What do we do now?"

"We head to Crol," Oren replied so sharply that the girls instantly lost all thought of saying anything else.

They followed him silently until he veered off the road to the right and after a few minutes of trotting, came upon a small stream. How he knew it would be there, they didn't question as he finally dismounted and led Titan to drink.

The girls did the same and relieved their horse of its packages before taking a seat on the ground. The ground was grassy with a few trees clustered in small groups sporadically around them. The horses could graze, and they could catch their breath on more forgiving surfaces then horse back and Dana was able to dress her aching wound.

The early morning sky was a kaleidoscope of reds, oranges and purples that was so spectacular it was hard to imagine that so much destruction and chaos was going on beneath it.

Gorn was dead.

He had died only hours ago and yet here they were, looking off into a sunrise as though nothing had happened.

Trista didn't want to upset Oren, but they needed to address it. She took a long drink from her water skin then refilled it before finally turning to Oren who was stood next to Titan absentmindedly stroking his mane, while staring across the stream. Trista cleared her throat,

"W-what did you do to your father?" he didn't reply for a long time, but she didn't push.

"I preserved him until we can perform the proper burial rights…as he deserves."

"Of course, but…how?" Oren turned his head to her and the look in his eyes wasn't pleasant. Trista felt her body and her power literally shrink away from him even as she looked in his bloodshot eyes; eyes that had cried hard as they'd ridden across the country.

"With a level of power that you have yet to understand or master."

"I didn't mean…"

"I don't care what you meant, Trista."

Trista's heart was pounding in her chest as she felt an intense rage practically streaming from Oren. She understood his anger, his father had just died but what concerned her was that the rage was unequivocally aimed at *her*.

"You blame me for this."

It wasn't a question but the scoff of derision that escaped him was answer enough.

"Oren, I didn't mean for this to happen; surely you know that!"

"I know that, of course I do!" he raged at her. "You never *mean* for anything to happen, do you? You just act without thinking and *that* is your very problem!"

He finally turned his entire body to her and he seemed to grow in size as his chest heaved with anger. She had never been scared of Oren before but this was as close as she'd ever come.

"You've spent the last few weeks telling me not to think too hard; to just be who I a—"

"There is a time and a place for both, and you need to learn the difference before you get us all killed!" he thundered at her.

Trista's heart was beating rapidly with fear and anger at the injustice of his ridicule but somewhere deep inside; with the guilt, she already felt because she knew he was partly right.

Those soldiers had been looking for her, they had meant to kill her, and countless other women had lost their lives as well as Gorn because of that. This was in many ways her fault but in the same breath, she hadn't asked to be who she was, so how could she be held accountable?

"I'm so sorry you lost your father Oren but this isn't my fault…I loved him too."

"Is that why you put him in danger? Why you couldn't follow orders and get away like I told you to!"

"People needed help! I stayed behind to defend them!" she shouted back. "What kind of saviour would I be if I had just left them to defend themselves?"

"That's not the point Trista, not everyone can be saved; this is war!"

"Not everyone can be saved but your father should be the exception?"

She saw her words hit home, even as she heard the sharp intake of breath from Dana behind her and had never hated herself more.

She watched the pain register on his face, a crippling hurt that made her feel like a monster. In an instant, it was gone and replace with…nothing.

His face was blank and without a response, Oren turned away from her and led Titan away from the bank of the river to anchor him to a nearby tree,

"Oren I didn't…"

She was about to say she didn't mean it, but it would only prove what he had just said: she acted impulsively and people got hurt.

"We'll rest then head for Crol. We get a boat, we head to Drem then straight onto Thelm."

"Oren plea—"

"If anything happens to me head straight to the Lithanian Council."

He was ignoring her, and she knew he would for as long as he wanted. She'd ruined any possibility of a friendship with him; or anything more than that.

Oren set his belongings on the ground and lay down with his head rested against one of the large packs, his back to them which didn't invite conversation.

Trista's eyes filled with tears as she looked over at him then turned to look at Dana who had stood in respectful silence during the whole ordeal. She finally came and stood beside Trista to hold her in a loose hug and whispered;

"Leave him be for a while…he'll come around."

Trista nodded but she wasn't entirely sure that he would.

***

"WHY ISNT SHE DEAD?"

Princess Briseis screamed out in the middle of her audience chamber as a messenger and Gardan brought her news of the attack on Priya. Energy streamed from her as she screamed, blasted everything in its path. It knocked the two men to the floor and whatever wasn't bolted to the floor over onto its side.

The princess was dressed in a black silk nightdress that left little to the imagination with a long satin robe over the top. Her white hair flowed down her back in a stream of elegant waves making her look dangerously beautiful as her grey eyes blazed with fury.

"Get up you imbeciles, I want answers. *Why* is she still alive?"

Gardan got up first, adjusted his sword and armour as best he could without looking like a complete idiot and looked her straight in the eyes.

"All women of the appropriate age were disposed of as you wished your highness…"

"But she was not among them Gardan, I can *feel* it! That little bitch is on her way here and I want her stopped now!"

"Yes your highness," Gardan responded although he had no real idea how he was going to carry out her request.

Briseis huffed her displeasure as she paced the length of the audience chamber, seething with rage and pent up aggression. She needed this woman dead and yet, she was still out there somewhere, trying to destroy everything Briseis was trying to achieve.

"When will Baron Dreston be arriving?"

"His fleet is a day or two away from Thea's Point, weather dependent. He shall be in the capital momentarily."

"That's one good thing at least," she mumbled as she paced her room barefoot, tapping the side of her plump lip in thought. "His previous men are all settled at camp?"

"Yes Princess; they arrived yesterday."

"Good…and the Six?"

"Training as you requested,"

"Good…good," Briseis was still in deep thought. "Any news on the Agmantians?"

"No response yet your highness,"

"Good, as long as that bitch Nucea keeps her nose out of other people's business I won't have to deal with her too. Leave me…I have much to think about."

Gardan didn't need to be told twice and exited the room with the messenger. He decided when she'd blasted them to the floor, that he'd wait to tell her that riots had begun in the streets of the city in support of the Samaian redeemer.

***

When the raven arrived with news of the destruction of Priya but not the demise of the Samaian threat; Baron Lyon Dreston was less than pleased.

In truth, he had no real care whether the Samaian so called Redeemer was alive or not; they merely served as a distraction for Princess Briseis.

While the young royal was occupied with that nuisance, it would keep her nose out of Lyon's business while he manipulated events in order to take the crown.

So far, he was in a marriage alliance with Baron Thelm and was already the richest man in Mortania. He led the largest private army and once he arrived in the capital, would have access to the Royal forces as well.

He had fealty from Lord Tyus due to his damning indiscretions but the same commitment from Lords Balkin, Weilyn and Rinly of Illiya, Thea's Point and Drem respectively; were a lot more difficult to obtain.

So far he had discovered nothing significant enough to black mail them to his side and they were much more dependent on the crown then Erik ever was.

As the third largest city in Mortania that had its own trade links with Coz and a variety of home grown produce; Thelm was in a position to cater for and defend themselves against the realm and himself.

Lord Weilyn of Thea's Point however, received the bulk of the trade to the country and the capital and served as the main entry into Mortania.

Ships from Agmantia and further east in Yitesh arrived constantly; bringing spices and foreign produce that sold for large amounts. It would be extremely difficult to convince Weilyn that things would be better under Dreston's rule than they currently were.

In addition, Illiya served as the only coastal town in the far west and so had its own appeal that Lord Balkin wouldn't want to part with. He had traders and merchants from Cotai; the country farthest west past Lithania, and had the occasional visit from the Phyn.

People travelled from across Mortania and the Known World to catch a glimpse of the water people as the Dyam Islands were not habitable for most, for long periods of time.

Lord Rinly of Crol on the other hand, while the lord of a much smaller province did have control of the Northern Pastures that had constant traffic from West to East if one were not travelling by sea.

He made a mountain in taxes from which he then sent a percentage to the crown. Perhaps not having to do so could be the angle to get Rinly to align with him against the Greybolds.

He needed to have a formidable force in place when he finally made his move on the princess and not capturing the Redeemer had its drawback. The princess could lose her faith in his abilities to get things done, and he needed her to trust him and bring him in her confidence so he could be close enough to kill her.

Lyon was no fool. It was clear that Princess Briseis was an arduous woman, a force to be reckoned with, but she was human like any other and therefore could be killed. She might possess the powers of the Everlasting but that wasn't anything for him to be concerned with. Curian had defeated Alexander Antonides without it and he would do so with Briseis. There was no question, that he would defeat her in order to claim the throne that may not be his by birth, but would be by force.

Baron Dreston and his household arrived at The Mark in the early hours of the morning and Lyon was awake to see it.

He had just left Geneiva's bed and not wanting to retire to his own cabin just yet, had walked onto the deck.

The crew acknowledged him accordingly as they went about their business, but Lyon paid them no mind as he observed the wonder of the scene before him.

He was not known for his sentimentality but there was beauty in the world that even he could not deny. Like the mixture of colour that could only be seen at the break of dawn that brought with it the possibilities of a brand-new day. The Mark loomed ahead of them; a large rocky island that served as a marker between the two sides of the kingdom. It was a day's sailing from this point on and then he would finally be in Thea's Point, ready to make his way to Tirnum and finally meet the princess.

Despite his intentions; Lyon was excited to finally be in her presence after so many years. He had seen her as a baby in the year he had remained in Tirnum after the war, but had no desire to return to the capital since.

Meeting Briseis, analysing her and discovering her weaknesses would finally set his lifelong dream of being king into motion and no one, not even the ominous threat of a long-lost princess, was going to get in his way.

WHAT LIES WITHIN

In the last two days of travelling, Lamya had felt nothing like the tremendous shift of power she felt around her, that could only come from the Antonides heir. Not only did she know that Trista was alive, Lamya realised that she was growing in strength and this brightened her spirits.

While the increasing strength of the princess could only be a good thing, Lamya questioned how she was doing it.

It was obvious that Avriel had neglected Trista's early training, so how had she managed to build her strength and power so quickly on her own?

If she was indeed in her own, it was a commendable achievement but if she wasn't, then who was helping her?

Lamya hoped she found the princess soon, so she could devise how deep her magic went and of course explain to her, all the information she may be missing about her heritage and her future. She wanted Trista to fully understand what she was fighting for, who she was fighting for and the foundations of her people and her powers.

Lamya sat astride her newly acquired horse and rode steadily through the open country towards Crol.

In the few short days she'd been travelling she had past small towns and villages, and even a caravan of travellers and showed them that change was coming.

The few Samai she'd come across were more than happy to listen to her tales of a lost princess coming to save them. Whether they believed it or not, she hadn't questioned, but instead revelled in the fact that they were listening.

She saw the hope in their eyes and smiles as she explained that they would be needed where possible in the time to come.

She told them to make their way to the capital if they could and take up arms for their rightful queen.

Along the Mortanian coast, Lamya preached the coming of Trista Antonides, of the young woman destined to overthrow the tyranny of the Greybold rule. While this brought happiness to many, it brought anger to more than a few.

It was in a small town of Eirenlough, that Lamya finally met with hostility from Man, a short distance from Crol.

"Leave this place or die," a man had said when Lamya had taken residence in the village square.

A few people had gathered to listen to her talk of the coming war and what they could do to protect themselves, whichever side they were on.

Lamya perched herself on the edge of a water fountain; the most elaborate construct in the small village. Everywhere she looked were wooden huts and stalls, housing people and produce; some doubling up as stores and homes.

"Excuse me?" Lamya had turned to him quizzically, wondering if she'd heard him correctly.

"You heard me! We don't want any of your sort around here stirring up trouble!" Lamya looked at him questioningly. He was a tall man, tall and thin; probably a bartender or innkeeper or some other non-physical profession.

"Oh…what sort would that be?"

"The kind that stirs up trouble;" he said pointing his bony finger at her. "We're a peaceful village. We don't want any part of what's going on out there!

"That's exactly why I'm here. What is going on out there, affects everything and everyone right *here*…there is no them and us; but all of us." He shot her down again,

"We've done alright minding our business 'til now; why should we change?"

"Leave her be Ben; she got a right to speak same as everyone else."

An elderly man who had been listening to Lamya speak since she'd started, called over to the man. Some nodded at his rebuke while others maintained their anger just as Ben did,

"My father fought and died in that Samaian war and she wants us to fight for them, Jon!" Lamya interjected,

"I want you to fight for what's right. At least I'm asking this of you; your king is demanding it!" there were murmurs across the now growing crowd and Lamya realised with horror that the news of Briseis' intent for the war hadn't reached the lower villages and towns.

"What do you mean?" a woman asked stepping forward. She was holding a young baby and from the looks of her, it was her first; probably newly married.

"Princess Briseis has enforced Conscription…men and women aged sixteen to forty-five will be commanded to fight."

Terror swept through the crowd as parents and young children worried about themselves and their young ones, but Ben shook his head,

"We haven't heard anything like that!"

"And how often do you contend yourself with what goes on *out there*?" Lamya looked through the sea of faces and drove her point home.

"I'm seventeen," the young woman replied meekly as she held her baby. "I've just had Aisla…surely I won't be asked to fight."

Lamya didn't respond, her face a picture of the pity she felt for the young woman and her new family,

"What happens in the capital does affect you and you need to be prepared for it. Change is coming Eirenlough, and you must decide which side you wish to be on when it does!"

More murmuring but not outright dismissal and so she continued,

"King Curian has no agenda that concerns your wellbeing but the Redeemer…the rightful princess, she wishes to see Mortania prosper and thrive once again!"

"Then where is she!" someone called out.

"Yeah, if she cares so much where is she?"

"Where was she when my crops failed for the last two seasons?"

"And when the rains wouldn't come?" said another.

Soon it turned into a din of abuse and screaming the frustrations all being aimed at Lamya rather than the true enemy,

"I hear your cries and the princess does too, but she needs your help to put things right!"

"What can we do?" another voice screamed, "We have no gold, not titles and lands!"

"Would it matter if you did? As you say, the rains barely pour and the ground isn't fertile, how long do you think you can survive that?"

"And this Redeemer can help us?" The young woman once again, seemingly the only one who was really listening. Whether of fear for herself or her family, Lamya wasn't sure, but it wouldn't matter in the end. If they didn't act soon, everything would be lost to them,

"Who knows of the Everlasting, of its power…its true power?" Lamya asked,

"A myth!" someone shouted

"A legend!" said another.

"No!" Lamya shouted. "Not a myth and not a legend but the very essence that makes Mortania thrive and the king and his vicious daughter are destroying it!"

She let that piece of information rest for a moment before going on,

"The royal family are directly linked to the prosperity of these lands; *your* lands. If they don't do something soon and return it to its rightful Keepers than your lands will perish. The Everlasting feeds off the goodness of its chosen people and Curian has abused that; destroying Mortania in the process; destroying *you!*" The murmuring stopped for the moment.

"You join forces against Curian and Briseis and the rains will come and the crops will grow." Lamya turned her eyes to Ben, "You might not want to fight for Curian or the true princess; Trista of House Antonides…but you should want to fight for yourselves, for your children and their children and the life you wish for them."

She held Ben's gaze and was shocked when he turned from her and approached the young woman with the baby, taking the small child into his arms and leading them away.

She reached her power out to him and felt his anger wane ever so slightly, but his pride wouldn't let it go completely.

Lamya stepped down from the fountain then pushed her way through the crowd to where she'd left her horse.

The villagers plagued her with questions and worry about the conscription, but she had nothing else to give. She'd told them more than their king ever had and that would have to be enough to get them to act.

There were a few who asked her about the Everlasting having not been exposed to the Samai or the hereditary power in this small part of Mortania; there wasn't even a Samaian population here. She explained to them as best she could but when the crowd began to get too intense, Lamya mounted her horse and left Eirenlough, hoping she'd left a lasting impression on the residents.

Crol in comparison was an entirely different matter. As she walked through the gates of the large coastal town, she felt the Samaian presence like a warmth washing over her.

There was a faint hum of power in the air that while she knew was not enough to pose a threat to anyone who would care, was still there. She approached carefully, observing the area and people around her with curiosity and excitement.

She had made good time travelling from Illiya and had arrived in the early morning. Seagulls flew overhead, through the masts of the few ships that were docked, swaying slightly in the move of the water.

While Crol was a port town, its only route was to and from Drem; a journey that took almost four days. The small dock could only hold four ships that left periodically; Lamya planned to take the next ship once she'd rested and eaten. It was going to be another long journey to Drem and eventually Thelm where she would be back in touch with the Lithanian Council and hopefully find Trista. Until then she had to keep her wits about her and continue to rally support where she could.

Lamya dismounted once she'd reached a tavern she was familiar with named Eagle's Wind. Once she'd paid for a young man to tend her horse and a day's lodging, she headed to the dock to arrange passage on the next available ship. It gave her enough time to arrange her affairs and buy any needed supplies once she'd rested.

With the ticket, safely inside her robes, Lamya returned to Eagle's Wind to get some rest. Hours later, she awoke and once again headed out, this time into the late afternoon sun.

It was the middle of summer but with the constant decline of the Everlasting power, a steady chill had spread across the southern part of the continent. Here in Crol, where the summer sun should have meant no cloaks or robes, there was a distinct chill in the air. Not nearly as cold as it had been in the capital, she knew but chilly none the less. The summer had truly abandoned them and Lamya walked now through the streets of Crol, wrapped in an additional shawl over her robe.

She headed toward the main street where she purchased two small books on the advantages of oak bark and the complete history of Samaian Kings: Volume One, a pair of gloves as hers had become rather threadbare and some dried and salted beef.

It was late by the time she returned to Eagle's Wind and it was as she sat down for her evening meal that her stomach lurched in the oddest way; a way she'd never experienced before but she knew exactly what it meant.

"She's here," Lamya breathed as she dropped her spoon with a clunk against the wooden table top. "Trista is here."

***

Curian sat in his encampment in the Imperial Lands, arranging his troops and banner men into their required positions on the field.

His map of Mortania was laid wide across a large oak table with carved wooden pieces to represent his men and the opposing force. The most obvious problem he saw, was that he didn't know where this force was coming from or even how many it involved.

Briseis had him preparing physically and mentally for a war that may never happen and for which he had seen no preparation from the opposing side!

It was all speculation and while there was something in him that maintained that his daughter was worrying about nothing; her use of her power made him question everything.

Briseis had said she could feel this person's power, where they were headed and that she was certain they were heading East. Who they were heading east *with* was another matter altogether.

Was this one person on a hunt for mere justice? Or were they travelling with a host of men set on revolt and taking the crown?

Curian hated being so unsure when before, when he had been fighting Alexander's army, he had felt so certain about what he was meant to do…

THEA'S POINT, MORTANIA
999A.E

"Alexander has positioned his men here, here and here," Rarno indicated the immediate border of the Imperial Lands, along the Chylar River and further south towards the coast on the map of Mortania laid before them.

"He seems to be focusing his energies on protecting the castle and the lands immediately surrounding it."

"Probably to protect the nobility and his friends," Curian spat the words as he looked down at their own positioning on the map.

They had entered through Thea's Point, having commandeered several ships from people who believed in his cause, namely Baron Lyon Dreston. They had been built in secret in the hot waters surrounding the Dyam Islands to avoid detection.

Men had died getting his fleet together and while Curian had known it was not going to be a war primarily at sea, blocking off the Samaian's easiest exit was a welcomed idea.

If Alexander and his men wanted to run, they would have to do so through The Pass, and that was never a good idea. The only people who regularly travelled it were merchants from Thelm and Coz in the north. They could charge more extortionate prices for their wares in the fertile land between The Pass and Tirnum, than they could between Thea's Point and Tirnum.

"We can use this to our advantage," Curian continued thoughtfully. "If he's protecting the castle, then there must be something there he wants to keep from us. We drive him back, into The Imperial Lands and to The Wide, meet him in open war."

"How Lord, would he be foolish enough to be driven back so far?"

Curian didn't answer straight away because he knew the answer was no; Alexander wasn't stupid, but he was sentimental.

Curian smirked,

"Get the trebuchets ready."

"Lord?"

"That poor excuse of a king will care more about protecting his people then he will his own head," he explained. "If we breech the city walls, he'll be forced to get as far away from the capital as possible."

Rarno nodded his head with a smile,

"I'll tell the men," Rarno immediately left to do his bidding.

Later that night Curian awoke suddenly to the lasting smells and sounds of a massacred city.

The hiss of dying flames still hung in the air as the remnants of thick smoke wafted over his camp from the burnt and burning buildings only a few miles away.

Rarno and his men had done an amazing job of destroying the city walls and even some of the city within it, enough so that it had drawn out the soldiers like vermin from a sewer.

While he had achieved destroying a chunk of the main city wall; he had lost many men to achieve it. The Samai had advanced on them with steel and magic and it had taken his best men to deflect the expert skill of the Samaian soldiers.

They fought with a precision and grace that was enviable. Curian had been reluctantly amazed at the array of colours on the field from their use of magic. A flame here and there; a colourful burst of energy used to block when a shield was down. Despite the destruction it came from, Curian couldn't deny that it was a truly beautiful sight.

The lasting impressions of those colours were still on his eyes when he woke in his darkened tent but knew instantly that he was not alone.

He reached for his sword and as he did so, a voice spoke to him through the darkness,

"If I was going to kill you, I could have done so already."

"Then, why don't you? If I were in your position, I would have."

"That, my friend, is where we are different".

Curian's eyes adjusted to the darkness as best they could as a tall figure stepped forward and he laid eyes on Alexander Antonides.

The Samaian king stood looking down at him in a cloak so dark in the unlit room; it looked like his face was hovering in mid-air. Alexander pulled back the hood he wore, and his large golden crown was visible atop his long black hair.

"We are *not* friends," Curian said simply, hatefully as he rose from his bed to face his foe; sword in hand.

As their eyes met, Curian watched as Alexander blinked and simultaneously a dim light appeared in the space between them and Curian's sword fell to the padded floor. Curian's fists clenched at his sides before he raised them in front of him,

"Fight me without magic and see who comes out the better for it."

Alexander looked at Curian's raised fists then back up at the man in front of him,

"I wasn't aware this was a fight…neither of us are armed."

Curian could feel his blood heating as he looked at the arrogant man before him. The man that had never worked for anything a day in his life; the privileged pampered prince who grew up to be a king.

"Why are you here, Alexander?"

Something changed in Alexander's eyes, something left them completely as he opened his mouth and said,

"I'm here, to end this ridiculous excuse of a war." Curian scoffed,

"How do you intend to do that?"

"I hope, by appealing to your better nature. I was taught we all have one."

"Were those the same lessons where you were taught you were better than everybody else?" Alexander didn't respond and Curian felt all the more ashamed because of it. His shame only made him angrier,

"I have a team of Empaths, Liya who work at the castle." Curian was unsure what this had to do with anything. "They told me what's in your heart Curian…what you truly desire."

Curian tensed but didn't reply,

"I am here to negotiate what you would consider accepting in order to stop this war."

"You have nothing I want."

"Not even Rowan?"

Curian's heart stopped in his chest as Alexander spoke her name. He was angered that the way he said it, was possessive and even more so, because he did in fact possess her. He tried desperately not to think of her, her perfectly sculpted face and hair as black as the ocean at night.

"I always knew you were a barbaric race but whoring out your woman is low, even for you."

Alexander smirked before relaxing his face, his green eyes flashing with a ring of blue flame before it disappeared completely, and he took one step toward Curian. Curian took one step back, knowing exactly what that flame could do and was rightfully afraid of it. His fear continued to fuel his anger because no matter how he fought this man with armies and vicious words, there was a strength and power *inside* Alexander that he could never have

"My *wife* is currently in my bed, nursing our child at her breasts; a child *I* put in her belly." Curian snarled before turning away from the taller man, unable to look at him a second longer. He hated that the words hit home, that Alexander knew how to truly hurt him.

"She has no desire to be with you or anyone else other than me...but you know that already."

Curian heard Alexander move in the shadows but still he did not face him; he didn't care that he had his back to his enemy. He couldn't look at the man that had everything he had ever dreamed of...the man who had Rowan.

"I didn't come here to trade insults with you Curian or to highlight the fact that Rowan is *my* wife and no matter how you feel about her; that will never change."

Alexander was now standing in front of him, his magical light having followed and was now between them once again.

"I came to make peace, for my country and my family I wish this to end!" Curian flared up at him,

"I don't. I started this, and I will finish it."

"It has to end with violence?"

"Yes, that seems to be all you understand!" Curian raged at the man in front of him, wanting him out of his space and out of his life. "Your people destroyed mine; took our lands and our homes and our right to decent lives and now you want peace? You can never have peace!"

Alexander's eyebrows knotted in the middle as he shouted back,

"You have a warped view of a thousand years of history Curian, but we have taken nothing!" Curian went to protest but Alexander cut him off, "The Everlasting *chose* us, the same way Liya were chosen for Lithania and Humans for Coz and Agmantia thousands of years ago. You would destroy your country, your home; kill *innocent* people to take something you were not given? This makes no sense!"

Curian scoffed and marched away from Alexander while the light he had created rose higher in the air and shone brighter to illuminate his tent that was filled with his belongings. Thankfully Myrenda had stayed home in the High Lands of the southern pastures. She would join him as soon as it was safe to do so, and she would finally give birth to their own child.

"What makes no sense is one type of person ruling over another!"

"Only if that person, is you?" Alexander's dark eyebrow arched but Curian shook his head in disgust,

"All you do is twist my words, but you will understand soon enough. You will know true power and then loss when I take this country back from your clutches!" He was enraged now and wouldn't let this farce of a conversation continue.

"I know who and what you are Alexander Antonides and I will destroy you and your entire bloodline if it's the last thing I do in this life!"

Alexander stared him down, saying nothing as his eyes focused on the shorter though wider man but said absolutely nothing. It was in that moment, his eyes saddened and what Curian saw there made him want to rip the other man's skin from his bones: pity.

"Then we have nothing left to say to each other." Alexander took a step toward him, "If you wish to re consider my offer of negotiations, send a messenger. If not...I'll see you in battle."

Before Curian could reply, the light Alexander had made extinguished and the tent was engulfed once again in darkness. Curian fumbled his way through it. to the thin line of light showing the opening to his tent was and pushed the canvas angrily aside.

He emerged into the torchlight of his war camp but there was no one outside his tent but the armed guards he had left there. Alexander had vanished.

"My Lord...is everything okay?"

Curian roared into the night, his anger now a pulsating thing in his veins. Alexander had managed to infiltrate his camp and to add insult, somehow no one had seen him do it or heard them arguing inside. His chest was heaving with fury,

"Wake Commander Rarno and tell him I wish to see him."

One of the guards left immediately to carry out his order while Curian stormed back into his tent. He set about lighting candles to get light in the room before Rarno came and vowed then and there that he would have Alexander's head on a spike before this war was over.

As for Rowan…he would deal with his demons for her once her husband was out of the way.

***

Curian slammed his fists on the table in front of him in frustration. He had known then, who and what he was facing, and his motives had been clear: destroy the man who had ruined his life.

The problem, Curian knew was that he no longer had that fight or rage in him.

Rowan was gone, Alexander was dead; their heir was missing, and he was king. It should have been enough and yet he felt more passion in getting rid of his psychotic daughter then he did in fighting this fake war.

Once he had word from Queen Nucea he could better project how he would handle Briseis.

Until then, he had to pretend to be on her side or pay dearly for it, perhaps, with his life.

CROL

"Why wasn't I informed of this sooner?"

Although her voice was calm, the men who had been in her service for many years, knew the storm that could erupt from her and so remained quiet. They were never sure what could trigger her anger and did nothing to deter being the cause of it.

Princess Briseis stood in front of them in the large meeting area of Sentry's Keep; the main entrance to Tirnum City. She made a point of visiting her guards unexpectedly to make sure none were slacking in their duties to her or the crown.

She had a meeting with Gardan and a few of his officers but had arrived a little early to see what they were up to. She had walked into a meeting where their commanding officer was sending them out into the city to quell some riots she hadn't even heard of.

Reluctantly, they had explained that riots had been erupting within the city walls and the surrounding lands and streets all the way to Thea's Point.

The inner city was strained with excess people who had come to trade before sailing away from Mortania to the next safest country, namely Agmantia.

Soldiers had taken to raiding ships and houses to prevent able bodied men from escaping Conscription. Man, Samai, Lithanians; all manner of people were fighting amongst themselves. The city was in chaos as people realised that war was coming, and they would have to finally pick a side.

"I did not wish to alarm you, Princess;" Gardan was saying. "I believed I had everything under control."

"You clearly do not Gardan!" she reprimanded him. "Was I unwise to appoint you as my General?" Gardan was humbled as he lowered his head respectfully,

"No your highness,"

"Then what do you suppose we do about these riots, so we can focus on more important matters. I can't very well fight two wars!" she hissed at him but Gardan didn't flinch, not because he wasn't terrified of her but because he knew he couldn't show it. He raised his head and looked at her determinedly,

"We increase The Sentry presence in the city; appoint more militant approaches and punishments for offences. These will be enforced by the officers you see here today. I will step down to devote all my attention to the war effort gathering in the Imperial Lands."

Briseis didn't say anything for a moment before a small smile appeared on her face,

"Good...very good."

She gestured with her hand and Endora, who had been standing behind her obediently rushed forward to wrap a thick fur cloak around her shoulders. She had discarded it once she'd dismounted Axus and now, as the wind blew mercilessly against the walls around them, she couldn't fend off the cold any longer.

Winter had truly come to the capital in the middle of Summer and no one ever mentioned it. From Tirnum all the way to the tip of Crescent Bay was covered in snow and ice and howling winds accompanied it. No one discussed it, no one mentioned the oddity of it even as the bizarre weather swept out further to Thea's Point and further North to Thelm.

Gardan adjusted his sword as the princess turned to him,

"Have all new recruits sent immediately to the Imperial Lands. I'm on my way there now and I want every able body in training while we finalise our plans."

"Yes, your highness," Briseis turned to leave then but Gardan called out to her.

"Your highness…may I have a private word with you?" Briseis stopped and nodded at Endora and the other few guards in the area. They all dispersed immediately, leaving them alone in the large room, closing the door behind them,

"What is it?"

"News…from Agmantia."

Gardan watched Briseis go completely still then let out a long breath. If he hadn't known any better, he would have thought she was nervous, but he knew she wasn't capable of such an emotion.

"Well?"

"There was only one line of response from Queen Nucea. It said, 'Shadows are destroyed by light but consumed by darkness. Shine so that Agmantia may see and darkness unleashed.'"

The confusion on Briseis' face was apparent,

"What the hell is that supposed to mean?" Gardan said nothing, clearly as confused as she.

"As long as Nucea keeps her nose out of my business, I have no need to worry myself about her."

Gardan watched uncertainty flitter across he face but said nothing. She was clearly going over something in her head that he didn't want to interrupt. She looked up at him suddenly, her grey eyes determined and stormy as manipulations cooked behind them.

"Continue to watch my father…there's clearly more to this and I need to know what."

"Yes, your highness," Gardan bowed his head and Briseis left Sentry's Keep as quickly as she'd come.

***

Curian unfolded the small piece of parchment he had received a few moments ago and read the few words printed elegantly on it in Queen Nucea's own hand.

Nucea was a proud woman, a powerful woman who would not involve herself with a war that did not readily concern her or that she could not benefit from.

Curian resolved that he would shine as Nucea requested and in return, rid Mortania of its own shadow.

***

It was early evening when they finally reached Crol and Trista was exhausted, physically and mentally.

They'd woken from an uncomfortable rest by the side of the road and travelled to the port town. He'd addressed Dana when he spoke, but Oren explained that they needed to catch the last ship heading to Drem.

"We can't waste any more time," Oren had said as they had trotted to give the horses a short break. "The sooner we get on a ship, the sooner we can continue your training."

Trista had only nodded, careful not to break whatever stalemate he had come to with her. They were the first words he'd spoken directed to her since she'd said such a horrible thing about his father.

At Dana's behest, she'd left him alone, but it was killing her that Oren was mad at her. She would do anything to make things right with him.

The Antonides Legacy II

They eventually came upon a road that was paved, rather than the natural beaten path, and saw Crol up ahead.

Torches lit up the road leading into the small port town and Trista watched as the people who owned the night congregated on the street. Brothels and taverns were bursting at the seams, while other establishments were dark, their candles snuffed out for the night.

Oren led them toward the congested street before dismounting and they followed suit. He led Titan towards a nearby trough and allowed the horse to drink; the girls did the same for their steeds.

"Dana," Dana looked up, "Find a stable for the horses and somewhere we can freshen up. I'll get us passage on a ship."

"Okay, but how will you know where to find us?" He let go of Titan's reins as he walked away,

"I'll find you," he called over his shoulder, disappearing into the growing crowd.

Dana rolled her eyes, sighing as she shook her head with a smile and took Titan's reins,

"Is it just me or are you glad he's gone!"

"Dana!"

"What, he's just so intense!" Dana stroked her horse's neck soothingly. "I know a lot has happened, but Oren scares me,"

"No, he doesn't," Trista veered her horse away from the trough and Dana followed close behind to lead them down a muddy street.

"Not seriously of course," Dana explained, nudging Trista wither her elbow. "You have to admit though, never knowing what to say to him is exhausting."

Trista was inclined to agree. She felt like she was constantly walking on eggshells whenever she spoke to Oren.

"I just don't want him to be mad at me anymore," Trista replied sadly. "It's hard enough talking to him and training with him, but this has just added another layer of resentment towards me. I don't want him to hate me forever." Dana looked over at her friend with a teasing smirk and wriggled her eyebrows,

"Because you like him," Trista blushed furiously and looked away from Dana without responding,

"I knew it!"

"Shut up!"

"Why," Dana laughed hysterically. "I think its sweet that you like someone, I mean, we don't know if you'll ever see Thorn again...have you thought about him much since we left?"

She knew the question was coming but it didn't hurt any less to admit to herself that she hadn't. In the beginning, Thorn was all she thought about; her feelings for him and whether or not she would see him again, but now, she barely remembered anything about Remora or Thorn.

Guilt set in because she knew she was beginning to forget Thorn because Oren had appeared in her life. She knew she was attracted to him; it wasn't hard to figure that out; he was an attractive man, but she didn't really know him. She'd known Thorn her entire life, she'd known Oren five minutes in comparison to that. Why she thought Oren even mattered was an issue in itself. She knew next to nothing about him.

Trista caught the eye of a few people, some of which were Samai who smiled warmly at her, but she couldn't return the gesture as her mind was someplace else.

She'd thought about Thorn but mostly in comparison to her feelings for Oren and she knew somehow that wasn't what Dana meant.

"I have thought about him but what does it matter? I'm some long-lost princess with a destiny to fulfil and I chose to leave him behind to do that."

She regretted leaving Thorn almost every day, but Trista continued to tell herself that it was for the greater good. This was beyond her feelings for him, no matter how much it hurt to admit that. Dana, seeing her disheartened response didn't comment further as they walked further into town.

They continued through the close-knit street, passing a small tailor's shop where Trista pretended not to notice Dana get extremely unhappy. Her face clouded over and Trista, feeling guilty said nothing; knowing it was all her fault.

They walked until the smell of bread caught their noses and the girls turned toward a tavern named Eagle's Wind.

"They have a stable," Dana observed looking around the side of the building and with a shrug, they both headed towards it.

The stable boy, in return for one silver coin and the other two horses they rode in on, gave them two rooms and meals for the evening. Once the horses had been exchanged and Titan settled down in his own pen to rest, the girls made their way into the tavern and found their rooms.

They unloaded their few belongings and weapons, had a quick wash and changed into looser, clean clothing before heading back into the tavern and taking a seat nearest the stairs that led to their rooms and got something to eat.

The room was heaving with people, most laughing and joking with each other over bets and the town gossip. There were whores floating in and out and Trista watched in fascination how they lounged over men and flirted with them in order to get them to part with their coin. In some cases, it worked and in others, the men were quite aggressive with their refusals.

Trista couldn't imagine being that way with any man and it fascinated her how easy it looked. She knew of course that Oren spent at least some of his time in places like this and she wondered, what kind of man he was in these situations. Was he aggressive or accommodating, who could say?

The girls continued to watch the other patrons; a rainbow of people including Agmantians and even a small group of people from Coz. Their angled eyes and pastel skin were unmistakeable amongst the tanned hues of the Men, Samai and Agmantians. Dana and Trista ate quietly in their corner, watching people discreetly until one person caught Trista's eye.

The woman was sat directly across the tavern in a dark robe that was covered over the shoulders by a stream of flaming red hair. Even from so far across the room, Trista could see the hazel glint of her eyes, shining like a wolf in the middle of her very beautiful face.

It should have been scary, but Trista found herself entranced by the woman who turned her eyes away and back to her plate of food. Trista did the same, suddenly feeling foolish for staring but when she found herself looking up again to catch a sight of the woman, she was gone.

"I wonder what's taking Oren so long?"

Dana shrugged as she shovelled some broth into her mouth,

"Oren's a big boy, he can take care of himself."

"I know that, I'm just worried he might not be able to find us." Dana smiled as she continued to eat,

"If you want to go and look for him Trista, just say so." Trista stuck her tongue out at Dana as she threw a crust of bread at her.

"Stay here?"

"Sure, I'll finish this then go up to our room."

Trista got up from her seat and headed out of the tavern into the night.

The night air was chilly against her skin as she walked freely through the streets. Her fighting leathers, ever tight against her frame were too restrictive and she was glad she'd changed into something more comfortable.

She caught the eyes of a few Samaian women as she walked, and they inclined their heads with a smile which she returned. It was still unnerving that people might know who she was without telling them, but she knew she would get more of it in the days to come.

Trista walked aimlessly, unsure of where to go until after almost fifteen minutes of looking down alleys and dimly lit streets, she came upon a God's House. The tall building at the top of some steps loomed over head and a strange sensation blossomed inside her stomach almost instantly. She knew instinctively that Oren was inside and with a happy smile, began to climb the steps. When she got to the large wooden door of the holy building, she pushed the door and quietly stepped inside.

The darkness was thick inside the building too, aside from a soothing glow at the far end of the chamber where hundreds of candles burned.

She could see even from so far back that it was the altar, surrounded by candles and people praying or giving offerings to the Gods, in this case; the Mother Goddess Thea. Her statue loomed at the far back of the chamber.

It made Trista laugh that while Man opposed Samaian rule, they worshipped their ancestors as Gods, as did their ancestors.

Thea and her five children, Alexander, Freya, Caia, Justin and Kriston were the six deities that Mortanians worshipped for various reasons. They were the Gods and Godessess of Earth/Nature, Sun/Life, Marriage/Love, Moon/Death, Wealth/Prosperity and War/Protection respectively.

Slowly, Trista approached the altar where she finally laid eyes on the large figure with two swords protruding from the holders on his back, knelt in front of the altar. Trista's heart caught in her chest as she realised that Oren was praying.

She watched in silence while a few other people prayed silently in the pews around her and on the floor in front of her. Some looked contemplative, others sad; lighting various candles for the blessings they wished to receive. Trista saw when Oren lifted his head and lit a spare black candle.

Tears welled in her eyes as she realised, the candle was for Gorn. The coloured candles represented different things: black for Death, while white was for marriage, red for love and yellow for pregnancy.

Not wanting to interrupt his very private moment, Trista turned to leave immediately. Feeling terrible, Trista ran down the steps of the God's House, her eyes filled with tears for Gorn and Oren that she didn't see the person she bumped into.

Trista wiped away her escaped tears as she fumbled her words towards the person she'd stumbled into,

"I'm so sorry, excuse me."

She looked up properly to smile politely at them but the smile fell from her lips as she came face to face with the creature of a man in front of her.

His face was disfigured from possibly having his nose broken one too many times and he had deep, vicious looking scars all over his face and neck.

Diverting eye contact, she made to step around him, but the man stepped with her, blocking her path.

"Excuse me," she went to step again and again the man blocked her path, this time grinning, exposing small, dirty and crooked teeth.

"Let me pass," she said more firmly but without responding, the man suddenly reached out and slapped her so hard across the face, she fell to the floor. It was a miracle she didn't fall down the steps completely, as he twisted her wrist from landing so hard on the uneven floor. The man twisted her onto her back almost instantly, covering her mouth with his large filthy hand to smother her scream.

With his other large hand around her waist, he lifted and dragged Trista down the God's House steps and into a nearby street.

Trista's head was spinning from his slap and the lack of air as his hand covered her mouth and nose. Fear consumed her as the lights around the God's House and the main streets disappeared into darkness as the man suddenly threw her down onto the hard, muddy ground. She banged her head, the pain ringing through like a bell, cutting off any scream she could have tried to make after taking in desperately needed air.

She was on her back, her head screaming in agony as the man loomed over her, now pawing at her clothes. Trista drew in the breath she so desperately needed and let out a piercing scream,

"HELP ME!"

Her sudden speech shocked him, and he slapped her again, this time, splitting her lip. Trista choked on the shock of the pain as she tried to fight him off even as he continued to claw at her clothing. He was between her legs, keeping them wide apart and ripped at her tunic, tearing it right down the middle, exposing her breasts. The man leered down at her as she tried desperately to fight him off before dropping himself onto her to place his mouth on her chest.

"NOOO!"

Trista screamed into the night, tears streaming down her face at the reality of what was happening to her. She felt him fumbling between them, untying his breeches she realised but she just couldn't fight him off, he was just too heavy. His knees kept her legs apart, while his body mass overpowered her own as he sucked on the mounds of her breasts.

"HELP ME PLEASE!" she screamed, the fight leaving her as she choked on her tears and felt him tug at her underclothes.

Just as the night air touched her skin, the pressure of his body was lifted, as a figure barrelled into him and knocked him off her, crashing into crates she'd never known were there but heard splinter into a million pieces.

Terrified, Trista rolled over onto her stomach and looked in their direction to see two darkened figures tussling in the dimly lit road. It wasn't until she saw the two protruding swords, did she realise it was Oren.

Trista scrambled away from the fighting, and huddled against the wall trying desperately to hold her ripped clothes together.

She looked on however as she saw Oren overpower the man and begin to pummel him with punch after bone crunching punch.

For a moment, she was so paralysed with fear and shock that she didn't register the sound of gargling blood that came from the man as Oren continued to beat him.

"Oren," her voice was small, hoarse from the screaming she'd done so he didn't hear her. When she heard, bones breaking she knew she had to stop this,

"Oren stop!" she cried out, both from the effort it took to yell and the pain in her face and jaw. Oren's fist stopped mid punch,

"You would have me show mercy?" his voice was vicious, unhuman as he crouched there enforcing his own type of justice.

"I would have you not be a murder!" she cried and she sat quivering on her cold hard ground. "Not for me."

Oren knelt there for a long time, breathing heavily before he growled down at the man and let him fall to the ground. Trista heard him whimper in pain and thanked the Gods, however ironic that was, that he was in fact still alive.

Oren got to his feet and walked to where she was crouched on the floor, weeping with shame and terror.

Oren bent down and without a word lifted her into his arms,

"I've got you," he said softly as Trista folded herself into his chest to shield her modesty and wept.

When the returned to the tavern, Oren knocked on their door and when Dana saw the state Trista was in, she immediately got to work, mixing some salves to help her. Oren sat Trista on the closest bed and wrapped one of the blankets around her shoulders as he went further into the room to draw her a small bath. He left and returned to the room a few times with buckets of heated water before he left them to it, telling them he would return when they were done.

Dana helped Trista undress and get into the bath. She helped her wash her body and hair before applying a salve to her split lip and a light cream to where her face was red from the slaps.

For a long time, the two girls said nothing as Trista washed the mud and dirt from her body and hair but they both knew, they couldn't wash it away from her mind.

Despite having used her power against the Tirnumese soldiers in Remora, deterred the men who tried to hurt them in Dreston and most recently fought her way out of Priya, Trista had never been personally attacked in this way.

"He would've hurt me," she whispered. "He put his mouth…" Trista wrapped her arms around herself before she suddenly grabbed the side of the bath and threw up on the other side. Dana rubbed her back soothingly,

"I'm sorry, I…"

"Don't worry about it…you're safe now."

Trista wiped her mouth, still leaning over the side of the bath feeling disgusted.

"If Oren hadn't been there, he would've…"

"Don't think about it anymore," Dana soothed. "You're safe now, with us."

"My powers were gone Dana," Trista admitted softly, turning to look at her best friend. "I couldn't feel them, I…I forgot I even had them."

Dana didn't say anything,

"What good are my powers if in a situation like this, I'm just as powerless as any other woman?"

"Trista?"

Two sharp knocks at the door followed by Oren's deep voice saved Dana from having to reply to her friend.

"She'll be out in a minute!" Dana called out. "Let's get you cleaned up okay."

Trista was out of the bath and in fresh new clothes in a few moments and helped Dana clear away her vomit and pack her things neatly away. Her lip still hurt and her wrist was sprained but it would all heal. Her jaw was stiff but soon enough, she was ready and when Dana opened the door, Oren was standing there waiting to come in.

He had changed too and was now in faded brown leather trousers and boots with a loose-fitting shirt open at the neck. His hair was loose, drying naturally as was her own and his leather cuffs were around his wrists, his forearms on show as his sleeves were rolled up to his elbows.

"I'll be in Oren's room. Just let me know when you need me."

Trista hugged Dana tightly before following her to the door where Oren was leant against the frame, waiting to come in. When Dana entered the room next door, he stepped into their room and closed the door gently behind him.

They stood there for a long time, looking at one another until Oren reached out and gently stroked the side of her face where her cheek was blossoming with a fresh bruise. His fingers were cool and even though it hurt, his touch was oddly soothing as well.

"I should have killed him."

"No," even as she winced from the tenderness of the bruise. "You shouldn't have. I wouldn't want that for you."

"Trista, he hurt you."

"Only my pride," she said lightly, trying to lighten the mood and get that murderous look off his face. Oren scowled at her, his eyebrows knotting together in pure rage. Trista saw a ring of fire ignite in his eyes then fade out.

"This isn't funny Trista! When I think of what he could've...what he wanted to..." he couldn't even bring himself to say the words as he raised his fist to the side of his mouth, trying and failing to stifle the growl that escaped it.

Trista saw then the bruising and scrapped skin on his knuckles and gasped, taking his right then his left fist into her hands.

"Oh my Gods are you okay?"

"I'm fine," he looked down at her as he as she looked in horror at his fists.

She ran her finger gently over the swollen skin and tears suddenly pooled in her eyes. She looked at him angrily,

"I don't ever want you to hurt yourself for me!" Oren took his hands away and shrugged,

"Trista come on, before this war is over, I'll suffer a lot more than bruised knuckles for you."

This time he tried to laugh the seriousness away, but Trista was furious; furious because she was terrified of exactly that.

"Oren..."

"Trista," he looked down at her, all playfulness gone. "I will always protect you. That's not up for discussion."

She didn't really know what to say, overwhelmed by the intent in his eyes and so, without thinking too much about it; Trista stepped into him to wrap her arms around his body and hugged him tightly.

"Thank you," she whispered into his chest. He hesitated for a second and for a moment, she thought he wouldn't hug her back but soon enough, she felt his arms wrap around her entire body.

She'd never really touched or held Oren before. They fought and trained all the time, but she'd never touched him without trying to hurt him.

He smelled wonderful, like outdoors and leather and that ever-present hint of metal. Mixed with his own bodily scent, he smelled...safe.

"I'd never forgive myself if anything ever happened to you." His deep voice rumbled above her head.

Trista hated her traitorous heart as it beat more rapid in her chest, anticipating what this meant. She lifted her head to look up at him, her eyes wide when he said,

"My father would never forgive me. I promised to protect you...and that's what I intend to do."

Trista let go of him and stepped away from his embrace, hurt and hating that she was,

"I see," she said quietly as her heart plummeted to her feet and she wrapped her arms around herself.

She hoped it wasn't obvious to him that she'd wanted him to care about her for an entirely different reason,

"Well you did your job and I'm thankful for it. I just don't understand something." She deflected the conversation quickly, "My powers...I didn't feel anything, they were just gone. What happened?" Oren shrugged apologetically.

"Fear, surprise? You're still so aware of how you use your powers Trista, and if in situations like this you're not prepared to use them, they can fail you."

Trista nodded her understanding but then questioned,

"They helped me even before I knew I had them," Oren smiled gently,

"Things happen a lot differently before we Ascend, its unpredictable. I'm sorry I don't have all the answers for you."

His small smile disappeared then, and he reached out to stroke her face again. She hadn't expected it and so she blushed before looking away,

"Get some rest," he said. "We leave first thing in the morning."

"The morning, I thought we were leaving tonight?" he shook his head,

"The evening ship was full, they only had space for one much less three of us and Titan. I was coming back to tell you before...everything." Trista nodded,

"Thank you," Oren turned to leave but she called out his name. He turned to her expectantly,

Trista smiled sheepishly up at him, wrapping her arms around herself as she said,

"I'm sorry...for what I said about Gorn. I loved him too and never meant to hurt you or disrespect his memory. I...I'm sorry."

Oren nodded his head respectfully,

"Thank you."

He turned to leave again and opened the door, but they were both startled to see a woman standing there.

Trista's eyes widened as she took in the red head woman from downstairs in the tavern,

"Pardon the intrusion but I can get you on the evening ship if you still require." she said gently. Trista looked at her quizzically,

"How did you know we..."

"Because she's Lithanian," Oren interrupted as though it were obvious while relaxing his hand that had immediately reached for his sword. "What do you want, Empath?"

SHIPS IN THE NIGHT

Lamya looked at the large Samaian warrior standing between her and Trista Antonides and knew exactly how the princess had survived this long.

"My name is Lamya Rubio. I'm a Lithanian Empath, a Liya as you pointed out sir...I'm here to help the princess."

Lamya looked passed the warrior's shoulder to where Trista stood, more beautiful then she could have ever imagined; even with a nasty bruise on one side of her face. She really was as beautiful if not more so than her mother, Queen Rowan.

The princess was wearing a simple black tunic and pair of trousers, her long curly hair a dark mass flowing around her head and her emerald green eyes shone innocently but expectantly.

It was really her and she was unharmed and seemingly unafraid, but then, how could she be if she had this mountain of a man protecting her.

"She doesn't need your help," the big man said curtly but Lamya watched as Trista stepped forward and placed her hand gently on his forearm, instantly stilling him.

"Why are you here Miss Rubio, and how do you know who I am?" Lamya smiled and curtseyed as she should have done before.

"Forgive me your highness, just Lamya will be fine. I know who you are because I can feel it. I've felt your presence ever since you Ascended, and I've journeyed to meet you so I can assist you to Thelm."

"Who told yo—"

"Trista, we don't know this woman." Oren said turning to her but keeping Lamya in his line of sight she realised. "Don't be so trusting."

"Asking her questions doesn't mean I trust her. How else am I meant to find out if she's genuine?"

The man grunted but said nothing as Trista turned her attention back to Lamya.

"Sorry about him, he forgets he has manners sometimes" Trista smiled warmly at her, "You said you could get us on the evening ship…how?"

"I'm an Empath and so have gifts that can help us."

"Us?" the man's eyebrow rose but Lamya nodded warmly at him,

"I've been sent by the Council to aid the princess in her journey." Oren stood a little straighter,

"The Council sent you?"

"You know of it?" the man was thoughtful before eventually saying,

"My name is Oren, my father was General Gorn Antos of HighTower, Captain of the Guard to His Majesty King Alexander. He instructed me to take Trista to the Council for further guidance." Lamya's smile was broad,

"Then it seems, Lord Antos, that our missions are one and the same."

Lamya bowed to him and when Oren responded with the same gesture, Lamya watched the confusion flit across Trista's face as her eyes darted between the two of them.

Lamya felt a sharp hit of resentment coming from Trista and as she reached out her powers, she understood why.

"Your highness," Lamya turned her hazel eyes to the princess and stepped closer to her. Oren, she noticed subtly stepped closer to Trista as well. "I am a scholar of sorts and I believe the Council wish me to educate you during our journey."

"Educate me?"

"Yes, I've been instructed to teach you the ways of the Samai, as well as the people you will one day rule. I can teach you about your history, your customs…all the things you were not able to learn as a child."

Lamya watched Trista's face light up,

"History?" Lamya nodded and felt as a cloud seemed to lift from her essence.

"So, if you'll permit me to come along, I can get you on that ship but we don't have much time."

"She's right Trista; we need to get out of Crol as soon as we can." Trista turned to Oren and nodded,

"So we can trust her?"

"If she serves the Council, then yes," Oren turned his eyes to Lamya as if to reiterate that if she were to prove him wrong; she wouldn't live to regret it. "I'll get Dana and the rest of my things." Oren turned his eyes to Lamya who took his meaning.

"I will meet you all downstairs."

She bowed to them both and turned to head down the hall and back down the stairs to the tavern.

Lord Antos and Trista met Lamya downstairs a few minutes later and they were accompanied by a girl with short brown hair and a pleasant face. She was dressed in simple grey trousers and a long-sleeved shirt clinched at the waist by a black leather belt that had various sized pockets and holders and walked with a large thick staff. The princess, in comparison, had less items strapped to her but a sword was against her hip.

Lord Antos, the imposing shadow that he was, was dressed in black with two swords strapped across his back. His hair was tied back in a ponytail and he had a large pack swung over his shoulder.

"Lamya, this is my best friend Dana Black. Dana, this is Lamya Rubio; an Empath sent from the Lithanian Council."

The two women shook hands with bright smiles,

"Wonderful to meet you Dana, are we all ready?"

"I need to collect Titan, then we can leave." Oren said and Lamya learned that Titan was Oren's horse. Once the retrieved the the four of them made their way back across town to the dock where a final ship was readying to leave.

"Wait here," Lamya prompted as they approached the gangplank. "I'll find accommodation but when you see me, approach without hesitation."

Everyone nodded as she turned and disappeared up onto the ship.

"Can we trust her?" Dana asked softly as Lamya's head disappeared from view.

"Oren says she's a member of this council and that makes her trustworthy." Trista turned to him for certification and he simply nodded,

"The Council are an ancient order, a group of learned Liya who have the power to do great things. Over millennia, Lithanians have been chosen by the Everlasting more often than any other race."

"Why aren't they the Keepers now?" Dana's eyebrows knotted in confusion.

"Years ago a Redeemer was needed but when they were killed, Lithania was destroyed. Everything, including Yzna-Tum and the Great Library there was lost forever."

"Yzna-Tum?"

"Their capital city; people from all over the world travelled there for knowledge and it was all gone in an instant."

"All because their Redeemer failed?" Trista asked this time as a million questions ran through her mind about what that meant. Oren didn't respond, and she didn't push him to.

The three of them went quiet until Lamya finally reappeared at the top of the gangplank and as instructed, they walked straight to her.

Oren led Titan up the plank and into the belly of the ship when Lamya directed him, and settled him down for the journey alongside two other horses.

When he returned to the deck, the girls were waiting for him and Lamya led them away to a row of doors a deck below,

"I could only manipulate the use of two cabins. Dana and Trista can share one and Lord Antos and I will share the other…if that's alright?"

"Umm, I don't think Lamya should be with someone she doesn't know,"

"She doesn't know any of us," Oren murmured sarcastically, "What you mean is, you don't think she should be with a man she doesn't know."

Dana blushed but shrugged,

"No offence,"

"None taken," although it was clear it had been.

"I can share with Trista if that's better?" Lamya offered but Oren immediately objected,

"I appreciate who you say you are, but I can't leave you alone with her just yet. I'll share with Trista."

Trista's heart raced as she fought to keep her face neutral.

"Very well, if there are no further objections, I would be delighted to share with you Dana. I think we should all get some rest and talk in the morning."

Oren nodded and with an indication from Lamya he turned to the cabin door on his left and opened the door,

"Trista?"

Before she turned to follow Oren to the room, Trista caught the mischievous look on Dana's face and realised what her friend had done. Trista turned from the girls, embarrassed and walked towards the door Oren held open,

"Goodnight," she called out to the girls before stepping under Oren's arm into the room and he closed it firmly behind her.

As she was now growing accustomed to, Oren instantly swallowed any small space with his size.

The room was barely as wide as he was with a bunked cot at the far end, a small bolted down writing desk with accompanying stool and two large chests for them to place their belongings.

In the left corner of the cabin, closest to them was a metal bathing drum with a foldable divider. She knew it would be a decent size for her but practically unusable for Oren.

"Well this is cosy," she thought out loud. Oren huffed his disapproval and stepped forward to drop his pack on the bottom cot.

"Take the top cot," he proceeded to unstrap his weapons from across his back and around his waist and putting them in one of the open trunks. "Get as much rest as you can."

Trista nodded even though he couldn't see her and started to unstrap her own weapons. She remained in the corner of the room until he was done and added her own things to the second trunk to keep out of his way as much as possible. Still, Oren was a large man and she couldn't completely avoid brushing against him to get to the trunk. She was thankful he didn't mention it every time she jumped just because his arm grazed hers.

Quickly, she rushed back to the other corner of the room and decidedly, began to unfold the divider. She rummaged through her pack for the nightshirt she'd buried somewhere in there. It was difficult to find anything in the dimly lit cabin and so she conjured a small ball of flame to hover above her head as she looked. Soon enough, she found the nightdress and, setting it aside she peeled away her leathers and underclothes.

Trista observed suddenly how interesting it felt that Oren was on one side of the screen and she was naked on the other. Unexpectedly, her nipples hardened at the thought, her skin suddenly feeling too tight and hot. Embarrassed by her reaction to him, she quickly stretched and pulled the nightdress over her head. She snuffed the flame out once she'd repacked as neatly as she could and stepped around the divider to find Oren standing with his back to her, his shirt already discarded.

She wrapped her arms around herself, feeling self-conscious and so to fill the thick silence and make him at least acknowledge her, she asked,

"Do you really not trust Lamya enough to be in the same room with me?" Oren shrugged, his back still to her.

"Until I know more about Lamya, I won't trust her completely, no."

"You left her alone with Dana,"

"Dana isn't as important as you …no offence."

She heard the amusement in his voice and smiled to herself, delighted that he at least had a sense of humour.

"Give it a few days," he added. "We can change if it bothers you that much."

He finally turned and she watched him throw some folded garments into the trunk on top of his weapons. He turned to the cots again without looking at her and began undressing the top one, pulling the sheets back and fluffing the two small pillows.

Trista swallowed as she ogled the defined muscles in his back and the sheer power that was shown there. His golden tanned skin was painted so beautifully down one arm with his tattoo that she found fascinating, but had never had the chance to ask him about.

"What does it mean?" she asked, dismissing his earlier comment. She wouldn't confirm or deny that she'd been elated that they were sharing a room, even if Dana had orchestrated the whole thing.

The feeling she got in her stomach whenever he was around, began to pulsate in the pit of her stomach in a way she'd subconsciously learned to ignore but now, she couldn't. It was suddenly beating like a drum, calling out to her and with a will she couldn't suppress she took steps towards him,

"It means a lot of things," Trista reached out to touch it, to touch *him,* but in that moment, he turned and she dropped her hand, ashamed of how much she'd wanted to be close to him. She didn't realise how close she'd walked to him until their chests were practically touching and she had to tilt her head to look into his face.

Oren towered over her now, his eyes suddenly staring into hers with a look she'd never seen before. Oren looked, tortured somehow, his eyes questioning but he didn't immediately say anything.

Confused and a little ashamed, Trista took a step back from him and clenched her fist to try and squeeze out the desire to touch him.

"I'll tell you when you're ready." Oren murmured. He didn't give her time to respond as he suddenly reached out, placed his hands under her armpits and lifted her onto the top cot.

Breathless, Trista quickly looked away from him, ashamed of how she was reacting, for no reason other than being nervous. Her palms felt clammy and she couldn't seem to breathe through her nose, instead feeling the need to pant. She snatched her bottom lip between her teeth, desperate not to make any sound.

With her on the bed, she was now looking down at him and for a few moments they just stared at one another. Green eyes clashing into green, taking each other in, not making a sound or acknowledging that something was clearly different between them. Trista watched as Oren slowly licked his lips,

"Goodnight…Princess," he turned away and with a wave of his hand, extinguished the few small candles in the room and she heard him climb into his own cot.

Trista lay in her bunk above him trembling from head to toe, desperate for him not to hear how heavy her heart was beating, threatening to tear out of her chest.

She *wanted* him.

In all the ways, a woman could physically want a man, Trista wanted Oren so badly she was terrified of it. She'd only kissed one boy very recently, and was now intensely attracted to a man who was her superior in almost every way.

You're his Queen; you couldn't be with him anyway.
Was that true?

Trista thought about how loyal Gorn and Oren were to her family and their roles as military men. It was more than likely that even if miracles were to happen and Oren returned her affections, he would rebuff them because she was royalty and he wasn't.

What about Thorn?

Thorn was still her fiancé as far as she knew, but if she ever made it back to him, would she still want to be his wife knowing how she now felt about Oren?

Oren lay on his back in his bunk for a long time after the lights were out, listening to Trista breathe. The sounds of her breath altered when she finally fell into a deep sleep, and when he heard the faint whistle that escaped her nose, he finally let his guard down and allowed himself to rest. He was constantly alert when it came to her, his senses on high whenever she was around and now she was asleep, he could finally get some peace.

His peace however was short lived, as his mind went off on a tangent and wondered whether Trista had known that while she was changing, her silhouette had been clearly outlined on the other side of the divider when she'd lit her flame.

He'd seen every curve of her body but when he'd seen the protrusion of her nipples, he'd had to look away for fear of what he felt and what he might reveal to her.

He knew this was going to be a long journey, not only physically but mentally, if he was going to keep his emotions intact, but he had to be strong. It didn't matter that everything had changed since she'd arrived in Priya, that his father had been right, and he had been so desperately wrong. It didn't matter that he no longer thought of Tysha or the nights he had spent with her, trying to drive away the inevitable.

The princess had arrived and now his obligations were not the only thing keeping him by her side.

TIRNUM CASTLE

Thea's Point, despite not being the capital was in fact, the heart of Mortania. People from all over the country and the Known World arrived every day on varying business and errands. It was a melting pot of cultures and races, buying, selling and always in a general rush to get from one point to another.

Gargantuan cargo and passenger ships entered the mix, monitored by docking captains and merchants; the skyline a mass of masts, ropes and sails. Various flags of provinces large enough to have them, flapped alongside the flags of noble houses and faraway lands in the sea breeze, high above the din of the activity below.

Baron Dreston stood beside the captain at the helm of his own ship and watched the small city come into view.

In the distance, far off atop a cliff overlooking the Aquatic was Tirnum Castle; a hazy shadow that although didn't resemble a castle from this far away, was a formidable sight up close. The centre of Mortania, the heart of its corruption and downfall and Dreston was finally heading back there.

"I trust your journey was comfortable, Lord?" the captain asked, and Lyon smiled, happier than he had been in days.

"Wonderful Captain Regus, although I am delighted to finally being going ashore."

"You do not have sea legs Lord; it is to be expected." The two men laughed good naturedly,

"My aid told me there was some trouble on the waters, we were fortunate not to have encountered any."

"That we are, Lord. A ship was capsized just a few nights ago. The *Mayflower,* was attacked by pirates looking for resources to their cause."

"What cause could that be, they're pirates no?"

"Pirating doesn't stop people being loyalists or in this case, royalists."

"They attacked in the king's name?"

"Not in his name but to fund their own causes for his side. The city is rife with rioting and fights among the small folk taking Mortania into their own hands."

Lyon was intrigued, he hadn't realised that the unrest had gone so far down. He rarely busied himself with lowborn issues, but it seemed he wasn't the only one Curian had insulted and upset.

"Lord!" Lyon turned to see Aml approaching them and bowed once he was close enough,

"General Beardmore awaits us at the dock. He will escort us to the castle to be received by her highness Princess Briseis."

"Then I must look my best," Lyon said with a smirk. "Come Aml, I must change before we disembark."

Aml bowed before he backed away and lead the way back to Lyon's chambers.

Within the hour, the baron was dressed in his most fetching attire; velvet black pants and doublet with a black cape lined with gold. The mighty fire breathing gold dragon was embroidered on the back which flapped in the wind as he walked. Long leather boots adorned his feet, buffed and shined while the finest longsword was strapped to his hip with a gold lined leather belt. Two large gems held his cape to his shoulders and a large golden chain hung between them resting comfortably on his narrow chest. His hair had been combed back away from his face, his beard trimmed and as he stepped off the ship, Geneiva by his side in a dress of the brightest gold, they looked like returning conquerors.

He looked out from the high deck onto the city and shivered as the winds cut through his clothing.

"Come my dear, our city awaits."

Lyon led Geneiva down the gangplank, Erik behind them, toward a rather young-looking man who stood waiting for them. From his very formal armour, it was clear he was General Beardmore, but Lyon had expected someone much older.

The man looked to be in his late twenties, maybe early thirties. He had serious eyes that bore into them as they approached him, before altering completely and looking warm and welcoming. This was a man to watch, Lyon thought to himself. Someone who knew how to play the game of wills and shield their emotions was a formidable opponent.

"Greetings Baron Dreston, I am General Gardan Beardmore here to escort you to the castle on her highness' order."

"Delighted General," Lyon replied looking at the remaining armed guard, four in total. "Are these enough men to accompany my entire household?"

"We are here to escort you Lord; others have left with your things so that they are ready at the castle. Your man Aml was quite thorough."

"Well, I pay him enough to be so." Lyon said turning to look at Aml who just bowed respectfully.

"Baron Thelm, so good to see you again and, forgive me my lady…I'm not sure we've met."

Erik nodded without comment, but Lyon offered the introduction,

"This is my wife, Lady Geneiva, daughter of Baron Erik. It is her first time visiting the capital."

Gardan was not quick enough to hide his shock at that revelation as his eyebrows rose to his hair line then went back down again.

"Forgive me Baroness Dreston, congratulations on your nuptials…and to you Baron. You have joined a truly mighty house. I hope you both enjoy your stay in Tirnum…however long that may be." Lyon didn't like the tone with which the General added his last words but didn't respond.

"I'm sure we will, shall we?"

"Of course," General Beardmore stepped aside where a stable hand, held the reins of four fine horses for each of them. Within moments, General Beardmore joined him at the front of the procession; while the other four guards took station beside each of them and soon enough, they set off towards the castle.

The ride to Tirnum was a long one, well over an hour at the snail's pace they took. They went first through the tight streets of Thea's Point before emerging onto Thea's Road, the main road that ran through the city and towards Tirnum; connecting the expanse of land that lay between.

Not wanting to ruin his clothing or become too sweaty, Lyon didn't push to ride faster but was growing increasingly impatient.

"Our apologies Baron, if the crown had known of your wedding, we would have sent a gift." General Beardmore struck up conversation as they neared Tirnum City gates. Lyon turned to look at him then back at the road ahead.

"It was a small affair; we did not want to make a fuss."

"Two of the mightiest and wealthiest houses in Mortania join in matrimony is very much a fuss…her highness will be delighted to hear of it."

Something about his tone told Lyon immediately that this wasn't true.

"And his majesty?" Lyon diverted the conversation to something he was more comfortable with. General Beardmore's eyebrows rose questioningly,

"The king?" Lyon didn't add anything else. "The king is busy with other matters…he'll find out soon enough."

General Beardmore didn't offer any more than that, but Lyon was too annoyed to care. He wanted out of this saddle and into an audience with the princess; he had things he wished to discuss.

They finally arrived at the city gates and were ushered through of course, without question. Once again, they had to trudge through the crowded city, filled with more high-ranking members of society but still too many of them none the less.

Buildings loomed all around him, buildings as tall as trees that attempted to block out the sun that beat down on the snow-covered ground.

Large townhouses were grouped together like a puzzle, everyone using every inch of land to be closer to the crown. The epicentre of the city, Tirnum Castle loomed over head, a gigantic structure of stone and glass that housed the power that made the world.

When they finally entered through the castle gates and into the castle courtyard, General Beardmore dismounted and turned to the Baron when he did the same.

"Would you not rather rest before meeting the princess?"

"No," was Lyon curt reply. He was tired of waiting; he was anxious to set eyes on the young woman he had come to hear so much about. "I will freshen up, then meet the princess."

"Very well, please." Gardan gestured to two servants who stood waiting for instruction. "Our attendants will show you to your rooms."

The servants led them to their chambers, Geneiva in the one adjoining his own and Erik and Aml housed somewhere else entirely.

Lyon combed his hair and wiped his face and neck in the basin of warm water that the servants brought him and General Beardmore was at his door all of twenty minutes later.

As they approached the Great Hall, Lyon observed the splendour around him. The tapestries and gold and marble on display within the stone structure, exposed the wealth of the city, the country and those that ran it. Dreston Castle was by no means a hovel, but this, this was something else entirely. Lyon saw himself within these walls, walking these hallways, a master of all around and within.

They passed liveried, armoured guards and countless servants running this way and that, doing the bidding of some higher person in the vicinity. It was a hive of activity and excitement, a far cry from the drudgery of Dreston Castle, that while he enjoyed on occasion, had grown stifling and dull.

Geneiva was by his side, her father a few steps behind and Aml a few steps behind him, a small procession of course but that was of no consequence.

His wealth was in gold and arms not a fancy entourage.

General Beardmore stopped outside the large wooden doors with two guards on either side and turned to face the baron,

"If you would wait here a moment Lord," and without waiting for his response, disappeared through the door, barely allowing enough space for Lyon to see inside.

Lyon stood aghast, turning to look at Geneiva, Erik and Aml but all said nothing; seemingly as confused as he.

Almost fifteen minutes went by before General Beardmore reappeared in the doorway and Lyon's outrage was momentarily stifled by the look on his face. Apology was plastered there but also something else that Lyon couldn't quite place...

"My sincerest apologies for the wait Baron Dreston...her highness will see you now."

Lyon cleared his throat to hide his displeasure and straightened his doublet as the large doors were finally pulled fully open by the guards on either side of it.

They stepped into what was clearly the middle of a banquet. There were rows of tables and benches and the appropriate arses to fill them, as Lyon glared around the room. A few of the men he recognised from various dealings around the kingdom, but there were many he did not know. Who were these men who dined within the castle walls while he had been made to wait outside like a peasant!

"Introducing Baron and Baroness Lyon of Dreston and her father; Baron Erik van Raylen of Thelm!"

The court announcer bellowed into the room, silencing any who wished to know who had arrived into their presence.

Lyon clenched his teeth in rage as Erik and the general both cleared their throats while Erik's neck turned a horrible shade of red. General Beardmore stepped subtly towards the court announcer who in turn cleared his throat and called out,

"...a-and her father, Baron Erik of Thelm!"

Lyon marched forward then, down the length of the long hall to the dais at the far end where two thrones were placed.

The thick black carpet beneath his feet was soft even in the boots he wore and after, he was sure, many other feet trampled over it. He kept his head held high, barely acknowledging those around him as he seethed at the incompetence of the woman he was about to meet. No one made him wait, no one.

"My love, you are hurting me," Geneiva murmured under her breath and Lyon loosened his hold on her hand. A few nobles, closer to the front inclined their heads in his direction but he declined to do the same.

When they stopped the appropriate distance from the dais and rose from their elaborate bow and curtsey, Baron Lyon finally laid eyes on the princess and she was…a *child!*

Lyon had always known her age of course, but to be face to face with a girl over half his age was an insult to everything he held dear.

Who was this child to not meet him when he docked, keep him waiting outside the door and attempt to embarrass his newly aligned family heritage?

Looking at her now, sat on her throne beside the one belonging to her father with a self-assured, lazy look on her face; Lyon knew she'd done this on purpose.

By highlighting Erik's original name, rather than the name he had taken for his family after the war; Briseis had highlighted how unworthy Erik was and by extension; him!

Before even speaking with him, she'd made it abundantly clear to everyone in the room that they were…less. Even if his own name carried inherited weight, it would never be enough.

Lyon tightened his fist again causing Geneiva to wince but he soon let go as he continued to stare at the astonishingly beautiful witch in front of him.

Despite her age and clear indifference to their arrival, Briseis *was* beautiful.

Her ice grey eyes bore into him from within darkened lashes and oval shaped angled eyes. Her slim face was smooth like porcelain and her hair was white as virgin snow. It hung either side of her face, straight but for two braids holding it away from her temples.

A small diadem was atop her head, silver; to match the silver gown she wore that clinched at the waist, thrusting her breasts towards the top of the low-cut bodice. The skirts were full, filling the width of the throne on which she sat and falling to the floor at her feet in a cascade of liquid silver.

She was leant on her left elbow, thumb beneath her chin and her index finger gently stroking her bottom lip. Out of nowhere, lust pierced his loins as he imagined her plump young mouth wrapped around his manhood.

She continued to stare at them, not saying a word as the rest of the nobles in the hall continued their meal and conversation. She knew very well that they were not permitted to speak until she addressed them and so she kept them waiting.

"Baron Dreston, so good of you to come."

Princess Briseis finally spoke and as she did so, she rose from her throne. Her voice was deeper than he imagined, husky even and had all the airs and command of any lord or baron he had ever met.

In front of her throne was a low table, spread with an abundance of foods and wines. She descended the five short steps in front of it to stand in front of him.

It was disconcerting to feel as though she were looking down on him although he was taller than her, Lyon thought.

"It is my honour to be able to serve you so personally your highness," Lyon took one small step toward her now outstretched hand, took it into his own and kissed the back of it. Her skin was warm, as though fire coursed through her blood and as his lips touched her tender flesh, his blood boiled with lust for her.

Was this young princess a virgin, supple and ripe for the picking, or was she as experienced in all things as she seemed to be in court politics?

"You have done well in coming to Mortania's aid…and mine," he released her hand. "While we wage this war and long after we have achieved our victory, know you are a true friend to the crown."

"You are too kind your highness. Might I introduce my wife Baroness Geneiva and her father Baron Thelm." Geneiva and Erik curtseyed and bowed again as was appropriate. She looked at them both but her expression told them nothing,

"Yes, Gardan told me you had been married."

Nothing else.

She continued to look at them as though waiting for them to say something else. Lyon was uncomfortable as he tried to find something to say. Before the response could come to him, Briseis suddenly clicked her fingers and seemingly out of nowhere, servants filed in with additional chairs and tables that were positioned on the table beneath her throne; clearly meant for their occupation.

"Come," Briseis said ignoring Geneiva and Erik completely and turning back to her meal. "Dine with me…we have much to discuss."

Lyon let go of Geneiva and took the seat immediately beside the princess.

It wasn't lost on him that General Beardmore who was stood behind the princess; breathed a sigh of visible relief.

What that meant, he could never really be sure.

YOUNG LOVE

For a long time after the war, he could never bring himself to use his newly acquired powers. Even then, after his victory; it had felt wrong. He didn't want to lose himself in it and so, he didn't.

He avoided the call of the magic inside of him, buried it deep down where he would pretend he couldn't feel it hissing, waiting to bubble to the surface…to be *free*.

All he had ever wanted was to be free. Free from the confinements of his early life and free to do what he pleased, free to be happy. When he had finally given in to the power, he realised finally that he could have and be and do whatever he wanted, just like Alexander had done.

Still, no matter the victory of the Samaian king, there was still something missing in Curian's life that no amount of power had ever been able to give him. What hurt him now, was that all he had done…he did for nothing. He still did not have the one thing he had wanted for what felt like his entire life; Rowan. He loved her. Curian had loved her from the moment he'd met her and every day since, growing up on her father's estate…

LORD'S MANSION, ILLIYA
982AE

It was the earliest part of a new day, when Curian quickly sat up in his straw filled bed and rushed on the wool cape that was meant to help stop the winter cold chilling his bones.

His father was asleep on the floor in the far corner of their cabin. Curian rolled his eyes at the high possibility that his father was drunk and so, without bothering to wake him, got dressed and went to start his chores.

His father, when he was sober and awake was a stable hand at the High Lord's Mansion in Illiya.

While they made a decent enough living, Curian realised early on that his father spent the majority of those earnings on ale and whores. His mother had died when he was very young and Curian had seen his father drink and whore his way into a stupor more times than he cared to admit.

There was a lot to be desired in their small cabin just off the main estate, especially when they saw how their betters lived in the big house.

His father complained constantly about how little they had while the high born had everything, but Curian never saw him do much to change it.

Even now, at the crack of dawn it was Magnus' job to clean out the main stables while Curian would feed and dress the horses. It was Curian who did it all now, waking as early as possible so their betters wouldn't think them slacking and turn them out into the street.

Curian also knew that it wasn't just his alcoholism and laziness that kept his father from doing his job, but that he had an innate distaste for the Illiyas and the Samai as a whole.

"They're usurpers and thieves," his father had told him on more than one occasion. "Using our land and making money from it while we barely have enough to eat. Samaians are savages Curian and can never be trusted, do you understand?"

Curian had nodded, eager to please his father and show him how he could be a true man, even more so now that he had turned eleven.

The Samai were the enemy and they only had to work for them until they had enough money to leave the estate altogether. His father had been telling him this since he was old enough to understand and yet, they remained.

It was spring but still chilly in the early mornings so Curian, now dressed as warmly as he could in his usual brown trousers, tunic and thin wool boots; headed over to the stables to start his work.

He had cleared the first stall before he heard someone speaking in one of the stables at the far end. He stopped moving for a second to listen, and while the person was speaking, they didn't seem to be getting a reply.

Curian put his pitchfork down and slowly approached the stable door that was a little ajar and listened,

"It shouldn't matter that he's a prince," came a tiny voice. "I still don't know him, so how can I ever learn to love him…what if he doesn't even like me?"

Curian's heart stopped as he peered into the last stall that held Aurya, the white Coznian mare that belonged to the young girl who was gently brushing her coat.

Lady Rowan.

Curian's mouth went dry as he stared at the back of her head, taking a moment to admire her before she knew he was there.

Her long ebony hair was curly which confused him because she'd never worn it like that before.

He cleared his throat and she instantly spun round, making his heart leap at the sight of her and her entrancing green eyes. Her face spread into a relieved smile as she saw it was him,

"It's just you Cur!" she said turning completely from her horse and walking up to him with a giggle. "I thought it was mother…she doesn't think I should be out here."

Rowan straightened her spine and looked down at Curian while wagging her finger, "The stables are no place for a lady," she said mimicking her mother.

Despite himself, Curian laughed and Rowan joined him, her laugh lighting up his heart,

"She's right you know…you shouldn't be here." Rowan rolled her eyes,

"Not you too Cur! I thought we were friends?" Curian's eyes widened. Of course, they were friends; he hadn't meant it that way at all!

"Of course we're friends but…you are a lady."

Rowan's playful grin disappeared, and it hurt Curian that he had made her sad,

"I know and one day…I'll be a princess."

"What do you mean?" Curian asked feeling stupid but Rowan just shrugged, lost in her own world again as she went back to brushing Aurya.

"I've Ascended," she said. "So I have to meet the prince."

"Ascended?" Curian had never heard this word before, was it meant to mean something? Rowan pulled at her now curly hair but didn't turn to look at him,

"It's what happens when we…" she looked at him but sighed, as though it wouldn't matter if she explained but he wanted to know, desperately.

"It means I have to go and meet Prince Alexander in Tirnum"

"You're leaving?" he said it too eagerly he knew, but he didn't care. Rowan was leaving Illiya possibly forever.

"Just for a year," she replied as she turned to him again and put a brave smile on her face. "I'll be back before you know it."

She'd smiled at him but he could see she was hiding something. What was so wrong with Tirnum if she was going to meet a prince, surely that was a good thing?

"I-I'll miss you Rowan" he said quietly, almost in the hope that she wouldn't hear him but Rowan just smiled and reached out, putting her soft and delicate hand on his cheek.

"I'll miss you too Cur…you're like a little brother to me."

If at eleven years old he knew what heartbreak was, Curian would have said that was it.

Rowan was thirteen and saw him as nothing more than a child, not a growing man who loved her and would do anything for her. He stepped back, hugging the handle of his pitch fork to his chest.

"I should go, I have work to do."

Curian stepped away from her and walked back to the next dirty stall.

"Goodbye Curian," she called after him but he didn't turn around to reply.

Rowan left for Tirnum that same day and a year later, she galloped back through the gates of the Lord's Mansion to greet her parents and older sister Renya. She'd been wearing a hooded cape of the darkest green trimmed in white fur with green leather riding gloves and boots.

As she entered the large court yard, the wind caught the inside of her hood and blew it from her head, allowing her long dark curls to stream in the wind behind her.

Curian, who had been watching from the side lines, ready to help her dismount and take her horse had fallen in love with her all over again, despite having told himself that he hated her for leaving and thinking him a child.

That resolve didn't last long, as she dismounted and ran into her father's arms for a long hug, then kissed her mother and sister.

"You look absolutely wonderful Rowan!" Renya had exclaimed as Rowan giggled with excitement at seeing her family again.

She looked absolutely beautiful Curian thought as he walked her horse back to the stables, without her having notice him at all.

Later that evening, Curian was in Aurya's stall brushing her smooth coat when he heard a sound and turned to see Rowan standing there with a huge grin on her face.

"Cur!" Rowan ran towards him and hugged him tightly and for the first time, Curian hugged her back.

Gods he had missed her.

Rowan stepped away from him, breathing heavily as she smiled broadly at him.

"Welcome home," he said.

"It feels good to be home. You're so tall now!" she acknowledged. "You're handsome too!" he blushed furiously but didn't reply.

Rowan realised she embarrassed him and quickly changed the subject,

"Listen, I can't stay long and mother wants me to get ready for my welcome home dinner. Rayne has come all the way from Agmantia for it but she'd just as bossy as ever!" Curian watched her laugh about her older sister, content in listening to her speak but Rowan must have realised she was babbling as she giggled and said,

"Anyway, I have something for you."

"What is it?"

Rowan handed him a small leather pouch and when he took it, it was heavy,

"Open it and see," he pulled the string to loosen it and poured the contents into his hand.

A small, grey stone fell into his palm; a perfect oval and smooth all the way around.

"What is it?"

"They call it a Briseis Stone. The legend is that a young woman was captured and taken as a prisoner of war but after years in captivity, she made it out relatively unscathed and one day became Queen."

Curian turned the stone over in his hand. It felt and looked like marble, with swirls of varying greys and light browns.

"That stone only gets that smooth after hundreds of years of the rock that's around it, has eroded…but the centre survives."

Curian looked up at Rowan's beautiful face and swallowed, unsure of what he was meant to say.

"Why did you give me this?"

Rowan looked uncomfortable for a moment but shrugged,

"I know we're different, that our…positions in life are so different that there's no reason we should be friends." Rowan shrugged, clearly getting embarrassed herself.

"I guess I wanted you to know that like that stone, you are special. Despite what's going on around you…with you father…"

Curian looked up then, not realising that she'd ever known he had issues with his father.

"You can do and be anything you put your mind to…I just wanted you to know that." Curian was silent for a moment as he looked down at the stone in his hand then closed it into his fist,

"Thank you," his voice didn't come out how he wanted it but he hoped she knew he was eternally grateful. Rowan smiled before leaning forward and kissing his cheek,

"I should go…bye Cur."

Curian stood there for a long time after she'd walked away thinking that not all Samaians were as bad as his father would have him believe.

***

Curian ran his thumb over the smooth stone that sat welded into his sword hilt and sighed deeply as he stared into the darkness of his tent.

If he couldn't have Rowan, then there was no need for this war or the woman who was orchestrating it, and he could only hope that Nucea answered his request in time.

The Antonides Legacy II

THE CHOSEN

"You look like her."

Trista looked up from the small table at which she, Dana, Oren and Lamya were eating their breakfast. They had awoken only an hour before to the harshness of the rising sun and at Lamya's instruction had gone on the hunt for food.

There were eating in quarters that were currently occupied by the Captain and the most important members of his crew. They didn't ask how Lamya was shielding them from questions about who they were and until it posed an issue; none of them felt the need to.

"So I've been told," Trista responded to Lamya's observation. Lamya looked on apologetically,

"I gather this is not what you want to hear about your mother. What do you know of her?"

Everyone was silent as Trista put her half-eaten slice of buttered toast back onto her plate.

"Nothing much...not really. I remember some things...small things." No one responded and so she continued,

"When Oren and I were training in Priya...I saw her. I saw her in a small cosy room rocking me to sleep. I saw her buying bread at a market while holding me in one arm and...I saw her give me to someone to take me away."

Lamya nodded, seemingly realising something she hadn't voiced,

"Your mother was able to use the Everlasting magic in many powerful ways, a truly special sorceress of her generation. Not as good as your Aunt Rayne of course, who did actually pledge to be Gifted but your mother was powerful."

Dana and Oren continued eating but looked on in keen interest, Dana more so than Oren who feigned indifference as usual.

"She loved to ride horses; she loved to read and had the most beautiful singing voice. She once performed at the Royal Music Hall in Tirnum in honour of your father's thirtieth birthday."

"Above all, Rowan was kind and honest as well as beautiful and the kingdom loved her. She was an asset to her family and to her husband and I hope that one day you will lead by her example."

When Trista didn't reply, Lamya tilt her head to the side contemplatively and asked,

"What do you know of your father?"

Trista was immediately attentive to Lamya's words. It wasn't that she cared more about her father, but she knew in her heart that she would meet Rowan someday; that she was alive somewhere.

Alexander was someone she could never touch or talk to and she craved him more, she supposed because she knew she could never have him.

"Mostly what Gorn told us about him being a great warrior and a just ruler." Lamya smiled,

"Well that much is definitely true, but what I can tell you is that your father was a lot like Lord Antos over there."

Everyone looked to Oren whose eyes widened,

"How do you mean?" Dana said with a giggle that Oren didn't find amusing,

"Alexander was confident, his enemies would say arrogant at times. He was aloof, guarded to those he didn't trust but above all very intelligent. He saw everything and everyone around him and commanded respect from every single person that was in his presence without even being vocal."

Oren scoffed and turned back to his food but he didn't look as offended anymore.

"Trista, your father was…magnetic; a true prince of Mortania and I believe you have a lot of those qualities in you."

It was Trista's turn to scoff as she poured herself some tea,

"Me, magnetic…I don't think so."

"I do think so…you're very special. When you discover that, I hope I'm there to see it." Trista smiled appreciatively but as they turned back to eating, Dana looked on curiously,

"Their cousins told us that Trista is a Maker…do you know what that is, Lamya?" Dana asked innocently but Lamya's eyes widened in wonder.

"How can that be?"

Trista explained what had happened to her at Gorn's house and Oren told her what happened while they were training,

"This is extraordinary Trista; we have to do some more research when we get to Thelm!"

"Will there be someone there who can explain more about it?"

"Most definitely! I haven't done much research on Makers but I know it is an important topic among my people who want to understand more about it. My grandmother is Chief Justice of the Lithanian Council, I'm sure she'll know of someone who can help us. Maybe even your own grandmother might know something when we finally get to her."

"What?" Oren winced as the girls chorused their confusion and Lamya looked at each of them in turn, not sure what had changed the mood.

"Your grandmother, you do know she's alive…don't you?"

"She does now," Oren mumbled, placing his cutlery down on his plate as he took a steadying breath, knowing Trista was going to explode.

"You knew, you knew and didn't tell me!"

"It would've distracted you from your training, you saw how excited you got when you found out about Naima and Nyron."

"And that gives you the right to keep things from me? I have family, living family; a connection to my past!" Oren didn't even look sorry,

"That stuff will come later, training and getting you ready to beat Briseis is more important right now." Trista couldn't believe what she was hearing.

"That *stuff* is my *life*, Oren! That stuff means something to me even if it doesn't to you because you had a loving family growing up; I didn't!"

Oren for once had the sense not to say anything.

"My parents loved me but only so far as was appropriate in Remoran society. Just because you had a father and cousins and uncles; how dare you take that possibility away from me?" she screamed at him but he didn't even flinch.

Trista threw her napkin on the table and marched out of the dining cabin, back to their room. The captain and his officers didn't lift their heads once at the entire exchange.

Dana turned to Oren with an intense look of disapproval,

"When she realises it was for her own good, she'll thank me."

He said stubbornly but Dana rose from her seat and looked down at him disgustedly,

"Don't count on it," before she went after Trista.

Trista slumped herself on Oren's bunk - it was too much effort to climb onto her own - and screamed into his feather pillow. It didn't help that it smelled like him but she wasn't going to dwell on that.

It wasn't until her cabin door opened and she sat up to see who it was, that her arm suddenly screamed in pain. Her face was still bruised from her attack the night before, her lip split but healing well enough. The arrow wound she'd suffered when leaving Priya was definitely better but still caused her pain every now and then. She would have to learn to fight through that pain once Oren started her training again.

"Your arm?" Dana asked, closing the door and coming to sit on the bed beside her.

Trista nodded as Dana peered under the bandage she'd previously put there. Trista was in her training gear, ready to train with Oren after breakfast so her tunic was sleeveless.

"I'll get some more salve for it," Dana offered and left her momentarily to get it from her room; when she returned, Lamya was with her.

"I'm not apologising for yelling at him," Trista snapped but Lamya only shook her head.

"I wouldn't expect you to. Lord Antos was wrong for not telling you about your family…so I will."

Lamya took a seat at the desk while Dana rubbed her salve into Trista's arm; and went into a tale of the Antonides family.

Her father's mother, Dowager Queen Freilyn Antonides was very much alive and lived on an estate on the coast of Tirnum.

She'd moved there long before the rebellion after her husband King Kriston had passed, but when her son was slain; she barricaded herself inside the estate walls and refused to leave.

For years, Curian attempted to flush her out, kill what he thought was the last of a dynasty, after Rowan and her child that he still couldn't find.

Almost ten years went by, with somehow Freilyn surviving on her estate when she sent a letter to Curian inviting him to her home.

When he left, the new king declared that the old woman was to never be harmed and that she would be catered to by the crown until her dying day. She'd been there ever since.

"Your father also has a first cousin," Lamya continued as Dana redressed Trista's arm. "Her name is Alexia Sentine and she is a good friend of mine; I was with her in Thea's Point before I came to meet you. She has twin daughters, Deena and Nesta, who are a few years older than you. Her husband Elijah was killed in the battle alongside your father and uncles."

"Uncles?" Dana patted her arm gently as she finished.

"Yes, your father like your mother had two siblings; brothers named Justin and Brennan…they also passed during the battle." Lamya asked the last part regrettably.

Once Dana had finished bandaging her arm, Trista took a deep breath and turned to Lamya.

"So many of my family have died for this…for the Everlasting and the throne and I don't even think I deserve it." Lamya shook her head,

"It's not a question of deserving; the throne is yours whether you want it or not but you should want it Trista. You should want it to claim back the family that you lost."

"I don't know if I'm good enough Lamya!" Trista snapped suddenly. "I've had my visions and training and history lessons and even small memories coming back, but in the back of my mind; it's all not enough!"

Trista stood from the bed now, angry at everything that had been taken from her before she even knew she had it.

"I wasn't raised like Oren or Naima and Nyron. I wasn't cut from the same cloth as them to be able to do all that needs to be done and I'm scared!" Trista was crying now,

"I'm scared that this will have all been for nothing; that my father and Gorn and even Rayne; Gods know where she is, have all died for absolutely nothing and I won't be able to make it right!"

"You will!"

"You don't know that, no one knows that! They want it to be true but I've got a trained fighter out there who doesn't believe in me and everyone else who believes in me too much!"

"If the ones who do believe in you are the majority, why bother with what Oren thinks?"

"He knew them that's why!" Trista exploded at them, tears streaming down her face, "He knows our ways, our people; he *is* me. He's the only person I'm close enough to who can help me understand who I really am, and if he doesn't believe I can do it then why bother!"

"Because I do believe you can do it."

Trista jumped at the sound of Oren's voice and all eyes turned to him as he opened the door fully and looked directly over at Trista.

"Get out Oren!" she screamed at him, embarrassed that he had heard how much she wanted him to approve of her.

She took two steps toward him before she lunged at him with her power but even as the pulse of energy hit him and he stumbled backward, he straightened and looked directly at her.

"Dana...we should go."

Lamya and Dana exited quickly and quietly, leaving the two of them alone in the small space, the door now closed.

Trista angrily wiped the tears from her face and pushed at him again with her power and once again; he didn't allow it to deter him.

"I want you to leave Oren…now!"

"If you wanted to hurt me, you could. Just let me explain."

"I don't want to hear anything you have to say!"

As the last word left her mouth, Trista's entire body erupted into blue flame knocking Oren harshly against the door and sliding down onto the floor on his backside.

Everything that wasn't bolted to the floor went flying in each direction of the small cabin, pressing at the wooden walls until the beam that held the bunks apart cracked,

"Trista, stop!" Oren yelled over the hum of the power in such a confined space as he shielded his eyes from the glare of it and tried to stand up.

Her power felt like the gravity had intensified and was pressing down on him; keeping him stuck to the floor.

"Trista! Stop!" Oren yelled again but she refused to listen, bearing down on him further, her eyes filled with flame as she directed her power and anger at him.

She didn't even understand what she was trying to do to him, she just knew that she would crack this entire ship in two if he didn't leave.

"TRISTA ENOUGH!"

Oren reached his palm out toward her, his arm suddenly engulfed in teal coloured flame that streamed out at her; knocking her back against the bunks and completely dousing her own flames.

Oren's flames disappeared as quickly as they had come, as Trista collapsed onto her hands and knees trying to catch her breath, feeling like she was choking.

"What did…what did you…you do?"

"It d-doesn't matter," he stammered as he finally got to his feet and slowly made his way to her. He tried to help her up, but she snapped viciously at him,

"Don't touch me!"

She could barely catch her breath, but she had enough to make sure he knew she wasn't okay with him still being here. She got to her feet, clutching her chest. He reached out to help her again, even as exhausted as he looked from whatever magic he had used to stop her.

"Let go of me!" her words were clearer now as her breath evened out but still, he wouldn't let go of her,

"No, I won't let go. I'm here to protect you!"

"Protect me from what, *you*?"

"Of course, not me," he said in horror. "I could *never* hurt you."

She made the mistake of looking into his face just as he said it, because what she saw there was too intense...too honest.

"How can you say that when you hurt me all the time by lying to me?"

"I don't lie to you Trista,"

"You don't tell me the truth either!" she continued to scream at him, fuelled by her rage.

"You keep everything from me. You didn't want to tell me about Nyron and Naima, you didn't tell me about my grandmother or my possibly being a Master. You don't even tell me about our people, *my* people. How am I supposed to trust you if you don't tell me basic things?"

"Of course you can trust me!" his grip on her tightened but as much as she felt it, it didn't register in the way it usually did. She hated him in this moment and wanted him gone. Her heart was beating too fast; her traitorous heart was thumping inside her chest at his being so close and looking so beautiful. Trista yanked herself away from him and this time he let her go and she knew he had indeed let her walk away from him. He could have held her there for eternity if he wanted to.

"Oren just leave…please," she begged him. She needed him to leave her alone so she could cry, so that she could hate him without wanting him at the same time.

"I'll leave Princess…but know this," she stilled, waiting to hear what he was going to say and she hated herself for it.

"I've waited most of my life for you; for the…idea of you that was built up by everyone around me who invested their dreams and survival in your name." He took a moment,

"It never occurred to me that you wouldn't have any idea about who you were and when I realised that…it angered me. I was angry that the same people who had put their faith in you, hadn't done enough to educate you. Instead of understanding that…I got angry at you, angry that you weren't as…ready as I was and for that…I'm sorry."

Trista didn't turn to face him; she didn't know what she would have said if she did.

"I said to you before that I would train you because my father wished it, but I'm training you now because I want to…because I believe in your abilities and your strength. I believe in the Queen that you'll become."

The feeling in her belly began to pulsate so hard that she had to grab her stomach. She wanted to go to him, to forgive him for making her feel so terrible about herself but something stopped her, pride stopped her.

"The Gods were right in their choice for us. I didn't want to admit that, but I can't fight it anymore…I don't *want* to fight it anymore."

The feeling slammed into the front of her stomach like a punch that had her ball over to stop from crying out. When she finally found the strength to turn to Oren, it disappeared, and he was gone.

Outside, Lamya looked intently toward the door of Oren and Trista's cabin,

"Interesting," she muttered

"What's interesting?" Dana looked up from the book she was reading and Lamya turned to her and smiled,

"The world and its many emotions, sweet girl."

Dana closed the book and looked at Lamya thoughtfully,

"What exactly can an Empath do? I mean, we know you're shielding us from these crewmen asking questions and surely that must take a lot of power?"

"An immense amount of power Dana, but I don't have to do it often. An Empath has many skills but they all rely on the feelings and emotions of others. For those that have trained extensively like I have, there are other gifts that are achievable."

"Such as?"

"Well, a standard Empath can read emotions, feelings etc. that can let you know if someone is lying for example. We can influence the thoughts of others to make them think things we want them to or choose paths we wish them to take to further our aims." Dana was impressed.

"A much more powerful Empath, like myself, can actually manipulate that power into actions or a complete covering of the mind...as I'm doing now."

"Rayne told Trista about something like that called Compulsion," Lamya nodded,

"Exactly, much like that." Lamya was impressed,

"Isn't that bad; making people do things against their will?"

"It can be, yes. Throughout our history there have been many Empaths who have abused their powers to make people kill or do other unscrupulous things without necessary provocation, but they have always been dealt with. The Council and I strive to uphold the reputation of our members and our race, but there is only so much we can do. People will do what they wish in the end."

Dana nodded her understanding but Lamya still looked at her with questioning eyes. The crew busied themselves around them, seemingly oblivious to the two women speaking quietly amongst themselves. The morning air was crisp as they headed north but all in all it was a beautiful day.

"You feel guilty…why?" Dana chuckled,

"Can't you tell?"

"I'd rather you shared it with me instead."

Dana smiled sweetly before losing her smile and looking speculatively,

"I feel guilty that I don't miss my family. I mean, I miss them because I haven't seen them in so long but not because I wish to return to them. I'm…" she was pensive for a moment, trying to find the right words.

"You're having fun?" Dana looked at her embarrassed but also relieved,

"Yes! I know how Trista feels and what she's going through but I'm enjoying learning and being a part of something!"

It was clear Dana had had this on her mind for a long time,

"I was nobody in Remora and now I'm somebody, somebody who can make a difference and heal people."

"There is nothing wrong with wanting better things for yourself, Dana. Trista has her burdens to bear but you are here with her through all of it and you deserve your own happiness too."

Dana tucked a strand of her now growing brown hair behind her ears as she blushed,

"Thank you, Lamya." Lamya smiled back at her just as Oren appeared from within the cabin. When he saw them, he immediately turned away and went to look out onto the water; not inviting discussion from either of them.

"It's going to be a long trip," Lamya said gently. "Why don't you show me what medicines you've learned."

THE SIX

Since their dinner in the Great Hall, Lyon had not laid eyes on the enigmatic princess again, but he was anxious to learn so much more about her.

In the short time, they had spent together; he had discovered things about the young royal that intrigued him. She was highly intelligent, clever, blunt and dismissive and entirely too bloodthirsty for his liking.

Still, there was something about her that resonated with him on a personal level and he couldn't help but want to learn more about the young woman who had grown men quivering with fear.

He saw that General Gardan both respected and feared her, as did the other men who were her close personal guard. People who entered the Great Hall bowed as was appropriate but made sure not to hold eye contact with her. They scurried to be away from her and even when her attention wasn't on them; they didn't give any cause for that to change.

There was a tension in the room the whole night that was palpable, so thick you could almost taste it; even as the princess engaged him in conversation and laughed at his terrible jokes.

He was not under the impression that she found him funny in the slightest, but she wanted something from him and if stroking his ego was the way to do it, then he knew that she would.

She'd been delighted at the tithe of soldiers he'd brought to the capital and told him as much.

"You have done well Baron, much better than a lot of the other lords you see around here." She gestured lazily to the open room and he was inclined to agree. He knew from Aml that many of the other more influential barons had yet to give the satisfactory numbers.

"Thank you, your highness, I merely wish to play my part."

"As you did in the last war," he nodded. "The last war for which you were not justly compensated. What was it...the failing efforts of a small few?"

She recited the words of his letter back to him and swallowing, suddenly unsure of the direction of the conversation; Lyon simply nodded.

Briseis stared at him then, stared directly into his eyes and ultimately to his soul. She stared so hard, he had to look away for a moment but when he looked back at her, she was still staring.

The smile that appeared on her face was feline, predatory before she finally tore them away from him to take a sip from her cup of wine.

"We will have many adventures you and I," she said more to herself than him and so he had said nothing. The princess didn't speak to him again for the rest of the meal.

Lyon had gone to bed more than a little annoyed. He had been disrespected by the princess on more than one occasion and as he had so much to learn about the politics of the capital, he had to bide his time before he made any real moves.

He awoke the following morning in his chamber, adjacent to Geneiva's.

He had visited her after the meal but after performing his marital duty on her less than appealing body, he'd gone on a hunt for the suppler delights of Alaina.

The young girl lay beside him now, asleep and as he looked at her, he noticed something that he had not been conscious of the night before. Immediately, he shook her awake. The girl looked bewildered for a moment as her eyes widened,

"What is this?" he asked pointing at her bare stomach... her slightly plump bare stomach.

"N-nothing Lord," she stammered, sitting up in the large bed and backing away from him. She didn't back further enough away as he reached out and backhanded her right across her face.

"Don't you dare lie to me girl," he hissed at her as tears escaped her eyes, but she said nothing.

"I-I am w-with child Lord," she mumbled just before he hit her again. This time she cried out as her lip split,

"HOW DARE YOU!" he thundered causing her to back away so far that she fell off the side of the bed completely. She scrambled to the corner and instinctively lifted her hands to cover her face.

Lyon dived over the edge of the bed, grabbed a hold of her hair and dragged her out of the corner. He curled her long hair into his left fist and punched her directly in the gut with his right one. Alaina grunted as he winded her, her legs curling up into herself as her head was held back by her hair

"Get rid of it!" he shouted again before releasing her hair and kicking her in her stomach as she hit the floor. "GET RID OF IT NOW!"

Lyon kicked her again and just as he raised his foot to repeat the action, the door opened,

"Lord!"

Lyon turned to Aml with eyes ablaze with anger but the man just stared on in horror. His chest was tight with rage as he looked down to the girl at his feet.

"What is it!" Lyon bellowed making Aml jump out of his trance and turn to his master,

"The princess…she is to ride to the Imperial Lands this morning. She has asked you to accompany her."

Lyon looked away from the blubbering girl on the floor at his feet, blood now flowing from between her legs,

"Well…we shouldn't keep her highness waiting," he said and walked away from the girl without a backwards glance into the adjoining privy.

Aml took quick steps to where Alaina lay on the floor, bleeding out, looking faint as she did so but did not make a sound.

She'd been so battered and abused, she knew to make any sound would bring more punishment,

"Flynn!" Aml called out and almost immediately a young man entered the room.

"Yes Senior?" Flynn, a young man newly appointed to the baron's service laid eyes on Alaina and gasped, "Gods above!"

"The Baron will be exiting the privy momentarily; he will be riding with her highness this morning to the Imperial Lands."

Flynn nodded although he couldn't take his eyes away from the beaten girl,

"Quickly man!" Aml ordered and Flynn went to get the baron's things together.

Aml ripped the sheets from the bed and carefully wrapped it around Alaina's legs before gently lifting her into his arms and heading to the baron's chamber door. Two guards stood there, careful not to look in his direction.

"Have someone come and clean this place up," he said as he passed them. "The Baron will want no trace of it."

The two men nodded before one took off to find a maid,

"Which way to the Infirmary?" the other guard told him and quickly, Aml made his way there with a bleeding girl in his arms.

Lyon Dreston was dressed in his finest and warmest furs and leathers later that morning as he prepared to meet with the princess. The air was brisk so early in the morning and where he had been prepared for it once they'd entered Thea's Point and then the capital, nothing could compare to the frosty wilderness of the Imperial Lands.

He'd made his way to the courtyard to retrieve his horse with one of his aids as Aml was off somewhere arranging Gods knew what, but by the time they reached the gates of the city, he had arrived; ready to meet the princess by his side.

Erik and Geneiva had remained behind of course, Erik to infiltrate the lesser lords and nobleman scattered about court to find out their true intentions and report back to him.

Briseis was at the castle gates with General Beardmore and she looked as magnificent as ever atop her white mare dressed entirely in white.

She had a white fur hat that allowed her pale white hair to frame her beautiful face. He could not see what she wore underneath, but she was covered in a white fur cloak that covered the rump of her horse and clasped together at her neck by a bright red gemstone. White leather gloves were on her delicate hands and high riding boots were on her feet.

Her resident guard dog, General Beardmore was on the horse beside her, talking animatedly to the soldier beside him. Lyon could tell that he would have a hard time getting through to the princess if her minder were constantly in the way.

"Baron Dreston, you made it!" Briseis called out as they approached her line of vision. He bowed his head respectfully.

"I hadn't thought early rising would be your thing." Lyon dismissed her subtle attempt to mock him and smiled,

"If it is worth my time, I am known to rise for many an occasion." Briseis raised a perfectly plucked eyebrow and stared across at him,

"It's delightful to know that you deem me worthy of your time Baron…isn't it delightful Gardan?" she added quietly.

"Absolutely your highness," Beardmore replied noncommittedly, and Lyon was irked as he knew somehow that he had lost some potentially high ground,

"I am but a meagre servant in your presence, your highness. You are undoubtedly worthy of everyone's time without question." Briseis didn't turn to look at him when she said,

"It's frightfully uncomfortable up here," Briseis remarked, causing Lyon to tilt his head in confusion.

"Your highness?"

"With your head so far up my ass," Briseis turned her eyes to him before turning them back to the gates that had suddenly began to open and when they were wide enough for her to get through, she set off.

General Beardmore signalled to the few men that were with them and set out after her. Lyon and Aml had no choice but to follow. The clamour of hooves departing the castle courtyard snapped Lyon out of his bewilderment, as well as Aml appearing by his side,

"Lord, we must stay close to the princess." Lyon knew the truth of it.

This was a test of some kind and he'd be damned if he failed it. So, with an irritated grimace, he kicked his horse in motion and flew out of the castle gates.

The journey from Tirnum to the Imperial Lands was a short one, much shorter than from Tirnum to Thea's Point and so they caught up with the princess within twenty minutes, galloping through the deserted land. The princess and her general had stopped just on the edge of the Imperial Lands. Far out, he could see the making of tents.

Briseis and the general had dismounted by the time they arrived and were watering their horses from a water skin. Briseis absentmindedly stroked her horse, a move that even though seeing it for the first time; seemed completely out of place. That she could behave so tenderly towards something seemed, odd.

"You managed to keep up I see," she acknowledged, allowing him to enter her presence by addressing him.

"You are an excellent rider, your highness," he chose not to answer her question.

"I have an excellent mount," she said it so matter-of-factly, it broached no further conversation.

So, she loved her horse.

"We are close to our destination?" he enquired just as the General took the skin from the princess' horse and gave it to his own.

"Soon…what I have to show you will be worth the wait." Lyon nodded appreciatively as Aml stopped a few metres away from them.

"We are on the border of what was once the most desired and fertile land in all Mortania." The princess continued, "That ruin was the residence of the last General of the royal army…before it was destroyed during the war."

"I visited the place only once before, a General Antos if I remember correctly." Briseis nodded her head briefly.

There had been, of course, many other establishments in the space they now occupied but they had since been torn down, burned, whichever was appropriate at the time. The

General's Mansion however had seemed too significant to completely abolish. There was something about its presence here that was a gentle reminder of what had once stood, and what had now been eradicated. The princess said as much,

"Whenever we approach these lands, I remind myself of how mighty a general and by consequence a nation, was brought down by my father and his armies."

She turned her ice grey eyes onto him and Gods forgive him; Lyon shuddered. There was something about that look that was entirely too calculated.

What was even more disconcerting, he knew it was a look he had given on more than one occasion

"Armies that you helped man, as you are doing now."

"I am but a servant to the crown, your highness," he said as humbly as he could.

She turned her attention back to the open space where hundreds of tents were being raised before getting into the saddle again. The largest tents he assumed housed her and her father and their belongings, but the rest were of the simple kind, housing the soldiers who would truly fight.

There was smoke, billowing into the sky from the campfires used for warmth as well as cooking and the constant movement of people, from here looked like ants in a colony. There were horses and logs of wood piled all over the place, as wagons travelled in and out of the trailed road with more provisions and materials to build their military base.

"I wonder...what do you wish to achieve by your continued support in this war Baron?"

Lyon saw General Beardmore lift his eyes in their direction before swiftly turning them away again and mounting his horse; signalling subtly to the guards around them that they would be ready to depart momentarily.

Lyon looked back at the princess; her eyes boring into him and for a split second he saw two flames billow in the depths of her irises. He blinked, losing the connection with her and cleared his throat,

"I merely wish to provide the necessary support to make sure the rightful ruler sits on the throne."

He wasn't lying, he was that ruler and he'd do anything to get himself on that coveted seat.

Briseis laughed,

"I'm sure you do."

With no warning, Briseis set off again towards the castle ruins but away from the war camp. Once he'd set off after her, they passed the camp completely and arrived into a secluded area with one solitary tent in the middle of the snowy clearing. Snow covered trees rose up all around them, closing them off from the rest of the army.

When she brought her horse to a neat stop, Briseis turned to eye the pompous, slimy and completely transparent excuse of a man beside her and felt repulsed.

If not for his contribution to her army she would have killed him the moment he'd arrived in the capital. His attitude, his sense of entitlement, his kiss ass behaviour all made her want to rip his skin clean from his bones. She hated everything about him, especially the way he thought he was smarter than her and could out do her.

As soon as she exhausted his uses, she would kill him; of that she was certain. She'd brought him here to show him the force of her army and the Six as a courtesy, as well as a warning that she was not to be underestimated. She wasn't a fool; she knew there were men twice her age with the experience to match who thought her juvenile despite their fear of her. Baron

Dreston was one of these men and to make matters worse, he was a lecherous little thing.

She'd seen the way he'd looked at her in the Great Hall as though he would gladly rip her dress off right then and there. Not in this or any lifetime, she thought to herself. She understood men like him, what they wanted and how they got it, usually by taking it by force and the fact that he couldn't with her would ultimately be a challenge in his eyes. Give him enough rope to hang himself and she knew the Baron would proposition her, but she would sooner die then give her maidenhead to that disgusting little weasel.

It had shocked the few who knew of her innocence but Briseis didn't care. Her body was her power along with her physical prowess, and she wouldn't give that up to some lesser man who would be able to claim the title as the one who'd deflowered the terrifying princess. Once she let a man inside her, all men would feel she could be won over with a promise of what was between their legs.

Yes, one day she would marry and produce an heir, but it was so far down on her list of important things, it didn't bode thinking about. She might choose to indulge in the pleasures of the flesh; but until she found a man that was worthy of her, that wouldn't be any time soon.

As she thought it, Gardan rode up beside her and her heart beat just that little bit faster.

"Sixteen thousand men, including your own of course."

"Against how many?" the baron asked.

Good question

"Unfortunately, that's the problem…we don't know. The opposing army is somewhat of a mystery."

"How can you expect to fight an army you've yet to see?"

Briseis turned to him with a smug smirk before kicking her horse into a trot, urging the Baron to follow. Gardan stayed behind so the Baron's manservant followed suit, leaving the two of them alone.

Briseis brought her horse to a stop and dismounted, the baron following her actions before watching her plant her feet firmly on the ground and call out

"Six!"

As the word left her mouth the princess ignited into grey flames, making Lyon jump back in fear, lose his footing and fall to the hard, cold ground. He instinctively shielded his face from the flames before realising they were nowhere near him. He peered from behind his arm in astonishment as the sounds of boots on trampled ground echoed around them in the open space.

The tent flap opened, and six young people rushed out.

From nowhere, Lyon watched as Briseis conjured a ball of fire in her hand and launched it at the teenagers. The ball disintegrated in the air before reaching them; something he realised that they must have done.

The six youths charged at the princess, firing their own fireballs which she deflected and attacked with her own energy blasts.

The seven of them engaged in a small though impressive battle, the likes of which Lyon had never seen. Even during the civil war, he had remained away from the heart of battle. Just because he could wield a sword, it didn't mean he had to. His prowess was better served in audience chambers.

The seven teenagers, the princess included, were truly a force to be reckoned with as the earth rumbled beneath their feet. Colourful flame flew everywhere, as they attacked and defended where necessary, against the attack from their opponent.

Even with six on one, the princess didn't seem to be faltering, until a boy, the tallest of the group planted his feet and roared, before a stream of fiery orange flame poured out of him and knocked the princess clear across the snow-covered ground.

Briseis crashed into one of the flat rocks that surrounded their encampment and it splintered. She shook off her daze, barely phased by her collision as she raised her legs and flipped them forward to land firmly on her feet.

She reached her arm out and from the scabbard on her horse, her sword flew into her waiting hand. No sooner had it landed there she threw it at a protruding boulder a few metres from the teenagers. The sword embedded firmly into the rock and Briseis darted towards it in three, clearly magically assisted strides and used the exposed hilt of the sword to propel her further into the air.

Briseis was now above them before she crossed her arms across her chest and sent a blast of pure energy down onto the teenagers.

All six of them raised their arms at exactly the right second and where Briseis' blast bore down on them, they deflected with power of their own.

Lyon watched in both fear and amazement as the six people were pressed into the ground; snow and dirt and buried root cracking all around them as the princess; still airborne pushed down onto them.

It was as though Briseis was resting on the energy she was pushing down, the force so strong it was like she was balancing on top of it.

The six teenagers had seemed to create an orb shaped shield, because the power Briseis was streaming was flowing around it. There was a distinct crack in the floor where their barrier stopped but even from where he stood, Lyon could see the group were faltering. It wasn't until one of the young women finally raised her arm into a punching motion, that there was a thunderous crack as the two powers connected, knocking Briseis out the sky.

The princess crashed to the ground, her white garments sullied immediately, and her power disappeared as the six of them extinguished their shield and approached her; bowing as they eyed her on the floor but not moving to help her up.

Slowly, the princess did just that and when she threw her head back, Lyon could see there was a cut on the side of her face. She raised her fingers to it and saw the blood but only laughed,

"Come Baron," the princess got to her feet, "Come see your salvation!"

Lyon didn't think twice to obey and rushed over to where she stood. When he got to her, he felt a thickness in the air that he realised immediately to be their power.

It pulsated in the area around them, a physical thing that slowly died away.

General Beardmore and Aml suddenly joined them and the eight of them stood deathly quietly as Briseis brushed the dirt off her arms and legs.

"These six incredible humans are my Six; an elite fighting force that I have been training to help defeat the Samaian army…however many that might be."

Lyon couldn't deny that he was impressed. This was power like he had never seen. Even during the rebellion, he didn't see what the Samaians were capable of on the battlefield.

"What you saw here today was but a small dose of what they will be capable of by the time the war begins."

"They...you...are truly magnificent."

Lyon was lost for words as he stared at the teenagers before him, four boys and two girls who looked no more than eighteen; he couldn't really tell.

"What will they do once the war is won? Surely all this power must not go to waste?" he eyed them up, thoughtful of their affiliation to Briseis.

Could these young people be swayed to his side with the right incentive? Who was to know until he tried?

"When I take my father's throne they will smite my enemies and fight my wars and one day, when I am done ruling and fighting and my son or daughter takes the throne, they will defend any who would wish to take it from them as well."

Lyon felt her eyes on him before he turned to look at her and when he did, he made sure to keep his face neutral. When he finally looked over at her, once again that predatory look was on her face and instantly, Lyon knew that she was on to him.

He didn't know how she knew but somehow, Briseis knew that he wanted her crown, and just, so he could remain alive long enough to even try to take it, he smiled graciously and said,

"May the pain of a thousand deaths befall whoever would try." and bowed.

WORDS LEFT UNSAID

Confined to such a small area, with only themselves to talk to and two of their group not speaking to each other, made for a difficult journey ahead for Trista and her friends.

The first and second day after their fight, while Trista continued her training with Oren without argument, it was strained. Her anger helped her determination to beat him and show him she could handle anything he dished out, but it made for an uncomfortable environment for Dana and Lamya.

While the Samaians trained, Dana and Lamya spent their time together; reading and learning. Dana was becoming quite skilled with her medicines and salves and Lamya praised her commitment to learning as well as her speed.

"You could join the Council one day if you wish," she commented while they read and discussed the various uses of nightshade one afternoon. Oren and Trista were training on the deck a few metres away, and the two women spoke under the afternoon sun.

The heat of the south was slowly fading away and instead, the days and nights were crisper and they each wore more layers. Lamya had explained to them that Thea's Point was completely cold and she heard that further north was already covered in snow.

For Trista and Dana who had grown up in the Remoran mountains, the cold was nothing new, but Lamya had told them to be prepared for the worst; the closer they got to The Wide, the colder it would become.

"It's not unheard of for other races to join and even take quite senior positions," Lamya was saying and Dana was intrigued.

"Really…you think I'm good enough?"

"Yes, you pick up things very quickly. They're always in the need for healers and medical apprentices. I think you would be a most welcome addition to the school."

"I'll definitely think about it, I mean…Trista won't need me once she's queen."

Lamya's eyebrows raised to her hair line in surprise,

"What on earth do you mean?" Dana shrugged shyly, turning her eyes to the book in front of her even though it was closed.

"What could she possibly want with someone from her past…her painful past from what I've now learned." Dana hung her head solemnly, "I never knew she felt so…alone."

Lamya felt her guilt and took her hand,

"You can't blame yourself for that Dana. Trista's experiences were her own, you didn't do anything to hurt her."

"I didn't stop others from hurting either," Dana admitted. "I was there when they excluded her from our conversations and didn't invite her to birthday parties, but I still went to those parties. I still did enough so that I wouldn't be cast out too. What kind of a friend does that make me?"

Lamya could see as well as sense the guilt that riddled through Dana and she knew there wasn't much she could do about it. Her heart went out to the young woman,

"There isn't much I can say that will change how you feel Dana but you're here now; by her side through all of this."

Dana nodded, logic winning out over her emotions before she looked across the deck to where Trista and Oren were going through hand-to-hand combat training.

Oren was throwing punches and jabs at her while Trista had to continuously block or deflect them. It was difficult to keep up as they were moved so fast; it was an incredible sight to see.

"I know you're right, it's just…the closer we get to Tirnum, the more she learns…"

Dana didn't take her eyes off Trista as the young princess held her guard up against Oren.

"I'm worried she won't need me anymore."

Dana turned to Lamya, her eyes wide with the effort it was taking her not to cry. "She's a Princess, soon to be a Queen and I'm…"

"Her best friend," Lamya added gently. "A woman always needs her best friend Dana. Whenever being queen, or a wife or mother, or even a beacon of hope for thousands of people gets too hard, she'll need you."

"You think so?" Dana asked hopefully as she wiped a betraying tear from her cheek.

"She'll need the person who knew and loved her before she became all those things, someone to keep her grounded."

And so Lamya fell into the role of confidant and teacher, teaching both girls what they needed and wished to know.

In the day, she sat with Dana learning about and mixing various ingredients to perfect the uses for which she needed them. In the evenings, she told Trista of her history, of her father and his family and of the Illiya family who ruled a large part of the southern pastures. She learned Samaian customs and rules and general way of life.

Through Lamya, the girls learned about themselves in ways that had previously been restricted. They blossomed into woman that were not only beautiful and smart, but confident and special in the gifts they put out into the world.

That night while they eat dinner once again, hidden from the crew by Lamya's abilities, Lamya asked Trista about Avriel.

They would be arriving in Drem the following morning and all were anxious to get off the ship and continue the journey to Thelm.

"Avriel?" Trista asked as she chewed some salmon, "What about her?"

"Well, how did she treat you growing up?"

"Fine I guess. She's married to the town leader; I only ever saw her when my father was around. She only really spoke to me after I got enga—"

Trista's eyes shot up and looked directly at Oren who looked right back; expectantly waiting for the rest of her sentence. Trista's face heated up as she looked down back at her plate,

"After you what?" Lamya asked. Trista cleared her throat and put on a quick smile.

"After I got engaged to her son," Trista answered softly.

"You're engaged?" Lamya was shocked as she looked at Dana for confirmation. Dana who sent her a small smile but didn't say anything.

"Yes…well, I mean I was when I left Remora but that was of course before…everything."

Trista tried not to look up at Oren but he had resumed eating and didn't seem to be bothered by her little revelation.

Wishful thinking, she realised but since their argument and his subsequent apology there had been a calm storm brewing between them.

They didn't speak much when they trained but there was an energy between them that couldn't be ignored. His movements, his power, his body, she felt it all as they trained and felt closer to him for it in a way she couldn't explain. When his hands clasped hers to make sure she was holding her weapons right or securing her various items of armour onto her body or holding her thighs to make sure her feet were in the right stance. Every touch, brief or lingered, she felt it everywhere.

The last two nights in their cabin had been hell, being so close to him and knowing she wanted something a lot more physical out of their situation than she was entirely ready for.

Sure, she liked him, but she was in fact a virgin and other than her kiss with Thorn, had never done anything remotely sexual. She knew what sex involved, she wasn't stupid, but as much as her body seemed to want it, she didn't know if her mind was ready for it.

Despite everything she was feeling, Oren was completely neutral to her so it was no use torturing herself over something that would never happen.

"Will you marry him once the war is over?"

The dreaded question that hadn't left her mind since she'd left Remora and knew what her journey would involve. Trista looked over at Oren who continued to eat his meal, paying her no mind.

"I don't...I don't know," Trista pushed her plate away, stepped away from the table to march out the door and to her cabin.

Trista lay in bed but was wide awake when Oren finally came into their room that night.

She lay with her back to him and listened to the sounds of him using the small wash bowl they had, then taking off his shirt and pants. She tried not to let the image of him topless come into her mind but it was futile and she was imagining the ripples in his biceps and down his back and the glorious tattoos that decorated his arm.

She thought of his beautiful green eyes and his thick black locks of hair and his full lips that looked so inviting.

The room suddenly went dark as he snuffed out the small candle and climbed into his bunk.

She knew he was awake for a long time, his breathing different when he was asleep, but something pushed her to ask him a question, something that might help or crush her. She turned onto her back, her hands clasped over her chest,

"Do you have someone…in Priya?"

"What do you mean?" his voice rumbled from below her. Trista swallowed, terrified to push this but knowing in some way that she must, to keep from going crazy.

"Do you have someone you left behind…someone special?" There was a pregnant silence before he said,

"Tysha…her name is Tysha."

Trista didn't realise she was crying until she felt the tears escape and roll down the side of her face and onto the flats of her ears before soaking into her pillow.

"I…I hope you return safely to her."

The silence was almost chokingly thick as Trista lay there, waiting for him to respond, the last chance for her heart not to shatter in two if he responded differently.

"I hope so too."

"Well…goodnight."

"Goodnight Princess," Trista turned onto her side and slowly created a sound bubble around herself, blocking any sound she made from within and let herself cry for the warrior she'd never had, but somehow lost to another.

The quartet finally arrived in Drem the following morning and didn't waste time in disembarking the ship. The air was thin and icy but with no snow to be seen. They elected to wear their warmest wools rather than add to their furs. They would have to buy more once they got to Thelm of course, but for now they were fine with what they had.

Once the ship docked, the four of them were packed and ready, and at Lamya's instruction they quickly walked the gangplank, finally onto dry land.

Oren held Titan by the reins, close to him and they immediately set off to find somewhere to gather their resources and of course buy three horses for the onward journey. From Drem to Thelin would take them another two days at least and they had to be prepared for whatever might befall them on the road.

For Trista and Dana, this was their first time so far away from home so was both exciting and terrifying for them.

Drem was not as big a town as Priya and their Samaian population was considerably smaller. Lamya had explained to Trista that not all inhabited areas were welcoming to outsiders whether that be Samai or anything else.

The world bustled around them as people waited to board the ship they had just disembarked. Some looked eager and excited while others looked afraid, some even curious when they laid eyes on her. Trista smiled back where it seemed warranted but was wary of the much larger men who looked at her with disgust.

She'd grown up in Remora where her peers continually left her out of their festivities, but none of the elders had ever been outright rude to her and Trista found it disconcerting. They looked at Oren with the same repulsion, but he barely seemed to notice. He walked ahead of them, his back as straight as ever; his swords across his back, uncaring who was bothered by them.

Trista looked at the activity around her and the tightly packed buildings that made up the town of Drem. Far off to the right she could see what looked to be a castle cut directly into the rock with various thatched roofed townhouses, inns and shops in the space between there and where they currently walked. Horses pulled carts and vendors yelled their wears in a din of activity that was invigorating.

Off to their left she could just make out a colossal statue, who from what she could see was Alexander Antonides, the God of Life.

"This way," Oren suddenly declared above the noise and led them deeper into the bustling town. They all saw the inn he had spotted quickly, and when he approached to negotiate their price, the man outside didn't put up too much of an argument. Whether that was because the price was fair or because Oren was so intimidating, who could know?

He returned to them and handed Dana a wooden token with a number carved into it while simultaneously showing another token with a different number in his other hand,

"Trista and I will be next door."

It didn't broach any discussion and considering how she felt the last time they had to share a room, Trista wasn't entirely happy about doing so again. Still, she said nothing; not wanting to give him the satisfaction of knowing that she didn't want to be around him or that he affected her.

"I'll get Titan settled in and meet you back here in four hours."

The girls all nodded as he handed Trista the token to their rooms and took off with his horse. Oren disappeared into the crowd and the girls disappeared into the inn to find their rooms.

It was easy enough, the inn opening up into a large open space with a bar at one end and a row of six doors at the other, all with numbers carved on the doors. The middle of the room was occupied by five large tables, placed around a roaring hearth and various stools and mismatched chairs around them.

A few eyes looked up at them when they entered and while some looked away unbothered, a few lingered appreciatively. Trista cleared her throat and approached the fifth room, corresponding with her token.

Lamya and Dana followed close behind and as they passed the hearth in the middle of the room, a whistle came from across the bar. The girls ignored it, not wanting to assume it was directed at them but when it happened again and someone called *Red*, they knew he was referring to Lamya.

They continued to ignore the whistles and cat calls until someone touched Lamya's shoulder and spun her around to face him.

"Hey Red, I'm talking to you!" the wiry looking man challenged as he looked at her, his eyes brushing briefly over the other two. Lamya shrugged her shoulder out of his grip,

"Keep your hands off me sir," the man chuckled,

"Sir? Oh, you're a high one aren't ya?" they assumed high to mean she was high born, not that it mattered. It was clear this man wanted to start trouble. Dana stepped forward,

"Leave her alone," the man turned his attention to Dana who was stood in the middle as Lamya had been bringing up the rear.

"And what are you going to do if I don't?"

Dana stepped in front of her and before anyone even registered she'd moved, she swiped her staff under his legs and sent the man crashing to the floor on his back. She stabbed the end of her staff into his chest, pressing down with her whole weight,

"Try it again and see," she warned him as he struggled to breathe. His hands gripped around the staff trying to push it away as she choked him.

"P…please!" he choked out before she finally released the pressure on him. The man spluttered as he tried to draw in breath while Dana straightened up and without a word, continued walking to the rooms. No one else said anything but Trista and Lamya smiled at one another, pride in their eyes

Once they'd unpacked, the girls met at the entrance a few moments later and headed into town. Lamya bought some books and ingredients she said was always good to have around, while Dana bought specific medicinal items she'd read about in the book Rayne had given her. They each bought new socks and hats and extra furs for the horses they would be using. They bought more food for the road, dried meats and fish; dried fruits and nuts that could be easily accessed in the saddle.

They'd done their shopping, returned to the inn to pack it all neatly for their departure when they decided to stay for a drink until Oren returned to them. The girls soon fell into an easy conversation about Lamya's travels around the world,

"You've seen a Phyn?" Dana asked astonished. While everyone knew, they existed, the sea creatures were very rarely seen. They were half human and half fish with long elegant tails of varying colours that glistened in the sunlight if one was lucky enough to see one.

"Yes, I spent some time with them while I was studying. It was a most memorable experience."

"What are they like?"

"Much like us really. They have their own language; I know a few phrases but I'm by no means fluent. They're quiet, spending most of their time in their homes underwater and are ruled by a King, Venelaus and his queen."

"Did they know my father?" Lamya nodded,

"Phyn live a lot longer than humans so King Venelaus would have known your father, grandfather and great grandfather if I'm not mistaken." The girls were amazed and impressed,

"I want to see them one day," Dana thought whimsically out loud. "I bet they're beautiful."

"They are," Lamya agreed before taking another drink of her ale.

The day wore on as they drank and talked when Trista suddenly excused herself,

"Where are you going?"

"Nowhere, I'll be back soon."

They didn't push her for a response even though it was clear they wanted to. Trista was thankful they didn't pry because she didn't really know what she would say, she just needed some time away. She left the inn and set off into Drem.

The day was relatively pleasant, and the people around didn't seem too hostile but she kept herself small anyway. She didn't want to have to get into another altercation. She was still hurting from her attack in Crol and she wasn't looking forward to taking on anyone other than Oren with her wounded arm.

Trista smiled to herself at the thought of her having battle scars. Only a month ago she would have been sitting in her room reading or sewing with her mother in the living room. She might have been running errands in the market, but she would never be nursing wounds.

She'd come so far in so short a time, but in many ways, she didn't feel any better for it.

She walked aimlessly now, looking through various shop windows and observing the people around her. Most were oblivious to who she was; not a princess or a queen but a woman who was about to alter their lives in more ways than one. It didn't matter if Samai or Man believed in her birth right, no matter who you were, she was going to affect lives.

With that depressing thought, Trista turned down a side road that looked more residential and was suddenly hit with the most nauseating feeling. Pressure pulsated at her temples, much like they had in Priya and sure enough, after a few attempts to regulate her now rapid breathing; voices erupted in her head.

"Once conscription is completed, we will have more."

"More but not able your highness. Many will be kitchen boys and the like."

"We need more able bodies Gardan!"

"I appreciate that your highness but unless we can conjure fully formed men in the next few days, there are not enough people in Mortania."

"You grow bold"

"I merely wish to be honest and serve you as best I can your highness. With the Six we have an extra advantage, but the men may not be enough, we don't know the breadth of the Samaian threat."

"That much is true...I need to find out their numbers. I need to know what we're up against and soon."

"How?"

"Who do we know in..."

The voices faded and with it, the nauseating feeling and pulsating in her head. Trista kept taking deep breaths through her nose and out through her mouth until she felt better.

She knew who she had heard of course, the same two people she'd heard before. They were trying to prepare for a threat that could be mightier than theirs. Smart, obviously but infuriating because she didn't know if she *was* mightier. The princess hadn't said how much arms she had to hand and Nyron had told Trista they had twelve thousand, but was that enough?

She would discuss what she'd heard with Oren but for right now, she just needed some peace. Away from voices in her head, and moody warriors and the pressures of her destiny.

Trista ended up at a Gods House and didn't know how she'd got there. Still, she entered the relatively small building compared to the one in Crol and said a prayer. She prayed for her parents back in Remora, for Dana and her family; for Lamya arriving to help her and of course for Oren and Gorn. She lit a candle for Gorn and with a sense of peace, made her way back towards the inn. She was almost there when something or rather someone caught her eye.

Oren was a few feet away from her, leant against the wall of a building that was so conspicuous because it was trying so hard not to be. The windows had been blacked out and the walls painted a murky shade of brown that against the vibrant colours and shutters of the shops around it, stood out like a sore thumb.

He was leant there, with a woman; a scantily dressed woman even in the chilly day time air who was nuzzling into his neck as he dropped something into her hand.

Trista tensed as she realised what was going on and a debilitating rage took over her as she marched over to him.

The moment she got near him, he turned to step into the street; the woman walking back into the establishment and when he saw her, Oren looked surprised.

"What are you doing here? I thought I told you to wait at the inn."

"What were you doing?" she didn't bother to reply she was so furious; furious because she was insanely and irrevocably jealous. Her blood felt like lava flowing through her veins.

Oren smiled guiltily, licking his lips, clearly remembering something.

"I don't think that really concerns you." He was right, it didn't but she wanted it to, desperately.

Trista clenched her fists so tight she felt her nail cut into her palm. Her hand began to feel hot as she took a step towards him.

"We're on our way to fight a war and you're here with some...some...whore!" The smile evaporated from his face as he took a step toward her, grabbing her arm,

"Keep your voice down!" he hissed at her, but she yanked her arm out of his grip.

"Don't touch me!" she snapped back, her eyes shooting hatred at him for doing this to her and not even caring, not even knowing that he was upsetting her. "So much for protecting me. Try doing it without your pants around your ankles next time!"

Trista marched away from him without a backwards glance all the way to the inn. It took all her willpower not to break down in front of Dana and Lamya once she made it back there.

"Trista?" Dana stood up from where she and Dana were still drinking at a table but she ignored her and went into her room.

She quickly wrapped a sound bubble around herself and screamed out her frustration, anger and hurt.

She hated that she felt this way, so irrational when she knew that what Oren did with other women had nothing to do with her.

He said he had Tysha back in Priya, although that hadn't stopped him being with the whore just now so maybe she didn't want someone who could do that to someone they loved.

Love didn't matter either way, she didn't love him; she didn't know him, but it hurt that he was completely oblivious to her attraction to him. So much so that he would indulge in carnal pleasures with her only metres away. It was clear, Oren had no attraction to her whatsoever and she had to deal with that no matter how humiliating it was. He was just a man, there were men everywhere and she was likely to meet one more appealing and nicer than Oren Antos.

When did being attracted to a man become so important anyway?

Trista took a deep and calming breath and dissipated her sound bubble before taking a seat on her bed, dropping to hold her head in her hands. She knew she'd overreacted just now and wasn't in the mood to explain it to the others, especially Oren.

As she sat there, two sharp raps echoed on the door and when she looked up, Oren stepped into the room.

Quickly, she stood, determined not to let him know how upset she was and steeled her eyes at him,

"What do you want?"

"We leave for Thelm tonight," he offered as he shut the door, looking over at her; his face stoic and unfeeling. "It's best to gain miles at night, less eyes will be upon us."

Fine, he wasn't going to address how angry she'd just been so she wouldn't either.

"Whose eyes?" she could be as indifferent as him, he wasn't the only one who didn't care.

Oren tilted his head to the side as he looked at her quizzically. He crossed his arms across his chest, resting his weight on his left leg and placed his right one forward.

"You really don't understand the threat you're under, do you?" Trista shrugged inflexibly,

"Why don't you explain to me then." Oren sucked his teeth,

"There are people out there who want to kill you Trista, you must know that."

"Of course, Briseis wants t—"

"No, not just Briseis! Her people, Man, the king's people, every one of them wants you dead. Didn't the attack on Priya show you that; the attack on Dreston even?"

"I'm not an idiot despite what you think!" she snapped at him then forced herself to calm down. "No one even knows we're here, what's the big deal!"

She wanted him gone and he just kept talking,

"So you think, but it never hurts to be careful? How else are you going to stay safe?"

She hated that she'd said it, but it was out there now. He had vowed to protect her on more than one occasion, but she'd accused him of not doing that because he was too busy with women. She didn't want to bring that conversation up ever again.

Oren readjusted his weight onto both feet before stepping toward her and without warning took hold of her hand. Trista's breath caught in her throat as she fought not to melt into the warmth of his touch. Her heart betrayed her as it sped up just at the feel of his hands on hers.

Oren stared his teal coloured eyes at her,

"I will always keep you safe Trista," the way he said her name made her want to whimper. The intimacy of it was so unusual, as was his touching her. He touched her all the time, but this was different, this was something he wanted to do she realised.

"I'm sorry," he murmured gently, still looking deep into her eyes but letting go of her hand..

"F-for what?"

"For…before."

She saw the faint blush on his cheeks and her heart flipped over in her chest,

"I was out of line and like you said…I should be focused on the task at hand. I was wrong and I apologise."

Okay, so it wasn't a declaration of his affections, but it was something. It was more personal than he had probably ever been with her and something in that resonated with Trista deeply.

Maybe she was too overwhelmed, maybe she was outright stupid but without thinking, Trista reached out and wrapped her arms around his neck, hugging him tightly; breathing in his wonderful scent.

The feel of his hair against her face, the feel of him in her arms was so wonderful, she felt almost giddy with it. She'd wanted to hug him again for so long and having him in her arms now, felt incredible.

He was hesitant as before; his arms still by his side but eventually, Oren wrapped his arms around her, pressing her into his chest. Trista sighed contentedly, and her heart raced as she felt him breathe her in. Oren squeezed her just before he let go of her. They both raised their heads to look back into each other's eyes,

"Trista I…"

"Yes?" she was practically panting, her heart in her chest as her arms remained rested on his shoulders; his around her waist. She didn't care how she'd felt only moments ago, this couldn't be nothing; they were practically breathing each other's air!

"Trista we…"

"Yes?" Oren seemed to be mere inches from her face and without warning, her eyes fluttered closed, desperate for him to kiss her.

"Trista!"

They sprang apart, Trista's eyes instantly open as there was a sharp knock at the door followed by Dana's voice,

"Trista, Oren are you busy?"

Trista and Oren looked at one another but neither said anything as Oren simply stepped away from her and opened the door. Trista's face was hot with shame at what she was very sure, she'd been obvious about wanting.

Dana's eyes were wide and frantic as she laid eyes on them,

"Dana what's wrong?" Oren asked.

Dana didn't reply, instead stepping back out of the open door to where the bar was now in plain view and coming back, holding someone's hand.

Trista's mouth went completely dry and goose bumps erupted over her flesh as she looked into the bright blue eyes of her fiancé, Thorn Remora.

THE PRINCESS AND THE GENERAL

Lyon spent the rest of the morning with the princess before leaving the Imperial Lands to return to Tirnum Castle. Once in his room, he requested a whore to be brought to his rooms and once he'd sated himself within her, he entered his seating chamber and poured himself a very large drink.

What he had seen…what she was capable of…he'd never seen anything like it and for the first time in his life; Baron Lyon Dreston was afraid.

Briseis, somehow, knew that he planned to overthrow her and that terrified him now that he knew what she could do and what power she had at her disposal.

The Six were a force to be reckoned with and if what he had seen was just the beginning of their training then they would be unstoppable once the war was completely underway. Whether he could get the Six on his side before they could be used against him, he still had to find out.

Briseis on the other hand was another issue altogether; her own power obviously exceeding that of the people she was teaching. The way she'd moved today, such speed, agility and power, was phenomenal.

Despite being in such obvious awe of her, he now understood why the other nobles and Erik had been so afraid of her. Lyon took a long drink from his glass before refilling it with the strong wine.

He should have listened to them, he thought. He should have listened to the other lords and taken heed of their information. He couldn't very well change anything now other than his course of action.

The princess right now, was happy to keep him alive and play as though she didn't know his true intentions. As long as he stayed alive, he could find a way out of this mess but first, he needed alliances.

Even though his men made up considerable numbers in the now accumulating army, he would need more to overpower the Six as their power outweighed any soldier.

He was bound by marriage to Thelm, so had a further three thousand from the North. A few were already within the princess' army but at an order from Erik, they would turn coat. He would, however, need more forces from the southern regions in order to surround the city with men loyal to him, or at least loyal to his cause.

The best way to do this would be to recruit Lord Weilyn who controlled Thea's Point and thereby the traffic in and out of the capital but how would he get through to him? He knew from their discussions in the Great Hall, that the princess proposed to have men stationed in Thea's Point in case any wanted to leave or fight their way through. This could be helpful.

As he took another full mouthful of his drink, there was a knock on his chamber door, but it immediately opened to admit the person.

Lyon was about to get extremely angry about the intrusion before he realised exactly who was standing there.

"Your majesty!" Lyon bowed immediately to King Curian.

He was told the king was at the slowly forming camp, so his appearance there was surprising for more than one reason.

Curian stepped forward, dressed in all black, his golden crown the only colour on his entire person, the door closing silently behind him. He surveyed the room casually and before waving his arm in an arch shape after which Lyon felt the very air go still. The king looked back at him, eyes firm and dark, serious as he spoke,

"No one should be able to hear us but then…she does have her ways."

"Your majesty?"

"Do not play coy with me Baron, I know your kind and what's in your mind…your heart."

Lyon placed the glass he was holding on the dresser and was interested to realise that where his hand reached to place it, his hand was cold. When he returned his hand to his side, it was warm again.

"Your majesty, I have no idea what you're talking about."

"Yes, you do and what's more…I wish to help you."

"Excuse me?"

King Curian the Conqueror stepped closer to Baron Lyon Dreston and despite the magical shield he had place around them, he lowered his crowned head and whispered,

"I've come to offer my assistance." Lyon didn't like what he felt deep inside he knew was coming, but asked anyway.

"Assistance with what?" Curian looked him right in the eye and said firmly,

"You wish to kill Briseis…and I'm going to help me to do it."

***

Despite the luxuries that were undoubtedly provided to make her stay the most comfortable; Briseis did not feel like spending the night in the Imperial Lands and so she made her way back to Tirnum Castle after spending the day training with the Six.

They were making amazing progress and even though she may not admit it to them, she was thoroughly impressed with them and their use of the Everlasting power. They would be a formidable force in the war and considering the argument she'd had with Gardan, they would be needed.

Briseis hated that she was still not closer to knowing how many men would constitute the Samaian army. They were preparing blind and it was a frustrating concept.

She sat at the desk in her study that evening, going through the finances for the war preparations and while they had enough for the men they had, she needed more in case the fighting went on for longer than anticipated. She was not so stupid that she would drain the resources of the capital in order to fund her war. She wanted and planned to win with strength in numbers, not endurance that would milk their resources dry.

Grain, furs, timber, steel; all cost gold and she had to make sure she had an abundance of it. Raising taxes was all well and good but even she wasn't stupid. She might not care how the common folk fared; but she wasn't completely ignorant to the fact that there was hardly anything left to be taxed.

The advisors and guards had tried to hide it from her and her father, but she'd seen how the banquets got smaller and the ale much thinner. Crops didn't grow like they used to and even this ridiculous weather was testament to what was going on in the world.

She'd been cold forever and she was tired of it; things needed to change and soon. They would need more food, weapons before this war was over and she had no idea when that would happen when it hadn't even begun. Baron Dreston was more important than he realised but in the grand scheme of things, she needed his money, not his life.

It was at that precise moment that Briseis doubled over onto her desk, spilling her ink and quills over the papers she was going over. Her head pulsated as her stomach cramped. As she squinted her eyes closed against the pain, she had a brief second to smile as she realised what was happening.

In moments, the pain had receded and Briseis was able to catch her breath,

"Guards!" she called out breathlessly, summoning a cup of water from across the room to quench her dry throat.

Two men barrelled into her rooms almost instantly, swords at the ready,

"Yes Princess!" Briseis gulped down the water, slamming the cup onto the table top when she was done.

"One of you bring General Beardmore to me, I need him now!" one guard immediately departed, fleeing down the stone hallway. Briseis turned to the other guard,

"Have Baron Thelm brought here as well…I wish to speak with him."

The other guard bowed before leaving as well and within seconds, she was alone again.

Briseis rose slowly from her chair, draining the last of the cup of water as she did so, slamming it back onto the table again with the weight of having to hold it up, finally being released.

She touched her fingertips to her nose and realised belatedly, that she was bleeding. This war had to start and end soon, or she didn't know how long she would last.

She was not a fool, she knew using the Everlasting took a lot out of her; it was part of the reason she was training the Six; so, they could use the power she wouldn't have to.

She would save her strength for the Redeemer, only then would she engage in serious battle; the battle she'd both consciously and unconsciously been training her entire life for.

The princess walked a few steps to regain her balance and composure and by the time Gardan arrived, she was feeling more like herself,

"Your highness," Gardan said by way of greeting and so she turned to him just as he was bowing.

"General, I need you to send a small party of men to Thelm and watch for any activity."

"Activity?"

"Yes, I had another of my visions and this time the Redeemer was much further North. I couldn't feel where exactly, but it seems to me that the attack will come from the North...through Thea's Reach." Gardan looked thoughtful,

"Forgive me your highness, but how can you know that for sure?"

Briseis' eyebrows raised at his boldness and the fact it wasn't the first time he'd been this way. She found she liked when he challenged her; when he had a back bone, but remained respectful. She watched him now in the dim lighting of her study, adjacent to her seating room and her bedroom and bathing rooms beyond.

He was incredibly handsome she realised, his uniform and weapons arranged on him in a way that was confident and prompted no questioning from his subordinates.

"You grow bold Gardan...it suits you." Gardan cleared his throat embarrassed but said nothing. "The last time I felt their presence was in Priya. If they were heading straight to the capital, they would have gone south in order to board a ship to Thea's Point," Gardan nodded his agreement.

"So, if they're not coming to Tirnum then the only other way to meet us in open war is from the north, through Thelm and ultimately the Reach."

"No army can get through there. It would be suicide."

"That, Gardan is not my problem. I only wish to be prepared for whatever does come out of the north."

"Yes Princess. I'll send my best men."

"See that you do, I wish to know everything that is going on in that city. We'll have the fastest ravens to report back to us." Gardan nodded just as the door knocked to her study.

"One last thing Gardan, have the gold we discussed sent to Remora."

Gardan nodded once again before Briseis waved her hand toward the door and it opened, showing Baron Thelm in the doorway looking somewhat terrified.

The Baron was almost physically shaking in his boots making Briseis roll her eyes.

"Y-you summoned me your highness?" she beckoned him forward.

Gardan moved to stand by her side and fleetingly, she noticed that she liked it. She looked at him briefly, at his strong jaw and deep brown eyes before looking away, back to the Baron.

"Yes, I did, please sit."

Briseis moved to sit on a large chair across the room with the twin across from her. Once again, Gardan moved to stand by her side.

Baron Thelm timidly took his seat but tried to maintain his composure.

"I won't keep you too long Baron as I have things to be getting on with,"

"Of course, Princess, how can I hope to serve you?" Briseis made sure Baron Erik could see her eyes when the flames flashed within her pupils. The man visibly shook and it made her insanely happy. She looked down at him, intensely and said,

"Sever all ties with Baron Dreston while you remain in the capital and pledge your fealty to me."

Erik was understandably shocked as he looked from her to Gardan then back to her. He was unsure what to do.

"Y-your highness, what do you mean?" the older man spluttered like a disgusting little worm. Briseis stared him down,

"In what way was I unclear?" Erik's eyes were shifty as found the words to say,

"M-my daughter, my daughter is married to Baron Dreston." Briseis nodded,

"Yes, General Beardmore informed me when you arrived of the secret nuptials that took place in Dreston. Nuptials, I assume, were discussed in order for Baron Dreston to assume the might of Thelm during his pathetic attempt to dethrone my father and myself when the time comes."

Erik stared at her, his mouth open wide before his eyes shifted to Gardan who remained stoic.

Without warning, Baron Thelm dropped to his knees and scrambled to prostrate at her feet. He gathered the hem of her skirts into his hands making Gardan draw his sword but Briseis stayed him with a small gesture of her hand.

"Please, your highness!" he wailed. "I beg you, please spare me and my daughter. We had nothing to do with his plans, Lyon planned it all!"

Briseis smirked down at him and nodded,

"I believe entirely that this attempt to amass power was all Lyon's idea and for that, I will spare you, your daughter and her reputation for marrying a traitor…if you do this one thing."

"Anything, your highness! I'll do anything!"

Briseis continued to look down at the pathetic excuse of a man and wondered how her father could have ever given him lands and titles after the war. His people seventeen years ago had been made up of rebels and pirates from the north who, while poor, were burly. They were men of big stature who had provided the strength she now needed in her own army. Her father had seemingly rewarded this miserable man for those numbers. It certainly wasn't his military or political expertise.

"I want you to do nothing Erik,"

"W-what?"

"I want you to do absolutely nothing." Briseis continued to look down at him, happy to watch him beg. "Remain in Lyon's confidence and report everything he says and does, back to me. Can you do that?"

"My daughter, she will be safe? She can re marry?"

"You're in no position to question or negotiate. I have said no harm will come to Geneiva and I meant it. Will you be my informant Baron Erik?"

"Y-yes, I will your highness." Erik lowered his head and kissed the hem of her gathered dress. "Thank you for your mercy."

"Fail me Erik, allow Lyon to know you work for me and you'll be begging for more than mercy."

Briseis fanned him away and Gardan stepped from behind her seat to drag the whimpering man to his feet before hauling him out the door. He turned to bow to her before exiting but Briseis stopped him,

"Wait," he stopped expectantly. "Stay awhile Gardan,"
"Your highness?" he asked confused.

Briseis rose from her position on the chair and walked determinedly toward him, stopping mere inches from his face.

"Have a drink before you return to Sentry's Keep or is my company not good enough for you?" Gardan was surprised but stepped into the room and closed the door behind him.

"Of course, your highness…as you wish."

Gardan bowed his head and went to take the seat that Erik had just vacated. Briseis went to pour them both a glass of wine before returning to him and handing him his glass. He took it from her and looked up at her; he really was very handsome.

"You're so refreshing Gardan. You do as I say, exactly when I say it without cowardice or hesitation."

She took the seat opposite him again and looked straight into his eyes as she sipped,

"I try to serve you as best I can your highness," he said, his deep voice smooth as he spoke assuredly before taking a sip of his glass. Briseis smiled as she ran her index finger over the top of her glass then sucked the wine from her finger.

"Where do you live Gardan, where do you go when you leave my service?" Gardan cleared his throat,

"I have a small cottage on the edge of the city, your highness, but admittedly, I don't spend much time there."

"Oh?"

"Yes, you keep me quite busy."

She almost smiled, laughed even at his humour but didn't. She took another sip before asking, the glass still at her lips.

"There is no one in this cottage waiting for you?"

"No," he replied, although it was almost sad. As though he wanted there to be someone waiting for him. "There is no one."

It was decided then, Briseis thought to herself. She might not wish to allow any man to have power over her by invading her body, but a man who was already in her service; a man who already respected her and had no possibility of outshining her, the idea had considerable merit.

AGE OF ANTONIDES

Queen Nucea Voltaire of Agmantia stood in the throne room of the Voltaire Palace before her three children: Crown Prince Rian, Princess Saicha and Prince Aslan. Her husband, Prince Consort Tagnan stood behind her, watching; listening to all around them.

The throne room was one of the oldest rooms of the palace, the others built around it in its eight-hundred-year-old history.

The Agmantian royal family had ruled Agmantian for thousands of years but not always from within the walls of the magnificent palace nestled in the Agmantian jungle.

What had begun as tribes of chiefs and shamans had evolved into the Voltaire family that ruled today, over the five other provinces that made up the country.

Nucea, for the past twenty-three years, had ruled these provinces with minimal wars and none of them had been started by her. She ruled with diplomacy and elegance and avoided fighting at all costs. Not because Agmantia was deficient in military strength, but because she believed in discussions to prevent death at all costs.

Nucea wore a white dress that draped elegantly over one shoulder, leaving the other bare, exposing her glowing brown skin. It flowed majestically to the floor, clinched at the waist by a thick gold band and rested lightly on top of golden sandals.

"We have received a request," Nucea began firmly, firmly that all attention was on her. "…a request to end the life of a royal of another land."

Her voice carried through the elegant though ancient room with the heat of the jungle all around and the call of the tropical birds in the air.

"How would you respond to that, my children?"

"What business is that of ours?" Aslan, ever rash and judgemental; the youngest of the three but always the first to speak.

"Why have we been asked?" Rian added, questioning, suspicious and always on guard; a true first born.

"What have they done to warrant death?"

Nucea smiled proudly at Saicha, her only daughter and if she'd been her eldest; her heir.

Saicha was cunning, smart, watchful and always questioning. It was why she'd done so well at the Guild and why now, at twenty-one, she was a fully-fledged Agmantian Assassin. The girl had begged to be sent to the remote city in the deepest mountains to train with the guild and even then, at nine; Nucea knew she could not deny her daughter.

She hadn't seen Saicha again for ten years. She'd now been home only two years and with this insidious request, she would have to leave home again.

"Good Saicha," Saicha bowed her head respectfully. "What could someone, anyone, have done to warrant a price on their head?"

Nucea descended gracefully down the few remaining steps of the raised platform where her throne sat. Tagnan, who remained a few steps behind her, followed and stopped when she stopped.

"This is what we must find out. I will not take anyone's life on only the words of their enemies."

Nucea held up the message she'd received from King Curian the Conqueror of Mortania. He had shone his light as she'd requested, and she would answer as she'd promised.

What she'd not told her children, or her husband, was that Curian had offered Agmantia the crown of Mortania, a crown Nucea knew he had no right to give.

"Saicha and Aslan will go to Mortania and determine the character of both King Curian and his daughter Princess Briseis. It will determine whether or not we answer this request and how."

"Mother, why are you doing this? Aslan is right; what does this have to do with Agmantia?" Rian questioned. Her son was ever practically and would make a wonderful king one day. He was handsome and brave and had been raised to know he would be king. There were a few Nucea knew, who hadn't had that same luxury.

"Mother, I must agree with my brothers. Why involve us with these foreigners? You've said yourself they have no morals."

Nucea nodded agreeably as she walked closer to her children and a look of intense sadness fell upon her face,

"You are all too young to have remembered the time before Curian, the Age of Antonides. A time when Agmantia and Mortania were more than just silent lands with an ocean between. You never knew a time when we were…truest friends."

Nucea went deathly quiet for a moment, her three children looked at each other puzzled at their mother's change of attitude. Within a moment, the passion had ignited back into her eyes and Nucea turned to them with a determined look,

"I lost my belief in humanity the day one friend was slain and another lost, lost with a life that had barely even begun."

The princes and princess watched as a single tear slipped down their mother's smooth brown cheek. "But if the man who caused that can seek redemption, I must know how…and why."

Rian was still confused but it was Aslan that voiced it,

"Mother, what exactly do you mean for us to do?" Nucea turned to her youngest son,

"I mean for you to go to Mortania discreetly and find out whether it is in our interest to ally with the Mortanians or not."

"Discreetly?" Saicha replied with a grin that even Aslan had to smile at. Nucea merely nodded and walked back up the steps to her throne, Tagnan followed ever silently and stood by her side. She reached out and took his hand, which he held firmly and lovingly. His presence was soothing, something she'd relied on all these years.

"While these two are away, what would you ask of me?" Rian asked.

"I would ask you to be prepared Rian, for whatever answer your siblings provide, for one of them…will mean war."

Pronunciation Guide

ANTONIDES - An-Toe-Nee-Deez
AVRIEL - Av-Re-El
BRISEIS - Bri-Say-Uss
CURIAN - Kerr-Ry-Yun
DRESTON - Dress-Tun
ILLIYA - Ill-Ee-Yah
IONA - Ee-Oh-Nah
JARN LAKE - Yarn Lake
LAMYA - Lah-My-Ah
LIYA - Lie-Yah
LYON - Lee-On
MORTANIA - Mor-Tan-Yah
NAIMA - Nay-Eem-Ah
NUCEA - New-See-Yah
OREN - Or-un
PHYN - Fin
PRIYA - Pree-Yah
RIAN - Ry-Un
SAICHA - Say-Sha
SAMAI - Sah- My
SAMAIAN - Sah-My-Un
THEA - Thay-Yah
TIRNUM - Ter-Num
YZNA-TUM – Eaze-Nar-Tomb